J. M. Ryder was born in London in 1959, and wrote her first novel at the age of 60. She has worked in both veterinary and dental nursing, but is now a cleaner and gardener. She lives with her husband in Dorset and enjoys walking, playing guitar, arty things, and the occasional pub quiz.

J. M. Ryder

A CHANGE OF HEART

AUSTIN MACAULEY PUBLISHERS
LONDON * CAMBRIDGE * NEW YORK * SHARJAH

Copyright © J. M. Ryder 2025

The right of J. M. Ryder to be identified as author of this work has been asserted by the author in accordance with sections 77 and 78 of the Copyright, Designs and Patents Act 1988.

All rights reserved. No part of this publication may be reproduced, stored in a retrieval system, or transmitted in any form or by any means, electronic, mechanical, photocopying, recording, or otherwise, without the prior permission of the publishers.

Any person who commits any unauthorised act in relation to this publication may be liable to criminal prosecution and civil claims for damages.

This is a work of fiction. Names, characters, businesses, places, events, locales, and incidents are either the products of the author's imagination or used in a fictitious manner. Any resemblance to actual persons, living or dead, or actual events is purely coincidental.

A CIP catalogue record for this title is available from the British Library.

ISBN 9781035884773 (Paperback)
ISBN 9781035884780 (ePub e-book)

www.austinmacauley.com

First Published 2025
Austin Macauley Publishers Ltd®
1 Canada Square
Canary Wharf
London
E14 5AA

Table of Contents

Introduction	7
Chapter One: Sunday	9
Chapter Two: Monday	13
Chapter Three: Monday	16
Chapter Four: Tuesday	20
Chapter Five: Friday	25
Chapter Six: Friday	30
Chapter Seven; Friday Continued	35
Chapter Eight: Saturday	41
Chapter Nine: Saturday	46
Chapter Ten: Saturday	51
Chapter Eleven: Returning to Friday Evening	59
Chapter Twelve: Back to Saturday Evening	64
Chapter Thirteen: Saturday Morning	70
Chapter Fourteen: Sunday	83
Chapter Fifteen: Monday	97

Chapter Sixteen: Tuesday	108
Chapter Seventeen: Wednesday	112
Chapter Eighteen: Back to Monday	119
Chapter Nineteen: Wednesday Evening/Thursday	133
Chapter Twenty: Friday/Saturday	143
Chapter Twenty-One: Friday/Saturday	158
Chapter Twenty-Two: Sunday	177
Chapter Twenty-Three: Tuesday	193
Chapter Twenty-Four: Wednesday	207
Chapter Twenty-Five: Wednesday Evening	226
Chapter Twenty-Six: Wednesday	234
Chapter Twenty-Seven: Thursday Evening	240
Chapter Twenty-Eight: Friday	251
Chapter Twenty-Nine: Friday	259
Chapter Thirty: Saturday	276
Chapter Thirty-One: Sunday	297
Chapter Thirty-Two: Sometime Later	307

Introduction

My name is Rick.

I am twenty-one, finished with education, and about to enter the University of Life.

Because two friends and myself are embarking on a 'gap' year, travelling around the world in the hopes of broadening our horizons before starting careers, I have found my thoughts lingering on life.

And on death.

What if something happened to someone in my family, or one of my friends, while I was away? I thought about my family; I knew my sister reasonably well, but I knew very little about my parents' lives.

I had never really considered this before. You don't, do you, when you just see them as the suppliers, managers and controllers of practically everything you do? You assume they were born into their widening middle-aged bodies, with an old and sensible mindset.

I spoke to my sister about this; we are close and know everything (more or less) about each other, and realised it was time we asked our parents about themselves; how they met, what they were like before they got married and decided to start a family, things like that.

I spoke to my best friends, Sam and Adam, too. It's the three of us that are going on this trip. Sam is a few years older than Adam and me, and they all think he'll be a steadying influence; they don't know him very well! Mum seemed to think Sam's dad was the same at his age, but I find that hard to believe. Sam's dad is fun, but ordinary.

No doubt we'll have to protect Adam from hordes of adoring girls; apparently, it was the same for his dad back in the day. He doesn't seem to realise the effect he has on the fairer sex. I wish I had it.

All our parents have been friends for years, and it turned out there was more to their connections than just meeting at school…

It turned out to be a fascinating tale.

This is their story, and the beginning of ours.

Chapter One
Sunday

It was 4 September 1994, 5 am, and Antonia was sitting in the lounge in her pyjamas, feet stretched out on the coffee table in front of her, mulling over Charles again.

She hadn't even bothered to switch the light on, and now a dim light was starting to filter out the darkness. The date had reopened the wound again.

Yesterday, her birthday, had marked a whole year since he had given her the card that now sat propped open between her feet. She regarded it with a mixture of bitterness and despair. It was a big, showy thing covered in kisses, and signed 'All my love, forever, Charles'.

She had been pleasantly surprised at this show of emotion, because Charles didn't usually do things like that. In fact, he'd never done anything like that before.

It had even crossed her mind that a ring may soon be decorating her finger. And then he had left.

Why had she even bothered to keep the damn thing?

She didn't understand what had happened, and still wondered now why he had done something so out of character. He'd just said he was going, that it was best. He had looked watery eyed and tense, and she had frowned, puzzled, not understanding what he meant.

Going? Going where? What did he mean?

He had stood there for a few uncertain seconds, then said Bibi was waiting and hurried off.

Bibi? Who?

When the door closed behind him Antonia rushed to the window with growing alarm and watched as the two of them drove away together. She couldn't contact him, she had no idea where they were going, and that was the last time she had seen him. By the time she had belted down the stairs and into the street they were gone.

Why? What had made him do it? What had she done wrong?

It had been so unlike anything he'd ever done before; he just didn't do things like that! There had been no warning, how could she not have known? First the card, then this.

It was that woman from downstairs! It had to have been her that instigated this.

Her thoughts, as always, were venomous as she recalled that unfriendly, handsome woman that had lived downstairs with her posh, sycophantic husband. It had to have been her doing. She'd noticed, of course, the flirting with Charles; it happened all the time to him. Antonia had assumed he was unaware of it, as he normally would have been. It was one of the things she had loved about him. Perhaps he was more knowing than she had given him credit for.

That was a whole year ago today, and the months of heartache and tears seemed embodied in that bloody card, a symbol of guilt at what he was intending to do. Right now, she had never felt so lonely. She crushed the card between her feet and tried to destroy it, along with the memories, then yawned, sighed and got up to put on a dressing gown.

Rain had slanted in the day before, after two months of mostly dry sunshine, and had continued throughout the night. She got up and looked out of the window, and even in this half-light she could see a green blush already beginning to spread across the patchy lawns across the road.

"Oh Charlie," she sighed, imagining his dark, glossy hair with the gentle curl. Cornflower-blue eyes, soft sensuous lips, perfect bone structure, all put together to its best advantage. He had always been completely unaware of the effect he had on her and other women, which just made him all the more appealing.

They had met in a queue, of all places. At the very moment Antonia had noticed him and gone weak at the knees, Charles had seen that pretty face with its enormous green eyes and the cloud of chestnut hair that surrounded it and discovered something stirring within him he had never experienced before. He imagined what that lovely hair would feel like if he touched it, bunched it in his hands. He'd never really noticed a girl in this way before, he was usually so awkward around women. They were always fussing over him and clutching at him or giggling inanely. He preferred a good book, if he was truthful.

They struck up a gentle conversation, ended up abandoning the queue for the Wimpy café next door and the next twelve years was history, as they say.

And then, just like that, all of it was gone.

He had just left. walked off with someone, it seemed, she could not possibly compete with. Perhaps he had finally realised he could have anyone he wanted, and it was no longer going to be her.

There were no more tears left in her now, and since he'd gone it had gradually dawned on her how dissatisfactory their relationship had become, how stale. They were just two dull people together, knocking along in tandem with no destination in mind.

This discovery had almost made her feel worse. Maybe that had been the problem all along, his eye had settled somewhere else because she was boring. All that wasted time, she thought angrily. She sighed again, she did a lot of that lately, and a small mist clouded the window for a few seconds. She drew a small face with a downturned mouth in it and walked away.

Charles was old for his years. He had never wanted to do anything but watch television and go to bed early to read. She remembered, cringing, how on his birthday she had put on some naughty underwear she'd been persuaded into buying, for a laugh, at an Ann Summers party, then crept into the bedroom to surprise him. He'd been asleep.

Asleep! Like some worn-out old geriatric. She shuddered to think of it, standing over him like a prostitute in red satin crotchless knickers and a matching bra with gold tassels. The next day, she had wrapped them in newspaper and a carrier bag and thrown them in the bin. What had ever possessed her to buy them in the first place? Thank God no one had ever known about it, even Charles himself.

They had been living together in a fur-lined rut, she could see it so clearly once she was out of it, and she had since decided that it was a good thing to live alone for a while and discover all the pros and cons about yourself and what you really wanted from life.

There were a lot of advantages to being part of a couple, and suddenly when everyone else was getting spliced and having babies that door had been slammed shut in her face.

She had gone back to square one at the age of thirty, which was a tiny worry. Would she ever meet anyone else? Single females past twenty-five tended to be edged out of the couples scene, unless there was a single male on the loose as well, usually a weird one that no one else wanted; so now she hardly ever went out and the only people who ever called were family. It was different for a man on his own, she couldn't just go waltzing into the local pub to find a bit of company. She'd get some alright, but not the sort she was looking for. It was most definitely a man's world.

So much for independence.

Perhaps she was just a boring person now. The old fun Antonia was now just boring, apart from when she was angry. Which seemed to be most of the time.

She moved through to the kitchen, putting all thoughts of Charles and that bloody woman out of her mind. Just enjoy being able to do exactly what you want, she told herself. That was the other edge of the sword.

Chapter Two
Monday

Next morning, Monday, she was awake at 5am again, dozing sporadically until the alarm finally alerted her at 7.30, a tiring pattern which had established itself since Charles' departure. At least she did now doze for those final hours, instead of lying there going over and over it all. Apart from yesterday of course, but she saw that as a year up, time now to move on.

She was up, washed, dressed and out in twenty minutes. The cycle ride to work took half an hour and was the best part of the day, taking her through quiet back roads and parks. It woke her up and prepared her for another challenging day with Dan and Susan at the dental surgery.

Daniel S. Murphy BDS, for whom she worked as dental nurse and receptionist, was, on the face of it, a big hearty Irishman. He seemed kind and solicitous to old ladies, witty and charming to his contemporaries and deferential when he needed to be.

Behind all that, he was taciturn and sour.

Antonia disliked him intensely.

He had been chatty and pleasant with her at first, but his true colours soon showed through and had left her confidence in her ability to read people a bit scuffed.

The first indication of this change of character came when, two days into her new job, he stood over a cavernous mouth moving his finger in circles and frowning at her. She was bewildered. What did he want her to *do*? Aspirate apparently, enlightenment coming when he snatched the instrument from her and nearly gave the patient a tonsillectomy as he plunged it into the back of the poor man's mouth.

Dan would only indicate with strange hand signals and odd facial contortions that he was displeased with something. This would always be when a patient was in the chair, and she was unable to reply. Sometimes she could have burst with humiliation or anger. Many a time, she had been tempted to tell him to shove his aspirator up his hairy Celtic backside. But she needed the job, which did pay well after all, so she would hate him in silent fury and think of the money. After all, £9 an hour was huge compared to what some people were earning as dental nurses; and Dan tended to take a lot of holidays too. She had had six weeks paid leave last year. In that respect, her boss was very generous.

One other body worked in the place. Susan, a forty-five-year-old spinster who lived with her ageing mother and was hopelessly in love with their unreasonable boss. She and Susan enjoyed a sort of tolerant relationship with each other, which never quite teetered into friendship. Antonia had tried to bond with her at first, but it was soon obvious where Susan's loyalties lay; she wasn't having any young thing coming in and usurping her position with Dan.

What she was waiting for was difficult to comprehend; that he might suddenly realise she was the woman of his dreams, divorce his wife and marry her? Hardly. An affair? Antonia imagined them bobbing up and down on the reclining chair together when they could snatch a moment between patients.

No, Susan was very old-fashioned, it would have to be marriage or nothing. Perhaps unrequited love was her thing, nice and safe with no disruption or mess. She had a point.

Every Friday, Antonia had scrutinised the situations vacant pages of the local paper, reading out possibilities to the back of Charles' head, which he would reply to with a grunt; it was like conversing with a wildebeest. Despondency had even knocked that weekly exercise off the agenda after he left. She must start looking again, she thought. Maybe she would buy a paper this Friday.

Anyway, these random thoughts were swiftly forgotten about five minutes into her journey when rain began to fall. Heavily. The only thing worse than rain was when it was accompanied by wind, which this was. By the time she reached the surgery, lashed on all sides as she struggled to pedal into the weather, the lack of a mudguard on the back wheel had resulted in an untidy line of filth sprayed up her back. Her underwear was soaked. The weather had been dry for so long now she'd completely forgotten about bringing a raincoat or spare underwear (having been caught like this before), so rather than spend the entire day in soggy discomfort, she removed her pants and stuffed them quickly into the bottom of her bag. Tights would do fine. After blotting her hair with paper towels and changing into her uniform she felt almost ready for the Monday morning onslaught. It was her week for chairside duty, Susan was running the reception.

"Morning," said Susan brightly, shaking an umbrella as she entered. She sucked air in through her teeth as she did this, an annoying habit she had. Susan glanced at the clock. "You're early." She made it sound like an accusation.

"Morning Sue." *She probably thinks I'm here early to catch Dan alone,* Antonia thought with amusement, when in fact she had pedalled like the devil to get out of the deluge.

Dan was also on time today, something of a minor miracle, sometimes not arriving until well after the first few patients should have been long gone. He had transferred his bulk into the surgery and was now scrubbing vigorously at his own teeth with an ancient toothbrush, its bristles separated neatly down the centre like a butler's parting.

"Morning," Antonia greeted her boss, who glanced sideways but continued scrubbing. "Nice weekend?" she enquired conversationally, determined to get a polite answer. "Do anything much?"

"No, not really," he offered finally, tossing the germ-infested brush into a drawer amongst some sterile instruments. "Let's have the first one in."

There were no further comments.

Antonia poked her head into the waiting room and called Mrs Cooper.

An old lady leapt from her chair and scuttled past, treading on Antonia's toe as she went.

Mrs Cooper was having new dentures made, in the hope they would stay in without help from fixative products. Lying back in the chair minus her present set made her look like an unwrapped mummy Antonia had seen once in an exhibition. And the curious smell emanating from her woollen coat only added to that image.

The afternoon passed uneventfully and at 5.30 Antonia was once again pedalling furiously in heavy rain, this time without fear of soaking her underwear which was still screwed up at the bottom of her bag.

Chapter Three
Monday

Just as Antonia was setting off on her damp cycle ride to work, in the flat downstairs Wendell Cornish was slapping a hand down on his alarm clock. He stretched, screwing up his face with the effort, yawned expansively and scratched his balls before slumping back on the pillows with a small groan. His head hurt and his mouth felt like it was carpeted wall to wall. His breath was probably rancid too. He huffed into his cupped palm, sniffed, and screwed his face up a second time.

Raising himself slowly so as to ease into the headache, he sat for a moment until his balance settled itself, then hoisted himself wearily from the bed and trailed through to the bathroom where he pointed his bits at the toilet, eyes half closed.

This had become the way mornings began in Wendell's world—with a hangover.

In the kitchen, dirty dishes and pans formed an exotic landscape in and around the sink, welded together by hardened food. Wendell carefully extracted one of the cleaner looking plates and ran it under cold water.

"What *is* that *smell*?" he asked himself out loud, as he rubbed the plate with a limp tea towel from which the pong was rising. He removed a final stubborn particle from the plate with a fingernail before putting a slice of bread into the toaster.

Since his wife had gone he had become an absolute slob, hopelessly out of his depth domestically. A Public School Upbringing may have taught him how to read Latin and quote the great philosophers, but when it came to wielding a hoover or keeping a kitchen hygienic, he was a complete dunce.

By the time he left for the office, however, he at least looked presentable, and it vaguely worried him that he was unable to attain this level of orderliness in his home. Perhaps it was time to move? Just leave the muck behind for someone else to deal with. He'd lose his deposit of course, but who cared. There were too many unpleasant memories here anyway. He ignored the notion that the cleaning problem would be a recurring one and accelerated off behind the wheel of his sporty car. He drove fast, impatient with other road users, pedestrians, traffic lights, in fact just about everything that might hold him up, late as he was yet again. Must set my clock earlier, he thought, as he shot past two cyclists drenching them both with cold, dirty water from a kerbside puddle. At least he was spared that flog into London now that he'd been transferred to the Surrey branch. Bibi hadn't wanted to leave the city, but as she didn't work, she'd had little choice in the matter.

Suddenly stationary at lights, he examined his face in the mirror. The eyes were a bit pouchy but otherwise there were not too many signs of excess alcohol. His hair, which needed cutting, was swept back and held in place by half a can of hairspray, forgotten when Bibi cleared her stuff out. If anyone cared to drop a rock on his head today, he would be saved by it for sure, it was almost a helmet. He was clean shaven, revealing the pocked skin of a teenage acne sufferer, scars he'd long got used to.

He hadn't made much progress since joining this branch, a fact which he dismissed airily, putting it at first down to Bibi and her constant demands to return to London at weekends. No one could keep that pace going. Then she left him.

His secretary, a widowed woman of fifty-nine, treated him like a wayward son, listening to his woes on a weekly basis with kindly attention and comforting him with a cup of tea and a biscuit. The general office opinion was that he was fast heading towards middle age.

He drove mechanically, eyes fixed ahead, brain barely awake. Months of heavy drinking, bad eating habits and lack of sleep was starting to take its toll.

At work he was absent-minded and yawned constantly, which had not gone unnoticed by his boss, and today, perhaps because it was raining or it was Monday or because of the awful weekend he'd just had with his menopausal wife, Bellingham was not in the best mood. So as he spotted Wendell creeping in quietly to slide behind his desk, he decided enough was enough. Not only was the man little more than excess baggage as far as his work was concerned, he was also unpunctual nearly every day. How did he manage to breeze in looking so dapper when he lived the life of Riley, wondered Bellingham with irritation. And why was he always fiddling with his tie? It irritated him.

"Cornish!" he barked from his office door, making his own secretary's blonde curls jump with alarm. She placed a well-manicured hand on her ample chest in an effort to steady her nerves and exchanged a sympathetic glance with Wendell.

"My office please," finished Bellingham smartly, marching back inside and closing the door behind him, thereby ensuring Wendell had to knock.

"Wish me luck," he mouthed to the blonde secretary in passing, and she raised an eyebrow in return without pausing her frantic typing.

Wendell's knock was followed by a moment of silence then "Enter!"

He entered, still fiddling with the tie.

"Morning Mr Bellingham," smiled Wendell, adjusting his tie again.

Bellingham was enthroned in an enormous swivel chair of creaking brown leather. A chair more suited to a boardroom than this tiny office, which it dominated entirely, but which gave the boss a great feeling of superiority. At present, his elbows were propped on the arm rests, fingertips interlaced. His expression was both thoughtful and grim and Wendell, waiting for the offer of a seat, asked if he had had a pleasant weekend.

It was the wrong thing to say, reminding Bellingham of the hysterical scene with his wife on Saturday evening in front of the neighbours. How he would ever face the Munssens again he didn't know. God, he'd do away with the stupid cow if he had the guts. No, he had not had a pleasant weekend and ignored the question.

"Sit down, Cornish," he waved an impatient hand towards the other chair, a small thing in comparison to the mighty swivel.

"Thank you," Wendell sat and waited.

"Cornish," began Bellingham, "how long have you been with us now?"

"Erm, not quite two years."

"Mmm…"

There was a pause, during which Wendell shifted uncomfortably on the little chair and rearranged his tie.

"Cornish," snapped Bellingham with renewed irritation, "what I am about to say to you is not…" His eyes roamed the inside of his skull for a suitable word, "…easy. But I feel the time has come to point out that your work output has been poor, and frankly your presence within this office has become a liability."

"Sir, I…" began Wendell, which was met with a cold stare and a raised hand.

"I haven't finished, Cornish," said Bellingham with bulging eyes.

"Excuse me, sorry."

"As I was saying. I hoped initially that it was just due to the transition, particularly in view of the glowing reference I received from Mr Marsh. He had great faith in you, Cornish. The only reference I could give at this time would be to highlight the dubious quality of your work and your constant tardiness."

He stopped, studying Wendell briefly and saw a sad, red eyed man with an almost greenish tinge to his complexion which he put down to the lighting. In fact, Wendell was feeling a bit sick.

"Anything you'd like to say?"

In a moment of clarity, Wendell saw the last year flash before his tired eyes. Bibi, his beautiful wife, waltzing off with that good-looking bastard from the flat above them, the late nights drowning his sorrows, the weeks of hoping for her return, the anger when she didn't, the slow decline into slobbery.

What was he doing for God's sake?

A dull headache became a thudding migraine. He felt old, tired and hungover.

"I don't feel very well. Sorry," he said quietly.

Chapter Four
Tuesday

The following morning Antonia was eating a banana for breakfast when she noticed that woman's husband climbing into his car outside. She stopped mid-chew for a few seconds and, rather hamster like, watched him.

So, he was still here then, that woman's husband. It had been so long since she'd seen him, she had assumed he'd moved. Neither of them had ever been particularly friendly, certainly not to her anyway. The last time she'd seen the pair of them together, they were dressed up like a cabaret act and he was helping his flashy wife into his flashy car. He had been fondling her thigh as she settled herself and she had smiled seductively, and playfully slapped his hand away. Not very long after, it was Charles who was rubbing her thighs for her.

Innocent, undemonstrative Charlie.

How had that woman *done* it? Managed to entice him to leave like that? Had they been at it behind her back? No, he couldn't hide something like that from her.

But what was the point of going over it all again, it had merely become a habit to think about these things, and she dismissed it without further thought.

She dropped the banana skin into the bin, grabbed her things and set off to work. On the way she struggled to recall the husband's name—had she even known it? Something stupid and pretentious she thought.

Today it wasn't actually raining, but the threat was there in the low clouds overhead, no doubt gathering force for the coming weekend. Last night there had even been a rumble of thunder, God feeling hungry as her mother used to tell her if she was frightened by it. She smiled at the memory.

Thankfully, she made it to work dry this time and greeted Susan with false cheerfulness. Sue would be on holiday next week, going somewhere with the aged mother, which meant she would have to do both their jobs and suffer Dan Murphy on her own.

At least the time would fly.

It was going to be a busy day by the look of it. Mrs Cooper's new teeth were being fitted and she was already complaining enthusiastically. They felt too big and too loose. The teeth looked darker than her old ones and the gums were too pink. Dan assured her they were identical to the last lot in every way and ushered her irritably out into reception, telling her with an impatient smile to wait until they had 'bedded in' and call if she had any problems. By this time, he was running about twenty minutes late and his mood was deteriorating.

The next patient, a nervous, weedy man with bad skin, had returned to have a tooth extracted. He had decided not to have the job done on the previous visit in order to 'psyche himself up for it', which he had managed so well he was now a quivering wreck. Beads of sweat glistened on his forehead and upper lip and his complexion was waxy.

Antonia spotted a possible fainter.

Dan rushed him into the chair, making no particular effort to hide his contempt.

"Open," he snapped.

The man opened his mouth wide.

"No, no, no," Dan shook his head irritably. "You must open your mouth, or I can't see what I'm doing. I could do you a serious injury."

Graham Pinfold's eyes bulged with terror, a mouse looking for escape and finding none. If he opened his mouth any wider his head would turn inside out. Sweat ran freely down from the corrugations in his brow and a couple of pimples had started to weep in sympathy.

The injection was administered, and things calmed down a bit. Antonia smiled reassuringly at him and received a pleading grimace in return. He then babbled some unnecessary apologies to Dan, which were largely ignored. Before he could speak further, Dan rammed a mirror into his mouth.

"Does that feel numb?" he enquired, poking about in the area with a sharp instrument.

"I think so." The patient tapped his cheek with a shaky finger.

"Put your hand down."

"Oh, sorry." He returned it to its firm grip on the armrest and Dan plunged straight in with the forceps.

As she regarded Dan Murphy battling with the tooth, she wondered afresh why anyone ever came back here. Her previous employer would have had the tooth out effortlessly in seconds, without sweat or tears from either participant. Even after twenty years practising, this brute was incapable of doing the job efficiently. Her heart went out to Graham Pinfold. If Dan would put aside his manly pride and admit he needed glasses, he might find he'd get on better. Anyone who needed to hold a newspaper at arm's length to read it should get his eyes tested, and quickly. Especially doing this job.

There was a loud crack.

"What was that?" squeaked the patient in the garbled tone of someone trying to talk with their mouth half open.

"Open please. Open, open!" roared Dan, dragging at the poor man's lower jaw with a bloody finger.

He had broken the top of the tooth away from its root, making the extraction immediately more difficult. Antonia had been expecting it, the way he was trying to lever it out with brute force, and now she expected him (as he usually did) to blame it on the patient.

Dan's expression darkened as he reached for another instrument and began digging the remainder of the tooth out bit by bit.

"You must keep your mouth open, Mr Penfill, that may not have happened if you had."

Graham Pinfold looked dreadful. His whole face was ashen and covered in sweat, white knuckles clung to the armrests, the room stank of terror. And now the poor man thought it was all his own fault.

"Come on, aspirate!" boomed Dan to Antonia, who was already doing it.

How draining and unpleasant all this was, the incompetence, the bullying. He should have found a different occupation, well away from the general public.

Dan removed the instrument and shook his head, tutting.

"You must open your mouth, Mr Pinhead; I can't work if you won't. We've hardly got anything to get hold of and you're making things very difficult when you keep closing. Do you understand?"

Not daring to shut his mouth, Graham Pinfold nodded vigorously. Considering the amount of time the wretched man had been stretching his jaws apart, Antonia thought he'd done pretty well. She looked again at his deathly pallor and decided again that he could well be a fainter.

She regarded Dan with loathing as he dug away. How did he get away with such incompetence? Had he done his training in a butcher's shop?

Finally, and to everyone's relief, he removed the instruments and sat back, sighing heavily. He washed his hands. Graham Pinfold tried to look sideways and see what was going on and a trail of slimy blood dribbled down the side of his mouth and onto his shoulder.

As he dried his hands with a paper towel, Dan turned back to the patient.

"Right."

Graham Pinfold's mouth shot open like a baby bird expecting a worm.

"No, no, we're done now, you can close your mouth."

He snapped it shut.

"Well, there's a small fragment of the root remaining but on balance I think enough of the tooth is out. Give me a shout if you have any further trouble."

With that, he shoved a cotton wool swab into the gap with the instruction to bite down hard on it. Ready to jump at any command, Graham Pinfold clamped his mouth shut on Dan's finger, then flung it open again and Dan whipped his digit out.

"Oh! I'm sho shorry. Shorry. Shorry Doc... Mr Murphy, Sir," he babbled.

"Keep your mouth shut."

While Graham Pinfold lay white and quivering on the chair, Dan whizzed through all the various instructions following an extraction, sprung the chair upright and turned to a lukewarm coffee, brought in unnoticed by Susan while the drama was in full flow.

"Are you alright?" enquired Antonia quietly.

He looked ghastly, but nodded and began to get up. His hair was matted with sweat and flattened where he had lain against the chair for so long. A damp and greasy patch indicated its recent position on the headrest. Dan took no further part in the proceedings and Antonia shadowed the patient out into reception.

The next lot were already in the surgery when she said goodbye to Mr Pinfold, a family of five whose little children had practically destroyed the waiting room while they had been there. She returned to the overcrowded surgery and began to wash instruments. The family's combined heads would have to soak up the sweat on the headrest, it was too late to deal with that as Dan had carried on regardless.

Susan's own extraction from Graham Pinfold was a hefty fee and then she sent him on his way.

Unbeknownst to them all, once out in the street, he fainted and was carried off in an ambulance fifteen minutes later.

Chapter Five
Friday

The short scene in Bellingham's office had given Wendell the proverbial kick up the backside he had been needing. He had stayed in all week, no booze at all, and had gone to bed at a reasonable hour. He was already beginning to feel the benefits and had arrived at work punctually each day, refreshed, and in a better mood.

On the advice of Beth, his secretary, he engaged a mature lady to come and clean the flat once a week, and now, early Friday morning, here she stood.

Mrs 'O', as she had introduced herself, was a well-worn, dumpy specimen of indeterminate age, armed with a selection of cleaning products and rags stuffed into a carrier bag.

Wendell showed her around, apologising profusely for the mess and excusing himself charmingly. Finally, he pointed out the location of tea and coffee and furnished her with a key. As he was leaving, she called to him with a voice that suggested years of cigarette-smoking.

"Where's yer 'oover, love?"

"Hoover?" he queried and rubbed his chin. It was a while since he'd had that out. "Oh yes, of course, in here."

He threw open the door of a small cupboard to reveal a dinosaur of a machine shoved in behind a pile of Bibi's old handbags. Mrs O regarded them, and then him, with a raised eyebrow.

"Yes, here we are," he cried, brushing off the carcasses of long dead spiders and their dusty cobwebs as he hauled it out onto the floor.

"Bags?"

Wendell looked puzzled.

"'Oover bags, love."

"Ah, yes, now, I'm not sure. In here maybe?" He rummaged further into the small cupboard unsuccessfully, not really knowing what they would look like. "Hmm, oh dear, I'm not sure if there are any."

"Alright love, I'll get some and leave you the receipt," said Mrs O with resignation and then mumbled, "If they still make 'em for that museum piece."

"Pardon?"

"Nothing love, don't you worry, I'll sort you out."

"Oh, would you? How very kind of you, thank you very much," he gushed.

The door closed and Mrs O. dumped her carrier on the nearest surface and surveyed the kitchen, hands on hips. She began by making herself a cup of tea and lighting a cigarette, using the encrusted crockery as an ashtray.

"'Alf is life a snob and the other 'alf a slob," she said aloud, as she strolled from room to room, tutting.

When the tea and cigarette ritual had been fulfilled, she donned a crisp floral pinnie, rolled up her sleeves and got to work. She had been engaged for two hours but by the end of that time had only managed to make any real headway in the kitchen. Everything had been sticky with grease and the floor had taken three quarters of an hour on its own. She huffed and puffed around the rest with a duster and polish, tried the ancient hoover which was surprisingly efficient, probably from the little it had been used, then left.

Wendell came in thoughtfully, after meeting his upstairs neighbour on the doorstep. She had lost her keys, then found them, then they had introduced themselves and she went to her flat and he to his. There was something slightly odd about her if the contents of her bag were anything to go by, but as soon as he stepped indoors all this was forgotten when he entered his clean and tidy flat. It was like properly coming home again and he realised just how depressing all the mess had become.

"This is wonderful, wonderful!" he exclaimed as he looked around.

"Right, now for some dinner." He clapped his hands together and rubbed them vigorously.

There wasn't very much in. In the end he opened a tin of soup and put it on to warm while he showered. When he returned to the kitchen, the soup was bubbling merrily, half its volume evaporated and with a fine crust forming on top. He transferred the glutinous mess into a sparkling bowl and threw the pan into the sink, momentarily considering whether to wipe away the few drops spilled on the table. But by the time he'd buttered some bread and sprinkled crumbs everywhere he'd forgotten all about that.

And as he surveyed his lounge, he let out a sigh of contentment. It was the first time in months that he felt he had some control over his life. He would be eternally grateful to Bellingham for that bollocking. When he'd explained all the things that had happened at the time he started working there, his boss had, surprisingly, almost seemed sympathetic. The enormous chair swung around towards the window and Bellingham said "women" in a strange voice.

In the end he had said they would speak again in a month, and review things then. During the week that followed, some wild and entertaining stories had circulated concerning Mrs Bellingham, and Wendell felt that his boss understood something about wife troubles.

Empty bowl, spoon and plate discarded to a sideboard, Wendell leant back and watched the news. After ten minutes he began to feel restless. A nice cup of tea should do the trick, he decided, and five minutes later he was staring out of the window, sipping the hot liquid with care. He looked at his watch. 7.30? Surely it was later than that? The wall clock backed up the watch. Strange, it seemed later.

People were heading out for the evening, determined clusters moving noisily along in lines like migrating geese, making Wendell feel suddenly rather alone. He picked up the TV magazine and scrutinised it. Nothing. Absolutely nothing. Friday night viewing seemed to be limited to children and the over 60s. Probably because no one of his age in their right mind would stay in and watch television on a Friday night.

He strolled back to the window, hands in pockets and stared out at the evening.

Without warning, Bibi came into his mind. What would she be doing tonight, he wondered? She would look beautiful, no doubt. Tall, slender, those gorgeous legs. He could almost smell the perfume she wore, almost feel her cool, silky skin against his. Perhaps she'd be having a cosy meal for two, followed by a club, a bit of dancing, then back to bed in the arms of that ponce. That ponce that would soon be just another notch on her bedpost, if he wasn't already. After all, it was a year now. At least he, Wendell, had lasted longer than the others. And now a whole wasted year had passed by. He sat down slowly, and for the first time since she had left, he put his head in his hands and cried like a baby.

Sometime later he woke, having nodded off after the blubbing, and found he was feeling better. Much better actually. It was out of his system, the first real tears he had shed since the whole sordid thing had happened. All the suppressed anger and humiliation seemed to have flowed out with his tears and given relief from the suffering, like the pus from some foul boil which had finally burst.

He wanted to go out, needed company. Women? Should he go to a nightclub? No, he didn't feel ready for that yet. What he needed now was male company.

He looked at his watch, an expensive gold-plated thing Bibi had bought for him. With his own money of course.

It was 8.45, still early really.

Wendell snatched up the phone before he could change his mind, and dialled the number of his old friend Barney. It was ages since he'd seen him, they had drifted a bit when both got married, but Barney was the kind of friend who wouldn't hold that against him. When you knew each other at school together, there were no barriers. Barney and Tracy had a new baby the last time he'd seen him and that had firmly put the lid on any nights out. As he thought of all this, the ringing stopped, and Wendell got ready to speak. But his spirits dipped as Barney's answerphone message began. At least that had remained the same. As he listened to the familiar recital churning out, Wendell felt deflated. Why had he expected Barney to be there on a Friday evening? However, before he had time to replace the receiver, another voice was shouting across the first.

"Just a second," said one Barney over the other, as he switched off the tape.

"Barney?"

There was a pause.

"Wendy? You old rascal!" yelled Barney loud enough to cause Wendell to wince. "I thought you'd been abducted by aliens. Where the hell have you been? I've been calling you for months, thought you'd moved."

"I haven't been in very much," confessed Wendell. "Thought it was about time I made contact."

"Too right, too right. So, how's things?"

"Yeah, ok. A few ups and downs," Wendell sidestepped the question. "But listen Barney, what're you up to tonight? Fancy making a night of it, boy's night out, you know?"

"Oh hell, no can do Wendy. It's Tracy's Birthday. We're going out to eat," he lowered his voice to a whisper. "I daren't change things now, it's been a bit... er, rough around here lately."

"Oh." Wendell felt depressed. "Never mind, another time maybe."

Hearing the dejection in his friend's tone, Barney suggested the following evening instead, partially restoring Wendell's spirits.

"Tracy's having some sort of Tupperware party, so you'll be doing me a favour." They both sniggered in schoolboy fashion, insinuating something about the strange things women enjoyed.

"Alright then Barney, see you tomorrow, eight-ish? Wish Tracy a happy birthday from me."

"Yep, yep, I will do. Bye then Wendy, better dash now. See you."

Bibi's name had been noticeably absent from the short conversation, so the grapevine had obviously been active. Sounded as though he and Tracy were having problems too then. He picked up his address book, a smart brown leather affair which had been another present from Bibi in the distant past, again paid for by himself. Other numbers produced equally limited success, so he cut his losses and stayed in with the television and a bottle of wine.

Chapter Six
Friday

There had been unfortunate repercussions after the Graham Pinfold extraction. During the Friday afternoon, the mother, an almighty woman dressed in angry red, stormed into the surgery ranting and raving about incompetence and negligence and a few other big words she had memorised specifically.

Antonia felt she had a point but kept it to herself.

"All you people are interested in is money," she bellowed at Susan, chins wobbling with indignation.

Dan appeared, nervous and pale, from the surgery and ushered her through into another room. The crowded waiting room had never been so quiet as people listened in on Mrs Pinfold's clearly audible voice behind the closed door. Whenever Dan managed to get a word in there was temporary silence. Finally, the door flew open, and she stomped out, almost steaming from the nostrils.

"And don't think you've heard the last of this," she finished, stabbing a finger at Dan. "I'm seeing a solicitor in the morning."

Dan stood rigid in the doorway throughout, his eyebrows dancing a jig with his hairline, saying nothing. Mrs Pinfold turned, thrust her jaw out and left, slamming the door hard enough to make the wall shake. All heads turned from her to Dan, following his rear view as he disappeared hurriedly into his surgery.

Unfortunately for Mrs Pinfold as she reeled furiously down the stairs, she slipped, shot through the open door and out onto the street, breaking her ankle and grating her carthorse-like buttocks on the pavement. Fifteen minutes later she was carried off in an ambulance, manned by the same crew that had removed her son earlier in the week.

"Don't think I'll make an appointment here," said the driver to his companion, as the vehicle screamed away into the traffic.

Inside the building, Dan's hands were shaking as he dealt with the next patient's filling.

"Aspirate!" He screamed, as Antonia sucked away the non-existent bits that only he, with his blurred vision, could see. Dan leant over and looked in, grimacing, then waggled a finger around in its circular motion above the patient's face. Antonia, leaning over for a better view, repeated the suction, even though she could see nothing. The patient's eyes were like dinner plates.

"Oh, for God's sake!" he snarled and snatched the aspirator from her. He shoved it so roughly down the patient's throat that the poor woman began to gag.

Antonia sat, once again seething with hatred, as she watched him rummage around in search of the invisible debris.

The patient snapped her mouth shut the second Dan removed the aspirator and coughed.

"Sorry," she said, opening her mouth once more. The new filling had fallen out and she had swallowed it. Dan let out a long deep breath but said nothing and started all over again. Eventually the tooth was whole again and as she sat up, the patient launched into an avalanche of apologies.

"Oh dear, I'm so sorry to have been so much trouble. I'm a terrible patient I know, you are good to put up with me," she grinned lopsidedly.

Dan ignored her and she continued.

"I know I'm a coward."

"No, no you're grand," he offered finally, shepherding her towards the door.

She smiled gratefully, relieved and comforted by these kind words and headed to reception, where Antonia overheard her praising Mr Murphy to all and sundry, to make up for the negatives that had steamed out of Mrs Pinfold.

What was the matter with these people? Why did they feel the need to apologise for shortcomings they didn't have? Must be nerves, Antonia decided.

After the chaos and drama of the morning, things quietened down and the failure of a patient to arrive for his hour long appointment left a pleasant break, during which they caught up timewise and Dan became almost human. They even had a bit of a chat. She could (almost) like him when he was like this. Susan, stuck on desk duty, looked green with envy when she brought in the coffee. At one point Dan even laughed, revealing a row of gleaming crowns that reminded her of an ill-tempered horse she had once encountered. She had never seen him smile before and it was rather frightening.

It didn't last.

Susan triumphantly managed to drive a wedge into this dangerous camaraderie by unearthing a chart from somewhere on which Antonia had undercharged the patient. Dan's good humour swiftly became a disapproving frown, and he snapped at Antonia to call the old man and tell him to send a cheque for the balance. It was in fact Dan's own fault as he hadn't included the item on the bill and the injustice of it, coupled with Susan's jealous righteousness, made her so furious she thought she would explode. Trying to explain made it worse and by the time she'd rung old Mr so and so and demanded the £1.75, she felt nearly suicidal. He'd been so sweet about it she could have wept. On impulse, she bought a newspaper before heading off, hoping her dream job would be in it.

She pedalled home like an Olympian athlete, rain lashing on all sides as she went, hating her job, Dan Murphy, old maids who ran receptions, the patients, in fact the rest of the world in general. And now to top it all, standing dripping and cold on the doorstep, she couldn't find her keys.

As Wendell drew up outside, he looked curiously at the forlorn figure on the step spilling the contents of a bag out onto the wet ground. She looked from her actions like a child having a tantrum, and he fiddled about with things in the car in the hope of avoiding her. It was that ponce's ex. Still living here then. She was obviously searching for her door keys. It would probably look odd to delay any longer, so he got out, locked the car and walked up the path.

Antonia, close to panic, didn't hear him. She was absolutely certain that she'd had the keys before leaving work. She'd used them to unlock her bike only half an hour ago, but she'd been in such a rage she couldn't remember what she'd done with them after that. The contents of her bag were littered across the doorstep, her address book open and flapping in the wind.

As Wendell approached, he could hear her repeating 'shit, shit, shit' over and over. She was just opening her mouth to scream out loud when she heard someone close by clearing their throat, and clamped it shut.

"Are you having trouble?" he enquired politely.

Antonia spun around, startled and red in the face. Her hair was escaping from its ponytail and lay in damp strands on her neck and cheeks. She turned back straight away mumbling something about keys.

"Well, at least I can let you in," smiled Wendell. She hated him too.

"Oh yes, sorry. Thank you. Sorry about that," she spluttered, wishing the ground would open and swallow her into its depths. She began to hurriedly gather up her possessions. Bugger off, she thought when he also bent to help her. Their eyes fell simultaneously on a pair of soggy black and white polka dot knickers caught just under the toe of his shoe. The pair of pants had remained forgotten in the bottom of the bag all week. He removed his foot wordlessly and she snatched them away and into a pocket while her cheeks burned. Had he seen them? Known what they were? She sincerely hoped not, while knowing full well he had and did.

How absolutely mortifying.

With everything now gathered up, he opened the door and stood back to let her pass.

"Thank you," she said dully. "I don't know what I could have done with my keys." She felt like crying.

"Er, look, would you like to come in and call anyone?" Wendell, ever the gentleman, couldn't help himself but he didn't really want this trouble on his shoulders.

The last thing Antonia wanted was to have to interact with that woman's ex and be beholden to *him*.

"Let me just check..." she said, vaguely recalling dropping the keys into a coat pocket.

They were there.

"Oh, thank goodness!" she exclaimed with relief, and smiled at last. It transformed her face completely and Wendell gave her a closer look.

"Disaster averted," he said, smiling back, and inserted his key in his own door. How strange that they shared a front door and all this time had never met there before. He was sure she was the same girl, the one whose boyfriend Bibi had gone off with. He had thought she had moved long ago. Different hairstyle perhaps.

"I'm sorry for the trouble, Mr Cornish." She'd seen his name on the outside bell. "Thank you for your help."

Wendell's charm surfaced. After all, damsels in distress were his speciality.

"Oh, do call me Wendell, please; after all, we are neighbours."

Wendell! That was it. He had a pleasant voice, educated, velvety, even if his name was ridiculous. She defrosted a little. "Antonia."

He took his hand from the door and offered it to her.

"Let's bury the hatchet Antonia, none of what happened was our fault after all," then he smiled at her in a friendly way and she decided she didn't, after all, hate Wendell Cornish.

Why had he said that? It seemed to have bubbled out without thought. He hoped he hadn't embarrassed her.

Antonia stared into his face. Tears stung and prickled. All the irritation of the past few hours and the torment of the last year welled up and threatened to spill over because of a kind word from a stranger. While she fought to control herself, she studied Wendell's face, noticing for the first time the shadows under his eyes, the fine lines on his brow, the tired expression, and was suddenly filled with compassion for this man she had so recently despised, realising that being consumed by her own self-pity she had not given a thought to his.

In this same moment he saw a frail, desperate girl, standing there soaked and dripping, with large tearful eyes. He wanted to put his arms around her and comfort her, tell her he knew. He'd been there too, but everything was going to be better now.

It was a moment of shared grief that bonded the victims of heartbreak.

Antonia took his hand and shook it.

"Come down here and have a coffee with me sometime," said Wendell brightly.

"Thanks," she smiled and was gone.

As soon as the door shut behind her, Antonia threw herself onto the bed and cried for a long time, not caring that she was still in her wet things and that the bed would get all damp. Afterwards, she absently opened the local paper she had bought, now dried out, and the first thing that caught her eye was a local dental surgery looking for a new nurse. It felt like fate and without her usual hesitation, Antonia phoned and made an appointment for an interview. She felt much better when she had done it, felt like she was actually doing something instead of just stagnating. Then she thought about the scene downstairs on the doorstep with her neighbour earlier, and sighed. What a mess her life was in.

Chapter Seven
Friday Continued

Bibi was feeling disgruntled, as she often did.

All Charlie wanted to do these days was watch TV and then go to bed for a quickie or, even worse, for an early night! Imagine *reading* while they were in bed together! And while she was always game for a romp, she wanted to be wined and dined, adored and cajoled as a prelude to it, which is what she had always been accustomed to. Strangely, it was one of the reasons Charles had lasted so long. She'd never known a man like him; he could be so infuriating. It was her that had been doing all the chasing and persuading, and now it was becoming a little tedious.

She thought about the 'reading material' *she* had supplied for him in an effort to get him going a bit, all those sexy men's magazines. She had popped into the shop she and Wendell used to use, knowing he had an account with them, and charged them all to him, after a quiet word with that shrivelled old hag in there. He probably wouldn't have been amused but who cared. They hadn't had the desired effect anyway, Charles was horrified. What a child he could be.

When Bibi had first spotted Charles, she had known she had to have him. How naïve the man was, she'd had to be pretty full on to gain his attention, but once he *had* noticed her, and she had forced things a little with that small lie, it had been a surprisingly easy conquest. She had felt a tiny pang of guilt about Wendell, but he'd been getting very tiresome anyway, and as for that mousy creature Charles referred to as his girlfriend, well, what on earth was he doing with someone like her? She'd done him a favour extracting him from that situation.

At first Charles had been happy enough as long as they were together (once he'd given up talking about his ex. Bibi had never let a man cry on her shoulder before). He did everything she wanted even if it wasn't something he was used to, or even liked, and she soaked up his admiration like a sponge, while being a bit put off by his neediness at the same time.

But now, a year on, it seemed his own personality was beginning to butt in strongly, and although she tried to convince herself otherwise, she was beginning to think him a little dull. But then again, with looks like his, she could forgive him anything. She enjoyed heads turning their way whenever they went out, even if he didn't.

Anyway, Friday evening was the start of the weekend and whether Charlie wanted to or not, they were going to make a night of it. She would dress to kill and flirt with him outrageously, make him her slave all over again. She smiled at the idea, fractionally disturbing the mud pack which presently adorned her face. A slice of cucumber rested on each eyelid and lying back as she was, with the peroxide hair pinned back tightly, long legs crossed at the ankles and the rest of her all wrapped in a fluffy pink robe, she could have jumped straight from the pages of any beauty magazine. Another couple of minutes and the mud pack would be done.

She planned what to wear. Red? She looked good in red, but Charlie didn't like it, said it looked tarty. She had slapped his face that time, it had been their first real row, but she didn't want to repeat it because he had not responded in the way she had expected. Instead of fussing over her, flattering and apologising and all the usual things men did, he had looked like a small child after a good hiding and sulked for the entire evening. She decided to wear the clingy black number with the silver earrings Wendell had given her when they first met, they were her favourites. Wendell did have good taste, she had to admit. The black choker would set it all off perfectly.

The alarm beeped; the face pack was cooked.

She rose gracefully and ate the cucumber, then went to start a bath. While the water ran, she cleaned her face then stirred the water and breathed in the scent of the expensive bubble bath with pleasure.

"Mmm," she purred, savouring the silkiness of her cheek with the back of an elegant hand, freshly manicured this morning. She lounged for forty-five minutes in the fragrant hot water and once out and with her hair wrapped in a towel, opened a prepacked salad and prepared to lunch.

She heard the front door open.

Oh no! She said to herself. What was he doing back so early?

"Darling?" called Charles.

She tutted irritably and didn't reply.

"Darling? Where are you?"

His head appeared around the kitchen door.

"Ah, there you are." He smiled, his eyes roaming over her with appreciation. How beautiful she was without all that make-up on. She was so untouchable when she'd just applied it all, right now she was perfect.

He leant over and kissed her, then smiled into her face. She smiled back.

"You're back early," she said casually.

"Yes," they're all off to enjoy the wonders of nature this afternoon. Some outing that's been planned forever. I forgot about it. But listen, darling, my parents are having a little get-together tonight, and I said we'd go along. They haven't seen us for ages. Charles looked quite animated for once at the idea.

"What!"

"I know what you're thinking," said Charles with a hand raised to stop the flow. "But put the last time behind you, they'll adore you when they get to know you properly."

Bibi would hardly forget that first visit. The boredom. Charlie's frumpy, twittering mother who kept throwing her unfriendly glances. The father, who just watched television all evening. Hours just sitting there with them after getting all dressed up. She wasn't going through that again.

There was a short uncomfortable pause.

"I had plans for us tonight," said Bibi in a pathetic tone. If he thought she was going to get all dolled up to go to some boring 'get-together' with a lot of old relics he could think again.

"Oh? What other plans?"

"Well, I thought we could go to Gino's for a meal, then on to a club. I've booked the table already, I was going to surprise you," she lied, and looked sorrowful. He didn't notice.

"But we can go to Gino's anytime," whined Charles, "my parents have offered the olive branch, I think we should take it."

Even worse! She was supposed to charm her way into the affections of his disapproving parents now. Whenever his mother phoned, she was polite but frosty, and there was no way she was going to waste this evening on that old bag.

"Oh, but darling," she bit her lip and rolled her eyes towards his pleadingly. "Darling, I can't just have this thrust on me like this. I need some time to prepare myself mentally. I just can't, not tonight, darling, please."

She looked so pretty sitting there all childlike holding her forkful of salad that Charles began to waver.

"Well…"

"Oh, thank you, darling," she said and stretched up to kiss him. She was still holding the fork minus the salad which had fallen off when she reached up. Charles trod on it as he hoisted her to him and swept her off to the bedroom.

When she finally managed to disentangle herself from Charles' grip, she went off to run another bath.

"Haven't you just had a bath?"

"I'm all sweaty now. Join me if you like?"

There was no reply and when, after another half hour soak, she wandered back to the bedroom it was to find him fast asleep with his long eyelashes resting on flushed cheeks like a sleeping baby. She bent over and kissed him lightly on the lips, not wishing to wake him. It was a bit annoying having to get ready with him there when she had expected the place to herself, but it couldn't be helped. If he slept for the next couple of hours that would be perfect.

She padded quietly to the lounge and closed the door then picked up the phone.

"Gino!" she trilled, using all her charm, and made a booking for 8 o'clock.

"Only for you, darling," said the man in accented English, heavy with lecherous suggestion. She imagined the glint in his eye as he spoke. They'd spent a passionate night together once when she'd been cross with Wendell, who'd thought she was at her mother's. How stupid men were.

By the time Charles woke, none the wiser, she was made up like Cleopatra and in the process of teasing her fluffy curls into shape.

"What time is it?" croaked Charles, eyes still shut.

"About six."

"Six! Good God," and he rose and walked naked into the bathroom. Bibi admired the view reflected in the mirror.

She heard the bath running for the third time.

"What time at Gino's?"

"Eight."

He wandered to the lounge, yawning loudly, still unclothed.

"Hello Mum, how are you?"

"Fine dear, can you still make it tonight?" she sounded hopeful.

"We can't, Bibi had something else planned. It was booked. We'll come another time. Sorry."

"Right." She was cross now, knowing full well that woman would have persuaded him not to come. They hardly ever saw him these days. Why hadn't he stayed with Antonia? That strumpet was no good for him.

"I'll drop in during the week, Mum. Got to go, my bath's running. Bye."

"Bye."

He ran to the bath and turned the tap off.

"What did you tell them?"

"What? Well, that you'd planned something else." Charles seemed surprised at the enquiry.

"You would," muttered Bibi as she fiddled with her hair, not intending him to hear. Couldn't he have invented something better; they were sure to realise she hadn't wanted to go. Oh, who cared anyway.

Charles got into his bath and lay back. It wasn't as warm as he would have liked, Bibi had used all the hot water.

They left the flat with half an hour to spare, Bibi looking stunning in the black dress with Wendell's tasteful silver earrings just visible under the mass of hair. A plain looking couple on the other side of the street, mesmerised with this handsome pair, accidentally collided with a lamp post.

Bibi let herself into the car as Charles had forgotten to open the door for her. Really! He had no idea sometimes. But she forgave him when he gazed at her and told her how beautiful she looked. He leaned over to kiss her, but she proffered a powdery cheek instead, not wishing to ruin her lipstick.

Gino ushered them through to a quiet table for two, greeting Bibi with an exaggerated kiss to her hand and escorting her to it personally with her arm linked in his. He ignored Charles completely, leaving him to trail along behind them like a pet dog. Charles felt stupid and inadequate and was furious at the way Bibi was also ignoring him. When they were seated and Gino had finally torn his swarthy face away from Bibi's cleavage, Charles said sulkily, "do you always have to flirt like that? It's embarrassing."

Colour flared into her cheeks. She did not like being criticised.

"It's the way to get what you want in this world," she hissed back angrily, "If, perhaps, *you* would lay on the charm once in a while, *I* wouldn't have to do it for both of us."

Fleetingly, Charles hated her. There she sat, arrogantly telling him, yet again, that he was without charm. He was getting tired of it. In some vague corner of his brain, he knew she was right, and it depressed him, but he didn't want it continually pointed out either. For the second time in ten minutes, he felt inadequate.

He picked up the menu and scanned it in angry silence. Bibi, noticing the two spots of colour in his cheeks, decided just to move on from the disagreement and forget it. She contemplated gaily what she would have. Charles remained sulky and finally she said in exasperation, "Well, if you're not interested in what I have to say, I'd better ask Gino."

"Can't you forget that fucking wop for a second?" he replied nastily.

Bibi recognised the danger signals and immediately began evasive action. She opened her eyes wide to allow them to get a little watery, then feigned a hurt expression, then bit her lip.

"Oh God, I'm sorry, darling," said Charles, moved by this display, and grasped her hand which had been obligingly placed on the table.

"Let's begin again, shall we? Come on, darling, I'm sorry, I didn't mean to swear."

She raised her eyes slowly to his and pouted.

"I've said I'm sorry," he smiled cautiously.

"Alright, let's start again," she smiled. "I'll start with the garlic mushrooms."

Chapter Eight
Saturday

Wendell woke that Saturday morning, dry-mouthed and a bit headachy.

How much of that wine had he drunk for God's sake?

The first thought to drift through the brain fog was that girl upstairs and their odd meeting on the doorstep the previous evening, possibly because it was the only thing of note to have happened all day yesterday.

While he was glugging down that sour tasting plonk, he'd been unable to stop thinking about it. He decided he would like to get to know her, it would give him some company for one thing, and she'd looked a rather helpless little thing standing there with her soggy underwear, the sort of girl any man wanted to be chivalrous to. She must have been as hurt by that good-looking boyfriend as he had been by his good-looking wife. His anger over the whole thing had been rekindled on her behalf and had made it an excuse to open the other bottle in his fridge.

Now he looked at his bedside clock. It was midday, this wouldn't do at all. He rolled into a sitting position and got to his feet, making the headache worse, but after a couple of aspirins followed by a late but large fried breakfast he felt properly recovered.

He ditched the greasy pan and everything else into a sinkful of hot water. After all, he wanted Mrs O. to be aware he was doing his bit. It wasn't a bad day out, so he strolled to the local shop to get a pint of milk and a breath of fresh air. People were everywhere, swarming in and out of the place laden with carrier bags and as he thrust through them, he was pounced upon by a small stout man in an overall who, as was his habit, was smoothing a few lengthy strands of hair over the top of a wide bald patch.

"Mr Cornish!" he declared; eyes wide with expectancy. "Haven't seen you for ages."

"No, how are you, Jim?" Wendell replied politely.

"Very good thank you, Sir. Yourself?"

"Fine thanks. Lovely day, isn't it?"

"Beautiful. Yes. Now then, I'm glad to have seen you. Your paper bill. We sent a letter; did you get it?" His mouth was smiling but his eyes were not.

"Oh? I'm sorry Jim, I can't remember. I suppose I must owe you a bit by now."

"Well, it has got rather high. I knew I needn't worry as it was you, Mr Cornish," he emphasised the word you, and Wendell felt a little sickened by this sycophantic attitude. Jim then lowered his voice, became conspiratorial. "Man's got to make a living you know." He finished with a grin, revealing yellowed teeth patched with old fillings, which reminded Wendell of mottled gravestones.

"Oh God, I am sorry Jim," Wendell replied in his most apologetic manner. "I had no idea it was so long; I really am terribly sorry."

Neither of them meant a word of all these platitudes, and both knew it, but there was a certain code of ethics to abide by, and both felt satisfied that they had achieved it. And in a way, Jim was secretly impressed by Wendell Cornish. Well-spoken and with charming manners, nice car too. It was enough to convince him that here stood a man of substance, of breeding.

"Let me settle up now," continued Wendell, rummaging for a tenner as he spoke.

Jim forestalled him with a raised hand. "Oh no, that's quite all right Mr Cornish. You settle up with Doreen at the till when you've done your shopping." A fleck of foamy spittle, whipped up by all the frantic talking, leapt from the corner of Jim's mouth and landed on Wendell's sweater, which he brushed away with a cuff and a wince before heading towards Doreen with a pint of milk and a mars bar.

Unlike her old man, Doreen was not at all impressed with Wendell and she had no hesitation in showing it. As he approached the till, she thrust the bill towards him with a stony expression. He had to take a second look. It came to £48.97.

He glanced up at Doreen, eyes wide. It couldn't be that long since he'd been in here, could it? Blimey, he'd have to write a cheque.

Doreen's unsmiling face stared up at him, a face like a little monkey, all brown and wrinkled with tight overpermed grey hair atop it. A hard face that had seen too much sun in its fifty odd years.

"I do apologise for leaving it so long," he tried, as he wrote the cheque. Doreen examined it closely, demanded a bank card and spent some time diligently scribbling all its information down before returning it to him.

"K'you," she said crisply as he left, still reeling at the size of the bill.

He was still puzzling over this as a group of lively boys flowed around him, shepherded by a thin, worried man with a ball and whistle. It reminded him of when he and a friend used to play football with their fathers at weekends. They would all return home starving and muddy to hot baths and a freshly baked cake. It used to be wonderful, that little ritual.

His parents lived in Spain now, one of the colonies of English couples retired there. It must be two years since he'd seen them, possibly more, he thought with a jolt. When had he last called them? He couldn't remember. Gripped with sudden remorse, he quickened his pace and went home determined to rectify it. But all this went out of the window when he glanced again at the paper bill. Listed among all the usual stuff was a great quantity of expensive 'men's' magazines and other things that he had no knowledge of at all. Bibi! That bloody bitch must have had a good laugh over buying those, no doubt whispering to Doreen that he needed them. His jaw dropped at the thought of her looking at him with those hard piggy eyes, imagining him salivating over pornographic pictures, how could he ever go in there again? No wonder the bill had been so high. It must have been ages since he'd been in there too.

Why on earth was she so vindictive, wondered Wendell? It was her that had jumped ship. God, she was a piece of work!

Wendell telephoned the shop and explained, telling Doreen that Bibi must pay for her own things now, and having always thought of Bibi as a stuck-up bitch and been suspicious of her sudden friendliness when buying those filthy magazines, Doreen gave him the benefit of the doubt and thawed a bit.

While he was at it, he also telephoned through to his parents. The call went through without problems but as he began to speak, he realised he was greeting an answerphone message. What on earth did they need that for?

"Hello? Hello? Anyone there?" He called impatiently across his father's slow and deliberate message.

"Wendell!" came his mother's voice suddenly and the message ceased abruptly. "Where have you *been*? We've been worried about you. Didn't you get my letter?" She was cross with relief. But before he could reply, another tirade spilled down the line. "It really is bad of you, Wendell, a postcard would have done. I suppose you forgot it was your father's birthday on the 15th. He was very hurt. Peter remembered."

He would, thought Wendell. Peter, the brother he hadn't spoken to for ten years at least and wouldn't be bothered if it carried on for another ten. The golden boy.

"Oh hell," groaned Wendell, genuine in his remorse. "Let me speak to him. Is he there?"

"He's on the toilet. Honestly, he takes longer and longer in there these days. I'll pass you over when he's done."

"Oh… dear." Wendell wasn't quite sure how to respond to this information. "I'm sorry about that. How are you?"

"I've been worried about you, darling. I've heard a rumour."

"About Bibi?"

"Yes."

"It's probably true then. She left me a year ago. Went off with our upstairs neighbour."

How well he could picture his mother, perched upright on a very English armchair wearing a very floaty garment, lips pursed and brow puckered, an Englishwoman abroad.

"A year! Oh, really, darling, you should have told us." She sounded cross again.

"I'm sorry, Mother, I didn't want you to worry…" *or interfere*, he thought but didn't say it. "I hoped at first she would come back, then as time went by and she didn't I just felt too miserable about the whole thing."

He filled in the details, and she made suitable comments throughout, then tried unsuccessfully to persuade him to come over for a holiday; then passed him on to his father, long finished with his ablutions.

"Hello Wendell."

"Hello father. Happy Birthday for the 15th, sorry I forgot."

"Oh yes, seems long ago now," replied his father with an air of dismissal. "What's all this about Bibi leaving you?"

Wendell had to repeat the whole saga again, but it was better for his father to hear it from him than the version his mother would have given.

"Always said she was a tart," he snapped, when Wendell concluded the story.

Wendell was surprised, shocked even. It was unusual for his father to express such a view, let alone use a word like 'tart' and he felt suddenly awkward. His father had always seemed very fond of Bibi. There followed a few pleasantries and promises to write, and the call ended.

He sat and mulled over his father's words thoughtfully. So, he thought she was a tart then. Well, well, well, you live and learn.

He switched the telly on. The football season had started so he stretched out on the sofa to watch the action and five minutes later was soundly asleep.

Chapter Nine
Saturday

Antonia's Saturday began with a luxurious lie in, the more so because it didn't happen very often these days. She woke around ten and relaxed for a few more lovely minutes while she became properly awake. Lying there in that half asleep state, she remembered a strange dream she'd had.

What had its sequence been?

She fought to recall the details. That man Wendell Cornish had been in it, yes, and Rob Murphy too. That was it—she had been at work, Rob shouting "Aspirate! Aspirate!" repeatedly. She couldn't seem to aim the suction tube properly and kept missing the patient's mouth. In her struggle with it, she inserted it instead into Rob's open one where it became firmly attached to his tongue. The patient was staring wild-eyed at him and screaming with terror. He merely made comforting remarks despite his handicapped tongue being dragged further and further out of his mouth.

Antonia panicked, pulling unsuccessfully on the offending instrument like a sailor hauling on a rope. Rob suddenly keeled over sideways and lay motionless on the floor, his tongue now reaching down as far as his breast pocket. She pulled again and the tongue scrolled out like a roll of toilet paper. She ran from the room looking for help and there was Wendell Cornish, so she shook his hand and hurried him into the surgery where he immediately took charge of the situation.

Rob lay motionless, eyes staring from a pale and sweaty face. He looked like one of his patients.

"Call an ambulance," demanded Wendell to the screaming patient, still in the chair, who became calm at once and called from the instrument tray, which had somehow become a payphone. A team of paramedics burst into the room, which was bigger than normal and full of unknown people in medical uniforms.

Wendell Cornish had his arm around her shoulders and seemed strong and capable.

"We'll have to operate to save his life," said one of the medics, swiftly producing a pair of gardening shears from a trouser pocket and snipped off the aspirator. The tongue began to shrink, there was sudden calm and Rob sat up and stared at Antonia.

"You're thacked," he lisped, as he whirled a finger around in a circular motion over his mouth.

"Never mind," interrupted the patient brightly. "You can come and work for me. I'm a dentist from down the road." She smiled, but her teeth had vanished.

Antonia turned to Wendell Cornish and gazed into his eyes. He was holding out a pair of pants to her with a silly grin on his face. Oh God, she thought, reliving the embarrassing scene from the day before. The dream faded. What a way to meet her neighbour. She felt odd about him, pleased that they had met at last and almost desperately hopeful that she may have found a friend in him. Throwing the covers off, she shoved her feet into some slippers and shivered. It felt cool this morning. The phone rang.

"Hello Mum," she said with a yawn, settling into an embryonic position on the armchair.

"Just got up?"

"How did you guess?"

"How are things?" This was a standard question, of course, but lately Antonia's mother had not received standard answers and was unsure what she would hear in response.

"Ok I suppose."

"You suppose."

Antonia outlined her week.

"I met the downstairs neighbour yesterday, that horrible woman's husband."

"Oh! What's he like?"

Antonia's mother worried continually about her daughter's single status and would happily have paired her off with Jack the Ripper had he been available.

"Nice, surprisingly. He's called Wendell Cornish." She pronounced it in a pompous voice and they both laughed.

"What a funny name, his parents must have had a sense of humour. Sounds like an insurance company." Antonia's mother laughed again then continued, "Antonia Cornish, yes, that has a nice ring to it."

"Oh Mum!" scolded Antonia, and quickly changed the subject, "Are you in this afternoon, Mum?"

"Yes, come over and have lunch with me."

"Ok thanks. I'll be there about one. In fact, why don't we go out and have something? I'll treat you."

Her mother agreed happily, and the call ended. Antonia threw on some clothes and went to fight it out at the supermarket with the Saturday crush, then prepared to set off for her mother's. For a horrible moment, she thought the car wasn't going to start but it eventually coughed into life and off she went, singing along to the radio. Traffic was heavy, there was a long jam right through the town. It would have added a bit of mileage to go around but, she decided, would probably have been worth it in the long run as the journey, usually twenty minutes, had taken nearly twice that. Would have helped the car to give it a run too. It was a nice day, that always brought the crowds out.

How green the fields were already, she thought, as she finally left the town behind her. To think that only two weeks ago everything had been so scorched and yellow. She felt unexpectedly melancholy about the summer coming to an end.

It was warm in the car though, so she opened the window and savoured the fresh countryside aroma of cut hay. Huge rolls of it rested in the fields, giant wheels drying in the sun.

She arrived at her mother's about twenty minutes late, only to find her in the bath.

Her mother was a terrible timekeeper, always had been. After the death of Antonia's father, she had become worse without him to chivvy her along.

"Mum?" Antonia tapped on the bathroom door.

"Oh dear, you're here already. Am I late? What time is it?"

The door swung back to reveal Antonia's small, fragrant mother resplendent in a fluffy striped robe and matching slippers.

"One-thirty," replied Antonia, adding fifteen minutes as she bent to kiss her mother's cheek, which smelled of soap and talc, familiar and comforting. This usually had the effect of hurrying her mother up. The length of time added corresponded to the importance of the occasion.

"Oh dear, I'm not ready, am I?"

"You never are," replied Antonia fondly and they both smiled. "I thought we could just go to the pub, ok?"

"Fine. I'll be five minutes." She disappeared back into the bathroom.

Antonia left her in peace, knowing from experience that despite the temptation to do it, hurrying her would not achieve anything.

Twenty minutes later she reappeared, made up and coiffured but still wrapped in the robe. It was when Antonia heard the kettle going on and washing up being done that she jumped up.

"Mum, Mum, for God's sake! It's 2 o'clock. We haven't got time for all that. I'll do it while you get some clothes on."

"I just want to get it out of the way, I don't want to come back to it."

"I'll do it," repeated Antonia, taking her mother from behind and shepherding her firmly towards the stairs. "You get ready."

She dispatched the washing up and began leafing through the TV magazine. What a load of rubbish there was on, again, this evening. All for families or kids. Nothing for a single person in need of entertainment.

Finally, at 2.30, her mother emerged, sporting a dark lounge suit which was new to her daughter.

"You look nice, Mum."

"Do you like it?" said her mother happily, then frowned. "You don't think I should put something else on do you? Something cooler? Is it warm out?"

"No, it's fine, let's go, they stop serving at three."

By the time her mother had selected a suitable jacket and been dissuaded from having another coffee, it was ten to. Luckily, the pub was only a two-minute walk away and they made it just in the nick of time.

"We've got plenty of time," cooed her mother as Antonia hurried her to the food counter. "It's not three yet."

I give up, thought Antonia, exasperated.

Amazingly there was still food left, albeit a little dried up, and they sat down to it hungrily.

The story of the soaking underpants was discussed.

"I was *mortified*!" said Antonia with feeling, shaking her head at the memory. "God knows what he must have thought. Probably thought I was a local prostitute."

"Go and explain it to him. Make a joke of it, break the ice."

"Oh no, I couldn't."

"Oh, you are silly," chided her mother, "always missing opportunities."

"What do you suggest then? Knock on his door and say hi, I'm Antonia from upstairs, remember? The one who chucks wet knickers in front of men to get attention."

"No of course not." She tutted. "No need for that filth, I was only making a suggestion."

There was a small silence, then the conversation turned to other matters.

After their meal they wandered to the local shops and had a look, arriving back just before six.

"I'm going to a little party tonight," announced Antonia's mother suddenly, as they sat down to relax with a coffee.

"Oh?"

"Mary. It's her birthday today."

"That's nice, what time?"

"Half past six I think."

"What! It's past six now."

"It won't take me long to get ready. She won't mind if I'm ten minutes late anyway."

Antonia rolled her eyes and got up to go, knowing it would delay things further if she sat there.

"Bye Mum." She kissed her cheek. "Have a nice time if you ever get there. Say hello and happy birthday to Mary."

"You could come too," she offered kindly, guessing correctly that her daughter had no plans for the evening.

"Thanks, but no, I've got things to do."

The last thing she wanted was to go to a gathering of over sixties, she would be a blight just being there. She would have to make do with the crap on the telly. Perhaps she could call on Wendell Cornish? Invite herself in for that coffee? Even as she thought it, she knew absolutely that she would never have the courage to do such a thing.

"Bye Toni, why don't you look in on your neighbour tonight?" Her mother said, as if reading her daughter's mind. She wasn't going to forget Wendell Cornish; in fact, she already had him lined up as marriage material.

"Bye."

After Antonia had left, her mum noticed that the washing up needed to be put away.

Chapter Ten
Saturday

At six-thirty or thereabouts, Wendell woke up feeling disorientated, imagining in that horrible way that sometimes happens, that he was late for work. When reality finally reached him and panic had subsided, he stretched and yawned, shut his eyes for a few more blissful seconds and then heaved himself into a sitting position.

As he rubbed his eyes with one hand, he regarded the cold cup of tea on the table, with its little islands of scum resting on the surface. For one tiny moment he considered drinking it, even going so far as to reach out and touch the cup. Stone cold. No, he couldn't.

He made a fresh one in a new cup and sighed with pleasure as he surveyed the tidy room, and the hot sweet liquid refreshed his dry mouth. Having wandered over to the window with it clutched in both hands, he looked out to see Antonia returning from her mother's, and studied her afresh from his position of invisibility, thinking how strange it was that he hadn't seen her for a year and now had seen her twice in as many days.

He was glad they had spoken, perhaps they would become friends. Who cared if she was a bit odd, he wasn't about to walk down the aisle with her. It would be so nice to have a female friend, and he was also curious as to whether she had suspected her good-looking boyfriend was playing away. Perhaps she'd be up for a no strings attached… oh God, what was he thinking! He'd been on his own too long. Nice hair. He liked long hair. His mind went once again to their 'brief' encounter of the day before and he smiled at the memory. Why did she have wet underwear in her bag anyway? Wonder what she's doing tonight?

Christ, if he was going to be at Barney's by eight, he'd better get a move on, no good standing about dreaming all evening. He left the window and threw down the tea in a final gulp, then got himself ready to go out on the town. By the time he was done he felt good and was raring to go. All the sleep he'd had had refreshed him wonderfully both in mind and body, and he was looking forward to seeing his old friend. He examined himself in the mirror one final time. The hazel eyes were bright, the puffiness was gone, or at least less pronounced than it had been. Even the slightly pock marked skin, those scars of teenage acne, did not look unattractive.

"Handsome devil," he said to his reflection, affecting a seductive grin. He glanced at his watch. He would be a little late but they'd got all night so what did that matter.

He grabbed a light jacket, stuffed a tie into a pocket just in case, and pranced out to his car before roaring away, pulling up exactly twenty-five minutes later outside Barney's house.

He approached the door with a spring in his step, then became aware of shouting emanating from the interior, which silenced abruptly when he rang the bell. After some delay, just as he was about to ring again, the door opened to reveal Barney's dishevelled figure, clearly not at all ready for a night on the town, and as his friend stared uncomprehendingly at him for a moment, Wendell suspected with a sinking feeling that he had forgotten all about their arrangement.

"Wendy! Oh my God!" He put a hand to his forehead. "Wendy, old man, come in, come in."

He was ushered into the lounge where Barney's wife, Tracy, sat enthroned on the sofa surrounded by a large collection of cushions, thereby ensuring that no one else had room to sit with her. She was bloated and very obviously pregnant and looked like she had been crying. She scrutinised Wendell through sullen eyes.

The room was in a state of terrible disarray. Newspapers and children's toys were strewn across the floor, the table was laden with used cups and beer cans and an ashtray piled high with debris was perched on top of one of them like a geometric mushroom.

"Hello Wendell," said Tracy with an effort at politeness. "Sorry about the mess, you can ask him about that," she shot a spiteful look Barney's way.

"Hello Tracy." Wendell leant across her bulk and planted a cautious kiss on her pink and puffy cheek. "You look... well, I had no idea you were expecting another one. Congratulations! When's it due?"

"A week ago, last Wednesday," she replied, beginning to cry. There was an embarrassing pause while Barney did and said nothing, so she heaved herself up, mumbled an apology in Wendell's direction and shuffled out of the room.

"Oh, er, happy birthday by the way," said Wendell, trailing off a bit towards the end of the sentence. Tracy was already gone.

"Sorry about that," said Barney with false cheerfulness. "Sit down, sit down. Would you like a drink? Tea? Coffee?"

"Thanks, I'll have the drink," he replied, more at home now Tracy wasn't there.

Barney laughed. "Ha, very good!" What'll it be then? I haven't got much in actually, had a bit of a session with Bill and Terry earlier. Beer ok?

"Fine." He removed a sticky toy from the armchair and sat down.

From the kitchen came the sound of glasses being retrieved from a sinkful of crockery, followed by a loud crash. Barney returned some minutes later with two cans of beer swinging from their plastic circles. He had a tea towel wrapped around his hand to stem a bleeding cut.

"Not my day Wendy, not my day at all," he said flopping into the space recently vacated by Tracy. "So… what's been happening? Haven't seen you for ages. You're looking very dapper, are you going somewhere?"

Wendell regarded his friend, subdued. He looked bloody awful. He'd put on weight in all the wrong places, and it didn't suit him. His waistline seemed to be in competition with Tracy's, he'd gone quite grey too and could do with a haircut. A shave too. It was painfully obvious that he wasn't going anywhere tonight. There were no signs of an impending Tupperware party either. Did he even remember their conversation? How awkward.

"Well, I've been a bit rough lately to be truthful, Barney, but I'm raring to go now. How about you?"

Barney was stifling a yawn and seeing Wendell had noticed, replied with an apology.

"Sorry Wendy, I'm so knackered I can barely think straight. Tracy's been an absolute bitch during this pregnancy. I tell you; I'll be bloody glad when it's out. Sam's been a little shit too. We've run the gamut of tantrums, I can't cope with it any more. I'm just going through the motions. Work's the only place I get any peace. Bill and Terry—you remember them?" He didn't wait for an answer. "Came over this morning and crow-barred me out for a lunchtime drink while Tracy was at her mothers with the kid. First bloody outing I've had for weeks.

We came back here for a swift one, as you can see." He waved a hand vaguely towards the table. "When she got back with that dragon of a mother, well, all hell broke loose. I think you've met her mother, haven't you?"

"Er…"

"Anyway," he took a long gulp of beer and wiped the foam off his lips with his tongue. "Anyway, I told her mother to leave us alone and stop interfering, bit of bravado with the lads here. Very stupid of me to do it really. I was probably pissed at the time too. That's what all that," he hitched a thumb in the general direction of upstairs, "was all about. Oh dear. Beware of mothers-in-law, Wendy, beware of mothers-in-law."

The monologue finished, Barney drained the beer can and lit a cigarette, inhaling deeply, a wisp of smoke rising in front of his face as he did so.

"I can see I've come at a bad time," said Wendell with resignation. "We can go out another time."

Barney turned towards Wendell and stared, enlightenment dawning, as his tired mind fought its way through the fog.

"Christ, I'm sorry, Wendy." He ran a hand through his hair, leaving the fringe standing to attention.

There was a short pause while Barney stared desperately into the carpet. He stubbed his cigarette out on a convenient saucer. "What can I say? I'm so sorry, we made an arrangement for this evening, didn't we? God, I am so sorry. I must be cracking up! Was it only last night we spoke? Surely not. I got the Tupperware thing all wrong too. God, I'm so sorry. I need a long holiday before I break down completely!"

He stopped. Ash fell from the cigarette onto his knee and remained there unnoticed.

Wendell felt sorry too. For Barney, for Tracy, but mostly for himself and his shattered evening. His friend looked like a broken man, slumped there amongst the pile of cushions with his empty beer can and half an inch of grey stubble.

There was a minute's silence, apt in the circumstances, during which Barney closed his eyes and began to nod off.

"I'm off then," said Wendell, rising from his seat. There was a jelly baby stuck to his trousers which he peeled off and placed on the table. "You need sleep."

"Sorry Wendy."

"I'll see myself out. Give me a call sometime."

"I am really sorry," slurred Barney, eyes still shut.

Wendell stared at him for a couple of seconds then left the house quietly, and by the time the front door closed, Barney was fast asleep.

Antonia drove by the shop on the way back from her mother's to buy the biggest bar of chocolate she could find. When she got upstairs, she put it reverently into the freezer then stood looking around her for inspiration.

She sighed, preparing herself for another boring evening on her own. The television held little of interest, but she put it on anyway. At least it was a human presence of sorts. Drifting from the kitchen with tea and a sandwich she glanced out of the window and saw Wendell Cornish leaping with purpose into his car. How strange that a couple of days ago she wasn't even sure if he was still living downstairs, and now she had seen him twice in the same space of time. She watched until the car turned the corner.

Where was he off to? Probably meeting some glamorous bimbette for a night on the town. Candlelit supper, a club perhaps, then back to her penthouse flat for a night of unbridled lust. He'd looked smart and quite attractive and completely out of her league, she thought miserably. Why was she on her own? Everybody else had someone except her.

The sandwich was rather dry and made her cough and the tea with which she washed it down was too hot and scalded her throat.

"Oh my God!" she exclaimed, clutching her neck and hanging out her tongue to cool it, which only made her dive deeper into self-pity. But the moment passed, and she made another cup of tea, wandering from room to room, bored. She brushed her hair and fiddled about with various styles, examining herself from all angles with the aid of a hand mirror. Finally, with this exercise exhausted, she left a pile of accessories on the bed and returned to the television. The documentary that had been running when she was last there was long finished and canned laughter rang out from a new sit-com, which she sat down and watched without a glimmer of amusement. As the credits rolled, she shook her head and announced aloud, "What utter crap," before remotely looping around every channel hopefully. Then repeated it in case she had missed something the first time.

"What utter crap and rubbish," she exclaimed crossly and switched it off altogether. The room was immediately engulfed in unbearable silence. She got up, switched off the light and stood for a moment staring out at the darkness of the street.

To her surprise, Wendell's car was just returning. As she watched, unnoticed, in the darkness of the room, he stepped out, locked the car and stood looking down the road, then across over the fields before trailing slowly to the front door.

So he was back then. Oh dear, had the bimbette stood him up? She smiled spitefully to herself. He had looked rather dejected. Could this be the moment for that coffee? She started tidying the lounge, a habit of hers when she was feeling a decision coming. No, he probably had other plans and it would be embarrassing. No, she couldn't. Come on, be brave for once she told herself, just say you wondered if he was in. Oh God, I can't. How did people do it? Was she really this desperate? Was this what it had come to.

Who could she call? No one, they'd all be out or occupied. She rammed a heap of papers into the bin, still undecided. After ten minutes she was sorry she'd begun the tidying and the idea of approaching her neighbour refused to stop nagging. What could she say?

Borrow a cup of sugar? No.

Ask him if he had yesterday's paper handy? No.

Would he mind removing a spider for her? No, he'd wonder how she'd managed before.

This was pathetic. How about "hello, I'm bored stiff, so I thought I'd come for that coffee you offered me the other day." Make him think she was completely nutty.

If only they could become comfortable neighbours, the sort that lived in close proximity and could easily just drop in on each other for a cuppa and a friendly chat, no ties. It would be interesting to find out his side of their story too, like whether he was aware that Charles and that tart of his were cheating on them.

She put a weary hand to her head, annoyed with herself. Just go down there, knock and say *hi, I saw you were in, so I wondered if you'd like to have a coffee with me?*

No, she just couldn't, it was impossible.

She shoved an untidy drawer roughly back into its hole and went back to the window.

Wendell Cornish had left his lights on.

"Oh," she said softly, lighting up herself.

"Perfect."

When he escaped Barney's house of horror, Wendell raced off as fast as he could safely manage needing, for the sake of sanity, to put as much distance between himself and the place as possible. He pulled into a lay by in a lonely spot a couple of miles on and turned the engine off.

"Christ all fucking mighty," he swore, thumping the passenger seat hard.

What the hell was happening to everybody? Whatever it was he didn't care for it.

First, Bibi buggers off with a 'sod you, I've been putting in time here until something better turns up' attitude, nearly driving him into alcoholic reclusiveness. Now Barney, 'rock steady dependable for a night out' Barney, had become some henpecked, middle-aged tramp fast heading into dementia. If that's what a wife and family do for you, forget it.

The anger he had felt was quickly turning into self-pity. He felt depressed and past it, then told himself not to give in to it.

So, what now? It was still relatively early. Maybe that girl from upstairs would join him for a coffee. Unlikely, she was already a recluse. The fact he was even considering her was a measure of his desperation for company. He pulled at his lip, watching a car full of laughing youngsters whizz past, and felt old and abandoned, and a trifle seedy sitting there like this in a lay by.

He could go into town. A nightclub? But then he'd have to get a train back at God knows what hour and back the next day to retrieve the car. No, too much hassle and he didn't feel like it anyway. What about a local club? No, he really didn't feel much like clubbing. Who was there to call? He couldn't think of anyone who would be available. The pub? No, he wasn't going back to that routine again if he could help it. He decided he would just go home.

He began to feel foolish, what an idiot he must have looked! All wide-eyed and expectant like a bitch on heat. Really, he must have looked ridiculous, they were probably having a good old titter at his expense at this very moment. He considered going to the pub once more and decided he probably would; after all, he could do with a drink after all this. But he would go home and get changed first, he was rather overdressed for the local.

He let himself into his flat and considered all the options again. There were only two. Go out or stay in. Surely it would only fuel the depression to sit alone amongst people enjoying themselves. This time last week he had been propping up the bar, getting quietly pissed all by himself and feeling fairly ok. This week the thought of it made him feel like ending it all. He poured himself a large scotch. As the warming liquid burned through him, he began to relax, and once again considered Antonia. Maybe she wasn't alone up there? There was no way he was going to knock, one rejection in an evening was enough.

He'd certainly never noticed anyone calling here for her.

But he didn't want her getting the wrong idea. Imagine some desperate clingy neighbour knocking every day and pestering him.

"This is ridiculous!" he said to himself with a tut and rose with determination from the sofa to go and see. She could only say no after all, no harm in asking. But as he was putting his shoes back on an idea came to him. He grabbed the car keys and crept out to where it was sitting, switched the lights on and slunk back inside, closing the door silently. Give it twenty minutes, that wouldn't drain the battery. If she was alone and bored upstairs, chances are she would look out of the window and see them on, if not he'd cut his losses and go to the pub. Let fate decide, he thought, as he flopped back on the sofa, kicked his shoes off and sat back to look at the rubbish on the television.

Chapter Eleven
Returning to Friday Evening

Bibi and Charles' evening out had not been a success. Just as they'd begun to feel comfortable again, Gino had glided up to take their order. Ignoring Charles absolutely, he launched once again into a verbal tidal wave of compliments.

"'Ow booteeful you look tonight, darleeng," he said into Bibi's eyes, and whispered other little intimacies quite unashamedly as he shoved his tiny bottom into Charles' face. In an effort to avoid a nasty situation, Bibi did her best to be standoffish and formal, but it wasn't really in her nature to ignore flattery and her quiet, self-satisfied smile only served to bring Charles' anger back to the boil all over again.

"May we order now?" he interrupted, fury making him bolder than usual.

"Sir?" Gino half turned, one eyebrow raised in question, and looked around his backside at Charles.

"I *said* may we order now. Please."

"Of course, Sir." Gino whipped around and took the order from Charles in a thoroughly professional manner. After all, they didn't want to lose custom even if this stiff boyfriend was completely unsuited to the delightful Bibi.

Then with a final wink at her, he minced away shouting things in Italian towards the kitchen.

"For God's sake!" She hissed at Charles. "What's the matter with you? He did us a favour squeezing us in here tonight."

"Well, just stop… stop throwing yourself at him then. It's embarrassing." Charles stopped and glanced around to check. "Anyone would think you were with him, not me." He stuck his lower lip out and began to sulk.

"Oh, for God's sake, stop being so bloody childish, Charles. I've known Gino for years. He flirts with all the women; you know what Italians are like."

"I didn't see him falling all over them," he said peevishly, indicating a trio of blue-rinsed crones at a neighbouring table.

"Keep your voice down, they'll hear you."

"So what? I don't care," he said loudly and sat back. Several eyes and a couple of heads turned in their direction, then back again when no more was forthcoming.

Finally, Bibi spoke, "Right, let's just forget this shall we?"

Charles brightened for a moment, thinking they would be going and could still make his parents' get-together.

She continued, "Let's have our meal with some cultured conversation and then perhaps you'll start behaving like an adult."

Charles had rarely felt so furious. First with Gino, carrying on like that with Bibi. And then with Bibi herself, who was treating him like a naughty schoolboy, indicating that the trouble was all *his* fault. He hadn't wanted to come here anyway, he'd only done it to please her, would have preferred them to go to his parents'. He felt as though his head was going to explode.

Suddenly he knew what to do.

"I'm not hungry anymore," he said, getting up and throwing the starchy cloth napkin onto his chair, "I'm sure Gino will join you for the meal as he's much more grown-up than I am. Here." He threw a twenty-pound note onto the table. "I'm going to my parents' get-together, where I know people will be happy to see me and might treat me with some sort of respect." Charles was so angry he felt he could weep and wanted more than anything to get out of here, with or without Bibi.

She caught his hand.

"Sit down. Please. Please sit down, Charlie." She looked up at him with big anxious eyes and he felt his decision wobble.

Still standing and with her hand in his, he said, "Say you'll come to my parents'. We can finish here first, then pop in just for half an hour. That's all. You know I'm not keen on dancing and clubbing anyway."

There was a heavily pregnant pause during which they both looked at one another, reading each other's faces. Bibi broke the gaze first.

"Charlie…" she began carefully, then fell silent again. He could see her mind frantically trying to come up with a good reason for not going.

"I see," said Charles finally and pulled his hand away from hers. He waited another five seconds, then took his coat from the back of the chair and left the restaurant without looking back. He'd never done anything so brave in his life and his legs felt like jelly, but he was proud of himself. It was time he took a stand; he was fed up with her constant criticism.

"You bastard!" She murmured to herself, humiliated beyond belief. How dare he leave her sitting here, people were whispering behind their hands. How *dare* he!

Charles drove straight home, now feeling a bit shaky and unsure if he'd done the right thing. He had probably looked a complete tit. Loneliness swamped him suddenly and violently, it was something that kept happening lately, even when he and Bibi were together. He thought of Antonia nostalgically and wanted to speak to her. He decided he could forgive what she had done, what had forced him to forget her and go with Bibi. On impulse he called her number, *their* number, but there was no answer. Maybe just as well. But he tried it twice more during the evening anyway. Where might she be? Her mother's? Why had he left her anyway? He should really have asked her for an explanation, but it had all happened so fast, he'd just let himself be led away, he'd been bewitched. At the time, he had no reason to disbelieve this tragic, appealing woman, but now and then he wasn't sure if she always told the truth. Bibi was beautiful and exciting, yes, but they didn't seem to have very much in common. And she was still married.

At least he'd saved her from that terrible abusive relationship, he told himself. *He* would never hit her. He loved Bibi, didn't he?

Did he still love Antonia? At this moment he felt as though he did, but he was feeling sorry for himself, so it didn't count. However, as soon as this thought was out, he was consumed with a desire to see her, to talk to her. Find out what was behind that note. Before he could stop himself, he was in the car driving around to the old flat. It was a whole year since he'd been anywhere near it and buried memories surfaced in his mind as he looked at the familiar façade. Perhaps she didn't even live here now. He was parked across the road, engine idling, handsome eyes glistening. The place was in darkness, but he doubted he would have knocked even if it hadn't been. After a few minutes of indulgent self-pity he drove off and, much to the delight of his mother, called in on the little party. Probing enquiries persuaded him to leave after an hour, so he made his excuses and went home. He would have to face Bibi sometime so may as well get it over with. Hopefully she wouldn't be in bed yet. But the place was in darkness and Bibi did not return at all that night. She was spending it with someone else.

Gino was not a man to miss an opportunity. As soon as Charles had vacated the restaurant, he glided gallantly across to where Bibi sat staring at the recently occupied chair with a glassy expression. He'd had his hot Italian finger firmly on the pulse of the situation as soon as the pair had arrived, had purposely fanned the flames in fact.

Bibi gazed into his dashing, swarthy face, into his dark eyes which flashed with expectation. He was handsome and he knew it, and now he was quivering with passion like a randy terrier. She knew what he was up to and was willing to join in with the game. She'd done it before to teach Wendell a lesson and had spent a wonderful illicit night with Gino being wined, dined and driven off to a posh hotel in a Ferrari, where they had spent the night locked in passionate embraces amongst the silken sheets. No strings attached. It was exactly what she needed.

Wendell had fallen over himself to make it up to her the next day, when she had told him she'd spent the night folded up miserably on a cold sofa at her friend Clara's place. Let's see what Charlie would do to make it up to her. And so she said and did all the right things and so did Gino.

"Very beezy tonight, darleeng," he said, as he brought her meal to her and a complimentary bottle of wine, then spent the next two hours flinging himself about the tables while she got slowly and miserably drunk. Finally, around about midnight when everything was more or less finished, he donned a jacket and propelled her, unresisting, to his car. She was stiff from sitting there for so long. She hadn't expected such a lengthy wait, but the wine had helped. She had at one point considered just going home in a taxi, but pride and the idea of revenge had kept her fixed to her chair.

Another disappointment awaited outside when, instead of the fast and flashy Ferrari, Gino invited her to step into a rather tatty brown hatchback. There was a dent on the nearside door which creaked painfully as Gino opened it for her and had to be banged shut. He hurriedly swept some crumbs, bits of foil and sweet wrappers off the seat before settling her in it. The car reeked of old takeaways.

"My cousin's car," explained Gino quickly, as her eye fell suspiciously on a baby's dummy lying on the dashboard.

"Where are we going then?" she asked with a coy smile.

"My booteeful Bibi, I take you to my house, we have some wine and wonderfool night toogedder. Tomorrow, I work early." They obviously couldn't go back to the lovely hotel he had taken her to the last time, having had his wedding there the previous year. Luckily, Gino still had a bolt hole at his cousin's flat. Hopefully Mario would be out.

"Oh." She felt deflated and annoyed, this wasn't what she'd had in mind at all. But she could hardly go home now. Oh well, maybe a jacuzzi or a pool awaited her, so she put all negative thoughts from her mind and smiled again. "Alright, let's go."

They went with a great deal of noise, because the exhaust had a hole in it.

The mansion house she had visualised turned out, in reality, to be a squalid flat above the butcher's shop in town. It was dirty and untidy and smelled strongly of animal carcasses. There were no carpets, just odd rugs lying here and there on the bare floorboards, but worst of all he said he had his cousin lodging there, at present sprawled across the sofa in his bulging underwear, watching porn and eating cold baked beans straight from the tin. She looked around her in frank disgust.

He had to be joking, surely.

There was a rapid conversation in Italian which sounded like an argument, but ended in laughter; so it probably wasn't. Gino's cousin, a fat, hairy, sweaty specimen, looked her up and down in silence then hoisted himself up and said, "Goodnight, Signorina" in heavily accented English before slapping his way out to his own room. The whole thing seemed suddenly horribly sordid. Gino whisked her away into his room which bore all the signs of a secret love nest but was at least clean and tidy, and smelled of some strong perfume which masked the butcher's shop from below. He poured them both a glass of warm wine, then began, without further preamble, to run his hands through her hair and kiss her neck. She let him do it, listless, resigned. This wasn't going to be like last time at all. He hadn't even had a wash and smelled of kitchen grease and cooking. Ugh!

Afterwards, she felt dirty and cheap, lying next to Gino's hot Italian body, vibrating with loud Italian snoring and then, to her disgust, loud Italian farting.

Oh, this was awful! She needed the loo but didn't want to bump into the cousin while searching for its unknown location. So she lay there miserable and uncomfortable and tried to get some sleep.

Chapter Twelve
Back to Saturday Evening

With a rush of adrenalin, Antonia darted into the bathroom and looked at herself. She quickly ran a brush through her hair then tossed it about in an effort to look casual. She managed to stop herself from running and plodded down the stairs, it wouldn't do to sound too eager. After all, it was only a bit of company she wanted. She knocked on Wendell's door, heard him padding towards her behind it.

"Antonia!" cried Wendell in mock surprise. "How lovely to see you again; to what do I owe the pleasure?"

"Hello Wendell," she forced out the silly name and felt her face heating up. "Do you know you've left your lights on? I've just noticed from my window."

"What? My lights? Oh God, how stupid of me. I was rather distracted when I got back, must have forgotten to switch them off," he smiled at her. "Not out tonight?" he remarked casually, as he rummaged in a coat pocket for his keys.

"No. Another boring Saturday evening in on my own."

"Oh, you too?"

"Sadly yes."

"Look…" he hesitated. Antonia held her breath.

"I've been let down tonight."

Images of the busty bimbette rose into Antonia's mind.

"By an old school friend. It would be funny if it wasn't so tragic."

The bimbette faded.

"I was just going to pop around to the local for a drink. You're welcome to come with me—just for a friendly drink with a neighbour. How about it?"

Antonia struggled for the right words. She didn't want to seem too eager but then again, there would never be a better chance for a new friend. It probably wouldn't happen again. And if she was too cool, he'd think she was only saying yes to be polite. She hesitated long enough for Wendell's hopes to plummet.

"Did you have something else planned? Don't feel obliged, it was only a suggestion."

"Oh no," she replied quickly. "No, I would love to go out actually, it's ages since I've been out on a Saturday night. Sure I won't cramp your style?"

"Good God no, I'd enjoy the company."

"Can I just change my shoes?"

"Of course, I'll get my coat and meet you down here."

How easy it had been!

Wendell was the first to reappear and he rubbed his hands together gleefully. Five minutes passed before Antonia thudded down the stairs.

"Sorry, I couldn't find the shoes," she panted, "that tells you how long it is since I wore them," she laughed.

What a transformation from the angry, bedraggled girl of yesterday thought Wendell, amazed at how nice she looked with her face so animated, and with a bit of make-up on. He quite fancied her.

It was ages since Antonia had visited their local, ages since she had been out anywhere like this, now here she was being escorted out by that woman's husband! She almost laughed at the irony of it, and as they walked along side by side chatting pleasantly, she once again silently thanked the Lord for the car lights.

"Your lights are still on!" she exclaimed, breaking the conversation mid-flow.

Wendell stopped abruptly.

"Oh, sod it!" he said without thinking. They both looked at one another and laughed as they turned around again. They were still laughing when they got there. Wendell reached in and switched them off declaring "Voila!" in a dramatic fashion, making Antonia laugh all over again.

"Right, let's start again," said Wendell as he bent to lock the door, at which point his stomach let rip.

"Oh dear," said Wendell awkwardly. "Do excuse me. I haven't eaten anything yet. That was another thing on the agenda that's gone by the wayside. How about you? Have you eaten?"

"If you call a dry cheese sandwich at 7.30 eating, then yes."

"Do you fancy getting a bite to eat first?"

"Well… I, yes that would be lovely. Look, are you sure I'm not in your way?"

"Not at all, not at all, I really am glad of the company. There's a nice place near the pub, the Continental Kitchen, do you know it?"

"Yes, we used to go there occasionally." She thought briefly of the times she and Charles had been to it.

As they approached, they were engulfed in food aromas.

"Mmm, that smells good," said Antonia. "I'm starving all of a sudden."

"Me too."

They crunched across the gravel and went inside where it was warm and buzzy, just like it used to be, and sat at a table by the window.

Wendell said, "I haven't been here in ages, used to come with The Wife." He said 'the wife' in a rather disparaging way, then apologised for bringing her into the conversation at all, while hoping it would open up a conversation about Bibi and Charles.

"Please don't apologise," she said quickly. "Now that we're talking to each other, Charles and your wife are bound to come up. We should either discuss them or forget them. I don't mind talking about it, but if you'd rather not, well, that's fine too." She was feeling much more confident now, enjoying being out.

This was much better than a date, no pressure to be perfect. And now they were about to talk about Charles and that woman, just what she had hoped.

For a moment Wendell said nothing. He was thinking she was quite unlike any girl he'd ever met. Why had he never met any real and honest women before? Perhaps he'd been looking in the wrong places, mistakenly thinking you had to meet gorgeous, high maintenance, sophisticated types to get on. He looked straight at her and felt an urge to kiss her.

Instead, he said, "What is there to say really? I admit here and now, hand on heart," he placed it there, "that Bibi probably instigated the whole thing. I should have known it would happen sooner or later. She was engaged to someone else when I met her. Not that she mentioned it," he paused to sip his drink, "leopards don't change their spots, as they say."

Wendell wasn't sure why he had told her that. He'd never mentioned it to a soul before. He recalled with an internal shudder the almighty scene outside a nightclub when her fiancée caught them together, the first Wendell had known of it. They'd avoided the place after that.

It had finished with her intended, Rupert, tearing the ring, which she had blatantly been wearing, from her finger and dropping it down a drain, then retreating stormily while she hurled abuse at him and tried, this particular time without success, to slap his face. Highly embarrassing, but Bibi had just shrugged her shoulders and said philosophically that it was just as well she'd found out about his awful temper before it was too late.

Wendell thought she was fantastic at the time and laughed at it all but, sobered up later, had wondered whether she would have gone through with a wedding and carried on with him as well? With the blindness of love and lust he had pushed the idea to some remote corner of his mind and chosen to leave it there.

He found himself telling all this, and lots more, to Antonia. All about the lies, his suspicions of her unfaithfulness, everything. It was a relief to talk about it, a relief to be laughing again.

"Would you believe, I didn't even know her name wasn't Bibi until we went to arrange our wedding?"

"What is it?"

"Brenda." Wendell laughed at the memory. "You should have seen her; she nearly went mad when I said it out loud. Said if I ever mentioned it again, either in front of her or anyone else, she would kill me. I think she may have meant it too, she certainly looked wild enough. You should have seen the registrar's face, I thought he was having a stroke."

Antonia listened with rapt attention and Wendell marvelled at how easy she was to get on with. He'd certainly never had a conversation like this with a woman before, perhaps it was because there was no notion of romance.

There was no awkwardness, and when she, in turn, told him about herself and Charles he listened with interest.

"The funny thing was that when I got over the fact that he'd left I wasn't really that bothered. Does that sound awful? I was terribly hurt, yes. Humiliated definitely, but I think our time had run its course, although we'd most likely still be shuffling around each other if your wife hadn't encouraged him away." She made a rueful face. "I sort of like being on my own, making my own decisions, eating what I like when I like, you know the sort of thing."

He did. But his had descended into drunkenness and disorder.

"Initially, I liked being alone anyway," she added, not wishing to give him the impression she was longing for everlasting spinsterhood. And because he was actually listening, she also told him about the birthday card. How that, somehow, had been the thing that hurt her most. The deceit behind the declaration of love. Telling that was like baring her soul. She couldn't look at him as she said it. He could clearly see the pain in her face and felt as though he knew what it must have been like.

Then there was a gap while they finished their food, both lost in silent memories.

"I'm very glad we've become friends," said Wendell between forkfuls. He would never have spoken with his mouth full, something else Charles had been good at, thought Antonia.

"Me too. I have felt a bit lonely, I admit. It's nice to be friendly, no strings attached. Especially a male friend," she glanced at him to see what his reaction would be. He looked thoughtful.

"Just tell me one thing, and please don't take this the wrong way," said Wendell, putting his fork down.

"Yes?"

"Well, why did you have a pair of wet pants in your bag?"

They both erupted into hysterical laughter, completely at ease with one another, which restored the earlier light mood and Antonia explained about the underwear. They left the restaurant still laughing and now fortified with good food. They had gone halves on the meal, Antonia had insisted, another new experience for Wendell. The pub had long since shut.

The night air was cool and fragrant with pine trees. Stars twinkled in the dark sky like jewels on black velvet. It seemed everything about this evening had been almost perfect. Still chatting, they wandered along by the river, its surface shining in the moonlight, and leant on the railings. There they fell companionably silent, enjoying the gentle sound of water bubbling along.

"Thank you for coming out tonight," said Wendell without turning. "I haven't enjoyed myself so much for ages."

"The pleasure has been all mine, truly," replied Antonia and they smiled at one another, then walked back.

The walk passed in silence while each thought about the time they had just spent together, completely spontaneous, surprised at how comfortable they had been with each other.

Outside the house they stood talking for a further ten minutes until it began to feel a bit cold.

"Look, would you like to come up for a coffee?"

Wendell accepted gladly and followed her up the stairs, his eyes appraising her neat behind. He liked her, he was keen on friendship and if anything more came of it, well, so be it. So they sat and drank coffee in the intimacy of Antonia's flat, and talked, and both felt like they had known each other forever by the time the first watery light began to creep into the room.

Antonia yawned. "Look at the time! Dawn's breaking for God's sake!"

"Time I went I think."

He stared at her and for a split second imagined Bibi there. She was nothing but a demanding, brassy tart next to this natural girl in her simple clothes. His father had been right about his wife, let her have her bloody nancy-boy. He's welcome to her. He almost felt sorry for him.

As for Antonia, she hadn't enjoyed an evening so much since she had first met Charles and she sincerely hoped it wouldn't be the last time they saw each other.

Wendell stood up preparatory to leaving, and she walked to the door with him.

"Thank you for a really lovely evening, I really have enjoyed it," she said warmly, "and morning," she added with a smile.

"I've enjoyed it too," he replied, "could we do it again sometime?"

Antonia blushed. "I'd like that, yes."

"Great."

Wendell leant over and gave her a peck on the cheek, hands firmly in his pockets, before disappearing down the stairs. She waited until she heard his door opening and closing before she quietly shut her own.

"Wendell," she said softly, fingering her cheek where he had placed his small kiss. Perhaps she could get used to the daft name after all.

Chapter Thirteen
Saturday Morning

Sleep evaded Charles that Friday night. Not only was he not tired after his long nap in the afternoon, but he was also plagued by anxiety about Bibi. Where the hell was she? What could have happened to her?

He felt stupid now. Guilty too. He should never have left her there like that. Anything could have happened to her. Should he call that fat friend of hers—what was the woman's name? Her mother? The hospital? Police? Round and round it went, his mind continuing the torture until he finally fell asleep exhausted with all the mental activity. He woke mid-morning and the whole thing swamped him again immediately. Where the bloody hell was she? Anxiety was giving in to annoyance. Should he call her mother? The idea of it only made him feel more wretched. If she wasn't there it would be embarrassing, and Bibi's mother was a bit intimidating. He certainly didn't relish the thought of a grilling by her.

Damn! Where could she be?

She had plenty of glamorous acquaintances that he knew by sight but had never really spoken to. What about that large girl? Clara! Yes that was her name. He'd seen her in town once, in the distance. Bibi had talked about her; they had been at school together, he thought.

Oh dear. He sighed and got up. Standing over the toilet for a morning pee, he suddenly discovered that he was ravenously hungry. He hadn't eaten at all yesterday evening, apart from the tea and two Jaffa cakes he'd had at his parents'. He hadn't even noticed last night, which was unusual for him, he had been too uptight. Now, with his stomach howling to be fed, he foraged around the kitchen finding only a low fat yogurt and two greenish tomatoes. Why did they never have anything in? There always used to be crisps and biscuits and just food in general when he and Antonia lived together. He ate the yogurt in desperation, sweetening it with a sachet of sugar which he found at the back of the larder.

He would go out for lunch. On his own. Sod Bibi and her tantrums he decided, let her come back and find *him* gone and see how *she* liked it. His hunger was making him feel vicious and unusually bold.

And so he took off to find somewhere where no one would know him. He felt daring as he drove along, he'd never done such a thing before, and he began to enjoy it. After criss-crossing the countryside a bit, he discovered a nice pub not teeming with children or tourists, and having parked the car where he could see it (couldn't be too careful these days), he strolled casually to the bar and ordered a beer. He hoped he looked nonchalant, a man of the world resting one foot on the rail as he waited. He was quite unaware of all the female eyes fixed on him as he stood there.

"Can I order some food please?" he asked the barmaid, who gazed at him from over made-up eyes then leant over him unnecessarily to reach a menu, making sure he got an eyeful of her ample bosom in the process.

"Sorry," she smiled, pinching her lips together in a tight smile as one of them brushed across his fingers. He removed his hand swiftly.

Slightly embarrassed, he quickly placed his order and paid. He indicated a table by the window and moved across to it with his drink. There was a large black dog minesweeping the car park but otherwise it was all quiet out there, so he began to relax and enjoy it once more as he examined his fellow patrons. The cronies at the bar were obviously locals, a middle-aged knot of beer bellies, bantering loudly with the landlord. Charles' gaze moved along, meeting those of the barmaid, who managed to throw him a sultry look before he averted his eyes. He wished he'd thought of bringing a paper with him, one needed something to do when eating alone. Must remember that another time. Then Bibi interrupted his thoughts again, and then the food arrived.

In his state of unaccustomed emptiness, he thought he had never tasted a finer roast dinner and was quite oblivious to the audience of women who watched him devour it like a pig at a trough.

"Everything alright, Sir?" enquired the barmaid as she wiggled across to remove the empty plate.

"Oh yes thank you. Delicious, thank you." Charles allowed her a small smile. Gravy bloomed at the corners of his lips.

"Anything else I can get you?" The question was loaded but he didn't notice.

Why not? He thought and was soon filling himself further with an enormous bowl of apple crumble and ice cream.

A balding, bespectacled gentleman who had just had a bowl of the same thrown down in front of him, wondered whether or not he should complain that his pudding was half the size of the one Charles had been brought.

"I like a man with a good appetite," purred the barmaid, before she shimmied back towards the bar, hoping he was getting a good view of her from the rear this time. He missed it because he was checking on the car. What a good idea this was, he thought, with a contented sigh. He would bring Bibi here next weekend to make it up to her. Charles' mood had lifted. Another half then home, where she would be waiting for him. They would fall into each other's arms, there would be apologies, a kiss or two and maybe more… He felt aroused by the thought and was suddenly keen to get back.

The barmaid was back, collecting the empty bowl.

"Anything else I can do for you, Sir? Another drink? Coffee?"

"No thank you." Forget the half, he wanted to get home now, but the buxom barmaid wasn't letting him go that easily.

"Haven't seen you in here before, you local?"

This was alarming, he couldn't get out while she was there. "Er… fairly."

"No one at home to cook your lunch then?"

"No."

"Live alone do you?"

"No."

"Work local, do you?"

"Fairly."

"What do you do?"

"Er, I'm a teacher." This was like an interview.

"Oh wonderful!" Her eyes lit up with feigned admiration. "I always wanted to be a teacher. I love kids. Although I'm not sure they're always lovable." She laughed heartily.

"No. Excuse me," he squeezed past her and headed for the toilets, forgetting her instantly.

He'd left his sweatshirt on the back of the chair and as he headed back for it, saw there were two girls pitched on the other seats.

"Oh! Is this your table?" said one. "Sorry, we thought you'd gone. I've just noticed your sweatshirt. Would you like us to move?" They were both grinning eagerly up at him.

"No, no, I'm just leaving."

Their faces fell.

"Haven't seen you in here before, are you local?"

"Fairly," he experienced a feeling of déjà vu. His eyes travelled over their heads towards the window and his car, where the dog was peeing against his wheel.

"Is that your dog?" asked the first girl. Charles regarded her quizzically. She was bony and blonde with bulging fishy eyes in an elfin face. Her hair had been strapped backwards and upwards into a tight bun adorned with accessories and welded together with copious amounts of hairspray. It looked painful and unattractive and as she moved her head it moved, sculpture like, with it. Charles was momentarily distracted.

"Sorry?"

"I said is that your dog. Only, you keep looking out there. I thought you might be checking on him."

"Oh no."

He'd had enough. The place was becoming claustrophobic. He turned to go but the second girl called him back.

"Don't forget your sweatshirt," she was holding it out to him.

"Oh thanks," he took hold of it, but she didn't seem to want to let it go and there was a short struggle for it. Were they all inbred here? Certainly odd. His route out took him past the barmaid.

"Bye, hope to see you again. Come midweek, it's quieter then. We can have a proper chat."

"Ah, yes. Thanks. Bye." He plunged for the door, deciding that perhaps he would take Bibi somewhere else.

"I think I'm in love," sighed the barmaid to her colleague, laughing.

The dog, now flopped on the grass verge, raised itself and sauntered across to greet Charles as he headed for the safety of the car. After a cursory sniff it returned to its siesta.

As he bumped across the gravel car park, his stomach now full, his anxiety about Bibi began to creep back. Surely, she must be home by now. He recalled his little daydream again, how they would make things up together, and he put more pressure on the accelerator. That one drink had made him feel randy. He was in such a hurry to get in that he failed to notice the absence of Bibi's car. He opened the door and called brightly, "Hello-o."

Nothing.

"Bibi?"

Nothing. Shit! Where the fucking hell was she? He was angry and stomped into the lounge, wondering hopefully if she was pretending not to be there.

"Hello? Anyone here?"

Nothing. Then he saw a note on the table which hadn't been there previously. He snatched it up.

"Charlie," it read, "As you've obviously gone out, have gone to see Wendell." It was signed 'B' with an angry line underneath it. No X.

"What!" he cried aloud, temples pulsing with an emotion he couldn't identify, something between anger and terror. "What the hell has she gone there for?" He reread the note and threw it on the floor in a temper. He didn't know what to do. Should he go around there? No, she must be bluffing, trying to put the wind up him.

Two hours later, after he had further tortured himself wondering what was happening and what he could do about it, he heard a key in the lock and almost whimpered with relief. Charles sprang up and rushed to greet her but came up against her outstretched hand.

"Stop!"

"Darling," he said, stepping back. "Where on *earth* have you *been*? I've been beside myself with worry!"

She regarded him coldly, saying nothing, then pushed by towards the bedroom, shrugging off his hand as she clattered past.

"Bibi..." he began. "I'm sorry, darling, let's be friends again?"

"You've been drinking, I can smell it." She opened a drawer and started rummaging. "You've got food all around your mouth too."

He ran his tongue, and then a cuff over his mouth. "There was nothing to eat here so I went to a pub for lunch. It was lovely, I want to take you there next weekend."

Bibi stopped and turned to face him, hands on hips. He didn't even try to make something up, what an absolute *idiot* the man was.

"Well, I'm so glad you had such a nice time," she hissed. "It wasn't very pleasant to come back to an empty flat."

No, he thought, remembering last night.

"I'm sorry, darling, but I had no idea where you were, I was going crazy wondering if something had happened to you. I nearly rang the hospital."

"You're a useless liar, Charlie."

"It's true! I nearly did! Where were you anyway?"

"Did you even see my note?" She stared at him defiantly.

"Of course I did!" He was silent for a moment. "What did you go and see him for?"

"So it did worry you!" she said in triumph. "I seriously thought of going back to him after that fiasco last night."

Charles was silent.

"I left that note to see what your reaction would be."

"So you didn't go to see him?"

"No."

"I was so worried," he embraced her, but she stood immobile, arms clamped to her sides, face down.

"Oh, please darling, let me make it up to you. I've felt wretched all day."

She was silent but less tense.

Wrongly thinking this meant things were back to normal, Charles smiled and pressed himself against her, which only reminded her of the ghastly night she'd spent, and she slapped him hard across the face.

"Oh!" He jumped back and put a hand against his cheek.

"You men," she spat. "You've all got your brains in your balls," and with that she flounced away and locked herself in the bathroom.

Charles moved his jaw with caution as he watched the door of the bathroom slam shut. He was bewildered.

"Now what?" he murmured to himself.

Bibi had lain awake most of the night wanting to go for a pee, in between thinking first about Charles and then about Wendell. Comparing the two, she had reluctantly concluded that Charles would never be the man Wendell was. If only Wendell had Charles' stunning looks or Charles had Wendell's interesting and charming personality. What did she have to do to find the right man? She decided that she would see how the land lay with Wendell. She'd heard he'd gone to pieces and started drinking, well she'd have to put a stop to that, in fact she could use it as an excuse to call him. If it was true. After all, he *was* her husband. She also considered just getting up and leaving, but she had nowhere to go and anyway, Charles had a lesson to learn. So she had stayed put.

At some unearthly hour an alarm had gone off. Gino rolled over and slammed a hand on it, then snorted unpleasant garlicky breath all over her before kissing her hard and running his hot hands all over her naked flesh. He touched her below and grinned, indicating that he had enough time for a quickie. His hair was greasy and he stank. Half an inch of beard seemed to have sprouted on his chin overnight and it sandpapered the delicate skin on her face. She certainly wasn't in the mood for this, so she pushed him off and finally visited the bathroom to clean herself up and have the long overdue pee. He was carefully arranging his hair with a greasy comb when she returned to the boudoir and asked him to call her a cab. He made the call and disappeared for work without even cleaning his teeth, let alone washing himself. How revolting.

She waited outside. The cab took almost an hour to arrive, by which time she was frozen and furious. She should probably have waited inside but couldn't bear to run into that disgusting specimen Gino had introduced as his cousin. That car was supposed to belong to the cousin too, but it was now gone with Gino. Where were the cousin's wife and kids that the car had borne evidence of? As she had passed his room, she had heard him snoring and prayed he wouldn't wake, he seemed like a single man. Had Gino lied to her? He wouldn't have been the first if he had.

Now she just felt tired and dirty. She could never see Gino again, those days were absolutely finished with, it would be too humiliating. Why hadn't she just gone home? Imagine demeaning herself like this. God, that *awful* flat!

When he finally arrived, the taxi driver looked as if he'd got out of bed specially, which in fact he had. He drove painfully slowly despite the absence of traffic, yawning loudly and scratching bits of himself as he did so. She had had to ask him to detour via the bank, suddenly remembering she had no money with her. She'd left the cash Charles had supplied on the table last night. Some tip, she thought grimly.

When she eventually arrived home, she was ready to let Charles have it. All this had been his fault completely and she was going to let rip. She knew how it was going to start, she had rehearsed it during her long, cold, angry wait for the cab.

But he wasn't there. Unheard of. The bastard! The fucking bastard! She screamed into the empty room then flopped onto the expensive sofa she had insisted on having, to cry out her frustration. Afterwards she felt much better for it, then got showered and changed.

Still furious at Charles' continued absence, she had scribbled a note out for him, then driven around to see Wendell. It would be the first time she would have seen him since she left, and she was prepared to put on a contrite act, he could never resist it. Yes, it would be nice to see him.

But there was no answer, despite his car still being there. She had stood on the step forlornly for a minute, unsure of what to do next. Perhaps he had moved and sold the car to the next tenant.

Where was everybody?

Then she just sat in the car for a while in the hope he might turn up. But after fifteen impatient minutes she rammed the car into gear and took off, spending what seemed like hours driving around aimlessly, before returning home exhausted and irritable.

And after all that, Charles expected her to just leap into bed with him! My God, he was insensitive, absolutely hopeless. She sat on the lid of the closed toilet and allowed tears to spill again. Hating the idea of him hearing her crying she ran the taps to cover any noise. There was a tap on the door. "Beebs?"

"What do you want?"

"Are you alright?"

"No." Silence. "Just go away, will you; leave me alone."

Charles listened at the door for a minute then ambled off to watch the football, ready to resume his usual life now that she was safely back.

When she eventually emerged from the bathroom, Bibi moved to the bedroom where she packed a bag and informed Charles coolly that she was going to visit her mother for a few days.

"Your mother?"

"Yes, the woman that gave birth to me, that's right."

"What for?"

She ignored this and was unmoved by his subsequent entreaties and refused even to kiss him goodbye, claiming she needed 'time to herself', she wouldn't even let him carry her bag which was very unusual. He followed her to her car, prancing about and plucking at her elbow.

"Bibi, speak to me. Bibi, stop. Stop." Charles stood in front of her.

"Get out of the way, will you," she said in a tired voice then shoved around him, got in her car and drove off.

"What have I done?" He asked himself, genuinely puzzled, then went inside and sat quietly lost in thought. He spent the remainder of the evening in front of the TV without really watching it, wondering whether he really loved Bibi at all.

Bibi told her mother that Charles was away on a course, but it hadn't fooled her for a second. She knew her daughter. But she said nothing and welcomed her with a token kiss.

They were two of a kind, Bibi and her mother. She had married Bibi's father when her first child was already well established in the womb, and he had stayed with them until circumstances became too intolerable to remain. He'd loved his precocious little daughter and spoiled her thoroughly, so they had kept in touch, albeit sporadically. There followed an amicable divorce, and the parents went their separate ways. Bibi had spent most weekends with him after that, pampered and spoiled to excess, only to return to her mother each Sunday evening to play second fiddle to whichever 'uncle' was in favour at the time.

When she was sixteen Bibi's father remarried. Furious at having to share him, she hated the new arrangement and was not afraid to show it. Joyce was quiet and unassuming and more than willing to be friendly, but had found the visits more and more trying and after becoming increasingly infrequent they had ceased altogether. Bibi had lost her father to Joyce and resented it more than anything that had ever happened to her.

There had been some letters, birthday and Christmas cards over the years, so she was aware that Joyce had died four years ago but pride prevented her from making contact again, and she had subconsciously been trying to replace his devotion from other sources ever since.

Her mother neither understood nor cared. She had her own life to think about and they were not close enough to discuss it. She still was an attractive woman, physically and financially, and generally had an entourage of men even now, these days much younger than herself. She took great care of her appearance and kept herself in good shape, in an effort to disguise signs of ageing for as long as possible.

"You look very thin," were her mother's first waspish words. "Are you eating enough?"

"Oh, don't fuss, I'm not ten years old now," snapped Bibi.

"Suit yourself. Drink?"

"What are you having?"

"G and T."

"Alright."

Her mother floated off to the kitchen. The truth was, she didn't care whether Bibi was eating or not, she just didn't want her looking too good when Guy turned up. Fifty years couldn't compete with thirty, (or was it thirty-one?), when one's offspring took after oneself. Her latest conquest was twenty-nine, virile and lantern-jawed in the way she preferred, and not altogether trustworthy. Guy had turned being a toy boy for rich, well-preserved women into his profession and would not have thrown away his gift horse for a younger woman who would expect him to provide for her, but he had no qualms about a younger bit on the side if it came along. They were both subtly aware of all this, but for the time being they were both getting what they wanted and were happy enough with the situation.

"You've changed your hair colour," commented Bibi as she swirled the ice in her drink.

"Yes, I got sick of that brassy blonde."

"The one I use, you mean?" Bibi shot back; certain her mother was trying to put her down as she always did.

"Do you?" was the uninterested response. Bibi suddenly felt weary of arguing and changed the subject, "So, how are you?"

Elizabeth was slightly taken aback at this query; it wasn't like her daughter to ask after her health.

"Oh, well, I'm fine. I've joined a gym."

"Oh really." Bibi hadn't particularly wanted to know how her mother was, it was just said to fill the silence.

Elizabeth noticed and felt irritated. What was the matter with the girl? Why was she always so prickly. She responded with well-concealed spite, "You should do something like that, your figure won't last without help. Dieting isn't the only thing you know."

"Can't you ever say anything without trying to put me down?" demanded Bibi, jumping up and slopping the G and T onto her clean blouse. "Damn it!"

"Do I?" said Elizabeth, as she held out a box of tissues.

"Yes, all the time." And with that, Bibi grabbed her bag and went upstairs.

Elizabeth recognised a touchiness when she saw it and let her daughter go without further comment, then poured herself another gin and tonic. Something had obviously happened again. She hoped her daughter wouldn't be staying too long this time.

In her old room Bibi lay on the bed and absently ran her hands over the silky bedspread as she examined the familiar décor and various trophies of childhood. On the bedside chest stood a photograph of her father, taken by her with the camera he'd given her for her twelfth birthday. He was laughing and holding a hand up, the fingers indicating victory, like Winston Churchill. She wondered what he was like now. Did he ever think of her? She let herself relive some of the times she had shared with him as a pampered child and felt nostalgic and emotional. It all seemed so long ago. In fact, it felt like the last time she had been truly happy.

She resolved to write to him. She had thought about it before but had not done it, this time she would. What if he invited her over? Would she go? She didn't think so, fearing an unsuccessful meeting would spoil her memories of those happier times. She raised herself up and began to rummage through the chest. There was the camera. She got it out and looked through the viewfinder, taking imaginary pictures of the room. There were piles of old letters there and she read a couple, smiling as she recalled their contents, feeling the words as much as reading them, returning to a time when life was somehow easier. The next letter was not in her father's elegant sloping script but in Wendell's loopy scrawl. Her mood became instantly serious.

Dearest Bibi,
It began.

Can it really be only half a day since we were together? The thought of tomorrow without you seems unbearable, but knowing I shall see you this weekend will keep me going.

And so on.

She laughed quietly. How corny, but then Wendell always had been. She read through a few more and found herself getting progressively more nostalgic, not an emotion she usually allowed into her life. Yes, we did have fun together, she conceded. What went wrong there? Charles of course! She thought of him with distaste. Damn the man and his godlike looks, why couldn't they have just had a secret fling, why did they ever end up living together anyway? He was far too childish and unsophisticated for her, no personality at all. All this was entirely his fault.

I *should* contact Wendell, she decided. Perhaps it was time to settle down properly. If not, it would be a pleasant interlude. Would he still want her? She'd waltzed off with Charles without a thought about his feelings, indicating Charles had seduced her. She thought back and could see him now, pleading with her to stay. If he didn't want her, she'd soon remedy that. She always could twist him around her little finger.

She had returned to their flat while he was at work and removed all her possessions and a few of his to furnish her new life with Charles. The one she now no longer wanted. Probably never wanted, truth be told.

Bibi felt quite excited about the idea, she would enjoy thawing him out and persuading him back to her, it would be just like when they first met. Well, almost like that.

Her mother was singing from somewhere downstairs. Why couldn't they have a 'normal' relationship? Where did one even start after all this time?

The doorbell chimed.

Bibi froze. Surely not Charles. Her beating heart threatened to stop her hearing who it was. She hurried across to the door and opened it a fraction to listen.

"Hi gorgeous," came a deep unknown voice.

Creeping out on to the landing, she looked down the curve of the stairs to see a muscular man approximately her own age attempting to suck her mother's face off like some hideous flesh-eating predator.

"God," she breathed with disgust and silently returned to her room.

Guy, one eye open as he engulfed Elizabeth, noticed long, shapely legs and a rather sexy behind disappearing from the top of the stairs.

Elizabeth clutched his leather clad buttocks with bejewelled fingers.

"Mmm... nice," she murmured. "Get yourself a drink, darling, I won't be a moment." She began to mount the stairs.

"I'd rather come with you if you're going up there," he teased, placing both hands on her retreating backside as he started to follow her up.

"Naughty!" laughed Elizabeth and they swept on and up into her room, where he threw her onto the enormous bed.

But she ignored his suggestive advances and gently pushed him away. "Not now, darling, I'm hungry, let's eat first, shall we?" It was a fur-lined order rather than a question. Guy knew the rules of the game and released her in a way that said he was terribly disappointed and frustrated. She was satisfied.

At Bibi's door Elizabeth called to her daughter, "Back later, darling."

As they walked towards Guy's flashy vehicle, he enquired after the mysterious visitor, now peeking through the curtains.

"House guest?"

"My daughter. She's had some sort of bust-up with her boyfriend and landed herself on me. It's the only time I ever see her of course, when she's in trouble."

They climbed into the jeep and departed.

Bibi, scrutinising Guy critically through the curtains, said "My God" to herself. It was disgusting, a woman her age with that young stud! He was straight from the pages of a catalogue, the men's underwear section. Mail order toy boy. Anyway, at least it gave her the place to herself she thought, sauntering downstairs. A whole evening to herself, what luxury! She began to unwind for the first time since Friday evening.

"Bloody men," she swore as she tucked into a packet of chocolate biscuits, but her feelings were half-hearted.

She spent the next three or four hours in front of the television, working her way through her mother's snack supply, and even found herself laughing at an amusing film that was on. How long was it since she'd enjoyed an evening so much?

Later, but not much because she was tired, she lay staring at her father's picture. Her eyes closed and she tucked the duvet around her comfortably, like a child might.

"Goodnight Dad," she whispered.

Chapter Fourteen
Sunday

Antonia's first thoughts on waking were of the previous evening.

She relived the conversation in its entirety, thinking that in one evening she and Wendell Cornish probably knew more about each other than she had ever known about Charles. She saw again Wendell's laughing face and began mixing it with other invented scenarios, one ending with the two of them locked together in a passionate embrace. She laughed out loud at the thought, although it wasn't an unwelcome one. Don't get carried away, she told herself. This is strictly friends only.

Finally, she got up. What would he be doing today, she wondered, unable at the moment to think of anything not connected with Wendell Cornish. She drew the curtains back, letting the midday light enter and was mildly disappointed, and then equally relieved, to see his car was gone. After a light lunch she went for a long walk. It was a lovely day, sunny, warm and with a hint of a breeze, just enough to sway the long grass at the side of the road. She smiled and greeted other walkers, enjoying these brief encounters. Upon reaching the summit of the walk she sat and raised her face to the sun, feeling more content than she had in a long, long time. People needed people she decided, and she was enjoying having found one in Wendell Cornish.

Below lay the picturesque village of Marshwick, so beloved of tourists, sprawled amidst the green and gold colours of autumn.

And now to complete her contentment she retrieved a bar of chocolate from her bag and placed it in front of her. As she bit into it, she concluded this must be what heaven was like.

The shadows were starting to lengthen by the time she got back, the time known to photographers as the 'golden' hour. She had been hoping Wendell would be back, only so she could knock and thank him for last night, but he had still not returned. Her phone started ringing as she opened her door and she raced to pick it up, shedding shoes and handbag on the way. Her sister's voice trilled down the line.

"Hi Toni, how are you?"

"Yeah OK. You?" she replied with suspicion. Antonia's sister generally only called when she was after something.

"Are you alright? You sound breathless?"

"I heard the phone as I was coming in, had to run for it."

"Oh," she swept on. "I tried you last night. Don't tell me you were out!"

How did Fiona always manage to irk her with these small observations?

"I am allowed out you know," she retorted.

"Really? Tell me more," she didn't wait to be told more. "Anyway, it seemed a while since I spoke to you."

"What do you want this time?" Antonia wasn't in the habit of being so abrupt, but she felt brave after the success of the previous evening and Fiona was getting on her nerves, because she knew she would want something, so why didn't she just say.

Faced with this unusual show of spirit, Fiona hesitated for a second. She felt uneasy now about the favour she was about to ask and struggled to find something else to say first.

"Er, well, how are you anyway?"

"I'm fine thanks. Are you?"

"Oh yes fine."

"Tom and the kids?"

"They're fine too." Fiona saw her chance. "Actually, we're off on holiday tomorrow."

Here it comes, thought Antonia, and waited.

"Hello? Are you still there?"

"Yes."

"Oh. Are you sure you're alright?"

"Never better."

"You sound strange. Different."

Antonia had been suppressing a laugh and now let it out, pleased to make her sister squirm for once. She was always so forthright and confident about everything, assured of having her way. Maybe it was what made Antonia the exact opposite.

"I'm just winding you up, take no notice. What is it you want? As long as it's not looking after children for a fortnight I don't mind."

Fiona paused again. This wasn't like her sister at all.

"Well, you remember Mum's friend Sheila? She's got a cottage on the Isle of Wight which she's letting us have for two weeks, free of charge."

"Where is it?"

"The Isle of Wight," replied Fiona loudly.

"No, I mean *where* on the Isle of Wight?"

"Ventnor."

"Lovely. I've never been there. Never been invited."

Oh no, surely she wasn't looking for an invitation to come with them? God no. What the hell was the matter with her? For the first time Fiona wondered how to proceed. But Antonia had had her fun and helped her out.

"So, what can I do for you then?"

Reassured at last, Fiona got to the point.

"Well, the thing is, Toni, that because it's such short notice, we've got no one to look after Ozzie. I was wondering if you'd have him, or come over and feed him?"

Ozzie was a large middle-aged black cat, the adored family pet. This was one of Fiona's easier asks.

"Of course I'll look after him, it'll be nice to have a moggy about the place."

"Yes, it'll be company for you."

Antonia bristled slightly.

"You have saved our holiday, why didn't I ask you first? I don't know how many people I've called."

I bet, thought Antonia.

"We'll be around later."

Fiona was just about to hang up when she had a sudden thought. "You will be in later won't you?"

"Yes, you know me. I never go out."

They arrived, Fiona and her eldest, a boy of six, at almost 11 o'clock p.m. Fiona's timekeeping, or lack of it, was something she shared with their mother. Antonia had been watching from her window and went out to meet them.

"Hi," Fiona sang, planting a perfunctory kiss on Antonia's cheek. "Thanks a million for this Toni."

She hauled the basket containing the wailing cat from the car, and headed up the stairs followed by the skinny child who was loaded down with armfuls of bags.

"Hello Matthew." Antonia smiled at her nephew and took a couple of bags from him. All she got in reply was a weary look.

"Say hello to Aunty Toni, Matthew."

"Hello," he said sullenly.

Fiona tutted. "Kids!"

"You look tired, sweetheart," said Antonia kindly and he yawned and nodded. "It is quite late."

She glanced at her sister.

"He's fine, yeah sorry we're running a bit late," said Fiona. "Come on, Matthew, hurry up," and she dumped the basket and everything else in the middle of the lounge where Ozzie continued howling. A bony paw reached frantically through the bars of the prison and Antonia bent to open it.

"Come on then," she encouraged the cat, reluctant to emerge now that freedom was offered.

"You're looking good," said Fiona. "Found a new man or something?"

Antonia reddened, annoyed.

She stayed crouched by the basket, pretending not to hear. "What's his routine then?"

Fiona produced a long list of instructions which appeared to be rather complex. The vet had advised a diet of boiled fish or chicken along with vitamin pills and a twice weekly dose of liquid paraffin.

"It makes him do enormous poos," said Matthew, giggling, "like giant sausages."

"Stops him getting bunged up," said Fiona, ignoring the boy.

Ozzie had by now ventured out of his basket and was cautiously exploring the new surroundings, sniffing. He seemed particularly interested in a light stain by the coffee table where once some take away curry had spilled. Eventually he raised his head, and his mouth was hanging slightly open in something akin to distress.

"Mum," whined Matthew, "can we go now."

"In a minute," said Fiona, still ignoring him. "Obviously, you'll have to buy the food fresh." Here's some money. She held out a twenty-pound note. "We'll be back two weeks tomorrow. That's all I think." Her brow furrowed in last-minute concentration.

"Mum, stop talking." Matthew had flopped onto the sofa and was thudding his foot up and down on it. Fiona ignored him.

"Thanks again, Toni, you've really saved my life."

"Mum!"

"What?"

"Can we go now?"

"Get up, Matthew. That's Aunty Toni's sofa you're destroying with your dirty shoes."

He remained sprawled across the cushions.

"Er, where's tomorrow's food?" enquired Antonia as she looked into a carrier bag. The last thing she wanted was fresh fish left in a bag on the floor all night.

"I didn't have time to get any, everything was such short notice. There's a shop just down the road isn't there? It'll give you a plan for the morning. It does open early, doesn't it?"

Antonia didn't know whether to be offended or exasperated.

"Blimey Fi, I do have work to go to you know."

Fiona made a reproachful face. "Yeah, sorry Toni. Thanks again though." She scooped Ozzie up and spent a couple of minutes smothering the unhappy animal in kisses. His front paws were resting on her chest, at full stretch, straining to get away.

"Be a good boy for Aunty Toni." She dropped him onto the sofa as he arched away from her which woke Matthew.

"Come on Matthew, get up. We're going. Look at the time, way past your bedtime."

He got up and clung to her. "I'm tired, Mummy, carry me."

"Carry you! You're not a baby." She was getting impatient with him as she made her way towards the door. "Stop it, Matthew, I can't walk with you hanging on to me like that." She grasped the boy's hand and pulled him out.

They walked to the car and waved as they pulled away.

"Send me a postcard," mouthed Antonia.

Wendell's car was still noticeably absent, and she suddenly felt rather tired and a bit cross, blaming it on the fact that she had to get up early and go to the shop for this damn fish. Honestly, Fiona could be so irritating sometimes.

Ozzie had made himself comfortable on the sofa and Antonia gently stroked his head, caressing him around the ears. He began to purr softly, and she decided she was going to enjoy his stay. Perhaps it would even encourage her to get a cat of her own. She made sure he was aware of where the facilities were and he obligingly made use of them, scattering bits of cat litter all over the bathroom floor as he covered the damp spot with great concentration and a lot of checking. This duty achieved, he jumped onto the bed this time and began to 'play the cello' as Fiona would have put it.

"Charming," said Antonia. Ten minutes later, they were both contentedly sleeping.

At just about the time Antonia was enjoying the bar of chocolate and comparing her day to one in heaven, Wendell was having one of the most hellish of his life.

It had begun with an early phone call from Barney, dragging him from sleep three hours after he'd gone to bed.

"Hello," he croaked into the receiver, laying it next to his head on the pillow.

"Wendy? Hello, this is Barney."

Barney? Oh God. "What time is it?"

"Oh. Yeah, sorry about that. Ringing so early I mean; it's been a bit of a night here. Tracy's in hospital, so I wondered if you fancied a lunchtime drink, make up for the other night. Sorry again about that, I felt awful."

Obviously, Barney was now the proud father of another screaming brat. Whoopee. He must feel like celebrating.

"Can we make it later, I only got to bed recently?" asked Wendell, eyes still closed. It was a bit like a reversal of the previous night.

"No can do Wendy, I have to put in an appearance at the hospital sometime. Not like you to refuse a lunchtime piss up. Come on, let's celebrate!"

Barney was maddeningly lively; he'd probably just had about fifteen hours uninterrupted sleep.

"What time?" asked Wendell, resigned now to getting up.

"11.30? Come here and we'll go around the corner. If you want to stay here for the night that's fine."

How long was this session going on, for God's sake? Wendell just agreed to everything in his longing to go back to sleep, then found to his annoyance that he couldn't. He opened his eyes. They felt like wheel bearings that needed changing and he kept blinking to rehydrate them. He turned to the clock; it was 9.15.

"Oh God!" he moaned. He did finally fall asleep again, waking at 10.30 feeling dreadfully tired. On his way to Barney's, he stopped for petrol and while he was at it grabbed a prepacked sausage roll, which at that moment seemed appetising and sensible before a lunchtime drink or two. He ate it driving along and decided not to include the greasy, puffy thing with its millimetre of processed mush in his fifty favourite snacks list. There was something hard in it too, and as he bit into it, an old filling disintegrated.

"Bugger!" he cursed, attempting to separate bits of amalgam from food with his tongue. He threw the half-eaten item aside and sorted the bits out with a finger.

Why was he doing this? he asked himself. After that fiasco last night, he should have left the bloody phone ringing. His thoughts as he nodded off last night had been of asking Antonia out to lunch next weekend. Delightful girl, he could fall for someone like that. He ran a hand through his hair, distributing flakes of pastry and sticky sausage roll into it in ignorance. Anyway, he was here.

He found the place in much the same state of chaos as it had been the previous evening, although this time Barney was sober and at least was expecting him.

"Wendy!" Exclaimed his friend, arms thrown wide. "Come in, come in."

Barney led the way and wiped crumbs and toys off the sofa with a sweep of his hand.

"Really sorry about last night, me ol' China," he joked with an attempt at a cockney accent.

At this point, Wendell decided to cut his losses and try and enjoy himself. He could sleep later after all.

"So, what did she have?"

"Who?"

"Well, Tracy of course! Boy or girl?"

"Oh, she hasn't had it yet."

Wendell stared at Barney's back, bent over the sink attempting to wash up and felt the first misgivings tickle his insides.

"Won't be a minute here," Barney called from the kitchen. "D'you want anything? Tea? Coffee?"

"No thanks, I'm fine." Wendell belched silently, tasting spicy processed food. He didn't even want a beer yet.

"Erm, what do you mean she hasn't had it? Is she alright?"

"She's in labour. Started early this morning."

"Hang on a minute, shouldn't you be with her, holding her hand or something?"

"Said she didn't want me there." There was a pause. "Called her mother. Besides, someone had to look after Sam."

As if on cue, a childish high-pitched voice came yelling from upstairs and was quickly followed by a noisy entrance into the room. He stood and stared at Wendell.

"Who's that man?"

"This is my friend Wendell," said Barney. "Don't do that Sam, it's dirty."

Wendell felt suddenly extraordinarily tired and slightly ill. A vague headache was settling over his eyes.

"Who's having Sam while we're out?" asked Wendell wearily, already fearing he knew what was coming.

"Us, old son, three men together, eh?" He ruffled Sam's untidy blonde hair in a fatherly fashion as he smiled down at him.

Wendell exhaled heavily. "For God's sake, Barney, what's going on? We can't have a session and babysit at the same time."

"There's a garden," replied Barney, as if this solved everything.

"Surely you should be at the hospital, isn't that what fathers do when their wives are giving birth?"

"Normally yes, Wendy," said Barney with feeling. "But my wife is not normal. Fact is she prefers to have her old lady stare up her fanny than me at the moment." There was bitterness in his tone.

"Daddy, what's a fanny?"

"Come on, we'd better get you dressed," said Barney, taking the child by the hand and hurrying him along the hall. His pyjamas, hanging around his knees, tripped him and Barney spent a further few minutes comforting the child, still repeatedly asking through sobs what a fanny was.

"It's something to avoid at all costs," Wendell heard Barney say as he carried Sam upstairs. "Won't be a minute Wendy," he added.

"Christ all fucking mighty," Wendell hissed under his breath and sunk his head into his hands.

Barney was right when he said he wouldn't be a minute. Fifty-eight of them later they set off for the pub. Barney took the car because Sam refused to walk, another delay.

But miraculously, the idea actually seemed to be working. The sun was shining, and Sam occupied himself playing with other children there. Apart from providing the boy with an occasional cola and bag of crisps, Barney ignored him absolutely and Wendell wondered why they were having another one at all.

"Shouldn't you at least call the hospital and see how she's doing?" At the back of his mind, Wendell's misgivings had grown, and this prompted him to make the suggestion.

"Don't worry so much," replied Barney, lighting up a cigarette. But he couldn't completely hide his own unease. He took a long haul on the cigarette and turned his head to look for Sam at last. After a moment, he turned back and stubbed the cigarette out while he spoke, so he didn't have to make actual eye contact.

"She made it very clear she wanted nothing to do with me. Called that fucking old pussy in. She wouldn't even let me drive them, called a fucking cab would you believe? I ask you."

He lit another cigarette, took a pull from it and downed the rest of his pint in one go. "Another?" Barney indicated his glass and stood up in readiness, but Wendell still had half of his own left and didn't respond.

"She may have changed her mind by now Barney."

"I don't care if she has. I've had it mate. Another pint?" He wove his way slightly erratically towards the bar and sometime later returned with two more pints. Resuming his seat, he gulped down a further half and licked his lips. He seemed to be mulling something over.

"Second thoughts, I think I had better call the hospital. Can you keep an eye on Sam for a minute Wendy? Thanks." He disappeared towards the bar once again, this time with determination. Wendell was torn between feeling almost painfully sorry for, and completely exasperated with his friend. He looked for Sam, who was still enjoying himself at the other end of the garden.

At the hospital Tracy was struggling and straining. Her mother, holding her left hand tightly, was trumpeting out advice from behind a surgical mask, while the midwife's bright words of encouragement came at her from the right. Intermittent comments of a medical nature came from the stern.

As she heaved and pushed in pain and misery, all she wanted was Barney by her side. Where was he? Why hadn't he come? Why had she been so spiteful to him this morning? Questions of a recriminatory kind swamped her; she was filled with remorse. He had his failings, but they did love each other and had made this baby between them and, goddammit, he should be here to see it arrive, and to see what she was going through in having it. She looked left, right and past her knees at the people surrounding her, all, more or less, strangers. Apart from her mother who was getting on her nerves.

"Mum?"

"I'm here, darling," she clutched her hand even tighter.

"Mum, I want Barney here."

"Now, never mind him, just concentrate on what you're doing." Her glasses were all steamed up over the mask, so she was unable to see the irritation on her daughter's face.

"I need him here. I want him here." Tracy was getting upset and the midwife tried to intervene.

The mother overrode her, "No, you don't want him, darling, I'm here for you, calm down and push."

"I want Barney," yelled Tracy, in time with the latest contraction. "Get him!"

Thinking she was becoming hysterical, both Tracy's mother and the midwife tried to soothe her. Tracy batted her mother's hand away with enough force to make her mother exclaim "Oh!" and start rubbing the back of it.

"Will you just fucking get him," shrieked Tracy, "or I'll get up and do it myself!"

Her mother, shocked, felt momentary pity for Barney.

"Somebody get him," wailed Tracy. "Please."

"Now don't you fret, darlin'," said the midwife, a large Jamaican lady with five children of her own, "Nurse iscahlin' him right now." She patted Tracy's hand.

By the time Barney did eventually get in touch, Tracy really was near to hysterical. The nurse had tried every number in vain, and even called down to A and E just in case.

"Mr Kennedy! We've been trying to contact you all afternoon," the receptionist said urgently.

Barney's blood froze. He sobered immediately. "Oh my God, what's happened?"

"Mrs Kennedy has been asking for you. She's still in labour as far as I know and would like you to be here with her." She managed by her manner to make him feel terribly guilty.

"Christ. Ok, I'll be there in a minute. Tell her to keep her legs crossed." He crashed the phone down and raced out to where Wendell was sitting, just taking a sip of the new pint.

"Wendy!" He yelled, making him jump.

"What's happened?"

"She wants me there; I've got to go." He grabbed his keys from the table.

"Hang on!" Wendell jumped to his feet and laid a restraining hand on Barney's arm. "Don't forget Sam."

"Sam! Oh my God!" He rushed over and dragged the child away from another boy who he was beating over the head with one of his shoes. Its partner had disappeared completely, probably buried somewhere in the sandpit.

Barney was in no fit state to drive, so Wendell gallantly offered to take them and was swiftly passed the keys. All the way there, Barney was poised on the edge of the seat repeating, "she wants me there" to himself in a slightly fanatical tone against a background of angry wailing. Wendell's head was pounding with tension and fatigue. After he'd got rid of them, he would go home and lie down with an aspirin, he decided. He tried to take his mind off the present chaos by thinking about his new friend, Antonia. What was she doing today? When he got back perhaps he'd call on her. Just to thank her for last night and ask her to come to lunch with him sometime. Just as friends of course. Today he needed rest. The idea of it was the only thing keeping him sane at the moment.

Wendell coasted up outside the hospital's main entrance and before he'd even come to a halt Barney was out, had banged the roof twice by way of a thank you, and was running towards the automatic doors like an Olympic gold medallist. Wendell scrabbled frantically at the window.

"Barney!" he yelled. "Barney!" But it was too late, he was gone.

A uniformed gentleman, eyes invisible under the peak of an immaculate cap, tapped on Wendell's window. He could hear the occupant of the car using foul four-letter words, and with a child in there too. Disgraceful. Wendell spun around and wound his window down.

"Yes?"

"I shall have to ask you to move your car please, Sir. This entrance must be kept clear at all times." He thrust his chin forward as he said this.

"Yes of course, sorry," spluttered Wendell, his temples pulsating. At least Sam had gone quiet at last.

"Is there a car park here?"

"Straight down there and to your left, Sir, follow the blue signs."

Tracy had always told Sam never to get into cars with strange men and now here he was being driven off by a very strange one. He began screaming hysterically for his Daddy. So did Wendell, but for entirely different reasons.

And now, as he toured the crowded car park, Wendell's patience snapped. Slamming a foot onto the brake he turned to the screaming child. Sam's grubby, contorted, purple face filled Wendell with loathing. How could anyone love that?

"Shut up, you little shit!" he roared above the noise. Sam's screeching ceased immediately, and he sat, lip quivering, regarding Wendell with something close to terror. The sudden quiet made Wendell's ears hiss.

"Right, that's better." He spotted a car vacating a space and eased Barney's into it. Then, calmer now, he tried to explain to Sam that they were going to find Mummy and Daddy and he must get out of the car and come with him.

First that strange man had driven him somewhere, now he wanted him to go with him. It was all too much for the child and he resumed the screaming with a vengeance while crouching as far away from Wendell as possible. There followed some half-hearted cajoling but, in the end Wendell gave up and dragged the wildly kicking brat bodily from the car. People stared and tutted at this unfeeling display, but Wendell was past caring. All he wanted was to dump the kid and go. He marched across to the entrance with Sam under his arm like a delivery driver with a parcel. The kid was still shrieking blue murder, so it was hard to make himself understood above the racket, but finally the receptionist responded frostily that both Mr and Mrs Kennedy were busy in the delivery room and, *obviously*, could not be disturbed. She pursed her lips and began rearranging some papers, thereby signifying that there was no more to be said.

Sam, safely amongst people again, had quietened and was now merely sobbing with despair.

"Are you going to take this child or not?" hissed Wendell through teeth clenched so tightly his shattered tooth began to hurt.

"Sir," snapped the receptionist, "do you see anyone with enough time on their hands to babysit for you? Hmm?" She stared at him like an angry chicken.

"Right," said Wendell in a dangerously quiet voice, before abandoning politeness and shouting, "Listen, you stupid woman, unless you want to have to save this brat from strangulation and me from the psychiatric ward, you'd better *find* someone to look after him because I'm going," and with that he lifted Sam onto the counter and walked away. His trousers clung to his thigh where the boy had wet himself.

"Nanny!" came a wail from behind him and Wendell glanced back to see Tracy's mother advancing with purpose towards reception, looking incredulously at Sam. Thank God!

Wendell fled to the nearest toilet to hide from her and to clean up his trousers, then headed with relief to the car park. When he finally located Barney's car it had a parking ticket on it. He removed it gently from the windscreen and stared at it. A parking ticket? Here? This just about iced the cake.

There was a brief moment of daydreaming, Wendell imagining a heart attack victim clutching his chest as he staggered, dying, towards the pay and display machine.

Throwing the thing on the passenger seat with the flattened remains of a biscuit where Barney had sat on it, Wendell drove off in a trance.

When he arrived at Barney's house, he posted the ticket through the letterbox with a twenty-pound note and hid the keys under a plant pot, in case it was their only set. He hoped that if the money didn't cover the charge, it would at least show he'd tried to do the right thing. He sat for a while in his own car, weary and unkempt, woke up half an hour later and drove home.

As he approached the front door, he glanced up at Antonia's window, seeing no sign of life there. Probably just as well. He'd contact her tomorrow when all this would be a good story. It was lovely to get out of his damp trousers, which he carried straight to the washing machine between finger and thumb at arm's length, then feel a hot bath cleanse him of sweat, urine and bits of greasy pastry. Afterwards he made a cup of tea and took two painkillers. He loaded the tea with sugar, having heard somewhere that it was what to give to people in shock, which he certainly had been. As the aspirins, tea and quietness began to work on him, the tension finally began to ebb and was replaced by indescribable fatigue. He slept soundly for an hour and finding only a half loaf covered in black pinheads in the kitchen, drove off to get a meal somewhere. Should he ask Antonia if she would like to come too? No, she would think he was pursuing her. He could just knock to thank her for last night and ask her then. She wasn't there and he found himself absurdly disappointed. Oh well, perhaps that's best, didn't want her to get the wrong idea.

As he turned the corner at one end of the road, she was just turning in from the other end.

Chapter Fifteen
Monday

Thankful that the work day was over at last, Antonia waited for Rob to leave before climbing into her decent clothes.

It was the day of her interview, and as she stood in the chilly toilet applying mascara and lipstick, she asked herself for the hundredth time why on earth she was bothering. She had decided she didn't want to be a dental nurse any more. She had been annoying herself thinking about Wendell Cornish all day, but was nevertheless hoping he would be at home when she got back, would see her arriving looking smart for once.

But forget all that, she must concentrate on this damn interview, which she was feeling nervous about. She wasn't sure why. The surgery was within walking distance, so she wheeled her bike along and chained it up nearby. The large clock in the window of the shop next door said ten to six. A bit early but it was getting cold out here. She examined herself in the same shop window, took a breath and entered.

Warmth and the smell of eugenolengulfed her. A thick royal blue carpet stretched across to where a chunky girl with a hat of glossy brown hair sat behind a wall of screens and other machinery. Comfortable but firm chairs lined the walls, which were painted a delicate eggshell blue and adorned with advertisements of attractive models with gleaming smiles. The whole place oozed expense. She made her way silently to the reception desk and stood in the clearing between the bank of computers and a display of toothbrushes.

"May I help you?" asked the girl, smiling to reveal a row of brilliant white crowns.

"Yes, hello, my name is Antonia Goldsmith. I have an appointment with Mrs Schafer at six." She glanced at the clock and added, "I'm a bit early."

"Take a seat, I'll tell her you're here."

"Thank you."

Antonia sat next to a table laden with glossy magazines. They were current too, all they had in Rob's surgery were two year old golfing stuff and the odd rambler's newsletter, left there by one of the patients. The receptionist returned with a clipboard and handed it to Antonia, requesting that she fill in the application form please.

As Antonia scribbled, she was aware of the receptionist's eyes on her. It would only have been what she would have done in her place, but it made her feel more uncomfortable than she already was. Why was she putting herself through this?

At five past six, Mrs Schafer appeared in her crisp white dental attire and with a surgical mask dangling around her neck. She advanced towards Antonia, who didn't know whether to stand, sit, curtsey or continue filling the form in. She stood.

"Miss Goldsmith?" Enquired the dentist and held out a manicured hand to her. They shook. Mrs Schafer had a grip like iron, there were white marks on Antonia's fingers when they were released.

"I'm running a fraction late," continued the dentist, fixing her with probing blue eyes. "Do you mind waiting a few minutes?"

"No, not at all," replied Antonia when she was thinking, *Yes, yes, I do mind. I want to go home.*

"Would you like a coffee?"

"Thank you, I'd love one."

Mrs Schafer turned to the glossy brown head. "Serena?"

Serena sprang into action, beaming. "Yes Mrs Schafer?"

"Make Miss Goldsmith a coffee, would you?" and with that, disappeared back into her surgery. Serena's smile faded and she ambled off, returning a few minutes later with some lukewarm sludge which she placed on the table next to the magazines.

"Thank you," smiled Antonia and took a sip. It was sugarless and tasted foul. At least the coffee at Rob's gaffe was better than this. Serena, now in her coat, waltzed past on her way home.

"Bye, good luck," she finished, smiling like the Cheshire cat. Antonia smiled back but said nothing. She had finished the form and now regarded the décor.

Eventually Mrs Schafer appeared again, dealt with the patient and ushered Antonia into a surgery so far removed from Rob Murphy's tatty workshop as to be from a different planet. It was space age in appearance, all brilliant white like Serena's teeth, except for the pale brown chair which seemed to be suspended in mid-air at the room's centre. The walls curved delicately into the floor, no chance of accumulating muck there, and soft classical music played from an invisible source just loud enough to relax without being intrusive.

Antonia placed herself into the chair indicated and Mrs Schafer launched straight into a practised monologue about how the practice was run, what was expected of the staff and all the general entitlements. Antonia, her face alight with fake interest, knew this job was out of her league. She would never achieve the 150% devotion to duty that Mrs Schafer seemed to be implying was a requirement of the job. She too sported dazzling crowns, this time in a sharp and strangely attractive face framed by pale red hair. There was a strength of purpose behind this feminine façade which said that Mrs Schafer would be an exacting boss.

She handed Antonia three items. "Can you tell me the names of these instruments and what they are used for?"

No, she couldn't. She fiddled desperately with them and felt herself getting hot. It was no good, she didn't have a clue. Dan Murphy always used the same four and these were not any of them.

"I'm sorry, I don't know."

Mrs Schafer made no comment.

"Is there anything you'd like to ask me?"

"Um, no, I think you've covered everything."

Antonia felt weary, she didn't want this job, Mrs Schafer knew she didn't want it and wouldn't have offered it to her if she had. What a waste of time.

"Well Miss Goldsmith, I shall be interviewing all week and shall contact everyone on Friday when I make my decision. If you feel the job is not for you, perhaps you would let me know before then."

There was a tiny trace of a German accent under the polished Oxford English, which probably accounted for the efficiency and professionalism of the woman thought Antonia, as she was led towards the door. She had the distinct impression she was not at the top of the shortlist, but she didn't care.

"Where are you working at the moment?" enquired Mrs Schafer conversationally. Antonia wondered why she hadn't asked before.

"Mr Murphy, just down the road here."

"Oh…" Disapproval was evident, Mrs Schafer looked like she had just caught a whiff of a bad smell, but the smile swiftly returned as she once again shook Antonia's hand in her vice-like grip as she bade her farewell, then locked the door behind her.

Antonia exhaled a sigh of relief, thank God that was over. It was past seven, she could go home and see if Wendell was in.

Monday lunchtime found Wendell relating the events of the weekend to his secretary over a pub lunch.

Beth was a comfortable middle-aged lady, who mothered him happily. They had an easy and friendly working relationship, uncluttered by the romantic undertones that often developed with younger women. When she smiled it lit up an otherwise rather ordinary face, and she was doing this now as she listened to the saga of Barney and son. She was dabbing a tissue to the corners of her eyes as Wendell finished the sorry tale.

"It was not funny yesterday I can tell you," he said rather seriously, which made her laugh all the more.

"I'm sorry Wendell," she said finally. "Oh dear, what a story. And after you'd had hardly any sleep."

"Yeah, but it was worth it for Saturday evening," he grinned.

Beth was glad to see such a change in him, she confessed. She'd been worried about him lately. Antonia sounded delightful; she was happy for him. She could see straight through the 'only friends' façade, and hoped something good would come of it.

Slightly embarrassed by this show of motherly misunderstanding, he changed the subject.

"When I got back to the car it had a parking ticket on it."

Beth hooted with renewed laughter and reached for her tissue again. This time Wendell joined in, feeling relaxed and happy as thoughts of Antonia filled his head.

"They had a pay and display system up there. How the hell was I supposed to know that? Would you believe it, paying in a hospital car park?"

"Yes, I know," said Beth, regaining her composure. "They'd let you die rather than allow you to park for nothing."

Wendell recalled his vision of the dying driver as he looked at his watch.

They rose and set off back to the office.

"Will you see her again?"

"Antonia?" said Wendell in an offhand voice. "I hope so. Just as friends, you know."

Beth knew.

The afternoon dragged. Wendell was sure Antonia would be in on a Monday evening, it would be the neighbourly thing to thank her and casually suggest repeating it. You never know what might come of it, he thought privately, all kinds of possibilities filling his head, then he stopped himself. No, just keep it friendly for now, she wasn't another Bibi after all.

By 5.37pm he was in his car and whizzing home, using every back road he knew to shorten the journey, astonished at how keen he was to see her.

She wasn't in.

He was disappointed. But then, it was only just after six, give her a chance to get in from work. He let himself in, listened carefully for sounds of the front door opening, and kept checking to see if a light was on in her window but there were still no visible signs of life.

Damn. So, she was out. Damn.

The phone rang and he answered it with disinterest. It wouldn't be her; she didn't have the number.

"Hello?"

"Wendy! Hi!" rang Barney's voice into his ear, full of fatherly joy.

This was all he needed.

"Hello Barney," he said in a flat voice. "Everything ok?"

"We have a daughter," Barney continued happily. "A real cracker, just like her mother. Lovely little thing she is," he finished with a laugh.

"Congratulations all of you," said Wendell, trying to inject some animation into his voice. He hoped Barney wouldn't mention yesterday.

"I'm so sorry about yesterday, Wendy. I was in a right old state, wasn't I?" He laughed. "Poor old Sam," he laughed more.

Poor old Sam! Bloody hell.

Barney flowed on, "I owe you one, Wendy. Have you eaten?"

"Er, well… no," said Wendell with caution. No way was he up to another Barney type fiasco.

"Excellent! Come over now and I'll treat you. Only around the corner but the food's marvellous, and no driving involved." He paused for breath then added as an afterthought, "You're not doing anything, are you?"

Wendell was hungry and the thought of marvellous pub grub was appealing, but...

"Come on Wendy, you can be here in twenty minutes."

"Well... I did have other plans for this evening, a good night's sleep for one."

"Cancel them. This is the last opportunity we'll have to go out for some time. Tracy's coming home tomorrow. Come on Wendy."

"Where's Sam?" Wendell asked warily. Even Barney wouldn't be able to take a four year old into a pub in the evening.

"Sam? Oh, he's catered for."

"Where is he then?"

"You sound as if you don't trust me," laughed Barney. "He's with Tracy's mum."

"And Tracy's at the hospital until tomorrow?"

"Yes. I've been there with her, told her all about yesterday, we had a good laugh about it. Funny thing, now the baby's out she seems to be her old self again. Marvellous."

Glad you thought it was funny, thought Wendell indignantly.

"Actually, it was Tracy who suggested I call you."

"Really?" It made him feel suddenly better about the arrangement. "Well, alright then. I'll leave now, see you shortly."

"Marvellous! See you soon. I'll be ready this time. Bye." The phone went dead, and Wendell wandered out to look at Antonia's window again. He knocked on her door on his way out, just in case, but no one answered. Tomorrow would have to do then. Wonder where she was?

So Wendell wasn't there again. Or he'd already gone out, thought Antonia as she locked the bike away. She was a bit disappointed. Had Saturday evening really happened? Perhaps it was really only a one-off.

Ozzie greeted her loudly as she entered the flat. She scooped him up and hugged him and he purred and quivered with satisfaction. She carried him to the kitchen where he howled for food and wound himself around her ankles.

"There we are, sweetie," she crooned as she placed the dish of cooked chicken, delicately chopped, in front of him. He bent his head and sniffed, turned and regarded her with as pitiful an expression as a cat could manage, then walked away.

"Oh, what!" she exclaimed, her shoulders sagging with exasperation. He'd hardly eaten a thing this morning either. The next twenty minutes were spent coaxing him into eating the stuff. It didn't look very appetising, she had to admit. She'd get fish tomorrow; he was bound to eat that stinking stuff. There was something black on her wrist. As she moved to flick it off, it sprang away of its own accord. Fleas. He had fleas!

"Oh God," she growled, scratching at the very thought, then spent the next twenty minutes chasing him around the flat with the can of spray so thoughtfully provided by Fiona. And she hadn't even taken her coat off yet.

Two hours later, Ozzie still refused to look at her, let alone stroke his now flea-free fur. She'd finally given up attempting to appease him and left him to come around in his own good time. Now and again he would attempt to wash the filthy stuff off his fur, but couldn't seem to bring himself to do it properly, and as a result it was standing up in sticky ridges where the spray had been applied.

Antonia stood and gazed out of the window again. Still no car, oh well. Sighing heavily, she returned to the sofa with the huffy cat, and they ignored each other from either end of it.

After the chaos of the previous two visits, Wendell was pleasantly surprised and relieved to find Barney dressed and ready, the house tidy and clean and Sam not in evidence.

"Who cleared up? Not you surely?" asked Wendell incredulously.

"Tracy's mother came in while I was at the hospital and did the lot. Marvellous woman, I'm very lucky there." He grinned and rubbed his hands up and down his chest as he spoke.

"I thought you said she was an old dragon?"

Another grin. "Yes, I did, but it seems she got a taste of my wife's more unpleasant side during the labour. We had a long conversation while Tracy was being stitched up."

Wendell grimaced.

"Seems she felt sorry for me, realised what a bitch her darling daughter could be. Sam was apparently at the reception desk, so she took him with her from the hospital and then popped around here and tidied up. The poor lad had wet himself, no wonder he was miserable. Anyway, good stuff. Are we ready then?"

Barney stopped rubbing his chest and clapped his hands together enthusiastically.

"Yes, let's go," replied Wendell and they walked off happily, two lads together laughing and joking. Just like old times, thought Wendell, forgetting Antonia for the first time all day.

Barney spoke excitedly of the birth, interspersing the dialogue with apologies about the weekend.

"It's wonderful Wendy, the birth of new life," said Barney philosophically, "and when it's part of you, it really is a special moment. Ever felt like starting a family?"

Wendell started to laugh.

As they ate, Wendell told Barney the details of his ordeal with Sam the previous afternoon, and the two of them were soon helpless with laughter. At the end of the story, their meals finished, Barney lit a cigarette and let the smoke engulf his head entirely. Ten seconds later a waiter hurried them into the bar as there was a no smoking policy in the eating area. They were accompanied by some cross looks from other diners, and Wendell did now recall someone next to them waving an irritable hand in Barney's direction as he'd sat there like Chief Sitting Bull with his pipe of peace.

They got settled again and began on a fourth pint.

"Life eh, Wendy?" Barney continued in his philosophical mood. "Let's hear about you now, what's life like without the lovely Bibi?"

"You heard about that then?"

"Yeah, Terry told me the other day. Shame. Beautiful girl."

"Yes, she was."

"What happened?"

"Would you believe, she left me for the guy upstairs."

"You jest!"

"Just buggered off with him one evening, the bitch." He stopped to sip his beer. "I should never have married her really, I knew what she was like."

He took Barney through the sordid details.

"I haven't seen or heard from her since, don't even know where she is. Quite frankly, I couldn't care less."

"Got someone new? Or are you on the prowl?"

Wendell smiled.

"You've met someone else." It was a statement rather than a question, delivered with a knowing look.

Wendell smiled back. "I've got a new friend, nothing more at the moment. She's my neighbour, the one whose boyfriend left with my wife."

"No!"

"Yes. Anyway, you did me a favour, it would never have happened otherwise."

Wendell, tongue loosened with alcohol, went through the details of Saturday evening, embellishing the end of the evening, as men do, with a passionate snog, just to keep his image intact. He suddenly wanted to see Antonia desperately, he really must see her tomorrow.

"What's her name then, this paragon?" slurred Barney, spilling beer on his jeans as he transported it to his mouth. A dark circle appeared there, and he tried to brush it away.

"Antonia."

"That's a nice name," said Barney, thoughtful suddenly. "Antonia."

"What have you called the baby by the way?"

"Nothing yet, we can't decide. But I think it might just be… Antonia. It's a lovely name, I think Tracy would like it too. Hmm, Antonia, yes, yes." He was rubbing his chest again.

"Good choice," slurred Wendell with a grin. He knew he would feel dreadful tomorrow but who cared. He hadn't had a good session for at least a week.

After the sixth pint the conversation started to lapse, mainly due to Barney whose eyelids were showing signs of giving in to gravity. His head was resting at an awkward angle on the back of one hand. Wendell was faring little better. What had happened to them? Age? God, this would only have been the introduction to a session in the past.

"Time. Gentlemen. Please," roared the landlord in their direction. Getting little response, he rang a large bell long and loud.

"Already?" Momentarily awakened from his reverie, Wendell looked at the clock and hiccupped loudly. It seemed they were the only people left in the bar.

The landlord, now towering over Barney's shoulder boomed his message out again.

Wendell looked upwards to this giant Elvis lookalike and waved a hand at the half-empty glasses.

"You'd better take them."

"Thank you, Sir," he said briskly as the glasses were whisked away.

Barney was sound asleep now; it took Wendell a good deal of shaking and slapping to rouse him. The barman finally gave him a hand and it was some unearthly hour of the morning when Wendell awoke on Barney's sofa engulfed in a duvet which had been laid over him sideways, so his legs from the knee down had been left uncovered. He struggled with the thing for a minute before finding he was dying for a pee.

"Oh, my head," he groaned, as he managed to raise himself to a sitting position. He looked at his watch and found it hard to focus in the dim light. 5.07a.m. and he was still feeling drunk.

He swayed up to the bathroom on feet stiff with cold and threw up.

After searching in vain for something that might alleviate the pain in his head, and having a second retching session, he decided to call a cab and go home to his own bed to be hungover in. His clothes smelled and he felt horribly nauseous still. He located the phone and the number of a local taxi service, and left Barney a short note, before quietly letting himself out. The chilly air revived him a little, but he was soon cold standing there in the dim, deserted street. His car was there so he sat in it, fleetingly considering whether he was capable of driving himself back. He decided not and wondered what on earth they'd been drinking to make him this overhung. Bit of a nuisance really. He'd have to get the train to work then come back later for the car. Damn. The thought of work in just over three hours was ghastly. Perhaps he should call in sick? No, he dared not with old Belly's eye fixed firmly on his every move. Maybe it would even look good, dragging himself in even though he wasn't well, devotion to duty and all that rubbish.

Approaching headlights broke his train of thought and he got himself back on the pavement. The cabbie, a short fat cockney seemingly oblivious to the cold in only a tee shirt, helped him into the taxi as though he were an old lady. He spoke cheerfully while a cigarette bounced up and down apparently glued to his lower lip.

"Blimey mate, you're in a two an' eight ain'cha?"

Wendell replied with a weak smile and sank gratefully into the warm interior of the vehicle.

"Awright mate, I'll getcher 'ome," finished cab man, spitting the dog-end off his lip and into the gutter with perfect precision.

Wendell felt strangely comforted by this friendly treatment of a drunk and gave the man a nice tip. As soon as he got indoors he was sick again and began to be concerned about the state of his liver. He took two aspirins, drank a lot of water and crawled into his bed. When his alarm roused him a very short time later, he knew he would make it to the office. The nausea had mostly passed and only a lingering headache and raging thirst remained. By the time Antonia woke and glanced hopefully out of the window, he had showered, dressed, breakfasted on aspirin and black coffee, and gone.

Beth was disapproving and sympathetic in equal measure and kept Wendell supplied with regular coffee and painkillers, for which he was very grateful. By lunchtime he was certainly over the worst, just dreadfully tired. At the end of the afternoon, he called Barney and asked if he could leave the car there until tomorrow.

Chapter Sixteen
Tuesday

The forecast storm broke just as Antonia set off for work the next morning, at about the same time that Wendell was wobbling wearily from his train. Overhead, thunder boomed from a dark, heavy sky, the low clouds broken only by occasional flashes of lightning. Once the rain started, it really thrashed down, filling gutters with small rivers and saturating anyone unlucky or daft enough to be out in it. Antonia, being one of this unfortunate group, now squelched up the stairs to the surgery ignoring the ringing phone in favour of changing first into something dry. After all, it wasn't yet nine. As she entered the waiting room with her wet jacket dripping all over the floor, Rob Murphy accosted her, in on time for once.

"Nasty morning," she said quickly and with forced cheerfulness as he was already wearing an expression of dour disapproval.

"You must answer the phone before you do *anything* else in the morning," was the sharp reply and she felt herself stiffen with anger. This was a good start; she'd got cold and wet and hadn't managed to thank Wendell Cornish for Saturday night. Everything in her mind just stopped her from being subservient. She turned on her heel to face her boss.

"Yes, normally I would, but it isn't even nine yet and I was soaked to the skin," she moved to continue to the coat rack leaving a dark wet patch on the carpet made by the jacket during this exchange, then stopped and turned again to him. "It's raining out there, in case you hadn't noticed."

"Aah, yes, aah." The overgrown eyebrows were propping up his hairline in surprise.

Antonia thought she heard a muffled 'sorry' as she shut the door of the spare room behind her. You bastard, she thought angrily as she arranged her wet clothing around the room.

Among the mail was a postcard from Susan, "Having a lovely time in Cornwall (despite the weather!), looking forward to getting back to work."

Stupid woman, she couldn't even stop thinking of work when she was on holiday. Antonia's buoyant few days were past history, she hated everyone again, even Wendell Cornish, as he seemed to have disappeared and she now felt he had just used her as a stand in on Saturday night.

She knew they had only gone out as friends, but she felt as though it had been more than that. Perhaps she had been wrong.

And now, she admitted to herself, she wanted it to be more.

As she pinned Susan's postcard up behind the phone and studied the picture of happy families on a sun-drenched beach, she could have cried. There was something lacking in her life that she thought she might have found on Saturday night. It would have been better if it had never happened, hope could be a cruel tormentor.

But there was work to be done so she pushed it all onto a back burner and smiled grimly at old Ma Cooper, back for the third time to complain about her new dentures.

Antonia made Rob a coffee and delivered it to his side while Mrs Cooper's lips, flapping like sheets in a strong wind, described in monotonous detail how these teeth were even worse than the last set.

Why the hell didn't the old bag go elsewhere?

The morning was a slow one with several gaps in it, which enabled her to catch up with a lot of accumulated paperwork. Mid-morning, Rob reclined the chair into a horizontal position and laid himself out in it, big hairy arms folded across his chest, and was soon snoring loudly enough to rattle the instrument tray. With all the administrative tasks completed, things began to go into really slow motion.

As Antonia fiddled absent-mindedly with the calculator, sounds of awakening filtered through from the surgery and Rob emerged, silently and briefly, to sort himself a golf magazine then disappeared once more without acknowledging her. She spent half her lunch hour queuing for fish at the supermarket. She'd been up at seven the previous day, dashing bleary eyed down the road for that overpriced piece of chicken at which Ozzie stared in disgust. As she stood and watched a lethargically slow cashier throw a box of eggs into the bottom of a carrier where, no doubt, they now lay oozing slime, she made a snap decision and reached out for a tin of cat food—just for emergencies. By this time, other groceries had been thrown from a height on top of those eggs, just in case any had survived the first assault. The timid woman buying them smiled anxiously but said nothing.

The afternoon threatened to be even more tedious than the morning session and there wasn't even any paperwork left to fill in the gaps. By three thirty Antonia was desperate enough to take a cup of coffee to Rob and try to engage him in conversation. For once there was a response and they had a reasonable chat which he then spoiled by reminding her she must answer the phone before anything else. However, time passed a little more quickly after that and she was soon pedalling home furiously to Ozzie and the odd few super fleas which had remained unaffected even after being liberally doused with poison. His hungry greeting was loud and enthusiastic, and she put the fish on to boil straight away while she enjoyed the feeling of him winding around her legs and butting her with his furry head.

"There you are, darling," she said sweetly, laying the carefully flaked and boned fish in front of him. She caressed his head to encourage him. He sniffed daintily at the delicate morsels then looked up sorrowfully.

"No!" cried Antonia in disbelief. "Eat it, you fucking fleabag!"

He sniffed it again and walked away, leaving the flat stinking of fish and Antonia about at the end of her tether. The following half hour was taken up with more gentle coaxing until she also stunk of fish. If Fiona thought she was going to do this every day for the next ten days she could forget it!

After she'd scrubbed her hands for the fourth time, and satisfied herself that she was now rid of the fishy whiff, she looked out for Wendell's car. She had purposely left it this long so that he would well and truly be back, but to her dismay there was still no sign of it. Disappointment overwhelmed her. She had been so sure he would want to speak to her, as she had him, sure there had been a spark between them. It made her feel all the more wretched.

Perhaps he already had a girlfriend that she didn't know about, it would explain why he wasn't there much, although she had never seen anyone there.

But then she hadn't seen him for a year either. He hadn't mentioned anything like that, but he was a man after all.

In fact, Wendell had left the office at 5.00, been in minutes before Antonia and had gone straight to bed, oblivious of hunger, thirst or romantic notions. While she sat lonely and wretched upstairs, he slumbered soundly in the flat beneath hers. The last thought that passed through before unconsciousness overtook his brain was that he would pin a note to her door in the morning. She must think he'd disappeared from the face of the Earth. He'd buy some flowers or something for her, yes, to stop himself feeling guilty for not at least thanking her for her company the other night. Why did he feel guilty? He barely knew her. He liked her, he wanted her to like him, he was pretty sure she had. These same thoughts had been on his mind as he sat with his head flopping backwards and forwards on the train home. The bland faces opposite had become hers and once he caught himself smiling involuntarily. Tomorrow, he had a meeting with Bellingham and later he would go and get the car, then perhaps they would make contact.

Chapter Seventeen
Wednesday

On Wednesday morning Wendell woke early after twelve hours of unbroken sleep, feeling much refreshed and ravenously hungry. After breakfast and a hot shower, he groomed himself with care, put on a clean suit, shirt and tie and set off towards the station with a spring in his step once more. As he stared at the blank-faced commuters Antonia came to mind again, and he remembered that he had meant to leave her a note. Damn! Oh well, he'd be able to catch her this evening, surely, she had said she hardly ever went out, hadn't she? And if not, he would leave a note then. And flowers. Or chocolates, something anyway.

Ten minutes into his journey he gave up his seat to a stony-faced secretarial type, who accepted it wordlessly and without a glimmer of a smile. He'd thought her rude but couldn't help admiring her long legs all the same. He hated the rush hour in trains, all those individuals squashed together pretending they were oblivious to the closeness of their neighbour, all nameless, faceless, expressionless, smelling each other's hair and clothing, invading each other's space. Thank goodness he would have the car back tomorrow.

The train hissed and squealed to a halt, and he was carried out with the rest of the crush, enjoying the cold air after the stale smell of the overcrowded carriage. He was at the office bright and early and gave himself a final preening before seeing Bellingham, the summons coming just as he had his lips to a cup of coffee. Never mind, it was too hot anyway. As he moved towards Bellingham's office, he dragged his tie about and with a final smoothing of the hair and clearing of the throat, knocked on the door.

"Enter," came the call.

"Good morning, Mr Bellingham," smiled Wendell charmingly.

"Ah, Cornish, sit down." Bellingham indicated the smaller chair opposite him. He was enthroned as usual in the leather swivel, elbows resting on its arms.

As Wendell seated himself, Bellingham rose, causing him to get up again.

"Sit, sit," Bellingham repeated with an irritated wave. Wendell sat.

Wendell was then treated to a lengthy monologue from his boss who never once looked at him, as he examined the view from the window. Wendell almost pulled a face behind him, then wondered if he was checking the reflection and thought better of it.

"Well Cornish, I must say, since our previous… discussion," he drew the word out with significance. "I have been most pleasantly surprised," he finally turned and faced Wendell, who smiled tightly. "Keep it up."

"Thank you, Sir." So that was all he'd wanted. "Our… discussion… gave me the push I needed, so thank you." Wendell readied himself to leave, smiling inanely.

"But that's not all I wanted to speak to you about." Bellingham returned to the window.

"Oh," the smile faded.

"We'll review all that later as I said."

Wendell waited while Bellingham turned and made himself comfy in the chair which made squeaky, farty noises as he manoeuvred his wide backside into it.

"I would like to ask you a favour."

"Oh?" He was alert.

"I would like you to entertain someone for me tomorrow. I have a young man from China staying, he's the son of an old friend and colleague. He wants to see a bit of nightlife. You're about his age so I thought this would be an opportunity for you. I'm too old for him—doesn't want an old fuddy-duddy like me to tote him around," he barked out a quick laugh at this attempt at wit.

Wendell stared. "Tomorrow?"

"Yes, tomorrow evening. You don't *have* to of course, but I would be *grateful* if you could." Bellingham's eyes, oversized behind thick glasses, bored into Wendell's own, daring him to say no.

The very last thing Wendell wanted was another session tomorrow. He'd only just recovered from the last one. And what about Antonia? He wanted to see her, it felt wrong to just leave things. Bugger it!

Bellingham was still glaring at him and doing something unpleasant with his lips, like a vicious dog about to go for the throat.

"I'd be delighted Mr Bellingham, delighted, no problem at all."

"Excellent Cornish, that's the spirit." The vicious dog had become a friendly puppy. "Speaks English, naturally. Expenses paid, of course."

He creaked out of the chair again, walked around to where Wendell now stood and placed a congenial hand on his shoulder, at the same time propelling him towards the door.

"Here's my address," he pulled a card from his pocket and handed it over, then opened the door.

So he had to pick the bastard up too. He glanced at the card; how long was it going to take to get there?

"He'll be ready at seven-thirty. Alright with you?"

Seven-thirty! Christ. Wendell was just about to suggest eight but was quickly interrupted.

"Splendid! Seven-thirty then," and the door shut swiftly behind him.

Wendell walked over to his desk, frowning. This was a bloody nuisance. Nothing to do for the past eleven months, and suddenly after meeting someone he really liked everything seemed to be getting in the way of it. He'd lose her before he'd properly found her. He really must make some sort of contact with her.

After work he commuted straight to Barney's intending to grab the car and go, after he'd said hello and admired the new arrival of course.

"Wendell!" It was Tracy who answered his knock. "Do come in." She was smiling and relaxed, quite different from the bloated, tearful creature he'd seen on his previous visit. Ok, there was some weight to lose but she'd just had a baby and all in all, the pretty, pleasant girl he remembered was back.

"Congratulations, darling!" said Wendell, hugging her gently and giving her a kiss on the cheek. "You look wonderful. How are you?"

She laughed delightedly. "Thanks Wendell, I'm fine now." She rolled her eyes. "Sorry about the other night."

"Forgotten it already."

She led him through to the lounge where Barney was seated with an impossibly tiny infant asleep in the crook of one arm, and the TV remote active in his other hand.

"Hi Wendy," grinned Barney quietly, so as not to wake his little daughter, then gazed down on her tenderly for a moment. "Here she is," he said proudly, "our little Antonia."

Wendell's insides fizzed for a moment. "Antonia?" he said stupidly.

"Ssshhh, don't wake her."

At this point, Tracy interrupted, "Would you like a cup of tea Wendell? I'm just making one for us."

"I would, thank you."

"Have you eaten yet?"

"Well, no, but…"

"Stay and have something with us, we've got plenty in."

"Oh no, I couldn't impose on you."

"You wouldn't be, would he Barney?"

"Eh?"

"That's settled then."

Wendell had to admit something did smell extremely good.

"Well… if you're sure," he had been persuaded, "hang on, where's Sam?" His guts fizzed in a different way with this thought.

"He's staying with his nan tonight, just until we've got Antonia settled."

Thank Christ for that.

He would call on the grown-up Antonia on his way in.

So Wendell stayed for supper, and very nice it was too. "Mmm, that was delicious, my compliments to the chef," he said, patting his stomach.

"Tracy's mum is a fabulous cook," said Barney, through a mouthful of his mother-in-law's lasagne. And then added quickly, "Tracy takes after her," and leant over to kiss her on the cheek.

"Thank you, darling," she smiled.

All very cosy thought Wendell, but not for me. He glanced at the clock; time was moving on. Give it a polite twenty minutes then go.

Baby Antonia, who had slept through until now, awoke suddenly and set up a raucous squawking which was quite alarming coming from such a tiny little scrap.

Tracy picked her up, settled herself with a couple of cushions then flopped out a large bosom and began to feed her. From his place at the table, Wendell had a front row view of the procedure, and he didn't much care for it. Embarrassed and uncomfortable, he tried not to look in their direction. Barney was droning on with his back to it all, quite unaware of his friend's discomfort.

"Well," began Wendell, when Barney finally paused for breath. His head was addressing a sideboard on his left. "I think it's time I left you good people to it." He began to get up.

"You're not going?"

Wendell scrutinised his watch. "It's getting late, I can't impose any longer. Many thanks, that was lovely," he addressed this last comment to Tracy, forgetting not to look for a moment.

She was absorbed in the baby and unaware of anything else going on around her, but Barney suddenly realised that Wendell was avoiding looking her way.

"You're not embarrassed by breast feeding, are you?"

"Er, no… not at all," he paused. "Well… actually," and they both laughed and moved into the kitchen.

"You old prude Wendy," said Barney, still teasing. "No one bothers to be discreet about it these days you know. I was like you when Sam was born." Alright with Tracy of course, but one day she had two friends over for coffee and all three of them sat there with their tits out. "I didn't know where to look."

"I bet you did," they sniggered again.

"Two weeks after that I wouldn't even have noticed. They all do it. It's natural. You'll find out one day," he finished.

"Hope not," muttered Wendell.

"What?"

"Yes, who knows."

"Another cuppa love?" called Barney.

"Yes please, darling."

"Things seem pretty much back to normal between you now," said Wendell, watching Barney pour the tea from a great height.

"Makes it taste better if you pour high," explained his friend, seeing Wendell's look of amusement. "Yeah, we're getting there."

They returned to the lounge, Wendell shuffling along in Barney's shadow, to find the feeding session finished, Tracy's bosom safely tucked away, and the baby propped up and awake on her lap.

"Meet your uncle Wendy," crooned the proud father, at which little Antonia belched and sent a dollop of partially digested milk flying from her rosebud lips onto her dad's sleeve.

Wendell averted his eyes, feeling slightly sick himself.

"Ooh, did you spit up then?" cooed Barney, wiping his arm on a convenient cloth.

Tracy attended to the baby, wiping her tiny mouth with another convenient cloth, and the parents fussed and clucked over her for a minute.

Wendell felt yet another kind of sick.

"That's what she thinks of her uncle Wendy then," laughed Barney.

"Charming. Seems to be my reaction from women these days."

They all laughed.

"How's your Antonia?" said Barney, winking mischievously at him.

"Fine," replied Wendell, slightly taken aback, until he remembered everything he'd said on Monday night. It was time to go. He was tired of baby talk and the smell of milky puke and he wanted to get away before Tracy got her jugs out again.

It took another ten minutes of profuse thanking and congratulations before he made it out of the door, acutely aware of the lateness of the hour. Antonia would probably have gone to bed. Damn. *Damn*.

"Come over anytime," said Barney. "Bring the new lady, we'd love to meet Antonia's namesake."

"What?"

"It was after you told me about that girl that I thought what a nice name it was, remember?"

"No, not really to be honest."

"We love it don't we Tracy?"

"Yes," she looked at the baby and smiled. "Antonia. It's perfect."

"Yes," said Wendell, thinking of another Antonia. What had given Barney the idea they were an item? What had he been saying? Would she still be up? If the lights were on he would knock, otherwise leave a note for her. He was filled with sudden urgency.

"Right, must get going, thanks again." He planted a quick kiss on Tracy's cheek, shook Barney by the hand and hurried off with a wave.

Antonia had already gone to bed when he arrived back. She had been tired and filled with despondency. Ozzie still wasn't eating without endless coaxing, and she was sporting a fine collection of red, itchy bites. Wendell seemed to have disappeared completely and her high hopes of a new friendship, perhaps leading to romance, had almost completely faded. She felt worse than she had done in ages. Absence really did seem to make the heart grow fonder it seemed.

During her lunch break she had called Mrs Schafer's surgery and told her the job wasn't for her. Mrs Schafer had replied, without conviction, how sorry she was to hear that and wished her good luck with her job search. As she sat now in front of an uninteresting television programme with Ozzie curled up on her lap, it occurred to her that perhaps Wendell's car was in for a service or something. Maybe he'd been there all along. But then if he had wouldn't he have called on her? She sighed. She had been so sure he'd liked her; how could she have been so mistaken? He had suggested meeting again, hadn't he?

She decided she must be turning into some desperate old hag. So desperate that anyone would do.

But this was crazy, sitting here wishing and hoping he would call. She had to find out if he was there, so before there was time to change her mind, she dumped Ozzie onto the sofa and clumped down the stairs, then hovered by his door listening but heard nothing from within. Now she was here she felt less brave. What if he had company in there? Female company. Well, they could have a good laugh at her expense, the mousy girl from upstairs who thought she was in with a chance. She knocked, then again, louder this time. Nothing. She knocked one last time just to make sure, listened again to the silence for a few seconds and then ran back up the stairs.

Chapter Eighteen
Back to Monday

It wasn't until the next morning that Charles, when dressing for work, discovered his ruined clothes. Bibi had taken out her fury on his trousers and shirts when she found him absent. His favourite cords were now a pair of ragged-edged cut-down shorts like something from a pirate costume, and several shirts were decorated with lipstick pigs.

"You bitch!" he shouted angrily as he rummaged about assessing the damage. Discarding things in heaps on the floor, he eventually located a pair of untouched trousers and a clean shirt and took himself off to work in a thunderous mood. He was more cross with his pupils than usual in the morning, which did not go unnoticed and when some young wag called from the back, "Wouldn't she let you have any last night, Sir?" he doled out an instant detention. A few of the girls who had crushes on him, envisaging one-to-one attention, tried hard to join the detention but he was more embarrassed by their laughing and sniggering and let it go.

At lunchtime, he sat on his own, chewing absent-mindedly on a rubbery carrot, when he was joined by Eve Tate, biology teacher, who'd been infatuated with him ever since she had first come to the school as an eager student teacher two years previously.

"Hello Charles, may I join you?" she said, plonking herself down.

"Oh, yeah, 'course," he pushed his tray to one side and continued chewing.

"You don't seem very happy today."

"Well spotted," he didn't face her as he spoke, just stared across the mass of heads and out over the football pitch.

"Bad weekend? Nothing too dreadful I hope?"

"Yes."

"Oh dear." She ate in silence for a few seconds, then offered her listening ear if he wanted to talk about it.

Charles liked Eve, she was easy to talk to and didn't keep grabbing his arm or try to push her face into his. A wide, big boned girl with blonde hair and freckles and very blue eyes under invisible lashes.

"New trousers?"

Charles snorted violently. "There's a reason for that."

He found himself telling her all about the row at the restaurant, Bibi's disappearance and what had happened afterwards. She listened avidly, delighted at this opportunity of extra intimacy. He did go on a bit, but he looked so lovely sitting there so forlornly she would have sat there for hours. It was all she could do to stop herself putting an arm around him.

"Look, I've got an idea! Don't sit there alone tonight, come and have dinner with me," she managed to say when the droning finally came to a halt. "I'd welcome the company actually."

Charles looked aghast. "Just a friendly suggestion," Eve added swiftly.

He declined politely, but Eve was nothing if not persuasive and after she'd worked on him gently for a few minutes she could see he was wavering.

"After all, that's what friends are for isn't it? I'm making roast chicken tonight, with crispy potatoes and all the trimmings," she smiled hopefully. "I often make myself a nice dinner mid-week, I look forward to it. Something to occupy me. You know."

She could have the fish fingers tomorrow, stop at the supermarket on her way home.

Charles finally agreed, but only if Bibi still wasn't back.

Bibi. What a stupid name thought Eve, disliking her.

"Bibi?" called Charles hopefully as he let himself in later, then sighed heavily and went to the bedroom. A landscape of clothing hillocks lay in front of him where he'd left them earlier. He sighed again and began to sort through and see if anything was salvageable. In his hand was a shirt given to him long ago by Antonia and he thought of her with pangs of remorse and a lot of nostalgia. He hadn't really thought about her in all this and for the first time, having now experienced it himself, felt sorry for the way he'd treated her. Even though, he reminded himself, it had been her own fault.

Several shirts, and all but the trousers he had on ended up in a black plastic sack, the remainder in the wash. He'd have to get some more clothes. Damn Bibi. Damn the woman!

He picked up the phone and called Bibi's mother's number.

"Hello? It was Elizabeth who answered."

"Hello Elizabeth, Charles here."

"Charles, hello. How's the course going?"

"What course?"

The phone was snatched from her hand before she could continue, and she left the room shaking her head. Really, where did that girl get her manners from?

"Hello Charles," said Bibi rather formally.

"Hello. How are you?" he spoke with caution.

"Fine. You?"

"You destroyed my clothes." When no comment answered this statement, he carried on, "I miss you." A pause. "When are you coming back?"

"Next weekend. Maybe."

"Next weekend! Oh darling… look I don't really mind about the clothes; I need new stuff anyway."

"I haven't finished."

"Oh. Sorry."

"It's nice to see Mum, we haven't had a chance to see each other for ages," she had more to say but didn't want her mother eavesdropping. If she went out with that action man again tonight, she'd call Charles back.

"Have you forgiven me yet?" whined Charles in an irritating childish voice.

"I've forgiven *you*, about the clothes I mean."

"Yes, I suppose so," came the testy reply.

"Well, come back, darling, I want you to come home."

"I said no," she replied acidly, keeping an eye on the door.

"You do still love me, don't you?" still the childish whine.

Really, he was pathetic sometimes! The last thing she felt like saying was that she loved him at this moment for a whole raft of reasons. She deflected the question.

"Listen Charlie, I've got to go. My mother's made me a special tea."

"Oh," he said flatly. "I'll call tomorrow then."

"Actually… I'd rather you didn't. Just leave me alone this week, I need some time to think."

"But Beebs... to think about what?"

"I think I may be having a nervous breakdown," she cut him off mid-flow with this dramatic statement.

"What! Oh darling, come home, please come home, I'll look after you. I love you," he sounded frantic.

"Why don't you listen?" she demanded, regretting having told this fib now. "I said I'm staying here this week. Don't call me. I'll call you in a couple of days."

Charles continued protesting to no avail and finally she hung up on him.

"Phew," she said, slumping back in the chair. Elizabeth was framed in the doorway, the hall light illuminating the meringue of hair from behind. For a split second Bibi wanted to laugh.

"Don't you think it's about time you told me what's going on?"

"It's none of your business." Bibi fixed her eyes on the television.

"It is while you are in this house. I know he's not on a course."

Bibi remained staring at the screen, arms crossed.

"Look darling, I know we've never been particularly close, but I am your mother after all. At least let's see if I can help you."

It was probably the closest her mother had ever come to being maternal and, to her alarm, Bibi's emotions threatened to overwhelm her. In an instant she would have flung herself into Elizabeth's arms to cry like a baby.

"Just leave me alone," she said quietly, staring at the floor.

There was a heavily pregnant pause, during which raucous canned laughter from the TV filled the room. Elizabeth switched it off and a deafening silence replaced it. She then came over and laid a hand on her daughter's shoulder. Sheer willpower held back the waterfall of tears behind Bibi's eyes.

"Shall we go out tonight? Just the two of us," said Elizabeth. "We could try the place around the corner, it looks rather nice."

Silence.

Bibi slowly turned her head, disbelieving, and looked up at her mother. Elizabeth noticed the sparkle of tears and something else, a childlike hope there which made her own begin to water.

"Go on, I'll treat you," she smiled.

"Do you mean it?" said Bibi guardedly.

Had she really been such an awful mother that her own daughter would ask such a thing?

When she'd heard Bibi say they were having a special meal it had been a lie of course, but it had set her thinking. It was time one of them made a reconciliatory move, try and forge a more normal mother-daughter relationship, and although she had been thinking more about the future, the opportunity just seemed to have arisen. So here they were, padding off along the road, side by side, in truth feeling slightly awkward with this sudden intimacy.

The Dolphin was one of the new breed of pubs, filled with plants, stained glass and mirrors, more up market than just a watering hole for single old men. The atmosphere seemed welcoming, and it was neither empty nor too busy.

They were greeted cheerfully by the barman, whose clientele did not generally include two attractive and sophisticated ladies. He ran his eye over both and took them and their drinks personally to a quiet table in a corner, leaving a warty old local waiting impatiently for a refill.

"There we are, ladies," he flashed a grin at Bibi who remained frosty, "just place your order over there at the end of the bar when you're ready."

They both fiddled with the menus, still awkward in each other's company.

The conversation was inane, comments on the weather, the pub's décor.

Food arrived, a welcome distraction. Elizabeth asked for a bottle of wine and their jolly barman supplied it happily, and as it worked its way into them it finally loosened their knotted tongues. The conversation began on a light-hearted note and seemed to halt there. Each recognised this unique opportunity but seemed unable to breach the gulf that lay between them.

"Have you seen your father lately?" Elizabeth threw in. Bibi was struck dumb, her mother had not once mentioned him since the day he'd left them, never asked how her visits had been and wouldn't be drawn when she had babbled on, excited to relay all the wonderful things they had done. In the end he had never been mentioned in her mother's presence again.

"I've been meaning to write," Bibi began, "but I've been busy."

"You know he's not well."

"Not well?" Bibi paused. "What's wrong with him?"

"I think he should tell you himself."

Bibi put her fork down and regarded her mother seriously for the first time since they'd come in.

"What do you mean? What's wrong with him?" Bibi was suddenly fearful. "Come on, tell me."

"Why don't you go and see him, he'd love you to, you know."

Bibi stared at Elizabeth. "Don't tell me you've kept in touch with him, I won't believe it." A note of irritation had crept into her voice at her mother's refusal to answer her question.

"We've been out to lunch once or twice, yes."

"What! Why didn't you tell me?"

"Sssh, you're shouting."

"Why didn't you tell me?" she demanded, in a lowered voice.

"Well, darling," Elizabeth carefully placed her knife and fork on the plate and wiped her mouth on the napkin. "That's just it, isn't it? We've never been able to tell each other anything have we?"

Bibi stared.

"Well? Have we?"

"No."

Bibi drained her glass and refilled it.

"Look, I know Charles isn't on a course. Why don't you start by telling me what's going on there and we'll move on gradually. Have you left him?"

Bibi felt exposed. It was rather shocking to find that Elizabeth had seen straight through her flippant excuses for visiting.

"Not yet."

After a tentative start and a few more glasses of the surprisingly decent wine, the flood gates had been opened. Bibi found it hard to stop. She even revealed the ghastly night at Gino's that started the whole thing, leaving out the night she had spent in that vile flat: That was too humiliating to mention to anyone. It was a huge relief to get it all out and to laugh about something instead of moaning and feeling full of anger and self-pity.

They were enjoying themselves. They had become closer in the last two hours than they had been in the whole of their lives together.

The wine flowed on, and they found themselves reminiscing, unearthing old grudges and misunderstandings and finally laying them to rest.

When they left the pub at closing time, it was arm in arm and the silence this time was companionable. Both sensed that some kind of minor miracle had taken place and were filled with wellbeing. Bibi felt better than she had done in years and was determined to go and see her father.

When they reached the house, Guy was lounging in his shiny jeep outside it, smoking a long thin cigar. The window was rolled down and a tanned, muscular arm hung out of it in a lazy fashion. At their approach he jumped out through it like an athlete, action man all over. Bibi's lips tightened.

"Hi sweetheart," he said, ignoring Bibi completely as he bent forward and planted a passionate kiss on Elizabeth's mouth. "Where were you?"

After freeing herself from him, Elizabeth introduced Bibi, "Hello darling, have you met my daughter, Bibi?"

Guy hadn't managed to furnish his life with luxury by being imperceptive. He noted the edge in Elizabeth's tone and swung towards Bibi.

"Hi Bibi, a pleasure to meet you."

"Hello," came the cold reply.

"Hey, I was passing," he addressed Elizabeth, "so I thought I would drop in for a nightcap." A slow meaningful smile lifted the corners of his mouth and Bibi despised him absolutely. The spell had been broken by this idiotic fancy man. Not even a man, a boy. Why did he have to show up now?

"How lovely, darling," smiled Elizabeth, "but not tonight, I'm tired. It's a girl's night tonight." She threw a quick, knowing look towards Bibi and noticed a hint of that childlike hope again.

Guy looked first incredulous, then cross, then anxious, and seemed at a loss for words.

"See you, darling," said Elizabeth, kissing him lightly, then she took Bibi's arm, and they went into the house leaving him to come to terms with a rare rebuff.

Inside, Elizabeth began to laugh. "He's such a poseur."

Bibi relaxed and they adjourned to the lounge to continue their special evening with a final bottle of wine.

Charles stared at the phone without seeing it, despondent, idly twiddling the hairs at the top of his chest, which were nestling against the open top of his shirt. This was a nightmare! Why wouldn't Bibi come home? She didn't even like her mother. Their conversation felt unfinished, but she'd said not to call. Before he could decide whether to try phoning again, however, it rang. He snatched it up.

"Bibi?"

"Er no, hello Charles." It was Eve. "I hope you don't mind me calling you at home?"

"Oh. No, of course not." He wondered briefly where she had got his number from.

"I'm just putting the dinner on. As I said earlier, I'd be very happy for you to come and have some with me, there's always far too much just for me."

"Oh."

"Is Bibi back?" Please say she isn't, thought Eve, eyes closed, and fingers crossed.

"No… but she may ring and wonder where I am."

"Oh, please do come Charles," implored the hapless Eve. "I've got a lovely meal here, roast chicken, stuffing, the works. Far too much for just me. Just eat and go, no need for anything else, we've both got to work tomorrow." If she could just get him in the door.

"Well…" He was weakening.

"And an apple crumble with custard to follow. All homemade."

Memories of Sunday roasts and apple crumble filled his mind.

"Ok, you've twisted my arm. I'll be over in about an hour if that's alright?"

"Great, see you later then." Eve gave him her address, put the phone back in its cradle and clasped her arms around herself in an ecstasy of expectation. Charles was coming to her home, thoughts of shagging on the shag pile filled her mind.

Thinking only of roast chicken and apple crumble, Charles flung himself into the shower. Thinking only of what to wear, Eve put a bottle in the fridge, then decided to put another in, then went to ready herself.

Two further attempts to reach Bibi at her mother's had met with failure, and Charles worried about it all the way to Eve's. He didn't really want to go, but as the door opened and the wonderful aroma of food engulfed him, he realised just how hungry he was and forgot all about Bibi for a moment.

"Charles do come in," smiled Eve. She was wearing a clingy black dress, a cheap version of the one Bibi had worn last Friday, which projected an unfavourable comparison, Eve possessing neither Bibi's stunning figure nor her shapely legs. Charles wondered idly what on earth she was thinking of, dressing like that.

"Hello Eve. Thank you for this, it smells wonderful." He shuffled past her and stood in awkward indecision by the stairs. She took his jacket and slung it over the banister, then led him through to a warm and inviting lounge. There was soft background music playing, and the lights were low.

"This is nice," said Charles, looking around him innocently, "that dinner does smell good I must say. I didn't realise how hungry I was," he smiled, and Eve felt her knees weaken.

"Let me get you a drink," she sashayed out to the kitchen and poured two large glasses of wine for them. "There we are," she said, handing Charles the bigger of the two.

"Lovely." Charles studied Eve's face as she sipped her wine. What had happened to her eyes?

The pale lashes had disappeared under what looked like a row of spider's legs. She was wearing lipstick too. Fancy going to all that trouble just to have someone around to dinner. Had she expected him to dress up too? Too late now. She seemed to be behaving oddly too, he was beginning to feel slightly ill at ease, this wasn't the Eve Tate he was comfortable with.

She refilled their glasses and raised hers. "To friendship."

"Bottoms up," he replied and gulped.

Yes please, thought Eve.

As the first bottle gave up its last drip, Eve went to check on the dinner. Charles looked at his watch and hoped they were finally about to eat. She returned with the second bottle, having put a third in the fridge just in case.

"Another twenty minutes should do it," she announced, as she pulled out the cork expertly.

Charles said nothing. He was so hungry his stomach seemed to be eating itself, making strange growling noises. Maybe the wine was stripping the lining. He would be completely plastered if he kept pouring this vile stuff down his neck without something to soak it up.

Eve herself was feeling pretty squiffy. Better slow down a bit, she thought, and left her glass where it was for the moment.

The conversation staggered on for another minute before Eve cut Charles short.

"Oh Charlie!"

He flinched. Being called Charlie was something only Bibi did, even Antonia had only rarely called him Charlie.

She continued, "Let's talk about something other than work for God's sake, we can do that anytime. Did you speak to Bibi?"

"Yes, I did," he was on more familiar ground now and continued, "In fact Eve, would you mind if I tried her from here? Just a quick call."

Yes, she did mind. Very much. Why had she mentioned the woman at all?

"Not at all, please go ahead, it's in the hall."

He let it ring many times but there was no reply. He also called their place just in case she'd decided to go back after all. He longed to hear her voice. He didn't want to be here with Eve, he shouldn't have come at all. He was starving and half pissed and there was no sign of food. Why hadn't he just picked up a curry instead?

When he went back into the lounge, Eve had moved over onto the sofa with him, so he sat in an armchair instead.

"No luck?" enquired Eve, straightening her dress.

"No," he regarded her blankly.

"Come on let's eat," she said brightly, getting up a little unsteadily and then giggling.

"Are you alright? Need any help?"

"Well, you could carve the chicken if you don't mind?"

"Right."

Charles had never carved a chicken or anything else in his life. When they finally sat down, they were both laughing over his efforts. The meat had been well and truly butchered, but it was nevertheless delicious, and Charles relaxed as he lorried it in. He complimented Eve on her cooking and the conversation revived once more. Eve made certain the glasses were topped up and soon Charles felt really quite drunk.

"So, what's Bibi doing?" enquired Eve with a boldness encouraged by alcohol.

"Doing? Huh, good question. I honestly don't know, Eve." He mopped up the gravy with a piece of roast potato.

"It sounds like she's trying to make you suffer."

Always ready to be persuaded towards martyrdom, Charles mulled this over.

"I do believe you're right. But why? I don't know what I'm supposed to have done."

"What did you say about Saturday evening?"

"At Gino's? Yeah, but that was just a minor thing."

"Perhaps she didn't think so." Eve leant towards Charles and opened her eyes wide. Her bosom, in the low-cut dress, was resting invitingly on the table in front of him. She was doing something weird with her lips. It reminded him of a goldfish he once had, that used to suck up pieces of gravel and spit them out. He sat back, averting his eyes.

"Can't think of anything," he said finally.

"Well," began Eve, trying to discredit Bibi, "maybe there's something else on her mind. Us females are moody creatures you know. It doesn't take much."

He was all ears. "What do you mean?"

"Well… sometimes a little incident like that can be the straw that breaks the camel's back. Has she been argumentative lately, for instance? Irritable? Short tempered?"

"Now you come to mention it, yes."

"Perhaps you should make her jealous."

"Jealous?"

God, this was an uphill slog.

"Yes, you know, flirt a bit with other women, make her think she needs to pursue you a bit."

"Oh no, I could never do that," he went back to his plate and chased the remaining peas onto the fork.

"You don't actually have to mean it! Just pretend. For example, tell her you had dinner here and embellish it a bit. Make her afraid she might lose you."

"Embellish it? How?"

Eve looked at him and smiled seductively. No response. Bloody hell, did she have to spell it out?

"You know, be secretive, insinuate that something may have happened. Be a bit distant with her."

"Oh no!" He felt suddenly rather hot and clammy, aware he had drunk far too much.

Eve regarded him over the plates in exasperation. No wonder Bibi had flounced off. He'd probably been driving her mad if he was as thick as this with everything. If he wasn't so bloody drop dead gorgeous, no one would want him. She collected up the crockery and went off to get the pudding, leaving Charles mulling over their conversation and belching quietly because of the speed he had been eating at.

Eve felt very drunk, and her opinion of Charles was altering rapidly. She'd given him every hint she could, and nothing had borne fruit. She would have to offer herself on a platter; after all, every man could be seduced in the end. Couldn't they? Copious glasses of alcohol made her certain of success.

"I don't understand how making her jealous would help," said Charles between mouthfuls of apple crumble, "she would think I was having an affair or something."

Eve burst out laughing. "Exactly! That's the effect you want."

"Eh?"

Eve snorted with exasperation. "Good God Charles, if she loves you, she'll realise she might lose you," he still seemed puzzled, "she'll fight for you."

"I don't like the idea of women fighting. Bibi can get pretty vicious when she wants to."

Eve roared with laughter. "Oh Charlie, you are naïve!"

He blushed furiously. Why did all these women treat him like an imbecile? And why did she keep calling him Charlie, he didn't like it. She flopped across the table staring hard at him.

"Perhaps you should *have* an affair."

"What?" he replied incredulously.

"I'm serious Charlie. Believe me, there would be no shortage of willing volunteers," she met his eyes long enough to convey the desire in hers, but he was lost in thought. Maybe working with someone did this, made you sexless in their eyes.

"What on earth do you mean?" he asked her.

"Oh Charlie, you kill me!" she laughed. "You must know how good-looking you are, half the females in the school have got a crush on you, and the others are probably dancing at the other end of the ballroom."

The wine had gone completely to her head, made her tongue loose, revealing things she would regret sorely in the morning.

Charles was looking at her in horror.

"In fact, if you did decide to embark on an affair, I might just be the first in the queue," she threw her head back and roared drunkenly.

Charles was suddenly sober. Jumping swiftly to his feet he babbled a thank you for a lovely evening, must get back, look at the time and so on.

"You've had too much to drink, you can't drive home."

"Taxi then."

She heard his call and the desperate whisper, "How quickly can you get here then?"

Eve sat at the table with her head in her hands. She didn't feel too well suddenly.

Why on earth had she thought this was a good idea? Had she really thought she could get a man like him? What a fool she'd made of herself, he probably wouldn't speak to her again.

Charles poked his head around the door at this point. "Ten minutes they said. Well, thanks again Eve, I'll wait outside. Save you having to sit up any longer. Don't get up, I'll see myself out."

"No, you won't, at least let me do that," she got up unsteadily and staggered to the door.

"Oh, don't bother," squeaked Charles. "I can see myself out."

He was scared of her! Actually scared of her, how pathetic. Running away. He hadn't offered to help wash up or anything. She felt cross, she would teach him a lesson. Moving with amazing speed she put herself between him and the door and took hold of his arm.

"Don't go Charlie, you can stay here tonight."

"Stay he… what? No, oh no."

"On the sofa of course," she gazed up at him through bleary eyes. The liberally applied mascara had smudged and what was left of the lipstick was concentrated around the edge of her mouth, revealing the pale lips beneath. She looked repulsive and dangerous, like another fish he'd once seen in an aquarium, a poisonous one.

"I couldn't put you to the trouble. Bibi might phone anyway," he tried to free his arm.

"Bloody Bibi!" shouted Eve. "Any half-wit can see she's thinking of leaving you. Stay here, I'll look after you. I love you." She had released the claw-like grip on his arm and was now clinging like a limpet to a rock around his middle, her rosy cheek resting against his chest.

"Let me go, I have to go," cried Charles desperately. "I feel sick."

Eve laughed. She'd blown it completely, she knew that, so she may as well have some fun.

"Let me go! Please Eve."

"You are gorgeous when you're angry," she said, tightening her grip. She was remarkably strong.

"Let me go," he repeated loudly, in a schoolmasterly manner.

"Bye then," she raised her puckered lips towards him. Now she really did look like that fish. "You can't leave until I get a nice kiss."

"Eve, please stop this. You don't know what you're doing. Let me go," he pleaded, struggling vainly to rid himself of her.

There followed a silent thirty seconds of circular shuffling, while Charles tried to free himself from her grasp without actually touching her. She was *amazingly* strong for a woman, a drunken one at that, and she hung on tight, giggling continuously.

"One kiss and you can go. I give you my word," she slurred, when they finally ended the dance. "Lighten up Charlie, for goodness' sake."

Every fibre of him rebelled against it, but he was so desperate to get away that in the end he leant quickly down and delivered a peck on Eve's doughy cheek.

"That's not a very friendly kiss Charlie," she drawled, and then in a swift and plotted manoeuvre, grabbed him by the head and pulled his mouth down to hers. As Charles reeled backwards on release, she lost her balance and they both crashed to the floor, knocking flat a side table and its dried flower arrangement with them. The vase hit Charles on the jaw and covered them both in a mattress of crispy leaves and stalks. Eve was kissing his face. He had had enough. He pushed her off roughly and jumped to his feet, grabbing his coat and escaping through the door without bothering to shut it behind him. From her spreadeagled position on the floor amongst the mess, laughing uncontrollably, Eve watched him run wildly down the path towards the cab, shedding dried flowers as he went.

The next day Charles had a dreadful hangover and a bruised jaw, and phoned in sick, unable to face Eve, also wanting to collect his car without fear of bumping into her.

Eve did make it in to work, feeling ill and shamefaced, so it was with some relief that she found him absent. The following day she waited until she saw him approach the staff room and stepping from behind a locker, showered him with profuse apologies and begged him to forget it all. Charles, pink around the gills with embarrassment, was twitching and making odd facial movements as he fiddled with his sleeve. After mumbling something in reply, he gathered his post and made a speedy getaway.

Chapter Nineteen
Wednesday Evening/Thursday

It was quite chilly outside and Wendell's breath puffed out little clouds in the crisp air as he rummaged for his car keys outside Barney's house. Yes, autumn was here alright.

It had been a long day, and he opened his mouth and yawned like a cat. He rehearsed once again what he would say to Antonia but was disappointed to see her lights already extinguished. Before retiring himself, he picked out a suitable outfit for the evening with this Chinese bloke. He was resigned to it now, just get it over with and earn a few brownie points with Bellingham. He might even enjoy it. Finally, he scribbled out a little note.

"Dear Antonia," it read, "I apologise for not getting in touch sooner. Can I see you tomorrow evening? This evening I shall be out, but will knock on my way in tomorrow."

He read it through and decided it was short and casual enough, then opened his door softly and tiptoed up to place it on the mat there before returning to his lounge to get a piece of tape to stick it to the door and to rewrite it without 'dear'. There, she couldn't miss it.

As he left for work early the next day, he looked up the stairs at the note and thought of Antonia. He really didn't feel like this excursion tonight, he would have liked to have just come home and spent the evening with her instead. Oh well, it would have to wait.

Bellingham's luxurious house was miles away out in the sticks, so he'd have to kill some time at the office before going there. No point in coming home first. Damn, what a bloody nuisance this all was.

Antonia woke up late on Thursday morning. Preoccupied with her thoughts the previous evening she had had difficulty dropping off to sleep. She had also forgotten to switch the alarm on and now it was 8.20, and she was flapping around trying to get ready in half her usual time. Ozzie, looking thin and scruffy, wailed pitifully for food.

Oh God, there wasn't enough time for this fish business this morning!

She grabbed the tin of cat food from the cupboard, it wouldn't kill him for once surely. Was it her imagination, or had his sunken eyes brightened at the sight of the tin? He was purring and swallowing as he massaged the mat with his paws. She placed it in front of him and he tucked into the muck with relish. Antonia laughed. So cats preferred junk food too.

On her way to work, she thought of Wendell again. She was fed up with him invading her mind constantly, just accept he's not interested, she told herself; it was a pleasant one-off, a nice evening that's all.

The note was still stuck to her front door unread. She hadn't noticed it in her haste. And now, having subconsciously believed she would be seeing Wendell at the weekend, the idea of it looming with nothing to do seemed almost unbearable. What else could she fill it with? She would have to think of something, or the boredom would kill her. She'd hardly spoken to a living soul all week apart from Rob Murphy, and he hardly counted. At lunch time she flicked through her address book. It was almost an embarrassment to call anyone now, it had been so long since she'd been in touch with any of her friends. With a deep sigh, she dropped the book into her lap and stared out of the window at all the busy midday shoppers, hurrying about like ants on a mission.

Returning home, she saw the note.

Hesitating for just a moment, she dropped her bag on the stairs and tore her gloves off to read it with a thumping heart. Her mood switched instantly, and she threw open her door, humming a tune to herself. Ozzie appeared, stretching, and she bundled him into her arms and twisted herself from side to side.

"Wendell wants to see me, Ozzie," she told the purring animal. "We're only friends, but who knows?" She smiled, contentment restored, then admonished herself for getting too excited.

She fed Ozzie the remainder of the tinned food in celebration and spent the evening happily sitting in front of the television. Every time she thought about seeing Wendell Cornish there were butterflies in her stomach.

Wendell's Thursday seemed much longer than normal with the prospect of the evening ahead in his mind, which he just wanted to get over with. Bellingham nodded in his direction upon leaving but didn't stop. Wendell nodded back in understanding and pulled out a paper to read as soon as the door had closed behind the man's bulky backside.

Why did older men have such wide backsides anyway? Probably too much sitting about letting wives do everything for them.

It would take probably half an hour to drive to Bellingham's place from here, so he had an hour and a half to kill. By six he was alone in the office, a cup of coffee by his side and his hands clasped behind the back of his head. He leant back and put his feet up on the desk, wondering if Antonia would be pleased to find his note. He hoped so. He read the paper, then spent a few minutes freshening up. His stomach rumbled and roared, crying out for food, so he had another coffee and the last of the digestives, wincing a bit as the heat of the drink found his broken tooth. Must get that seen to, he thought idly. He would have loved a cigarette even after all this time of having given up. Good thing no one here smoked, or he might have tried to find one.

Finally, he was heading down darkened country lanes, trees flying by tall and ghostly. By the time he eventually located the place it was twenty to eight.

How were you supposed to find a house without a number for God's sake?

Ivy Cottage now stood before him, the only likeness to a cottage as far as he could see being the neat flowery garden and white picket fence surrounding it. It was more like a mock Tudor mansion from where he was standing. But there was certainly plenty of ivy, barely a square inch of brickwork could be seen through the dark green shroud. Bellingham's BMW and a rather nice orange sporty vehicle were parked in the driveway. It made his old banger look shabby in comparison. Was that the wife's or the daughter's, he wondered with indifference as he crunched across the gravel. He pressed the bell and after what seemed like ages, the door swung open to reveal his boss looking smartly casual in a Pringle sweater and cords, every inch the country gent.

"I thought we said seven-thirty, Cornish."

Wendell was taken aback and not a little annoyed by this terse greeting, after all he was doing the bastard a favour here.

"I do apologise, I had a little trouble finding your house."

"Never mind, you're here now," Bellingham replied in a kinder tone of voice. Cornish wasn't the first to have had that particular difficulty.

"Lung's been waiting for you; the Chinese are very particular about timekeeping."

At this point, Lung himself appeared from behind Bellingham where he had been standing unseen, grinning enormously to reveal a mouthful of large and overcrowded teeth, a big square oriental head surrounding them. Introductions were done on the doorstep and with a pat on Lung's shoulder and parting words of "enjoy yourself," the door closed. Not even 'yourselves' plural, thought Wendell with irritation. He felt like a chauffeur. He had at least expected to be asked inside.

"Right then, er… Lung, was it?" he began. This poor chap had a worse name than he did. It conjured up in his mind innards that he'd seen once in a biology lesson at school, pinned to a board. One of the girls had fainted.

"Shall we?" he said politely, holding out a hand towards his car.

As he drove, Wendell opened a conversation, "How long are you in England for Lung?"

"Onny fye dace," replied his passenger. "What you do for Lolan?"

Lolan? Who or what was that? Wendell hadn't yet got his head around Lung's rather thick accent. Ah! Roland. Roland Bellingham. Wendell smiled and explained his job with vague brevity while Lung smiled and nodded.

"Do you like England?"

"Ah yes, velly mutts," he enthused, the smile widening, "diss my four visit."

"And what do you do Lung?"

"Teacher of martial art."

Wendell took a quick look at his passenger, and decided he must teach infants. Either that or he taught martial arts to make up for being so small.

"What would you like to do, Lung?"

Lung's smile threatened to turn his head inside out. "Meet grrss."

Grrss? What on earth was that? Guests? Grass?

Wendell wasn't sure and ploughed on, "How about a play? Would that suit you?" Wendell didn't know much about what was on, but they could find out.

"Pray?" the smile dropped momentarily. "Night crub better."

"Oh!" Wendell knew all about those. "In that case, I know just the place."

They continued the journey in pleasant conversation, during which Wendell managed to get the hang of the accent and eventually stopped near a trendy restaurant he knew and liked.

"We'll have a bite to eat first, shall we?" Wendell leapt out without waiting for an answer, he was starving.

"Here we are." The last time he came here he had been with Bibi.

As Wendell examined the menu, Lung was scrutinising the clientele.

"Ah, velly good," he grinned at Wendell, "ruvry grrss."

As they entered, Lung advanced towards two barely clothed girls in a window seat announcing, "We sit wi' dem."

Wendell was just in time to steer him to an adjacent table, but he continued to eye the two girls anyway, grinning broadly.

Lung was a fast eater. He also downed two whiskies in quick succession and began to get lively.

"I go to ravatry, Corniss," he said suddenly and disappeared into the crowd.

This could be an interesting evening, thought Wendell as he looked at his watch for the hundredth time, and twisted around to keep an eye on his charge. Two babysitting jobs in one week, at least he was being paid for this one. Now that his stomach was full, he felt more relaxed, sleepy even. What would Antonia be up to? He hoped, again, she had been pleased to see his note. He ordered two coffees and drifted into a pleasant daydream about the evening to come tomorrow, when all this was done with. He was halfway through his and beginning to wonder what had become of Lung, when the man appeared by his shoulder with a leggy blonde on each arm.

"Ah Corniss," he cried, "company tonigh'."

The word 'grrss' suddenly became alarmingly clear. Girls.

Wendell stared, appalled. Christ, no. He greeted the girls politely and sat them down. This wasn't at all what he had planned, how could he get rid of them? He hoped he wouldn't be expected to pay for them either.

Lung was still grinning. "Diss Corniss," he indicated Wendell, who couldn't be bothered to correct him. The girls introduced themselves as Dawn and Karol with a K. This seemed to be vitally important to her and she repeated it several times.

"Nice to meet you Corniss," they said together and laughed.

"Actually, it's We—"

"You rike derrink radies?"

This sent them into fits of giggles and Wendell smiled, despite himself. They weren't a bad looking pair, may even be sisters with their carefully sculpted blonde curls, rosebud pink lips and tiny, clinging dresses. The yuppie uniform. Underneath it all they were just two girls out for the evening. The drinks arrived, whereupon Lung threw a third whisky down and completely took over the conversation, some of which was rather obviously sexual in reference. The girls hadn't yet got to the point of understanding everything Lung was saying and kept giggling, so he carried on regardless. Wendell was starting to feel uncomfortable and slightly out of control of the situation, especially as he was the only sober member of the party.

When they rose to leave it was already getting late. In Wendell's original plan, they would have soon been on their way back. Oh well, they could get going now.

"Thanks for the drinks," trilled Dawn and Karol with a K, gathering up their tiny handbags and moving away. "Bye Corniss."

"Goodbye, nice to have met you." Wendell was suddenly energised, ready to go home, but Lung pounced on the girls.

"Radies, you come wi' us," he looked towards Wendell and back, "we go nightcrub, yes?"

"Er… well…" Wendell looked at his watch, it was already quarter past nine. "Er… well, we haven't got too much time." Lung's smile fell for the first time and Wendell's returned.

"Ah yes, you come. We have derrinks, dance, rots of fun." The grin was back.

Lung looked ridiculous standing there, the two girls regarding him from on top of their lamp post legs. As this persuasion continued, the butterflies returned to Wendell's stomach.

"Come Corniss," commanded Lung finally, having eventually persuaded Dawn and Karol with a K to accompany them for one drink. Wendell hurried off to pay the bill, wondering how much 'expenses' would run to. He stowed the receipt carefully away and hurried off to the car, where Lung stood wedged between the two girls, their arms folded in an attempt to retain some warmth. Why did women never bring something warm to wear over their skin tight dresses anyway?

Wendell sat alone in the front of the car; Lung having shoehorned himself in between the girls.

"To Runden Corniss," cried Lung, lifting an arm like Henry V going into battle.

"Hey, wait a minute," came a shrill female voice, all trace of yuppiness forgotten for the moment. "No, not London. We're not going to London mate, some of us gotta work tomorrow."

"But Runden is best for nightcrub," retorted Lung.

There was a moment of silence.

"We go Stlingfellow."

Everybody spoke at once. Dawn and Karol with a K protesting about going to London and Wendell gasping, "Stringfellow's? I don't think expenses will run to that."

In any case, it would take half the night to go to London and back from here.

"Expenses?" said one of them indignantly. "Expenses? We're not two tarts for hire you know. I think we'd better go home if you don't mind." The plumminess had returned to her tone.

"No, no," cried Lung. "You go home now and Rung defrated." He laughed at this obviously well used joke and soon had the two girls in giggles again. Finally, they agreed to a club nearby, so everybody piled out again and trotted down to a lovely place by the river which Wendell knew of. It was jammed solid for midweek which was a surprise. Wendell left Lung pressing himself against Dawn and went to get some drinks. The Chinaman's intake of alcohol seemed to have little effect other than to make him more animated. Wendell returned to find Karol with a K standing alone with a cigarette while Lung had Dawn in a clinch out on the dance floor, his head nestling comfortably against her bosom. She was laughing over his head towards her friend, who smiled back in acknowledgement.

"Here we are," Wendell said cheerfully, realising he may as well put a limit of 2am on things and just go with the flow.

He handed Karol with a K her drink.

"Ta," she shouted across, avoiding looking at him. Dawn was obviously the dominant one of the pair.

"Do you live around here?" Wendell shouted back, in an attempt at conversation.

"Not far," she shouted back, her gaze fixed on Dawn and Lung. She dragged hard on her cigarette; brows pulled together in concentration.

"What do you do?"

"Eh?"

"I said WHAT DO YOU DO?"

"We work in a boutique."

"Oh, how lovely. What's it called?"

"Zips."

Her eyes had not left Dawn and Lung during their brief and boring conversation, and Wendell felt tired. He stopped bothering to address her right ear and sipped his orange juice instead. That tooth seemed to be nagging a bit, he'd ring his dentist in the morning and fix an appointment.

Lung was now in full swing and raring to go on, Wendell was longing for his bed. He looked at his watch. 10.40. Shit. Lung and Dawn came panting back, breathless, Dawn fanning herself with a hand. Lung downed his drink in one and turned to Karol with a K. "You now," and grabbed her before she could say no. The last Wendell saw of them was Karol's hand raised above her head with the remainder of the cigarette still smouldering between two fingers.

"Phew!" panted Dawn as she flopped into the vacated chair, clearly the chattier of the pair too. "Where does that guy get his energy from? He's hilarious. Where's he from anyway?"

"China," Wendell shouted back. Dawn sipped her drink.

"Phew," she said again. "Don't you want to dance then?"

"Sure," came Wendell's surprised reply, and they moved into the crush of bodies. As the evening went on, Lung seemed to be getting wilder with every drink. It had got very late now, and Wendell was praying for it to end. He was tired and sober and began to make the intervals between drinks longer and longer in the hope of calming the Chinaman down a bit. Accosting the latter in the gents, he enquired politely what time he would like to get back.

"When we leddy." And with that he zipped up, grinning, and departed.

When he got back to their perch, he found Lung standing on the edge of the dance floor staring into the crowd with a look of astonishment on his face. Karol with a K had another cigarette on the go and was also staring into the throng, envy written all over her face as she watched her friend folded into the arms of a tall muscular Germanic blonde. Lung's face darkened, Wendell moved towards him, slightly concerned, but he had disappeared and was plunging through the bodies towards Dawn and her dance partner. Wendell pushed through behind him in time to see Lung grab Dawn's arm and shout out something about her being with him. The tall man with her stared down on Lung with disdain and turned his back on him, which freed Dawn's arm.

"She wi' me," bellowed Lung with a mouthful of teeth snarling skyward and landed some kind of karate move on the unsuspecting man.

The effect was unexpected and immediate. The blond muscleman released Dawn and crumpled to the floor clutching his ribs and moaning. Dawn bent down to help him, but Lung had other ideas and grabbed her, trying to get her back into his arms.

"Get off me," she shrieked, pulling away, "what are you *doing*?"

The other had by this time been helped from the floor by his friends. He'd been made to look a fool by that gargoyle, and in front of everybody too. And whatever he'd done to him had bloody hurt, still did. The pack were regarding Lung murderously.

"Let me go, let me go, I wanna go 'ome now," wailed Dawn unhappily. Wendell sidled up to Lung and suggested it was time to leave.

"Yes, let's go, I wanna go," shouted Dawn, still imprisoned in Lung's grip of iron and only too aware of the ugly situation developing around them.

"Help!" she cried desperately as the big chap, now mostly recovered, lunged towards them intent on revenge. With a final desperate struggle, she managed to break free just as a huge fist swung into Lung's jaw.

"Oh Christ," hissed Wendell, trying to prevent Lung from falling. Everybody hurriedly moved away to the edge of the dance floor, leaving the combatants staring at one another.

All hell broke loose.

The big blond and his mates all rushed forward en masse, roaring like warriors on a battlefield. Doormen and staff threw people out of their way as they rushed to intervene and Wendell, having been pushed back with the crowd, now stood rooted to the spot, frozen with horrible indecision. A glance over his shoulder revealed Dawn and Karol with a K getting into a taxi outside. At least that was them out of the way.

Suddenly there seemed to be bodies flying about all over the place, big men crashing down onto flimsy peripheral tables and chairs, women screaming and men shouting. It was like a scene from a hundred bar room brawls in any western. In the centre of the action stood Lung, legs apart, hands held ready, chopping and kicking at anyone who approached him. An enormous shaven headed bouncer in a dinner jacket, complete with flattened nose, tattoos and battle scars, parted the crowd and headed purposefully towards Lung, only to be sent reeling backwards with a high kick to the chin. Foolishly, he returned to the arena and was quickly felled. The crowd were now cheering Lung on and enjoying the spectacle. Wendell could hardly believe what he was seeing, Lung really was a martial arts expert. It was impressive he had to admit.

Reinforcements quickly arrived and Lung was finally overpowered by four great big bouncers. A fifth lay whimpering in a shrimp-like position nursing his balls. Wendell found himself being driven outside with the crowd, and as they dispersed Lung was flung bodily from the place by four pairs of beefy arms. He landed in a heap on the pavement.

"If I ever see you even *near* here again, mate," snarled the biggest and bravest of the posse, as he held Lung to the pavement by the neck, "I will personally rip your nuts off and stuff them up your hairy yellow arse."

He stared into Lung's face with menace for a further five seconds then rejoined his team and they all stomped back inside dusting themselves off, victorious, jaws jutting out, like modern day gladiators.

Wendell hurried over to where Lung lay motionless on the pavement, his heart pounding. Anxiety stemmed from two things, firstly how the hell would he explain all this to Bellingham and secondly, would he now have to spend half the night in some hospital waiting room?

"Lung?" he bent over him.

The Chinaman's eyes opened, he shook his head and the huge grin returned.

"Ah Corniss! Velly good," he sat up and looked around. "Where are grrss?"

Wendell helped him up and Lung brushed himself down.

"They've gone."

"Ok," Lung sounded resigned. "We go home now preese. Sank you, Corniss."

Wendell led him to the car where he almost immediately fell fast asleep. Thankfully, he seemed to have suffered no more than ruffled hair. Any bruising would hopefully be disguised by his sallow complexion. Wendell silently thanked the Almighty that it was finally over as he glanced over at the collapsed Lung.

The man was indestructible.

Chapter Twenty
Friday/Saturday

After the discovery of Wendell's note the previous evening, nothing and nobody could dampen Antonia's spirits. Rob Murphy's continuous fault finding glanced off her without leaving a scratch and she was smiling and chatty with the patients. What a difference a day had made.

At lunchtime she skipped out of the surgery with a cheerful "See you later" and sat by the river to eat her sandwich which she shared with a friendly robin. Her thoughts were with Wendell, her stomach fizzing with excitement at the thought of seeing him again. The only shadow was the thought that he wasn't feeling anything more than just neighbourly, while here she was all fired up with romantic expectations.

What would he be doing at this moment? Had he thought of her at all?

She glanced around at all the other people. Office girls giggling together, couples meeting, mothers with small children. Everybody had somebody it seemed, and perhaps now there was a possibility of her finding someone too.

She returned to the surgery at 2 o'clock precisely. Rob would certainly never again be able to complain about her punctuality. A look of relief settled on his craggy features as she appeared, he'd mistaken her joyful demeanour and unusual lunchtime disappearance for leaving him in the lurch. Ha! He must have been a slave to the phone for an hour too, with no one else there to answer it. Served the bastard right, let him see what their lunch breaks were like.

"Alright?" he enquired cautiously.

"Fine thanks," she replied, smiling up at him, realising he really must have been panicking a bit.

The afternoon dragged on interminably. As five o'clock crawled ever nearer her stomach seemed to be doing somersaults. She wanted to go. Wendell was going to call on her on his way in from work. What time would that be?

At five, the phone became lively again, a regular Friday afternoon occurrence. All those idiots who had put off calling all week, now feeling they couldn't last the weekend. Rob's policy was rigid. No one to be seen after five on a Friday if at all possible. Absolutely not if they were not one of his patients. His reasoning for this was that if they had been putting up with the problem for weeks and left it until this last minute to call, they could wait another two days.

At five twenty-five the phone rang again.

"Hello, Mr Murphy's Dental Practice."

"Oh hello," came a voice like a ventriloquist in full flow. "I er, I losht a filling last week and itsh hurting rather badly. I don't suppose I could come and see someone thish evening. Itsh rather an emergenshee."

"Are you a patient here?"

"Well, no, but I—"

Antonia cut him short. "I'm very sorry," she said with false sympathy and a stuck-up phone manner, "but we're just closing."

She furnished the caller with the number of the emergency dentist for the weekend and hung up, completely unsympathetic. The answerphone was swiftly put on and she got ready to go.

At the other end of the line, Wendell held one hand gingerly against an overheated cheek and crashed the phone down with the other.

"Thanksh for that, you snotty bitch," he said through an immobile mouth, the intake of air only making the tooth spasm with pain.

The amalgam filling he had lost with the questionable sausage roll had given rise to sudden and vicious pain. His own dental surgery hadn't even answered their telephone and he'd been going through the directory ever since. He couldn't possibly wait until Monday; the pain was intolerable. He had noticed it nagging a bit last night at the club, all that cold orange juice and shouting seemed to have set it off, but he'd been able to ignore it then with all the other things going on. After he'd decanted Lung from the car at Bellingham's gate and driven home, he'd taken a couple of painkillers and fallen into bed, and now, overtired from the previous evening, pain had taken hold in a big way. Beth came to his desk, the telephone directory hanging open over one hand.

"Who was that you just tried? Any luck?"

"God knows, shum shnotty piece answered, thash all I remember. Oh, I've got an emergency number."

"I'll try it for you. Here." She handed him a glass of water and a couple of painkillers and returned to her desk to get dialling.

"Thansh Beth."

As Antonia opened the door to leave, an attractive brunette woman appeared in it.

"Hi," she beamed. "Jill from Buck & Partners."

"Hello." Antonia smiled back, liking Jill immediately. Buck & Partners was a dental surgery about five miles away and they had often spoken on the phone but, until now, never met.

"Nice to see the face on the end of a phone at last."

"Yes." Any other Friday, or any other day in fact, Antonia would have welcomed a chat but today time was pressing, so she kept the conversation brief. It seemed Jill had somewhere to go as well, as she handed a briefcase to Antonia and said in parting, "Here's the mobile then, nice to have met you at last. Hope it's a quiet one, byeee."

"Bye."

Jill was gone. Antonia stood for a second and stared at the briefcase as though she'd been handed a bomb. She stepped sideways into the surgery where Rob was already in his jacket and practising his swing. An evening golf game lay ahead of him, prior to a session with some of his cronies. His jaw dropped visibly at the sight of the briefcase, then the face above it clouded with anger. Without speaking he pushed past Antonia and began shuffling around in the reception area. Eventually finding what he was looking for amongst his untidy pile of papers, he scrutinised a long list of names and dropped his hand to his side, allowing the paper to float to the floor like an autumn leaf.

"It's my weekend for the emergency phone," he addressed the wall.

Antonia, still cradling the briefcase, was finally enlightened.

"It's your job to remind me of these things," he began, spinning around, needing someone to attack. "You should notice things like this."

Antonia's eyes narrowed. She could feel her face heating up. If he dared to try and blame her for *this*, she was more than ready to defend herself. In any case, it was up to Susan to remind him of 'things like this', not her.

"The emergency phone procedure has never even been mentioned to me," she began slowly. "I did not know that list existed until a moment ago."

Rob was not in the mood for a confrontation, and by the tone of her voice he could see Antonia would be.

"Oh no, sorry, sorry," he spluttered, while relieving her of the briefcase, its shiny surface now covered in sweaty fingerprints.

There was a pause before he turned to face Antonia.

"Unfortunately, this means you will have to work tomorrow."

He stared defiantly at her, eyebrows drawn together, daring her to refuse, and she stared back at him with undisguised loathing. What a bloody nuisance, why didn't the stupid bastard ever pay attention to anything? She wanted to scream, and he could see it.

"Er... sorry about that," he said a bit sheepishly.

"Oh," replied Antonia finally. "I'll just have to rearrange all my plans for tomorrow then."

"Yes, me too," he cleared his throat. "Sorry," his eyebrows returned to their usual neanderthal position, and he heaved a sigh of relief. It meant he could still get in a game of golf tomorrow, late afternoon.

"Right," he ended briskly, "be here at nine and book in all emergencies from ten onwards, at ten-minute intervals." He showed her how to work the mobile phone and as he plugged it in it began to ring. They both regarded it and looked at each other. "I'll be here at ten tomorrow then."

"What about this evening?" she asked, remembering how many people had been dished out this number.

"I'll have to leave it here; I'm playing golf at seven-thirty. No one's going to die of toothache overnight, it'll be fine."

With that, he pulled his keys from his pocket, sprinkling fluff all over the floor, and left.

"Bye, enjoy your game," said Antonia sarcastically as the door closed behind him. She moved across to the window and watched him saunter off down the road with her hands on her hips. "You horrible bastard," she said through clenched teeth.

The phone was still ringing as she left and she told herself it was Rob's business, not hers, to answer it. Anyway, she did agree that no one had ever died of toothache, so they'd have to wait. She had other things to think of tonight.

All thoughts of work dismissed, she headed for home looking forward to seeing Wendell Cornish again.

Beth tried the emergency number several times without success.

"I'm sorry Wendell," she said anxiously as she prepared to leave the office. "I must go. I've got the family coming for dinner tonight."

"Thansh Beth," replied Wendell without moving his mouth.

Unable to think of anything except numbing the pain, he went straight to the nearest bar and ordered himself a brandy. A colleague had told him this would help. Nick, the barman, a large hearty Scot, greeted him jovially.

"Well, well, long time no see. What can I get for you? Pint?"

"Brandy," whispered Wendell without moving his jaw.

Nick frowned. "Are you alright?"

"Toothache."

He laughed. "Oh so that's it."

He gave Wendell a double. "Here, you'll need it" and, leaning a hairy arm on the bar, went on to regale him with a tale of a dental disaster experienced by his wife's friend while holidaying in Germany.

Wendell didn't really want to hear it, but he was a captive audience. It would have taken too many words to halt the man anyway.

After the brandy, things did become fractionally improved, so he ordered another, managing this time to swill it around the affected tooth without suffering too much. Yes, it was working, there was less throbbing. Numbing up nicely, just like his brain.

Three doubles later found him talking again, this time slurred for a different reason. His mind was focused on Antonia, who seemed to have taken on the persona of a goddess in his drunken thoughts.

The note.

In his ocean of pain he had quite forgotten about that. He looked at his watch and found it hard to focus.

"What time is it, Nick?"

"Nine thirty precisely."

Damn! She would think he hadn't bothered. What was her surname? He could phone her. Goldman? Goldfinger? Goldsmith, that was it. He asked Nick for the directory and searched in vain, the entry being still in the name of Waterman. There was nothing for it, he would have to go.

"I hope you're not thinking of driving, Sir," called Nick, suddenly officious, as Wendell swayed towards the door.

"No. Bye Nick." He would just doze for twenty minutes then get going.

About midnight, when he woke, Wendell was stiff and freezing cold. His head and the tooth were locked in a throbbing competition. Waves of nausea washed over him. He felt sweaty and sick. When it all subsided a bit, he rubbed his eyes and ran his hands through his hair, knotty with hardened hair gel, then drove away slowly, feeling wretched. He was vaguely aware of the car's heater smelling of burning dust, it was the first time he'd had to use it this year, and it was making him feel sick again.

Finally, he was home. It was silent but for the distant barking of some nocturnal dog.

He let himself in quietly. He felt ghastly, and guilty too that he'd forgotten about calling on Antonia, but it couldn't be helped. They were only friends anyway, not joined at the hip. At least there was no dog shit forced through his letter box. It wasn't like they'd made a date or anything. He would call on her in the morning, after he'd seen a dentist.

He took three more pain killers with copious glasses of water and slumped onto the bed, only to wake a couple of hours later with the pain. He paced the room in agony, holding an ice cube in a tea towel to his cheek. He must get to a dentist. The emergency dental number was etched across his brain, so he began dialling it every five minutes from eight o'clock, with fingers crossed. At ten seconds past nine it was finally picked up.

"Dental surgery, good morning."

"Thank God," he cried, forgetting not to move his jaw and wincing. "I tried thish number all lasht night and this morning, I'm in agony, I need to shee shomeone urgently pleash."

"Can you be here at ten?" she relayed the address.

"I'll be there," he threw the receiver down. The effort of all that talking, with the air rushing in and out of his gob had set the bloody thing off again.

"Your name?" said Antonia, but he'd already hung up.

"Dammit," she hissed, and wrote stupid bastard in the slot, then crossed it out again and replaced it with a question mark. Oh, who cared anyway? She'd spent half the previous evening in a state of nervous excitement, then anger, despair and God knows what other emotions. Thank goodness for Ozzie, if she hadn't had him to weep all over, she might have felt dearly like ending it all there and then. Why did men always let her down? She was better off on her own.

While she continued with these miserable musings, Wendell was staring into his bathroom mirror and Dracula's last meal was looking back out at him. Dark shadows under bloodshot eyes in a pale and hungover face. He badly needed a shave, which wasn't going to happen. Just imagining the feeling of the razor vibrating against his cheek made him feel quite faint. He raked a comb through his hair and twenty-four hour old flakes of dried gel fell onto his shoulders. Was it his imagination or had his cheek swollen up? He was still in yesterday's clothes which were crumpled and must pong. Perhaps the smell of stale alcohol and halitosis would mask it. He'd come home and sort himself out when he'd got this tooth seen too. He scribbled out a quick explanatory note and stuck it on Antonia's door, he certainly couldn't face her looking like this.

Wendell arrived at the dentist at ten to ten, looking and smelling like an old dosser. He opened the door and was engulfed by that peculiar smell which pervaded all dental surgeries as he crossed to the reception.

She was on the phone and Wendell gazed absent-mindedly at the top of Antonia's head in a haze of pain and weariness.

"See you at ten forty then, goodbye." She replaced the receiver and looked up into Wendell's eyes.

"Hello."

Recognition came to both simultaneously. For a moment they just stared silently at one another, then Antonia raised herself up. She was blushing slightly and felt a bit light-headed for a moment.

"Wendell?" she said incredulously.

"Antonia," he replied with utter despair. This really was the end of any hope of impressing her.

"You look awful!" She came around from behind the reception and led him to a chair, her heart fluttering. The appalling evening she'd spent by herself yesterday came and went before her eyes. She wasn't sure what to think.

"I left you another note," he said feebly. "I tried to call you yesterday but you're not in the book."

"Oh God, you poor thing. Don't worry, he'll be here any minute." Rob was late as usual.

Another patient arrived, the ten past ten, and she left Wendell while she dealt with a sullen teenage girl dragged in by her mother.

As she filled out a chart for Wendell, she had to bend down close to hear what he was saying. She smelled gorgeous, clean and lightly scented, while he smelled of body odour and stale booze.

"I do apologise for the shtate I'm in," he whispered, "what must you think of me?" He couldn't bring himself to meet her gaze in case she caught a whiff of his undoubtedly vile breath.

"Don't worry, we'll soon have you sorted out."

The phone was ringing again, and she went back to her station to answer it, mulling over at the same time what could have happened to him to smell that bad.

In his state of tiredness and pain, Wendell almost felt like crying. He wasn't a bad person, was he? Why then did fate always seem to be against him? He glanced furtively in Antonia's direction and thought how lovely she was, like lots of others he rather liked a girl in a uniform. Why did this have to be where *she* worked? In a moment of clarity, he admitted to himself what he had known since last Saturday, that he would like them to be more than just friends.

And now he'd blown it for sure.

Rob Murphy breezed in at ten fifteen.

"Mr Cornish," he called, and Wendell shuffled into the surgery, arms limp at his sides like an ape man. He lay back in the chair, fragile and dejected, pain throbbing steadily.

Rob poked about and grunted.

"It's had it I'm afraid, it'll have to come out. I can do it now for you."

"Do anything."

As the anaesthetic began to take effect there was a merciful release from pain and Wendell began to feel terribly tired. Free from the preoccupation of the nagging ache, his feelings of mortification sharpened. What was he thinking of coming out in this unwashed state?

"Open."

He opened.

Suddenly she was there. He could smell that fragrance again as she sat close to him throughout the procedure. His hand, clenched to the armrest, almost brushed her thigh.

The extraction was an easy one and ten minutes later it was all over, and he hadn't really noticed what was happening.

"Here, bite on this," said Rob, placing something that felt like a pillow into his open mouth.

He bit down cautiously.

"Don't try to talk. Bite on that until you get home. No spitting, no rinsing, and definitely no alcohol for twenty-four hours," he said this rather pointedly, "then saltwater rinses for about a week. Goodbye."

Rob shot the chair upright, making Wendell's head spin.

"Are you alright?" enquired Antonia anxiously.

He nodded and rose shakily.

Rob, washing his hands, wanted to get shot of these people quickly, so he could rejoin his golf buddies on the fairway. The sullen girl went in while Antonia led Wendell to a chair. The waiting room was fairly full now with other scruffy types, which made Wendell feel slightly better. At least he wasn't the only one not appearing at his best.

"There's £30 to pay," she said quietly. He looked up at her, pale and forlorn, one cheek puffed out with the cotton wool swab and "Uh" was all he managed around it.

Numbness seemed to have spread up to his eye which felt droopy and huge, he must look like Quasimodo. He certainly felt like it. A lady on his left, sitting bunched on her seat trying not have to touch anyone, scrutinised him critically and wrinkled her nose.

"No money," he managed to mumble. "Forgot. Shorry."

"Never mind, sort it out later," smiled Antonia. She was already thinking this would give her an opportunity to call on him and see what had happened. Wendell was thinking the same thing exactly. "Will you be alright getting home? I can call a taxi for you if you like," she said quietly.

"I'll be fine," Wendell replied and began dragging himself home, weary with fatigue.

Antonia watched his retreating form from the window. She wanted to go home and look after him. At least she felt slightly better about everything now, the explanation would be interesting if nothing else. Hopefully he wouldn't turn out to be a completely unreliable closet alcoholic.

"Don't suppose you'll ever get paid from him," came a voice loaded with contempt from behind her.

Antonia turned and faced the woman. "He'll settle up with me when I see him at home later."

"Oh!" the woman turned brick red and began examining a nine month old golf magazine with great interest. Antonia turned her back and strode to the reception desk.

Wendell woke several hours later. There was still some pain, but of a healthier kind. The cotton wool swab was still in his mouth. He removed it with care, thankful not to have swallowed it and caused another problem. His jaw felt a bit stiff but at least it was mobile again. He rubbed it gently and his fingers rasped across two days beard growth.

As he made a cup of tea, he was suddenly aware of how clean the place was.

The cleaner! He'd forgotten to leave Mrs O's money out yesterday. He called her immediately to apologise and found her pleasant, if a little reserved. They agreed he would leave double next time.

As he lay in a warm bath sipping tea through a straw, he began to feel human again.

By the time all the emergencies had been dispatched it was nearly twelve. Rob disappeared hurriedly into the toilet, reappearing moments later in the most ridiculous purple and yellow check golf trousers, and instructed Antonia to stay by the phone and book anyone else in from five. Five! What time was she expected to work till? She was cross, what a waste of the day, and all so his game of golf wouldn't be interrupted. All the emergencies must wait until five when she should be on her way home. Damn the man, she really should look for another job. It also meant that it would be much later than she'd hoped before she could see Wendell. With a bit of luck, the main crush of patients had already come and gone.

There were only three more calls during the afternoon, but time moved as slowly as a lake of treacle. At one point she was certain the clock had stopped. At least she had Wendell's details now, including phone number. She wrote it all down on a piece of paper and put it in her bag.

Should she ring him? No, he might be sleeping, he'd looked exhausted.

Thankfully, all the patients arrived punctually, more than could be said of Rob who blustered in at twenty past five with an expression which suggested he had lost his game. He was met with a trio of angry stares from the waiting threesome and a sullen greeting from Antonia, also annoyed because now they would be held up even longer.

However, Rob was anxious to get away and dispatched the patients all in the space of five minutes, a record even for him, furnishing each with a prescription for antibiotics and telling them to contact their own dentists on Monday morning. He left hurriedly, stopping only to hand Antonia a £20 note as an extra, and grunt out his appreciation.

"Oh, thank you," she said in amazement.

"Yes, well, you don't need to come in tomorrow, I'll take the mobile equipment home with me. If anything urgent arises I'll call you in."

No, you won't, she thought, thinking quickly.

"Oh, I'm so sorry but I can't tomorrow," she lied. "I've promised my sister I'll pick her up from Heathrow. I can't let her down, sorry." She looked up with big innocent eyes in a face creased with fake concern.

"Oh, well… never mind, I'll manage. My wife can fill in if necessary." He frowned involuntarily as he said this, obviously hoping he wouldn't need her.

"Maybe it won't be busy anyway, sorry about that. If I'd known in advance…" she left the words dangling between them.

"Ah, yes. Well, see you Monday."

"Bye Rob, thanks for this," she waved the £20 in the air and smiled.

"Bye." The door closed behind him and she got her coat on.

Pedalling home, Antonia's thoughts raced. There were butterflies in her stomach and a jumping bean in her heart. She was panicking to see Wendell and then panicking in case he had felt better and gone out. What if he had company? The butterflies went wild at this new idea, and she told herself she was being ridiculous and to calm down. He only wanted them to be friends anyway, she must stop thinking of it as more. And anyway, he hadn't been very reliable yet had he? Don't want to get into something I might regret, she thought.

When she got there, his car was parked at the front but there were no lights visible in his flat. Her heart sank.

Inside the shared front door, she listened intently for sounds of life and heard none. If he was there, at least there would be no one with him.

Unless they were up to something quiet… oh stop! She told herself. It was just after six-thirty now and he'd had no sleep and a tooth extracted, surely he wouldn't have gone out? For God's sake stop this, she thought, relax. She went up to her flat making enough noise to alert him to her return, and fed Ozzie, who was eating happily at last on a mix of white meat and tinned cat food.

She read Wendell's note. It just said, "Sorry about last night, problems with a tooth, hope to see a dentist today."

She decided to shower and eat before knocking downstairs, which was accomplished at speed and again with as much noise as possible.

At last, hair washed and brushed, washing up all done, she took a deep breath and headed downstairs.

She knocked, waited, her heart beating fast.

Nothing.

She knocked again, louder this time, but there was still nothing and she cursed quietly and stood there with limp arms, not knowing what to do next. Eventually she turned and began to mount the stairs despondently.

And then there came the magic sound of a door being opened and she turned to speak from halfway up the stairs. "Wendell?"

He looked up. His hair was all ruffled and he was pale and sleepy looking.

"Oh Antonia, you don't know how glad I am to see you."

And he was. He felt a warmth spread through him at the sight of her.

Antonia was almost overwhelmed; it was all she could do to speak, "How are you feeling?"

"Oh, much better now thanks," he replied, placing a hand lightly against his cheek, "still a bit sore of course, but nothing like earlier," then added, "Would you like to come in? I think I owe you an explanation."

Yes, she would, she definitely would!

She followed him to the lounge. Typical bachelor pad, put together in a purely functional way. Stacks of papers on the coffee table and wires from the stereo trailing all over the place. At least it was clean.

There had been pictures and ornaments once, but Bibi had taken everything she could carry when she left, including certain things which were his, and he hadn't bothered to replace any of it.

"Have a seat," he gestured towards the sofa, and she perched awkwardly at one end. Thank God Mrs O. had tidied the place, he thought with relief.

"I'm not interrupting you, am I? I just wanted to make sure you were ok. Throw me out if you've got plans."

He regarded her closely. Did she want to stay or go?

"No plans," he said finally, "certainly not after last night."

She smiled shyly and his heart seemed to leap. What on earth was the matter with him? He was behaving like a nervous schoolboy. He covered the moment with an offer of coffee which she accepted happily, and while he clattered about in the kitchen, Antonia scrutinised the room properly. It seemed larger than her lounge upstairs, probably an illusion due to there being less in it. The walls were pale yellow, the carpet pale brown. All rather insipid but comfortable. The TV and stereo system, ensconced royally in a large, impressive unit, dominated the wall facing the sofa and that was about it, apart from the coffee table with its piles of papers. For some strange, unfathomable reason it made her want to titter.

She rose and looked out of the window. The edges of the carpet there bore signs of furniture now removed. A rock hard, scarlet pool of nail varnish adorned the window sill, a legacy of the days of Bibi perhaps. She turned as he entered with the coffee and sat down again.

"So how are you?" she repeated.

"Most definitely better for seeing you," he smiled.

Antonia blushed furiously and felt very foolish. Had he noticed?

He had and thought of it as a promising reaction.

"Actually," he began, "I'm very glad to see you. I wanted to apologise about last night for one thing."

"What happened?" Antonia could not bring herself to say it didn't matter, when it had mattered so much.

Wendell filled her in on the events of the past week, from losing his filling on that inedible sausage roll, Barney and Sam and the business at the hospital, Thursday night with Lung to the frightful day that had followed it.

"I don't think I've ever felt as near to death as I did in that dentist's chair this morning," he finished. "I think I would have welcomed it."

It all seemed hilarious now, sitting here relating it to Antonia and they seemed to constantly be laughing. He loved the way she laughed, the way her nose crinkled up and her eyes sparkled. She had nice teeth. Well, she would, being a dental nurse, he supposed.

"Is something the matter?" she asked, suddenly serious, and Wendell blushed this time, when he realised he had been staring at her, sheep-like, for some moments.

"What? No, no, I was just thinking I owe the dentist some money, don't I? Listen Antonia, I also wanted to apologise about the state I was in this morning, I've never been so embarrassed. What with yesterday and then arriving like that I was certain you'd want nothing more to do with me. You probably thought I was some deranged alcoholic."

She had considered it, yes.

"Don't worry, I've seen people in a worse state than that, believe me. When you're in agony nothing else matters."

"Really?" Wendell was genuinely surprised. "But I must have looked and smelled like some old wino. When I couldn't get to a dentist yesterday, I drowned the pain in alcohol."

They looked at each other and paused.

"I had seen you looking better," she started, with a giggle in her voice. She felt young and silly for a moment, but Wendell was grinning along with her.

Antonia went on to tell him about the dreadful Rob Murphy, having to work Saturday at the last minute and after Wendell's call, what she'd called him when he didn't leave his name. Wendell thought this particularly funny coming from her.

At midnight, Antonia got up. "I'd better go."

Wendell accompanied her to the door where they stood facing one another expectantly.

"Antonia?"

"Yes?"

"When I've recovered from all this," he waved a finger in the direction of his mouth, "could I treat you to an evening out somewhere?"

"I'd love that," she replied instantly, pleasure filling her till she was light-headed from it.

They both grinned.

"I've been trying all week to contact you actually," admitted Wendell.

"I thought you'd gone away; your car wasn't here."

So she had noticed!

"Look, how about Sunday lunch tomorrow. But this time… a proper date… if you would like to, I mean?"

Please say yes.

He rushed on eagerly, "I know a really nice country pub not too far from here. I may have to go easy but who cares?"

"That would be… great!" she stuttered, absurdly pleased by this hoped for development.

"I know we did say friends, but if you would like to come out with me on a date, well, great!" echoed Wendell, thinking how awful it sounded.

He badly wanted to kiss her.

Antonia so badly wanted him to kiss her.

"Right, see you tomorrow then. About 11.30 alright?" he finished. "It's a nice drive."

"Great!" *Stop saying great*, thought Antonia, *it sounds ridiculous*. "Night then."

She flew upstairs, her heart on fire. What the hell was happening? Why hadn't he kissed her? Should she have kissed him first, was that what he was waiting for? Maybe because of the tooth…

Wendell sat on his sofa glowing with contentment. What a lovely girl she was, he didn't want to mess this up. Incredible that all this miserable time she'd been living above him, and he'd never noticed her before. He should have kissed her, but he didn't want to put her off by rushing things. He would tomorrow though.

His phone rang. Who on earth could that be calling at this late hour? All kinds of unpleasant ideas flitted across his mind, then he wondered if it was Antonia calling just to say goodnight again. He picked it up quickly and listened.

"Hello?" enquired a voice at the other end, which didn't sound like Antonia.

"Hello. Yes?"

"Wendell? It's Bibi."

Chapter Twenty-One
Friday/Saturday

The weekend at last, thought Charles, dropping gratefully into a chair. He felt tired and stressed after what had seemed the longest week of his life.

Why was Bibi doing this, he kept on asking himself? What had he done?

In case of bumping into Eve, he had avoided the staff room all week, remaining in his classroom during breaks.

On the other hand, Eve's obsession with him had done a U-turn and she found she was despising him for being so utterly ridiculous! Love and hate were close companions it seemed. He was a grown man for God's sake, not a silly child!

He pretended not to see her whenever they passed in the corridor, but of course she knew he had, not least because of his suddenly slightly pink and alarmed look. Friendly smiles fell on stony ground, and she would send her pale eyes skyward in exasperation. Ridiculous. Any other bloke would probably have taken an illicit shag if it was offered. She felt slightly unhappy with this thought, truth be told. What was wrong with her?

When he went back to work, he had been jumpy all morning and after Eve had accosted him in the staff room, he'd had the runs all afternoon, which he unkindly blamed on Eve's food.

The flat looked like a bombsite. No dishes had been cleaned nor clothes washed. Every surface was accumulating muck and piles of papers, and the remains of his clothing still lay in flattened heaps amongst a minefield of shoes on the bedroom floor. It distressed him even more to see the place like this, but he'd never had to do any housework for himself, always having had an attendant woman, and he didn't really know what to do. He had no inclination whatsoever to clean up, that and a deep-rooted Dickensian idea that it was not a man's job to do all that stuff in any case.

He had called Bibi every evening. Elizabeth always answered and until Wednesday had said Bibi was 'out'. From Thursday she had said that yes, she was there, but didn't want to be disturbed. The pleading that followed had fallen on deaf ears, Elizabeth deftly giving vague and sympathetic replies while she poured herself another G and T. It was only the thought of Bibi returning at the weekend that kept Charles from going there straight away.

He was not a happy man.

For Bibi, the week had been a good one. She had, at last, made contact with her father and driven over to visit him. Emotions welled up as she turned into the familiar road. Most of the houses looked as they had done when she played there as that pampered child with the best toys, the prettiest dresses and the grandest birthday parties. The only real difference to the road was the number of parked cars. That was new. No kids would be able to play on the road nowadays. Oh well, what did she care about that.

And here was the house, plain, modern, square, just the same. The garden looked a bit neglected, that was unusual. Her father was always proud of his garden, used to be anyway.

Bibi stepped from the car and locked it with a clammy hand. She was wondering how they would get on after all this time when the door opened in welcome, a smiling white haired old man framed on its threshold. He'd been watching out for her.

"Dad?"

"Hello darling." The blue eyes twinkled in the thin face. Suddenly she was in his arms where they clung together for some time, oblivious to the twitchy curtains in the house opposite.

"Just look at that!" exclaimed a nosy neighbour, snorting with disapproval. "Him over the road cuddling some young woman with the door wide open! I thought he'd given up on all that at his age! It's disgraceful how people carry on these days. He's no better than those long-haired louts that call themselves students. Just look Jack!"

Jack, momentarily distracted from his newspaper, turned to see his wife quivering with indignation, her flaring nostrils poking through the parted net curtains, and rose obediently to look.

"Hmm yes." Lucky bastard, he thought.

When Bibi and her father finally released one another, she had mascara running all down her face. He removed his glasses and dabbed his eyes with a mass of handkerchief from his trouser pocket. He chuckled.

"Dear oh dear, what a pair we are. Come in, my darling, let's have a drink."

How terrifyingly fragile and elderly he was, and his hair, although still thick, was snowy white.

He took her by the hand as he used to, and they adjourned to the kitchen, where Bibi settled herself on the stool she had always sat upon and watched him while he made the tea.

When the teapot was under its cosy and everything ready, Bibi spoke.

"Well..." she struggled to think of something to say. "Er... how are you, Dad?"

"Oh, so-so, none of us is getting any younger you know."

He smiled, but she was aware of him avoiding her gaze and felt afraid.

"Mum said you hadn't been well lately."

"Did she, now? And how would she know that?"

"Well... I don't know. Are you well?"

He chuckled again and stared at her on the stool.

"You look just like a little girl perched on that stool, with your eyes all red from crying. What's all this black stuff then?" he brushed her cheek with his finger.

"Oh no!" The mascara was drying in streaky lines, and she spent the next ten minutes repairing the damage to her make-up.

"You've redone the bathroom," she said, returning.

"Oh, ages ago. I never did like that green colour. That was Joyce's choice," he glanced at her briefly. "All that green. Green bath, green sink, plants everywhere, it only needed a couple of parrots to turn it into a tropical rainforest."

They laughed together.

"It's good to see you, Dad," said Bibi before she could stop herself and was almost overcome by emotion again. Only the thought of her mascara prevented more tears.

"You could have come anytime you know. After Joyce died I thought you might, I hoped you would. I've really missed you, darling," his voice wavered.

"Don't!" cried Bibi. "I'll ruin my make-up again."

Her father laughed heartily. "Same old Bibi."

She pouted, nicely.

They spent a pleasant day in each other's company, Bibi driving them to a local restaurant where they lunched by the river. It was a sunny autumn day, not too hot but bright. Being midweek, they were undisturbed by screaming children and their disinterested parents, so it was all very civilised. They returned mid-afternoon and had tea in the garden while they caught up on the years. When the air began to cool, Bibi reluctantly decided she should go. Her father looked exhausted, and in the sunlight the unhealthy pallor of his skin was obvious.

"You look tired Dad, I should go."

"I get tired easily these days, darling."

"What's wrong with you? Tell me, I'm worried about you."

He was silent.

"I'm not a child any more you know! Come on, what *is* wrong with you?"

He took her hand in his and patted it gently. It seemed to Bibi that this old man was the only person she could feel safe and loved with, could drop the prickly outer shell she usually wore, and now she was terrified she might lose him.

"Dad?"

"I'm still here."

But for how long?

"I've got cancer," he finished at last. The words seemed almost to strangle him.

Shock fizzled from the top of Bibi's head down to her toes, she couldn't breathe properly for a moment; it was a strange and unpleasant sensation. They stared at one another in silence.

"I've got cancer, darling; I've been given about a year at most. And I'm bloody well terrified, I admit it."

Speechless, and numb with shock, Bibi knelt at his feet and rested her head in his lap the way she used to as a child. Everything was peaceful in the familiar garden, with just the sound of birds chattering and he laid a gentle hand on her head while she came to terms with what he'd just told her.

When Bibi got back to her mother's she avoided her, heading straight upstairs for a long soak in the bath, feeling extraordinarily drained. In her room, pale without make-up, she sat on the bed, desolate and childlike.

There was a tap on the door and Elizabeth entered without waiting to be invited. "He told you then."

"Why does everything go wrong in my life?" Bibi replied angrily as she stared at the floor. Elizabeth's eyes rolled skyward but this was not the time to point out it wasn't about her. She chose to do the motherly thing this time. So she sat beside her daughter and rested an arm gently on her shoulder.

"If he only has a short time left to him, shall we both try and make it nice for him? Hmm? I don't want to have to reproach myself when he's gone, and I don't think you want regrets either do you?"

"No of course not."

"Let's make this time the happiest of his life. With us."

Bibi looked at Elizabeth and said, "Yes" very definitely.

After that, Bibi visited her father every day. They had begun to know each other again, had got to the point where they could happily disagree without awkwardness or fear of further estrangement. She realised he was, and only ever had been, the one person she could do it with.

"I liked the sound of that fellow," said her father wistfully, when she admitted she and Wendell were separated. "Pity I never actually met him."

"Don't start, you didn't know him," came Bibi's quick retort.

"Your mother spoke of him often, I liked the sound of him, that's all," then added, "Marriage shouldn't be entered into lightly, darling."

"You're a fine one to talk!" Bibi flared, unwilling to admit that she may have made a mistake in leaving Wendell, and not liking her divorced parents discussing her relationships.

"Believe me, darling, I put up with… a lot of things before I left your mother. More than you can know."

Bibi imagined that toy boy of her mother's and thought she could guess.

They had been sitting in the garden again, and now sat companionably listening to birds twittering in the autumn sunshine before the serious business of winter began.

That night, lying in bed, she thought a lot about Wendell. They had had some really good times together now she looked back, especially at first.

He knew how to treat women properly, unlike that idiot Charles who seemed sometimes like a soppy boy rather than a grown man. She was confident that Wendell had been besotted with her and, in her own way, she imagined she had loved him. For the first time, she felt a twinge of remorse about the callous way she had treated him when she walked out. She could picture his anguished face, pleading with her not to go, asking what he had done wrong. She mentally swatted the picture to one side.

She also considered Charles and realised just how utterly sick of him she was, although it hadn't yet occurred to her that she was, in a parallel way, doing to him what she had just regretted doing to Wendell. If he hadn't been so damned attractive, she wouldn't have given him a second glance. In fact, without him in front of her to look at, she almost despised him. No personality, that was his problem. It was embarrassing sometimes. He didn't fit in with her kind of people, had no manners and certainly no fashion sense. God, the clothes he used to wear! She smiled, remembering destroying those hideous corduroy trousers, she'd actually done him a favour getting rid of those appalling articles. No, it was all over, she couldn't go back to living with him now, they had absolutely nothing in common. Her marriage break up had been all his fault, she could see it now. If he'd just been a 'normal' man and had an occasional sneaky romp with her, no one would have been any the wiser, she would never have been saddled with the idiot.

The following day she consulted her mother about Wendell in an offhand way.

"Wendell? Well, at first, I thought him just another of your wine swilling womanisers, but it was an unfair judgement, he grew on me. He had potential, I was sorry when you parted."

What did she mean 'your wine swilling womanisers'?

"What about Charles?"

Elizabeth laughed.

"Do you really want to know, darling?"

"I wouldn't have asked otherwise, would I?" she snapped back, a faint, angry pinkness in her cheeks.

"Gorgeous, darling, but dull as ditchwater, it was never going to last. I'm surprised it's gone on as long as it has."

Elizabeth stopped and refilled their glasses while Bibi sat lost in thought. She felt foolish but wasn't quite sure why. The idea of people making judgements about her was distasteful, she didn't like it.

"We all make mistakes, darling," said Elizabeth tartly and took a sip from her wine glass.

"Well, *you* certainly have. I'm going to bed now." Bibi rose with her head high and flounced out.

Elizabeth bade her daughter's back goodnight and rolled her eyes. What on earth had she produced in that girl?

"Answer, damn you!" Bibi was up early that Saturday morning and was calling Wendell. This was just about the time he was dragging himself down to Rob Murphy's surgery, hence the lack of an answer. She tried again later while her mother was out shopping but there was still no reply, and she banged the receiver down angrily. By this time, Wendell was soundly asleep and would not have woken if the ceiling had come down on him. Elizabeth had come back so she let the matter rest for the moment. She would try later, and if no one answered she would have to assume he had moved. But she had to get *someone* to answer to know for sure.

"Will you be here tonight, darling?" trilled Elizabeth casually.

"Where else would I be? I'm not exactly busy at the moment, am I?"

"I've got Guy coming around for dinner. I had no idea you would still be here when I made the arrangement."

Elizabeth was busily putting the groceries away as she spoke, purposefully not looking at her daughter, whose temper was beginning to bubble.

"You don't want me here then? Why didn't you just say?"

So, that muscular creep took precedence over her then? Her lips tightened and she went upstairs before she said anything worse.

What could she do tonight? She hadn't been out once since she had been here, apart from the evening with her mother. And the days with her father, of course.

Her father? No, he got so tired by six, the reason she had come back to her mother's so early every day.

Gino? She closed her eyes and shuddered to think of that ghastly evening. No, never again.

Perhaps she should get Charles over with? No. She didn't really want to see him, just sneak in for her things sometime, even he would eventually get the message.

She wanted to try Wendell again, but she didn't want Elizabeth knowing, so she shelved that too.

Was there no one she could call for a Saturday night out? It was unheard of. No man to take her out. Why was everything always against her?

Clara! She hadn't seen *her* for at least a year. She'd do. Clara, a dumpy, jolly girl who had attached herself to Bibi and her set of friends at school. She had become a sort of mascot, and they had all delighted in treating her like their own personal servant. She had been over the moon to be included and had never even suspected that they just let her hang around with them for a laugh. It was mostly Clara's own efforts that had kept her in touch with Bibi, who would otherwise have forgotten she existed, But Bibi knew for certain she would be delighted to see her. She called her straight away.

"Bibi!" shrieked Clara. "How super to hear from you, darling! Please say you'll come over, Tessa and Tina will be here, we're going out for a meal at Gino's! It'll be the four of us, just like old times!"

Bibi felt physically sick, there was no way she was going anywhere near there.

"Did you book, darling?" Please say no.

"Not yet, we've only just decided."

"Didn't you know, darling, he's packed up? Closed down and gone back to Italy."

"Gino? I don't believe it!" Clara sounded distraught.

"No, I went past it last week. The place was all dark and shuttered."

"Oh no!" Clara exclaimed, and Bibi could almost see her, the back of a pudgy hand against her forehead, gazing up with a tear glistening in the corner of an over made-up eye.

"How about Meggie's? It's alright there."

Clara brightened immediately. "Of course, I'd forgotten that! We're all meeting here at seven. Do say you can make it, darling!"

"Fab, I'll be there, darling."

"See you later, darling," sang the ecstatic Clara and was gone.

Good, thought Bibi, completely unrepentant of her appalling lie, Gino deserves that. She was pleased at the thought of a proper evening out, even if it was just Clara and the other two. Sitting in front of a television all evening was for the Charles' of this world. She decided she would call him after all, he was so thick he would keep on phoning otherwise.

Yes, she would call him tomorrow sometime and tell him it was all over, that would be the end of that. He'd probably go running back to that mousy creature he used to live with before, she was welcome to him as far as she was concerned.

Guy arrived just as Bibi was leaving and they faced each other at the gate. He looked her up and down and ran his tongue around his lips as she stared back with venom.

"Hi babe," he drawled. So, she was still here, was she? Elizabeth's feisty daughter was upsetting his plans with the mother. This had been a pleasant little number until she showed up. He hadn't seen Elizabeth all week and the cash flow was getting a bit low.

"You'll have to come for a drive with me in your ma's jeep sometime babe." Her ma's jeep?

Guy noticed Bibi's attention sharpen and carried on, "Great birthday present, don't you think?" A smirk slowly worked its way across his face.

Thinking briefly of the fifty-pound cheque she had received on her own birthday, Bibi was filled with violent loathing for this arrogant, sponging bastard.

"Get out of my way, monkey dick!" she spat, striding off to her car. She shoved him sideways with the gate as she went. Guy watched her leave, still smirking. That little snippet of info should set the cat among the pigeons and begin the rift, he thought.

Furious by the exchange, Bibi roared away, driving erratically, and narrowly missed two ramblers examining some plant at the side of the road. Unaware of the abusive shouts and rude hand gestures, she sped on towards Clara's. By the time she arrived her anger had hardened into a cold longing for revenge. She'd work something out later.

As she approached the door, she could hear the party already in full swing and was determined to enjoy her night out. Clara's puppy like devotion usually put a smile on her face. Screams of laughter and loud music brayed from the open window, and she could already smell the cigarette smoke, which was belching out of it into the evening air.

"Bibi darling!" squealed Clara, flinging herself against Bibi's cheek, one arm held straight out behind her with a cigarette smouldering in its fingertips. "Darling, you look *absolutely fabulous* as always."

"Yes," agreed Bibi, satisfied to see that Clara hadn't lost any weight. A harmless, cheerful girl, the bulbous Clara today had her bleached curls in a ball on top of her head, accentuating the plump face beneath. She sported multi coloured trousers and a blouse patterned with leopard skin spots. The two items clashed horribly and revealed fascinatingly bulbous buttocks which would not have looked out of place on a small horse. Every fingernail was painted a different colour. Bibi took all this in with a practised eye as she allowed Clara to take her coat.

Tessa and Tina, identical twins with oriental eyes in small pert faces framed by long straight dark hair, were draped at either end of the sofa like a pair of art deco bookends. Both dressed in identical black, they each held a half-smoked cigarette above their heads. Secretly, they had always found Bibi rather intimidating and now adopted their trademark haughty expression to cover it.

The room seemed to be engulfed in cigarette smoke. Clara returned and lowered her massive buttocks to the floor in a yoga-like movement, then stubbed her cigarette out vigorously.

Bibi chose a chintzy armchair to display herself in and studied the twins. It was a while since she'd seen them, she'd forgotten that irritating aloof expression they always put on.

"Hi," Bibi said, "long time no see."

"Hi. Yeah," they both said in unison, dropping their haughty façade at last, and that ended the conversation for the moment.

Bibi accepted the glass of cheap wine offered to her without comment.

"So, come on Bibi, what's new? It's simply ages since we caught up." Clara stopped to take a gulp of wine. "Do tell."

"Oh, this and that, you know, darling," she replied enigmatically, before taking a sip from her own glass. Yuk! It was barely fit for sprinkling over chips.

"How's the gorgeous Charlie?" drawled Tessa, the wordier of the twins, from her end of the sofa.

"Who? Oh him? I left him."

Three mouths dropped open in amazement. Dump the gorgeous Charles? Was she insane?

"Oh wow, Bibi, I mean, oh wow!" Clara reached for a cigarette. She pulled one from the packet and offered them to Bibi. "Go on, darling, I think you need one."

Bibi hadn't smoked since she and Wendell had given up three years previously, but in this moment of weakness she convinced herself one wouldn't hurt. And since everyone else was puffing away…

"Just this once then," she favoured Clara with a smile as she pulled one from the packet and allowed her to hold the lighter for her. The first drag made her light-headed but she enjoyed it, enjoyed the image of herself smoking like some Hollywood film star of the forties.

The evening turned out to be surprisingly good fun. While they ate, the conversation became raucous and entertaining, men in general being the main ingredient. Nevertheless, Bibi was sparing with the alcohol, she wanted to be able to drive back to her mother's so she could try Wendell again before she went to bed.

"Oh, do stay and have another bottle with us!" implored Clara. "The twins are staying over. They've got the spare room but the sofa's quite comfortable."

Bibi nearly laughed. "I must get back, darling," she replied breezily, and without further explanation planted a kiss on Clara's doughy cheek, then the twin's bony ones, and said her goodbyes.

"Fancy dumping that guy," said Tina, as soon as Bibi had gone. "No one in their right mind would dump him. She was too casual about it. He's dumped her I reckon, that's why she's suddenly reappeared."

The others were quietly impressed.

Tina didn't say much but when she did, she was usually right. The fact that in this case she wasn't, was neither here nor there.

Bibi seemed to be exuding cigarette smoke. Her hair and clothing reeked of it and taking one hand from the steering wheel, she covered her mouth and exhaled. "Yuk," she said and coughed, the smell of several cigarettes growing stale.

Guy's jeep, or her mother's, was still outside she noted with annoyance, but the house was dark and quiet. The remnants of an exotic dinner were piled by the sink, filling the place with aromatic scents, but the diners had obviously gone to bed. Good. Now she could call Wendell in peace. Midnight was as good a time as any to catch him. If she woke some stranger up she'd just claim a wrong number and hang up. She gently closed the door and dialled.

Eventually someone picked the phone up but didn't speak. Had she been cut off?

"Hello?"

"Hello. Yes?"

It was unmistakably him, her heartbeat quickened.

"Wendell? It's Bibi."

There was silence.

"Are you still there?"

"Yes."

"How are you?" It was as good a start as any.

"Huh," he snorted. "Well, just fine. How are you?" His voice was heavy with incredulous sarcasm.

"Oh Wendy. Don't be horrible, I've been trying to get you for weeks, you're always out. I know it's late, but I need to talk to you."

"Really? What for?"

"About us."

"Us?" he said in a voice higher than usual. "Us doesn't exist anymore. Your very words if I remember correctly." The space where the tooth had been extracted began to throb slightly.

"No... wait. I just wanted to say this. I've been doing a lot of thinking. I've changed Wendell, I've been through a lot myself that you don't know about, and I realise I treated you very badly. I want to apologise for that, I won't sleep until I've said sorry."

He shook his head and sighed. Why didn't he just hang up?

She continued, "I can see now what an absolute bitch I was. I don't expect you to forgive me, how could you, but perhaps we could at least be on speaking terms. How about it?"

She did seem different, he had to admit. He found himself, cautiously, softening a bit. After a pause he gave a cautious "Ok."

He was thawing, as she had known he would.

"I'm so sorry," she said, managing a small catch in her voice.

"Where are you calling from?"

"My mother's. I've been staying with her."

"Oh? Have you and whatshisname split up then?"

"Who? Oh, you mean Charles. We parted ages ago. I soon realised I'd made a dreadful mistake, but my pride wouldn't allow me to call you. I felt so awful about the whole thing, allowing myself to be taken in by him like that. Then I found out my father's only got six months to live," she shortened the time for effect and gave a small sob. "Sorry Wendell, but it's just been one thing after another," she finished pathetically.

Wendell's kind heart did feel some sympathy for her, and despite himself he found he was imagining her sensuous lips as she was speaking, her long legs. Perhaps he had been wrong about her, people could change.

But he wanted Antonia now, didn't he? Yes. For a moment he felt caught between the two.

"Well, I'm sorry about your father," he said at last.

"What a shame you never met him, you would have liked him I know. I feel so guilty about cutting him out of my life for years, and now we've made up I'm going to lose him. In fact, it's what's made me think back on all the other people I've hurt over the years. I truly am sorry, Wendell."

"Well, if there's anything you need, money or anything."

Genuine tears came to her eyes. Dear Wendell, she had forgotten how kind he was.

"Thank you," she choked. "I'd better let you get some sleep then. I suppose you've been out on the town tonight?"

He laughed and her heart leapt.

"Actually, I'm just recovering from having a tooth pulled."

She laughed in the way he remembered so well, and a pang of nostalgia sprang from somewhere inside, at the same time as he warned himself to be careful.

There followed a few minutes of guarded but friendly chat before both fell silent.

"Suppose I'd better go then," said Wendell a little awkwardly. "I'm glad we've buried the hatchet, it'll make... well, sorting things out easier."

Bibi ignored this comment and said, "Thank you for not hating me." When he didn't reply, she went on, "Wendell?"

"Yes?"

"I don't suppose... oh no, of course not, forget it."

"What?"

"Nothing. I just had a thought, that's all. It was stupid to think it."

"What?"

"Well... I wondered if, well, if you would like to have lunch sometime? Oh, what am I saying? Of course you wouldn't! Forget I said it. Sorry. I'll say goodnight."

"Hang on, don't get worked up," he said quickly.

She had him.

"I don't see any harm in a friendly lunch one day." He was thinking of discussing divorce, something which had been put on a back burner.

"Oh Wendell!" she cried joyfully. "Will you really? I don't know what to say, and after all I've done to you! You're so good to me. How would tomorrow suit?"

Wendell was not only taken aback, but he also suddenly recognised, in a moment of revelation, what she had just done. It was what she always did, twisting people into doing what she had in mind at the very start. He'd seen it a hundred times. What a fool he was.

"No, I'm busy tomorrow, some other time."

"Monday?"

"I still work, and anyway, Monday is our busiest day."

"It'll have to be Tuesday then. I'll meet you at your office, then there will be a time limit."

"Well... I..." What would Antonia think of this? He wouldn't tell her; she didn't need to know.

"Tuesday it is then," cried Bibi while he hesitated, before he could concoct another excuse. "Oh thank you, Wendell, I'm so looking forward to seeing you. You've really cheered me up. One o'clock?"

"Ok," said Wendell, resigned. Might as well get it over with.

There was a click, and she was gone. Wendell sat holding the phone to his ear, listening to the sound of nothing for a moment before carefully replacing it in its cradle. Damn you, Bibi! Why now, just when he was turning things around? He sighed heavily and went back to bed then lay there wondering what had just happened.

He decided to keep an open mind until he'd seen her. Tomorrow he would be taking Antonia out to lunch.

Charles had not left the place all day. Bibi had said she'd be back at the weekend, and he didn't dare risk her finding him not there again. Reluctantly, and against all his instincts, he did the washing up and tidied up. The ruined shirts and trousers went out with the rubbish. He even hoovered but was beaten by the ring of accumulated muck around the bath, which required more than a duster to remove. When he was finished, he was surprised to have gleaned a certain satisfaction from the work.

He tried Elizabeth's number again without success, no reply at all.

"Fuck it!" he shouted furiously. Charles didn't use swear words on a regular basis and hoped no one had heard the uncharacteristic outburst. He threw the phone to the floor in temper. There was an alarming crack and when he retrieved it the earpiece was dangling from its mounting by a couple of puny looking wires.

"Come on you effing thing," he swore again, as he tried with clumsy fingers to put all the bits back together. It fell into two pieces in his hand. He put it to his ear and was greeted with silence.

"Well, that's just abso-fucking-lutely marvellous," he screamed, not caring now if he was overheard. He hurled the phone across the room where it smashed into some stupid glass ornament Bibi had placed there. No phone. No ornament now either. Disaster.

He grabbed his keys and fled to the car, this time leaving a quickly scribbled note.

Driving into town on a Saturday was something to be avoided if at all possible, and he swore continually and with progressively more filth, finding in doing it a certain release of tension. At this rate walking would have been quicker. Twice around the centre, clutching the wheel like a dear friend, he craned forward in the hope of spotting somewhere to park. The air in the car was blue. Eventually, he managed to squeeze into a tiny gap between a mini and a motorbike, leaving it rather poorly parked with a back wheel obstructing the pavement. He sprinted to the phone shop. There seemed to be only one person serving, the same taking great pains to explain the workings of an answer machine to an elderly couple, obviously suffering from advanced dementia. By the time his turn came he was almost ready to explode.

As he dashed back towards the car, a warden was just tearing a ticket from a pad.

"Wait!" shouted Charles. "I'm going."

A lantern-jawed female traffic warden, immune to the good looks of any man, replaced Charles' windscreen wiper and handed him the ticket instead. Charles stared incredulously and made no move to take it from her. She put it under the wiper after all and began to walk away.

"Just a minute," called Charles over the bonnet.

She turned back.

"Would you mind telling me why you've given me this ticket?" He held it up towards her.

"Your car is obstructing the pavement."

"What? Oh, come on, it's only been there for five minutes." He was beginning to lose his temper. "It was an emergency," he added.

The warden consulted her notebook. "Thirty-five."

Charles looked at his watch. Good God, she was right, he'd been ages. Bibi! What if she'd come home? Without a word, he jumped into the car and started it, no time to lose. It jumped forward, just touching the motorbike, which rocked for a moment before crashing onto its side, making a woman with a pushchair leap back.

"Fuck!" he screamed, throwing the gears into reverse. If he could just prop the thing up and get away before the owner of the bike returned.

But it was not Charles' day.

The owner of the bike, watching from the chippy across the road, stormed over wiping bits of batter from his beard as he came. By the time this leather clad monster made it over, Charles was back in his car, having failed to lift the bike from its recumbent position. As he turned to look behind him before moving off, the window was filled with a dreadful face which seemed to have a swastika tattooed on its forehead.

"Open this effin' window, mate, or I'll smash it," he yelled.

Charles didn't doubt it. A small group had begun to gather. The window moved down an inch and the fearsome biker forced it down far enough to grasp Charles by the shirt and partially drag him through it.

"You stupid wanker, look watcher done to my bike," he shouted into Charles' face, sending a particle of masticated chip straight into it. The nasty bushy beard straggled against Charles' face and smelled of engine oil and cooking fat.

"Sorry," croaked Charles.

"Sorry! You will be mate. Watcher gonna do about it?"

"Well," spluttered Charles, "if you would kindly let me go, I'll help you get it upright and we'll see if there's any damage."

The biker loosened his grip and pushed Charles back roughly, reaching in and removing his keys as he did so.

"Hey…" began Charles.

"Just for a moment mate, don't want you doin' a runner."

Charles climbed out warily, smoothing his shirt back down. By the time he reached the bike, it was already upright, the great fists and arms of the man having hauled it from the ground single-handedly. Unbelievably, it seemed remarkably unscathed; thank God for crash bars. The biker took what seemed like forever scrutinising the machine minutely from end to end, occasionally throwing a vicious glance at Charles. The crowd began to thin out, realising there would not be a punch up after all.

"Hello Mr Waterman," shouted a childish voice from the pavement. Charles turned to see two giggling second-years watching. He groaned. Why did they have to see him? This would be all around the school by Monday morning.

"Hello girls," he replied with as much dignity as possible in the situation. They moved off.

At last, the examination completed, the biker strode across to where Charles waited impatiently. He thrust the malodorous beard back into Charles' face and pronounced, "Yer lucky, mate."

Then, holding the car keys between a massive thumb and forefinger, he dropped them over a drain, mounted his bike and roared away.

By some minor miracle, the keys had not slipped completely through and Charles was able, carefully, to retrieve them. He drove off pale with humiliation and headed straight for home to connect the new phone. As he listened with relief to the crisp dialling tone, he poured himself a large scotch and waited.

Bibi finally called him on Sunday morning by which time, almost suicidal, he had convinced himself she had come and gone during his unplanned interlude in town the previous day.

"Bibi! Oh Bibi, my darling, how I've missed you." Tears of relief coursed down his cheeks.

"Hello Charles," she spoke calmly, formally even.

"I'm in a right state, it's been such an awful week. Come home now and let's get back to normal."

Normal! What was normal? She'd been prepared to be kind, but he was irritating her already. If he'd confessed to being out every night, visited old friends, shagged some other woman, she may have felt a vestige of respect for him. But predictably, he must have moped about wondering what he'd done wrong and droning on about his misfortunes to whoever would listen. It sounded like he'd been drinking too.

She interrupted the flow of tearful entreaties and spoke in a calm and firm tone.

"Listen to me Charles. I've done a lot of thinking this week. I don't want to come back, I…"

"What! No! Bibi, why are you doing this? What have I done?"

"Listen, just listen will you!" she snapped. "My father's ill, he's only got a couple of months to live." A year, six months, two months, it was all the same really. "For the first time in my life I'm on good terms with both my parents and I'd like to spend some time with them."

"Your father? Well, hang on, how long are you going to be there?"

"As long as it takes." A lump came to her throat.

"What about me?" he whined. "What about being with me? When will I see you? When will you be back?"

The lump disappeared.

"Didn't you hear me?" she shouted down the phone, losing all control. "I said he's *terminally ill*. He's going to *die*. And you just whine on about me, me, me, me, ME!"

"But why do you have to stay there? You can see him from here, can't you?"

"What? With you making me pander to your every whim, and wear myself out in bed three times a day?"

"No, I didn't mean…"

"That's all you want, isn't it? A female robot, no demands on you, always ready to wash, cook and clean for you, willing to hop into bed day or night while looking like a film star. When was the last time you took me out? You probably can't even remember, can you?"

"We went to Gino's last weekend."

"Oh my God. Charlie, you are so *stupid*! I can't think what I ever saw in you!"

"Don't call me stupid!" Charles hated being called stupid. "You haven't even got an 'O' level."

Bibi laughed cruelly. "You just don't get it do you?"

He didn't.

"Bibi darling," the pleading tone was back. "What will I do here all on my own? This place is too big just for me."

"For Christ' sake! Move then. Or get a lodger or another woman. Your old girlfriend's probably still available. Or that freckly biology teacher you work with, she's obviously in love with you, move her in."

Charles, shocked into silence, especially at the mention of Eve, said nothing in reply.

"Look, I'm sorry Charlie, I didn't mean it to be like this, but you really are terribly thick skinned. The fact is I'm not coming back at all. It's finished. Over."

"But…"

"No, I've made up my mind. I'll come and collect my things sometime."

"No! No! Bibi! Don't do this, please. I love you."

She was silent.

"I know you still love me; you just won't admit it," he said finally.

"Why would I not admit it? The fact is I probably never did love you. I thought I did but I was fooling myself. Once this is all over, you'll probably realise the same thing, we had infatuation not love, different altogether. We should just have had a quick affair, then no one would have got hurt. It's better this way, you'll see that in time."

A quick affair? What on earth was she saying, they'd saved each other from awful situations, hadn't they? "I know you still love me, and you'll come back, I know you will."

Bibi exhaled and tutted with exasperation. Would he ever get the message?

"I don't and I won't. Goodbye Charles."

The line went dead.

"Hello? Bibi?" Charles called her back straight away, but it rang without being picked up. When he tried again it was engaged. He sat back and swilled down the rest of the glass of scotch.

"She'll be back," he said to himself with great confidence.

Chapter Twenty-Two
Sunday

From the slice of bright light visible between the curtains, Antonia could see it looked like it was going to be a nice day. Good, that was an excellent start anyway. Everyone looked better without a huge jacket over everything, while their hair was being blown into a bird's nest. She had slept restlessly after leaving Wendell, unable to prevent going over and over things they'd said. She sprang out of bed and headed straight for the wardrobe. It was early yet, plenty of time to get ready.

She wandered around naked straight from the bath, with a towel wrapped around her hair, and after much deliberation she selected smart blue trousers, a navy blouse speckled with red dots and a colourful sweater, just in case it was cooler out than it looked. She paraded herself before the mirror, twisting this way and that to examine all angles, then threw the whole lot off and put on a skirt and jumper which showed off her figure rather nicely. Now for the hair, which she was going to make sure Wendell saw at its best today. As she lay on the bed, head hanging over the edge while she dried it to give it fullness, she thought again of the previous evening. Had she ever felt like this about Charles? She couldn't even remember. Drudgery had clouded any excitement by the time he disappeared. She didn't think so.

Antonia rolled from the bed and stood up, feeling pleasantly light-headed for a second. A brisk workout with brush and comb sorted out the knots and left her hair a thick and shining cascade of ripples, the colour of horse chestnuts newly out of their prickly pods. She was amazed at how long it had grown. Charles had always said it was her hair that had first made him notice her.

What time had they said? She was jolted back into the present with the thought. Had they even said a time?

Yes, eleven thirty.

Better be ready by eleven, or quarter to, to be on the safe side. She began to feel nervous. Was she overdressed? It was only a pub lunch. She opened the wardrobe once again and rummaged about, pulling things out and putting them back, finally settling on smart black jeans and a different sweater, which showed her shape more. Why on earth did she keep all these clothes? She hardly ever wore any of them. Her bedroom looked like a changing room after a sale. She must go through it all and get rid of some stuff, she didn't need all this, didn't even like half of it.

By the time she had finished fiddling with make-up it was almost eleven thirty. Antonia thought about the let downs of the past week and her stomach lurched. Suppose he didn't turn up? If it got to twelve she would go down and knock.

There was a knock on the door. It made her jump, but she walked calmly to it and opened it to find Wendell there, smiling at her.

"You look beautiful." It was said because it was what Wendell always said, but Antonia wasn't used to being complimented and glowed with pleasure.

"Thank you, how's the tooth? Or should I say gum."

"Fine now, no problem at all," there was a pause, "shall we go then?"

"I'll just get my shoes. Won't be a second." Antonia had left the shoes on purpose. Didn't want him to think she'd been sitting there waiting.

"I'll wait downstairs then."

Wendell absent-mindedly took in the rear view as she retreated. He had stayed in bed until nearly ten thirty, just thinking about Bibi's call. Why had he agreed to meet her? He didn't want to rekindle the past. He had been attracted to her, maybe even loved her once, but that was history, Antonia was the future. He felt differently about her, felt he could trust her, talk to her.

Why had Bibi reappeared right now to complicate everything? Did Antonia even know she was on the loose again, maybe her ex had tried to contact her too?

Antonia flew down the stairs, startling him from his reverie, and landed with a thud at the bottom.

"Sorry," she apologised, "not very ladylike, force of habit."

He laughed at her big eyes looking so serious and forgot all about Bibi.

"I've often wondered what that thump was," he said. "Now I know."

Antonia smiled.

"Right then, lunch awaits," said Wendell, holding open the front door to allow her to pass.

They drove out to a nice country pub that Wendell had often used in his bachelor days. It was, in fact, the same one Charles had eaten at during his exploration of aloneness the previous weekend. Antonia liked it immediately. Wendell installed her at a table in the window, by coincidence the same one Charles had sat at, and went off for drinks and menus. They both opted for a roast dinner, just as Charles had, only this week it was lamb rather than chicken. Antonia studied Wendell's back view, then averted her eyes to the clientele as he made his way back.

A pot-bellied group had commandeered one end of the bar area and the two women who had tried their luck with Charles stood at the other end, attempting in vain to attract the attention of the barmaid. The place was obviously popular, they were lucky to have got a table at all by the look of it.

"I'm starving," declared Wendell, rubbing his hands together as he dropped into the chair opposite Antonia. "I haven't eaten very much this week, what with this tooth and everything else."

"Is it ok now?"

"Yes, fine thanks."

There was a small awkwardness going on, she had noticed it during the drive there and it was making her feel nervous. Had he changed his mind about this, had she got the wrong idea?

How could she know that Wendell was trying to push Bibi to the back of his mind?

How annoying, thought Wendell, all week trying to see Antonia and now they were here the spectre of Bibi was hovering between them on its broomstick. Bloody woman.

Something was waving in front of him. It was Antonia's hand.

"Hello?"

"Oh God, I'm so sorry, what did you say?"

"You seem miles away. Are you sure that tooth is alright?"

"Yes, really."

She shouldn't have asked again, she thought. He would think she was fussing. Everything was going wrong. He was different, uninterested. There was something on his mind, that much was obvious. He was almost cold towards her, quite different from the other night. Her buoyant mood began to wane, perhaps he had had second thoughts about suggesting a proper date. She could almost be angry if she thought about it hard enough.

"Is anything the matter?"

Wendell looked her in the eyes. Perhaps he should tell her?

"No, not at all."

The food arrived, steaming, held by the waitress with a tea towel.

"There we go," she said cheerily. "Mind, them plates is hot."

They ate in relative silence, making the occasional pointless comment about the crispiness of a potato or the tenderness of the lamb, superficial remarks. The barmaid returned for their plates, her cleavage rippling momentarily in Wendell's vision. Antonia noticed a faraway look in his eyes as he stared at it without interest.

They ordered a dessert, apple crumble just as Charles had, and Antonia wondered why men ignored her like this. Charles used to do it too. Wendell was now looking out of the window, chin in his cupped hand as he rested an elbow on the windowsill, his expression glazed. There was a dog sniffing the car tyre.

What the hell was the matter with him? Her desperation to please turned into sudden despondency and she sat back and said nothing. The apple crumble arrived, and she began to eat it.

Wendell peeked at her guiltily. Poor Antonia! It made something in his heart break to see her sitting there with that pudding. She had looked so radiant when they set off, now she was pale and sad. He knew he was ignoring her. Bloody Bibi, what on earth was he going to do? She could even make things difficult when she wasn't around. Why had he agreed to meet her, he thought once more; what a fool! Momentarily distracted by the delicious apple crumble, he missed the dog peeing against the side of his car, which was coincidentally parked in the same slot as Charles' car had been.

Antonia studied him furtively as he struggled with his conscience, and she felt suddenly tired. Why were they here? She felt stupid, all tarted up and coiffured. Thank goodness she hadn't worn that first outfit, she would have felt really overdressed. She almost asked if he was alright again, then stopped herself. She would just wait for him to say something.

With the last spoonful of dessert suspended over his bowl, Wendell looked across at Antonia, the silence properly attracting his attention at last.

"Another drink?"

"Thanks," she managed a tight smile, then looked out of the window, where the black dog was now arched over, thrusting out a turd by the car door.

"Everything alright love?" the barmaid said with a wink as she collected the plates.

"Lovely thanks." Antonia was feeling positively angry now, fed up with being emotionally dragged this way and that like a child between arguing parents. Men! They were all the same. You built up your hopes, then… they were all the same.

She watched the barmaid head straight for Wendell, ignoring the two girls who had been there long before him. He was oblivious, and was now responding to her flirtatious chat, laughing and joking with her. Unlike Antonia, who wasn't enjoying herself at all. She thought of the lovely walk she'd had the previous Sunday when she was feeling so positive, and suddenly longed for the emptiness of it instead of this crowded, smoky pub with someone who was just going through the motions with her. Could that really only have been a week ago? She began to make a mental list of all the times during it that she had been let down by Wendell.

"There we are." Wendell smiled, placing the drinks down on the table gently. "Isn't it nice here? I haven't been here for some time, I used to use it a lot."

Maybe that explained the chattiness of the barmaid.

"Really?" replied Antonia flatly.

It was his turn to regard her. Poor sweet Antonia, she looked fed up. Oh God, and after the way he'd let her down on Friday and all the other things. Quickly, think of something to say.

"Back to work tomorrow?" he continued with a forced smile "Oh, I must give you the money for the dentist."

"Yeah."

Oh God, folded arms, she was pissed off. No wonder, he'd made no attempt at conversation. Just been sitting there with his lip jutting out, preoccupied with his own problems.

"Are you?"

"Sorry?"

"Back at work tomorrow?" Antonia wasn't sure whether she wanted to laugh or cry as she asked him.

"Oh yes. Monday, worst day of the week." Why had he said that?

"At least when it's over the others aren't so bad." Why had she said that?

"Are you alright, Antonia?"

She looked at him and began to laugh without humour.

"What is this?" She paused and looked at him, unfolded her arms and flopped them into her lap, "we're sitting here asking each other if we're alright. I was, but I seem to have been infected by your mood."

It sounded rude, but she didn't really care.

"Sorry Wendell, I didn't mean to be rude, but you don't seem to want to be here." She could feel her face reddening and her eyes filling.

"No, no, I'm sorry," began Wendell desperately. "I've been preoccupied with something. Sorry," he caught her hand, "I'm really sorry, it's me that's being rude."

"Oh?" she took her hand away to sip from her drink, relieved for a moment. "Do you want to talk about it? Can I help?"

Wendell took a long gulp of his drink then sighed heavily, revolving the glass between forefinger and thumb so that it whined against the table.

"Bibi called me last night. My wife, Bibi."

He paused, not looking up.

So that was it.

The atmosphere around them receded, conversation became a distant hum, like bees. Antonia wanted to leave, dejected beyond belief. He was back with his wife, and he had still brought her here, not knowing how to get out of it. Bloody unbelievable! She felt ridiculous and angry and a whole lot of other things and didn't say anything immediately.

"She and Charles, your ex, are no longer together," explained Wendell.

Yes, she knew who Charles was, thank you. Was he suggesting she and Charles could rekindle their relationship too? Surely he couldn't be that insensitive.

"Oh."

"Yeah. She told me all about it. Talked me into lunch." Antonia shook her head in disbelief, and he glanced at her quickly. "Tuesday. It seemed like a good idea at the time, to bury the hatchet, get a few details sorted out, you know."

"Yes, I know." She must get out of here into the air. All her pathetic little dreams were unravelling before her eyes. That bitch! That fucking 'Brenda' had ruined it all—again! Well, if he wanted her back after everything, good luck to him.

"I… I really despise your wife," said Antonia quietly, simmering with fury, "she seems to be a permanent thorn in my side."

"Oh!" Wendell was wide-eyed. Here was Antonia as he'd never imagined, eyes flashing with suppressed anger. She looked strikingly lovely, so animated, like a wild animal cornered in a beam of light. Dangerous but alluring.

She stood up and picked up her bag. "Shall we go, it's getting stuffy in here?"

A foursome nearby began preparing to grab the table before another couple also on the lookout could get in first.

Wendell gulped down the remainder of his drink and hurried after her disappearing figure. She seemed terribly cross; surely she couldn't think he and Bibi were getting back together? Good God.

"Antonia," he called as he managed at last to exit the pub. She stopped by the car but didn't turn to answer him. "I don't want her back!"

She hung her head, noticing she had nearly trodden in a pile of dog poo, and stepped away from it. Tears were welling up; she pinched her arm to distract herself from crying in front of Wendell. Then there were hands on her shoulders. Wendell turned her to face him, then took her hands.

"I stopped wanting anything to do with that harpy pretty soon after she flounced off with your ex. She seems to be a serial cheat I'm afraid, I could never have trusted her again."

Antonia raised her head and a single tear escaped from one eye. Wendell caught it with a finger.

"Sorry," she said quietly. "I just thought…"

Wendell's heart almost broke, he had made Antonia cry. Something glacial inside him melted, releasing a tidal wave of emotion and suddenly he loved her, loved her so completely and hopelessly it hurt beyond belief to see her upset, and to know he had been the cause of it. He put his arms around her and held her tight, nuzzling the soft hair as he'd so longed to.

"I love you. *You*," he whispered.

Silently, she slipped her arms around his waist, and they stood there entwined, while the black dog sauntered over to investigate. Antonia glanced at the dog.

"Wendell?"

"Yes, my darling Antonia?"

"You've trodden in dog shit." The laughter and relief and joy were bubbling out.

"What!" Wendell looked down and discovered his foot was right in the middle of the orangey heap, so that the filthy stuff had risen up and over the sides of his good shoe. "Oh bloody hell."

He released her and went to wipe it on the grass verge in that embarrassed way people do when they've trodden in something nasty.

What was it that was so funny about people doing that? Antonia pinched her arm again, this time to stop herself from laughing at him. It wouldn't have been a good moment just now to start having hysterics.

It was weird and electric in the car. Neither of them spoke. Wendell was wondering why he had said what he had. He'd only known Antonia a few days really, it was just something about her. He didn't regret having said what he had, but she hadn't replied in the way he had expected or hoped, just laughed and told him he had trodden in dog shit.

Bloody dogs, why didn't their owners clear up after them? There was a lingering whiff in the car which made him try to keep his foot off the floor, his leg was beginning to ache with the effort.

Although outwardly still, Antonia was having palpitations every time she thought of Wendell telling her he loved her. Would he have kissed her if she hadn't mentioned the dog poo?

Did she want this? Alone suddenly seemed so safe from hurt even if it was boring. Did she feel the same way about him? She didn't know, couldn't bring herself to examine her own feelings too closely. What was going to happen when they got back? She was both excited and terrified.

Wendell's loins, redundant since Bibi's departure, had decided to make themselves known again. He hoped Antonia wouldn't notice, that would be embarrassing. What was she thinking? Had he just made a monumental idiot of himself? He reached over and stroked her hair.

"You have beautiful hair," he said, just to break the silence.

"Thank you."

"Sorry about that back there; you know, what I said," he said awkwardly, clearing his throat.

"What you said?" Antonia was teasing him now; she knew what he meant but pretended otherwise. "What? About your wife phoning you?"

"Oh that, well, yes, I should explain, shouldn't I?"

"Yes, please do."

Wendell outlined the late night conversation with Bibi, the resulting lunch arrangement and it suddenly dawning on him that he'd been manipulated again by her.

"She is the devil's spawn, that woman. I cannot believe I nearly fell for it," he finished.

They were back chatting happily again.

"And the other thing you said," said Antonia with a seductive glance at him. "Well, what can I say? I have been thinking about you too," she laid a hand on his thigh which did nothing for his increasing passion and, ignoring the shitty shoe, he pushed the car faster so they could get back and be on their own for once.

Antonia pretended not to notice but was filled with an excitement she had definitely never felt with Charles.

"My place or yours?" she grinned, as they arrived back.

Wendell fumbled with his shoes, leaving them both on the doorstep. "Whichever is closest," he laughed.

"Come up to mine," said Antonia, already climbing the stairs with her key at the ready.

Wendell followed her up and she let them in. Once inside there was a small hiatus while she put her keys and bag down and then they were in each other's arms, kissing passionately.

"Oh, Antonia darling," breathed Wendell, "you are so beautiful."

Antonia could not remember ever having felt so happy. Charles had never called her darling and she discovered she liked it. She ran her hands over Wendell's hair and was surprised to find it crisp with hairspray.

"Your hair's all stiff."

"It's not the only thing."

Antonia laughed delightedly.

"Come on, you seductress." Wendell swung her into his arms and kissed her.

"Oh!" gasped Antonia, literally swept off her feet. "In there." She turned her eyes towards the bedroom and they both grinned at each other.

He placed her gently on the bed and kissed her again. Antonia wanted him desperately; she'd never felt like this for Charles either. What on earth was happening to her?

Something black suddenly shot past Wendell and landed itself on the bed between them. Ozzie purred and meowed and rubbed his bony head against Antonia's chin.

Wendell, his hand over his heart, had stopped what he was doing and gone pale.

"Christ Almighty, what was that? It nearly gave me a heart attack."

Antonia fell about laughing at his shocked expression and he joined in. Ozzie came over to sniff at him and he stroked the happy cat. They both made a fuss of him.

"I didn't know you had a cat," said Wendell before kissing her again.

"He's my sister's. She should be collecting him fairly soon."

"Not *right* now."

"I sincerely hope not." Antonia leant over the cat and kissed Wendell back.

"Come on you little devil." She swept Ozzie from the bed, but he bounced straight back up again, and they flopped back laughing.

"I'll feed him, that's what he's after, poor thing."

Wendell used her brief absence to loosen his trousers which had become uncomfortably tight. Antonia closed the door behind her and said softly, "Now we really are alone."

Laughter ceased.

She moved towards the bed kicking off her shoes. She could hardly believe what she was doing, this just wasn't like her at all, but she wanted Wendell so urgently she couldn't seem to stop herself. They were locked together, kissing and removing clothing, it felt like a scene from some cheesy Hollywood romance.

Wendell, finally free of his trousers, undid hers and helped her wriggle from them. Antonia kicked them off the bed with a foot. This was all happening so fast. Wendell pressed himself hard against her and kissed her breast where it showed above her bra, while he fumbled with its catch.

These bloody contraptions were always so difficult to open, he thought. Anyway, what was the rush, make it last. Oh, she was lovely, he could hardly bear it.

Antonia ran her hand up and down Wendell's back. No acne scars there, his skin was delightfully smooth.

Finally! He had the bra open. Antonia had her hands down the back of his pants and was slowly removing them for him.

The phone rang.

They both stopped and laughed.

"Would you believe it?" said Antonia. "I only get one or two phone calls a week."

She frowned. "Hmm, I suppose it may be important, hang on a moment," she grasped the phone.

"Hello?"

They were still locked together, Wendell exploring her neck with the tip of his tongue.

"Toni, thank God! It's Charles."

"Charles? What's happened?" She shot into an upright position, holding her bra to her chest. He sounded absolutely desperate, something terrible must have happened, must have for him to phone her out of the blue like this.

Wendell laid back on the bed, one hand behind his head, the other gently stroking Antonia's back.

"Oh Toni, I made a terrible mistake leaving you, I don't even care about what you did. Bibi's gone, she said she would come back but now she's not. She ripped all my clothes up while I was out, it's been so awful, she is a right bitch."

"Hang on, hang on, when did all this happen? And what do you mean 'what I did'?"

"A week ago!"

Surely Wendell told her they had split up some time ago.

"I realise I should never have left you, darling!" Darling? Charles never called her darling. It sounded wrong, she didn't like it.

Antonia cut him off abruptly.

"Listen Charles, this is not a good time for me. Can we talk another time?"

"What? Didn't you hear what I said? She's gone, just upped and left me."

Antonia half laughed and shook her head. "Yes, I knew that anyway."

"You *knew*? How did you know?" Charles almost sounded indignant.

"Wendell told me." She turned and grinned at him over her shoulder.

"Who's Wendell?"

"The husband your girlfriend, sorry ex-girlfriend, dumped for you. The downstairs neighbour."

Wendell laughed silently, leant across and kissed Antonia's shoulder then lay back with both hands behind his head, savouring the revenge.

"That bastard! Is she back with him then, after all the terrible things he did to her? I knew there was something behind all this. You wouldn't believe the awful things he made her do."

Antonia laughed incredulously. She had only ever seen the woman from afar, but she had begun to know her this week and had concluded she would say anything to get what she wanted.

"Why are you laughing? Who's there with you?"

This was priceless. "None of your business. Now, if that's all I'm busy."

"I'll come over, shall I?"

"I don't think so!"

"But darling, I told you I made a mistake."

Antonia pulled a face. "Do I understand this correctly? You actually think I'm going to welcome you back? Look Charles, I'm sorry for you, I really am. I know what it feels like to be abandoned, it's what you did to me, remember?" She paused. "There's no way you're coming back into my life now, you'll have to learn to stand on your own two feet for once."

Lying there listening to all this, it dawned on Wendell that he'd been lied to by Bibi and fallen for it again. It was not ages ago they had parted; their split was recent. Maybe that story about her father had been made up too, God, she really was a piece of work.

"Anyway Charles, I must go now, call another time when you're more settled."

"Let me come over, we need to talk now."

"No. We don't."

"Oh please, if you only knew what a state I'm in."

Antonia was speechless. The stupidity of him! She was becoming impatient now.

"Actually Charles, I do know what sort of state you're in because I've been there. I was distraught the day after you took off and for a long time after that too, so you'd better get used to it. I'm busy now, I've got to go."

"No! Oh darling, don't be so cruel. I still love you."

Darling again. "Don't keep calling me darling."

"Oh, er, sorry," said Charles awkwardly, realising what he was saying at last. "Just let me come over for half an hour."

"No."

"Just half an hour. I promise. I can be there in fifteen minutes."

"Absolutely not!" she cried in alarm. "I'm going out."

"Can't it wait? Surely our future is more important."

Antonia nearly choked.

Wendell was still lying back, one hand still behind his head, the other extracting fluff from his belly button. He felt a bit cold and pulled the duvet over himself. That lying bitch. Right, he would keep the lunch date, find out the truth, have the satisfaction of catching her out and watch her squirm, he wouldn't fall for it any more. While he was at it, he may as well bring up the subject of divorce. He had been too drunk and depressed before but now it was time to break all ties and move on.

"Charles? Listen!" Antonia was shouting now. "Don't you dare come around here. I don't want to see you, don't ever contact me again. I've moved on, you grow up and do the same."

She slammed the phone down before he could answer and faced the wall angrily. Who the hell did he think he was, demanding to come around? Talking about their *future*, after what he'd done! Who had left who for God's sake? She burst into tears.

Wendell held her to him until she calmed down.

"Bloody bastard!" she said finally. "Fuc… goes off without so much as a goodbye, doesn't contact me for a whole year, then expects to be welcomed back when it's all over. Incredible. He said he didn't even care about what I did, what on earth does that mean?"

She looked around at Wendell. "I'm cold."

Wendell pulled the quilt over them, and they lay together in silence for a moment. She liked it, just lying there, their skin touching.

"I think I might have a guess at what he meant by that," said Wendell.

"Do you?"

"Yes, Bibi might have made up some lie about you, something that would have persuaded him to leave with her. She's very accomplished at it."

Everything suddenly made sense. It had always bothered her that Charles, usually so reserved, innocent even, would just make off with someone else's wife. It had been so completely out of character.

"He said I wouldn't believe the things you'd made her do, the awful things."

"I don't doubt it," he replied, sighing. "Shall we forget about them now?" He smiled.

"Yes," she turned to face him, and they kissed again. Antonia's passion had cooled but she was happy to rekindle it.

The doorbell rang.

"Oh no!" They said in unison, looked at each other without laughing this time.

"Ignore it. Are you expecting anyone?"

"Oh my God! Charles? No, he wouldn't? Surely not. Hang on a minute." Antonia pulled on a tee shirt while the bell rang and rang in the background. She tiptoed through to the lounge and peeked out of the window.

It was Charles, one finger pressing the bell and his face pressed to the glass panel in the front door.

"It's him!" cried Antonia. "He's off his head, what am I going to do?"

"Call the police?" suggested Wendell wearily. He had pulled his shirt back on.

"Oh no, not that. Not yet anyway." She began to pull on her jeans.

There was an odd sound in the lounge which turned out to be gravel being thrown at the window, but at least the bell had temporarily stopped. Ozzie darted behind the sofa in alarm.

"Right," said Wendell, leaping up and dragging himself into the rest of his clothes, "let's get this sorted out."

How masterful he was. And how cruel fate could be.

The bell started ringing again.

"Be careful Wendell, he might think it's you who made Bibi leave him."

"What? That bloody woman! What else has she told him? Is he the type to believe it all?"

"Definitely."

Wendell hurtled down the stairs, muttering obscenities. He unlocked his own door and left it ajar before flinging open the front door furiously.

"What the hell do you think you're doing?" he demanded of Charles, who sprang backwards in alarm. Wendell bent and picked up his shoes.

"Oh, sorry, er, I was ringing upstairs. Er, the bell must be broken or something." Apparently, Charles was no liar.

"The bell's alright, it's you who's the problem. What do you want?"

"Oh. Is she in?" Charles pointed towards Antonia's flat and made as if to come in. "Antonia, I mean, the girl living upstairs."

Wendell blocked his path.

"Unless she's gone profoundly deaf, then no."

"Oh, well it's just... her car is there."

"Maybe she got a lift."

"Any idea where?"

Wendell was incredulous. How had Antonia endured this idiot for so long?

"No." Wendell shut the door, leant against the wall and ran his hands through his hair. His bare feet were cold. He took his shoes into his flat and put some slippers on then glanced through the window to make sure the coast was clear and was annoyed to see Charles still hovering on the step.

Stupidly, Charles tried the bell again. And Wendell tore the door open.

"She's not there," he said with quiet menace. "If you don't go away, I shall call the police and have you forcibly removed."

Charles had spotted the curtain moving upstairs. He knew Antonia was there, but how could he get past this objectionable git? Antonia had indicated they knew one another, why on earth would she be friendly with someone like this? Especially after the things Bibi had told him too.

Charles deliberated while Wendell stood in the doorway with his hands in his pockets.

"She is expecting me, I've just spoken to her," began Charles again. "If I could just go by."

"Maybe she doesn't want to see you."

"Well... I don't think that's any of your business, is it?"

"It is, and she doesn't. Go away now or I will call the police."

Charles could finally see that he wasn't going to get past Wendell and began to shuffle backwards. "Ok, if you see her, can you tell her I'll drop in on her at work."

Wendell laughed and Charles regarded him with a frown.

"I don't suppose Bibi's here, is she?"

Wendell stopped laughing and his jaw fell open in disbelief.

"Bibi? Are you having a laugh?"

"Is she here?" Charles tried to look past Wendell's shoulder and then sideways at the downstairs window.

From upstairs, peeking carefully through the middle of the curtains, Antonia heard a muted slap before Charles flew backwards and overbalanced into the flower bed. She gasped, clamping her hands to her mouth.

The top of Wendell's head appeared and leant over Charles, still prostrate among the remains of the border plants. She couldn't hear exactly what was being said but it was possible to guess by the aggressive stabbing of Wendell's finger towards Charles' face.

"You *dare* to come around here asking for Bibi? I never want to see either of you again, do you hear me? If you're not away from here in the next twenty seconds I'm calling the police. Go on, fuck off, and don't come back!"

Charles scrabbled to his feet and wordlessly headed for the car, flexing his jaw as he went. It had only just stopped hurting from where it had hit that vase at Eve's.

As she watched him retreat, earth and leaves dropping from his trousers, Antonia felt rather sorry for him. Poor Charles, he was so naïve and helpless. It was one of the things that had attracted her to him in the first place. Maybe she should agree to meet him, just once, to draw a line under everything, help him to move on and find out what lies had been told about her.

She watched as he drove off and a few seconds later, heard knocking at the door. Wendell stood there, red-faced from all the exertion, raking a hand through his hair.

"What did he say?" asked Antonia anxiously, plucking at her lip.

Chapter Twenty-Three
Tuesday

Nine thirty Tuesday morning found Bibi already preparing for her lunch date with Wendell. Lying back in a bubbly bath, face pack and cucumber slices in position, she considered recent events and decided to go dressed in sombre, easy to remove (after all, one never knew) clothes. She arranged her hair, longer now than when she'd last seen Wendell, into a straight, sleek style rather than fluffy curls and applied discreet make-up in subdued shades, every inch the sophisticated woman struggling to be brave and cheerful despite the awful problems she was having to face. When she spotted Wendell exiting his office building, she felt a frisson of excitement. She'd forgotten how attractive he was.

Bibi approached slowly giving him a cautious smile, which had been rehearsed earlier. "Hello Wendell, thank you for this. I appreciate it."

An expression flickered for a moment across his face, of what she was unsure. He looked a bit hostile. Well, she would soon sort that out.

"Hello," he replied in a flat voice. "Do you mind the pub? It's the closest place to get a bite. I'm rather busy this afternoon so I must be back by two."

"Oh." A pub? Was he joking? "Oh, well, er of course, that's fine."

Wendell noticed she seemed a bit put out by the suggestion, but he didn't really care. She had probably had some trendy, intimate place in mind. She'd just have to lump it.

They walked in silence for a minute. Bibi had expected Wendell to ask her how she was, but he hadn't said anything.

"So how are you?" he forced out.

Bibi had her speech all ready. "Oh well, you know, bearing up I suppose," she replied sadly, rolling her eyes away and biting her lip.

The play acting was lost on him, he was tired and irritable, preoccupied with the events of the previous few days, particularly Sunday, as he hadn't seen Antonia since.

She had been so quiet, so serious, after he'd sent Charles reeling. They had had a bottle of wine between them, but the earlier mood of excitement was destroyed. In the end, Wendell gave her a peck on the cheek and left. He had knocked on her door yesterday after work, after thinking all day about seeing if she was alright, but she was out all evening.

Avoiding him? Maybe. He hoped not.

He had wanted to call this lunch thing with Bibi off altogether but somehow hadn't got around to it, so here they were.

Wendell held the heavy door open for Bibi before following her in then absent-mindedly let it swing back into the face of a startled man entering behind them.

"Oh dear, I'm terribly sorry," said Wendell as he hauled the door back again. The red-faced man mumbled something as he went past and trod heavily on Wendell's foot in revenge, while saying witheringly, "Oh dear, I'm terribly sorry."

As usual, all heads rotated in Bibi's direction as she glided across to a table, sat down and crossed her legs elegantly, giving Wendell the opportunity to admire them. He had always loved her long legs.

"What would you like?" he enquired, having seen it all before.

"Dry white wine please, darling. You choose some food for me; you know the sort of thing I like," she smiled up at him innocently.

Bibi watched him as he walked to the bar. He'd lost weight, it suited him. She glanced around her. Why on earth had he brought them here, to this spit and sawdust dive? There were plenty of fashionable little places around here they could have gone to. She was a bit put out that he hadn't complimented her on how she looked either, but it was early yet. She'd have him eating out of her hand in half an hour. She glanced around her again, feeling rather out of place. Wendell returned with drinks, wine for her and an orange juice for himself. She regarded it with surprise.

"Orange juice?" she exclaimed. "You have changed," she tried the innocent smile again.

"Yes, there have been changes since you ran off," he stared at her.

Wendell was finding her abhorrent. How had he ever thought her sexy? She was just an up market strumpet, with her tanned legs and flirty glances, so sure of getting her way. What the hell was he doing here? He didn't want to play these games any more, he'd left the playground. She was now pretending to flick a bit of fluff from her short dress, no doubt hoping to attract his attention to the legs again. It would have worked once, but not now.

"What was it you wanted to discuss?" he said bluntly, before taking a sip of his drink so he didn't have to look at her.

Bibi stopped picking at her dress and began stroking it carefully instead. Wendell almost wanted to laugh.

"Only that I'm sorry and perhaps we can be friends. I realise now that life's too short, let's just start again, shall we?"

"Start again? Start what again?" demanded Wendell.

"Calm down Wendy, no need to be so prickly," Bibi replied pleasantly, while privately admitting to herself that this may not be as simple as she had predicted.

"So, when did you say you and whatshisname parted?" asked Wendell casually. He studied her carefully as she replied.

"Charles? Oh, ages ago. I knew straight away I'd made an awful mistake. I'm so sorry, Wendell, for going off like that. He told me lies about you. Said you'd been cheating with his girlfriend. I… I was just so upset."

Her eyes were lowered as she waited for the soft reassurances which would surely follow.

"And so you bloody well should be."

For a moment she forgot the dramatics and looked up, startled and surprised. What had he turned into? How dare he speak to her like that!

"What did you say?"

"I said so you bloody well should be upset," he was looking towards the bar as he spoke, nodding to a colleague standing there.

Silence.

Wendell turned to face Bibi; his manner icy. "I know damn well you've only just broken up."

He had plenty more to say but was interrupted by the arrival of the food. Bibi was thankful for it; it would give her a chance to think about this unexpected turn of events. Under the make-up her face was white with fury at being caught out.

Wendell had ordered her a steak and kidney pie, chips and two veg. She looked at the steaming mountain of stodge with confusion and disgust and for a fleeting moment he almost pitied her.

But saying nothing, she nibbled daintily at a chip while Wendell shovelled his own down quickly, wiped his mouth and finished off the orange juice. Halfway through he glanced up to see her studying him with a blank expression. Half the chip was still in her hand.

"Not hungry?" he enquired. She didn't answer and he continued, "Why lie to me? That moron was at the flat on Sunday asking for you."

"What!" Her eyebrows shot up. She dropped the chip.

"Yes, unbelievable, isn't it? So I know you've only just left him, though after speaking with him for ten seconds I could well see why."

"You've changed," she said, still staring.

"Of course I've changed! Who wouldn't have after what I went through? Listen Bibi, I don't know what you hoped to achieve from this meeting, but I think it's better if we just call it a day," he was worn out with it now.

Bibi was furious, all pretence gone. "What else did Charles say?" she demanded.

"Nothing much. I got the impression you'd told him some fibs too. He was looking for Antonia at first, as a matter of fact."

"Who?"

"Antonia, that nice girl he left for you."

The way he said 'Antonia' and 'nice girl' had not gone unnoticed by Bibi. "So what happened then?" she said furiously.

"He asked if you were there, so I thumped him."

They stared angrily at one another for a moment before Bibi began to laugh uncontrollably. Wendell, surprised, couldn't help smiling and suddenly they were both laughing. When it finally ceased Bibi dabbed at her eyes.

"Oh dear," she said, still smiling. "Sorry about that, but it must have been so funny. Charles really is a complete idiot."

"Now we are in agreement."

Seeing Wendell relaxing at last, Bibi plunged in while the going was good, "Wendy, I know you must hate me..." She paused, waiting for him to respond but nothing happened so she hurried on, "Wendy, look, I would really like it if we could be friends. I want to make it up to you." She recrossed her legs for his benefit. Couldn't help herself.

Did she really think he would fall for that again? "You lied to me."

"I know, it was stupid. But we'd been in separate rooms for months, it felt as though it had been finished for a long time. You know, I've thought a lot about how awful I've been for ages, I wanted to contact you but somehow couldn't. I just knew I had to try and sort it all out," she glanced up quickly then fiddled with her wedding ring, replaced specially for the occasion, and spoke softly over the now congealing pie and chips. "After all, we are still married," she blinked her eyes up at him appealingly.

Wendell shook his head. "I could never trust you again, never," he said decisively. "In fact, was all that stuff the truth? Look, I don't mind being on friendly terms, that's fine, but that's all. It will make the divorce easier when the time comes."

"Divorce!" Bibi exclaimed, alarmed. Strangely, it had never occurred to her. Perhaps subconsciously she had always known she would want to go back to Wendell when the fling with Charles had run its course.

"I want a divorce; I might want to marry again." Wendell crossed his arms.

Bibi's eyes narrowed. So that was it. Another woman on the scene. Some brassy bird had her talons into him. How shallow men were. Well, whoever she was, she could be dealt with. The thought of him wanting someone more than her made her even more determined to get him back.

"I really think we should at least give it a try Wendell," her eyes pleaded with him, glistening with crocodile tears. Wendell looked away awkwardly.

"Face it Bibi, it's over. Be practical. It's pointless remaining hitched to one another."

"Not if we patch things up, we've both had this time to grow. We're different people now." A strange emotion had overwhelmed her. Rejection. It had never happened to her before. As Wendell drew away, her desperation grew. This was new to her. Resorting to what she knew, drama, she dabbed her eyes again.

"Sorry," she mumbled pathetically.

"You'll never change," said Wendell, unmoved.

"You're… you're heartless."

Wendell blew out a breath. "You're a fine one to talk!"

One or two heads turned in their direction but neither noticed it. Popping a final rather withered chip into his mouth, Wendell stood up.

"I've got to get back to the office."

Bibi rose silently, her meal, bar half a chip, untouched.

"Didn't you like it?" enquired Wendell with mock concern.

"You bastard."

"That's more like the Bibi I remember," smiled Wendell. "Let's just agree to be friends then, shall we?"

There was no reply. When he glanced sideways at her, Bibi's lips were set in a tight line and two angry red spots had managed to melt through the foundation and were now decorating her prominent cheekbones.

He had to admit she was beautiful when she was angry.

"Suit yourself." Wendell rammed his fists into his trouser pockets and carried on walking towards the door in silence. Bibi followed him, head held high.

"Bye Wendell," she mumbled as they reached her car. Her eyes were still glistening. Genuine tears? Hard to tell.

"Bye darling," he replied and gave her a peck on the cheek. "By the way, I forgot to say you look fabulous." She looked slightly less furious. "Friends?"

She lowered her eyes again. "Why can't you believe me when I say I've changed?"

"It would never work," he said quietly.

"How do you know?"

"I just do. I could never trust you," he was tempted to tell her he'd met somebody but decided it was wiser not to.

"Let's have an evening out and see how we get on," she smiled, innocent and animated like a little girl.

Wendell wasn't fooled this time.

"Oh no."

"Oh why not? It would be fun, like old times! Afraid you might still feel something for me?"

"No."

"Oh Wendy," she implored him. "One evening! What have you got to lose?"

Everything.

"No. I must go now. Bye," he turned and was gone. Anyone would think it was he who'd left her!

"I'll ring you," she called quickly, watching as he navigated the traffic, willing him to turn. When he did not, a cold fury seized her again. How dare he treat her like this! She'd made a complete fool of herself, almost pleading with him. The humiliation! As soon as she had driven far enough away from his office for anyone to know her, she let rip.

"Bastard!" she screamed into the windscreen. "The fucking bastard!"

She decided then and there to make his life hell. No one treated her like that and got away with it! That disgusting meal in that common pub, the offhand manner. By God, if he had another woman, she'd certainly sort her out, then she would make him beg to be with her before she cast him off again. And she would have the best laugh she had ever had while she slipped the dagger in.

Wendell was slightly disturbed for the rest of the afternoon. Antonia obviously still felt something for that idiot, which was a bit worrying. It appeared that good looks overrode everything. He was uncharacteristically jealous.

He also felt a little guilty about Bibi. Perhaps she really had changed? He hadn't enquired after her father either, that was a bit remiss. His thoughts bounced back and forth like a table tennis rally. Perhaps he should meet Bibi just once more? No, not a good idea.

He was very keen to speak with Antonia before she thought about making it up with that idiot ex of hers.

He happily agreed to a drink with a colleague after work, just the thing to clear his mind of women. It was much later, as they were tucking into a chicken vindaloo at a handy Indian restaurant, that he found Antonia popping back into his mind.

"Won't be a minute," he told his friend, as he wiped his lips with a napkin as thick as roofing felt. "Just remembered I've got a phone call to make."

"Bit late, isn't it?"

Wendell looked at the wall clock, a large beaten gold plastic square with Indian dancers embossed all over it. Eleven pm. Good God. Oh well, give it a go.

Antonia was already in bed, nearly asleep when the phone rang, sending Ozzie plummeting from the bed and waking her in alarm. Her hand reached automatically for it then stopped. What if it was Charles again? It stopped abruptly as Wendell changed his mind, and she eventually went back to sleep.

Back to Monday

What a peculiar weekend. After Wendell had punched Charles, they had talked in hushed tones over a couple of glasses of wine before Wendell left. All the earlier passion had left them both and it had felt more like the aftermath of a funeral. It had seemed unbelievable, when she considered it, that only an hour or two earlier they had been almost naked and locked in each other's arms in her bed! What would have happened had Charles not called? Neither of them had mentioned using anything but she was no longer taking the pill, so perhaps it was a good thing they hadn't gone any further. She hadn't even thought about it. Would she have done it anyway if she had thought about it? Normally never, but she had been so carried away that she wondered whether, yes, she might have taken the risk. Should she go back on the pill, just in case? Ridiculous, no, just take things slower. If there were going to be any more 'things' that was. Wendell had said he loved her. Did he mean it? Or was he one of those types who would say anything to get their leg over? The trouble was they didn't really know one another.

No, she decided, they must get to know one another better before being so stupid again.

It was hard to stop thinking about him though, and she got a rotten nights' sleep because of it. Well, she would see him later and find out what was what. This resolved, she got up and fed Ozzie then went to work. She went to see her mother after work, having changed her mind about speaking to Wendell. Let things cool a bit first, give her a chance to think straight. Wait until he'd had his lunch with the wife.

Tuesday

Tuesday was here, she would find out what happened later come what may.

Nine fifteen came and went, this was late even for Rob Murphy, and a lot of tutting and looking at watches was going on in the waiting room. Every time the door opened, and all heads turned towards it her stomach fizzed, in case Charles came barging in declaring undying love. She'd have to take a pain killer soon, it was giving her a stomach ache. Presumably he would now be at work, which made her feel calmer. How draining all this was. Perhaps being a lonely spinster indulging in unrequited love, like Susan, was the better option after all. Maybe she should speak to Charles, get the true story out of him and make it clear she didn't want him back. If he did call again, she decided, she would.

She yawned, just as the nine thirty arrived, a nice old man who had parted company with his false teeth during a particularly rough Channel crossing. The teeth had presumably drifted to the sea bed along with his dinner, seriously affecting the rest of his short break, not to mention his pride. Today he was having his new set fitted and was feeling jolly.

"Late night, eh?" he addressed Antonia gummily.

"Sorry."

"Is he here yet?"

"Not yet, any minute though."

"Ah, I don't know, these dentists. Probably getting in an early round of golf," he guffawed, enjoying his own joke, then wandered off to squeeze in between a large tense lady and a spotty youth in his early twenties who was examining the inside of an ear with his little finger.

By nine forty, another patient was seated and the first had left in a temper, saying she could wait no longer and would rebook. Antonia didn't blame her, this was ridiculous. Come on Rob, where are you? It was beginning to feel like more than just normal lateness.

Mr Parker, the patient collecting his false teeth, stood up and looked out of the window for a few seconds, before addressing Antonia.

"Is he always this late?" The earlier cheerfulness had given way to concern.

The phone rang.

"Well, no. Something must have delayed him. He hasn't called, unless this is him. I'm very sorry, everybody, for this delay," she addressed this last remark to the room generally.

It wasn't him. Come on Rob, you moron.

"Alright love, not to worry, I'm not in any hurry." Mr Parker returned to his seat and began talking to the spotty youth. Another patient decided to rebook. The phone rang again.

"Good morning, Dental Surgery."

"Hello dear," came a lilting Irish accent, "this is Mrs Murphy speaking."

"Hello Mrs Murphy, how are you?"

So, the coward was getting the wife to call in sick for him. How typical! Hearing the name Murphy, the waiting patients were suddenly eavesdropping.

"I've been trying to call; the line has been engaged. I'm afraid I have some bad news. My husband had a heart attack in the night and died in the early hours. I've recently come back from the hospital."

"Oh my God!" Antonia's hand flew to her chest. She felt as though all the breath had been knocked out of her. "Oh, I'm so sorry." She didn't know what to say, but Mrs Murphy continued, brisk and businesslike. Must be the shock, thought Antonia.

"I'm sure you and Susan will know what needs to be done there, cancellations, notices and so on. Come in as usual tomorrow if you would, and I'll be in to see you in the morning sometime."

"I'm so sorry," repeated Antonia, in shock herself.

"Thank you dear, bye for now," and with that she was gone.

Antonia looked up, eyes wide, and regarded the room. She was pallid and sort of numb. Her hands were trembling. She didn't know what to do. For once she wished Susan had been here.

Something about the manner of the phone call had relayed a disaster into the room, and Mr Parker, who seemed to have become the patients' spokesman, loomed over her expectantly.

After she had concluded her small speech there was a moment of quiet before everyone began talking and gasping. A woman with a small child perched on her hip entered. Antonia went over and enlightened her, glad of the distraction.

"Oh, my goodness," twittered one red-faced woman. "Poor Mr Murphy, he was such a lovely man."

"Yes, he was. And so young."

The newcomer left hurriedly, inconvenienced only by the waste of her time, having never been to this surgery before and Antonia found herself standing there wondering what to do again. Why didn't these people *go*? Ten minutes ago they were all complaining about being in a hurry. She returned to the reception area where Mr Parker stood rigid by its window, torn between sympathy for the dead man and despair that it couldn't have happened after he'd collected his new teeth.

"My teeth," he whispered.

Free of Rob's disapproval, and of Susan who was still in Cornwall, Antonia ushered Mr Parker into the surgery.

"Can you fit them?" he asked hopefully.

"No, I'm sorry," his face fell, "but it seems ridiculous for you not to have them," his face brightened again, "try them, and if they don't feel right, drop in down the road and they will be able to ease them for you."

Mr Parker slotted the proffered teeth into his mouth and clacked them together a few times.

"How are they?"

"Fine, I think. I've forgotten how to speak properly," he laughed, embarrassed by the slight lisp.

"Don't worry, you'll soon sort that out."

Mr Parker paid up and turned to leave, then remembering what had happened added, "Sorry about, you know, old Murphy. Thanks dear," he winked at Antonia and left, whistling through the new set with building confidence.

Two women still sitting there had run the length of sympathetic cliches and were awaiting further instructions.

"Ooh," fluted one, a stout specimen in tweeds. "Who would have thought it, a strong young man like Mr Murphy, it just goes to show."

"What about our treatment? Can you do it?" interrupted the other, having seen Mr Parker dealt with.

"No, I'm afraid not. I shall have to call Buck and Partners down the road here," she waved a hand in the general direction, "and see if they can help us out temporarily, until we know what's happening."

"Mr Buck!" announced the stout woman. "I won't go to him," she pursed her lips.

"It's entirely your choice, perhaps a friend can recommend someone."

"Oh," she sounded deflated.

It took forever to persuade the two ladies out of the door, during which time several more people had come and gone. If she heard Rob Murphy referred to as a 'lovely man' one more time, Antonia thought, she would scream. By lunch time her head was pounding. She had spent the previous two hours attempting, with partial success, to cancel the afternoon appointments. It had seemed prudent to explain why, especially when people started to get cross, but then they wanted to know all the details, and everything was taking so long that she just began with 'due to circumstances beyond our control'.

She wanted to go out, get some air, but she could hardly leave the place unattended, so she took two headache tablets and waited it out.

When she got home later that evening, she was relieved to see Wendell's half of the place still in darkness, she couldn't deal with anything else today. There was a postcard addressed to herself and Ozzie, which she read as he ate his coley and tinned cat food, and she forced down a cheese sandwich. It said that he was being missed terribly and that they couldn't wait to see him. There were little paw prints and kisses after this message and a tiny afterthought, 'Hi Toni', squeezed into the bottom left-hand corner in Tom's writing. Nice to be considered, she thought wryly. What was it about her?

As soon as the sandwich was finished, she drove over to her mother's.

Any long buried sweetness Bibi had possessed after spending time with her parents had evaporated. Simmering with bile and venom against Wendell, woe betide anyone who crossed her now. She slammed the door of the car behind her and the sight of the red jeep in the driveway only served to enrage her, if it was possible, even further. She banged the front door hard behind her and waited to see what effect it might have. Her mother's coiffured head appeared around the lounge door a moment later, looking startled.

"Oh, it's you. You made me jump."

Bibi said nothing, just marched through and turned on the television, ignoring both her mother and Guy, who was seated on the sofa in leather trousers and a skin tight shirt, with his legs apart and a muscular arm stretched along the back of it.

Elizabeth reseated herself next to Guy and the two regarded Bibi curiously. Her mother had seen this mood before and knew better than to enquire anything of her daughter. Guy, on the other hand, was considering how to use the situation to his advantage.

"Hi Bibi," he called to her and waggled his fingers in a small wave. Elizabeth rested a hand on his thigh.

Bibi did not respond and for a minute no one did anything.

"Right." Elizabeth stood up, crossed the room and turned the television off. She looked at Bibi.

"Guy was speaking to you," she said coldly and their eyes locked.

How alike they are, thought Guy as he sprawled on the sofa to enjoy the show.

"I was watching that."

"Guy said hello to you."

"So?"

"So you reply to him politely or you can leave now."

Bibi's lips tightened into a grim line. She turned slowly. "Hello Guy," she sneered, dragging the name out.

"Now you listen to me," said Elizabeth firmly. "I don't know what's put you into this foul mood, but you're not taking it out on us. This is my house; Guy is my guest and I expect you to be civil."

"Your *guest*? That's a good word for it. It's disgusting."

In a swift movement, Elizabeth crossed to Bibi and slapped her face hard, then stepped swiftly back to avoid retaliation. Bibi looked murderous, her hand against her cheek. Her mouth hung open in disbelief. She closed it slowly.

"Don't you *dare* speak to me like that!" Elizabeth said, cheeks flaming. "Guy is my invited guest, *you* are not. If you cannot behave like an adult, I suggest you leave right now."

"Chuck me out on the street then, you don't care. You never have. You only care about yourself and that... that... Gold-digger."

"Get out!" screamed Elizabeth, a manicured hand rattling with gold bangles pointing the way.

Bibi, a little daunted by her mother's temper, lowered her voice but could not stop herself hurling a final spiteful comment.

"Maybe I could borrow your jeep? Until I get another roof over my head, I'll need something to sleep in."

"What are you talking about?" Elizabeth was confused.

"That marvellous jeep you bought for *him*," she stabbed a finger in Guy's direction, who was by now keeping a low profile.

There was a pregnant pause. Elizabeth spoke first and with more control.

"What I choose to do with my money is my business."

"You think more of him than me then?" Bibi stood up and they stood there, face to face.

"And I wonder why that might be?" Elizabeth's hands were on her hips.

Before she did something she would really regret, Bibi turned and headed for the door. Fifteen minutes later, bag packed, she slammed the door again and drove away without saying goodbye.

"Damn," said Elizabeth under her breath, as she watched from the window.

"And you can wipe that smile off your face," she said, noticing as she turned, the amused grin on Guy's face. "What were you thinking telling her about the jeep?"

Guy caught her hand and pulled her to him. "You're beautiful when you're angry," he whispered.

Bibi's wheels squealed against the tarmac as she sped away. At this rate she'd soon need new tyres. Tears of anger and frustration welled up in her eyes. She was careful not to let them spill, this make-up had taken ages to apply this morning. Instead, she resorted to abusing the windscreen again.

"Fucking bastards. All men are fucking bastards!" She banged the steering wheel with a flat hand. "Fuck, fuck, fuck!"

She drove without direction, finally coming to rest in a deserted car park. It had begun to rain, and she sat still, watching the tiny beads run down the window like the tears she would have loved to shed. The tinny pattering on the roof seemed to have a calming effect, either that or she had finally run out of steam. She reflected solemnly on the events of the last couple of weeks.

What on earth had happened? Here she was all but homeless, no one to take care of her. She'd made friends with her mother and now blown it in the space of ten minutes. It was all that bloody toy boy's fault. Yes, he started it by saying hi to her, he knew what he was doing. Maybe she should just go back and patch things up with Charles, at least he wanted her without demands. But she didn't want him. She wanted Wendell now that she couldn't have him. Bloody Wendell! How dare he take her to a pub and order steak and kidney pie for her, the nerve of it!

"Bloody men," she said aloud, her voice sounding harsh in the confined space. And now the damn car was all steamed up. She cleared an area and looked out. There was a wide expanse of green to her right and she had a sudden urge to walk out on it and let the rain drench her. So she got out and did just that, letting it soak her thoroughly, not even caring about her ruined make-up. In the middle of the field, she stopped and screamed until her throat felt sore, then squelched back to the car, cold and bedraggled. She was lonely and wretched. Where could she go? She started the car and let the heater warm her while she thought about it.

Chapter Twenty-Four
Wednesday

Antonia's day had mostly been spent between trying to process the death of Rob Murphy, its possible repercussions for her, and trying to push Wendell from interrupting those thoughts. Having not seen him since the evening of the bedroom farce, before that horrible business with Charles, she was worrying again.

Was it all over before anything had even begun? She should have faced him on Monday evening. Every time she thought of them rolling around on her bed, she closed her eyes with shame and considered she had had a lucky escape. She wouldn't be taking risks like that again! But she still yearned for Wendell and wanted things to continue.

Mid-morning, Mrs Murphy had appeared, dressed all in black and barely concealing the joy she felt.

"I'm so sorry about Mr Murphy," Antonia had said again, in the absence of anything else to say.

"Oh yes, thank you," smiled Mrs Murphy, regarding her with the piercing blue eyes of a red-headed Irish woman. "Now then, what's been happening here?"

Antonia updated her.

"Right, let's see," the petite Mrs Murphy said to herself as she shuffled around in the reception area. She took a lot of paperwork out of a drawer and shoved it into a carrier bag to take away with her. She appeared to be very capable, more so than Rob had been.

"Not very organised, was he?" she remarked as she worked and Antonia smiled awkwardly.

"Can I get you a coffee, Mrs Murphy?"

"No thank you dear, I'm in a bit of a rush, there's a lot to do. When does Susan get back by the way?"

"Next Monday."

"Grand," she had got what she needed and now stood clutching the bag to her chest. "Can you come in for the rest of this week? I'm sorry it will probably be rather boring, but I'll be in and out sorting things and you can keep the patients informed, if you would. Once I've been through this paperwork and other stuff, I'll sort out your wages. Are you alright for the moment?" She fixed the blue eyes on Antonia's own.

"Yes, for the moment. Is there anything you specifically want done while I'm here? I mean, can I help with anything?"

Mrs Murphy looked around her. "Chuck out all this rubbish," she indicated the pile of golf magazines with a dismissive wave. "He's in the local obituaries this week. Perhaps you could do an answerphone message and make a notice for the door? I'm sure you know the sort of thing; you seem to be an efficient girl," she smiled at Antonia radiantly.

"Yes of course." Antonia, never one of Rob Murphy's fans herself, was nevertheless rather taken aback at Mrs Murphy's obvious pleasure in her husband's demise.

"Well then, that's it for the moment," she put a hand on the door handle then turned back. "You have my number in case of difficulties?"

"Yes."

"Right dear, bye for now," she turned to leave, then turned back again. "Oh wait now, give me your home number, would you?"

Antonia wrote it hurriedly on the back of an appointment card, gave it to Mrs Murphy and listened to her clatter away down the stairs.

"Hmm," said Antonia to herself as she viewed Mrs Murphy just about skipping down the street, "not much grief there."

She made herself a coffee and gladly ditched all the magazines into the bin, then got started on the answerphone and notice for the door.

When she got home, Antonia knocked timidly on Wendell's door then stood there disappointed. Now where was he? Perhaps he was avoiding her? She dragged herself upstairs and was happy to be greeted enthusiastically by Ozzie.

"At least you love me," she said to the cat, sighing, then added, "but only because I feed you."

Back to Tuesday, late Afternoon

While Bibi, soaked and sulking, was heading in the direction of her father's house, the man himself was busy entertaining friends from the chess circle. He didn't do this sort of thing much these days for obvious reasons but having a 'good' day he had suggested they all come to him and was, in fact, rather enjoying himself. It was some time since he had played chess with his old friends, and it seemed something like old times. He'd had someone from the local bakery drop off some cakes and was determined to forget illness for the afternoon. He might pay for it later, but it might be the last time he could manage it, having lied about how long he'd got left, so he was going to push out the boat a bit.

"Can I help with anything?" wavered a female voice, loaded with hope that she could not.

"Everything's under control thank you Sylvia, Kate's been helping me," said Bibi's father, as he came in with a tray of fine china tea things and fancy cakes.

Kate, a large bosomy cheerful type, was bustling around the kitchen in a manner suggesting she thought it wrong for a man to know what he was doing in there. Her husband, Ivor, understood this and was more than happy to leave her to it. After refreshment and some catching up, they would get out the boards and sit down to a nice afternoon of quiet gaming.

"I say!" exclaimed Ivor as he examined the array of delicious cakes displayed in front of him. He was by nature a jolly chap, which had accelerated his recovery from a stroke the previous year. Apart from using a stick, the only souvenirs of this event were a faint whistle as he bent over and a tendency for his right eye to twitch.

The final member of their foursome was the twittery Sylvia, always ready to offer help but never willing to give it. She had been the local lollipop lady since her own children were at school twenty-five years previously. Everyone knew Mrs Sylvia Fish, small and chunky with soft steel grey curls that tended to behave chaotically in a breeze. Sylvia's digestion played havoc with her these days, and she did all she could to help the problem by taking antacid tablets at every meal and sometimes in between, leaving a semi-permanent white tide mark around her lips. She popped one into her mouth now before carefully selecting a cream éclair to enjoy with her cup of tea.

"You have done us proud, Bill," said Sylvia as she bit happily into the éclair. A blob of cream surged out unnoticed and dropped onto her chest.

Kate chose a delicate pastry and Ivor perched a farmhouse slice on the edge of his saucer.

"Not partaking, Bill?" enquired Ivor as he chomped into the slice.

"In a moment, let the tea grease the passage first."

They all knew the situation, of course, so no one would castigate him should he choose to abstain.

"Saw a funny thing in town last week," began Ivor jovially. "Young chap knocked a motorbike over with his car." There were polite murmurs of 'oh dear' and 'really?' at this, before Ivor pressed on, "Yes, poor chap. A great thug appeared, one of those hells angels, you know." They all nodded, still chewing and sipping. "Great big lump, must have been about six foot five, in height and circumference. For a moment I thought there might be fisticuffs. Right yob he was, the hell's angel. The other looked like a pansy. In the end it was just a bit of pushing and shoving. Haven't got it in them these days." He leant forward as he said this, emitting a protracted whistle.

"No one seems the same anymore," put in Kate sadly as she brushed crumbs from her skirt, then launched into a fit of coughing. Sylvia patted her on the back, but Kate held a hand up and shook her head.

"Yes, I really don't know what this world is coming to," continued Ivor, when the coughing had subsided. "When I was their age, I was in the army. That would sort them out." He jutted his jaw out proudly and the others nodded their agreement.

Sylvia had dispatched the éclair and was now drowning it with tea. Bill leant over with a grunt and offered her the plate again.

"Oh Bill," she twittered. "I really shouldn't."

"Oh, come along Sylvia, you only live once," the other two glanced awkwardly at him but Sylvia didn't seem to have noticed.

"Oh well, you only live once," she echoed, and this time picked an overfilled cream meringue carefully off the stack. The thought of it made her stomach gurgle like an air lock in a pipe, clearly audible above the conversation, which had moved on to the demise of an acquaintance of theirs who had recently been sent to a care home by her son. No one paid any attention to it; they were well used to Sylvia's plumbing.

"Dreadful place it is," exclaimed Kate with feeling, "they get you in there, treat you like a deaf old fool, and you must put up with it from young bits of things whether you like it or not. You have no say at all."

"Mind you, she had completely lost her marbles. Told me the Pope got into bed with her every night the last time I saw her," put in Sylvia.

"That's no reason to suffer indignities," said Kate, coughing again. "It's the Doctors I blame. They get you in those places and use you as guinea-pigs. I've seen it happen so many times."

Ivor's chest whistled into the ensuing pause as he put his cup down, accompanied by a drum roll from Sylvia's overloaded digestive system. The doorbell rang unexpectedly to complete the symphony and as Bill hoisted himself out of his chair to answer it, he released a musical fart as an encore.

Rapid babbling erupted to cover the embarrassment.

"I say, are we expecting anyone else?"

"Perhaps Arthur and Christina have made it after all."

"Hope they've brought a board with them."

A young female voice drifted in from the hallway and they all fell silent, poised to listen in. Sylvia's lips were pursed at the edge of her cup for several seconds in case she missed anything.

"Bibi!" exclaimed her father in surprise. "What on earth's happened? You're soaking wet."

"Oh Dad," she moaned. "I've had such an awful day." Before she could elaborate a long whistle followed by the chink of china reached her ear.

"Who's that?"

"I've got some company love, just the chess group." Oh dear, this was awkward. Bill wasn't feeling too good suddenly, with all this going on and the mental activity it had conjured up. He wasn't used to it any more.

"Oh," her face darkened. Visitors. Could this day get any worse? Some bunch of old fossils playing chess of all things! When did he ever have visitors? Why was everything always against her!

"I'll go then," she said pitifully, not meaning it for a second. She had nowhere else to go after all.

"No, no. Come in and get dried off and I'll cut this short, I'm feeling tired anyway. And he was. What had begun as one of his good days was now turning into a bad one. He had over exerted himself in both mind and body."

"Sure?"

"Yes love, go upstairs and I'll dispatch this lot," he patted her affectionately on the behind as she started up the stairs leaving a trail of wet footprints behind her on the lino.

Bibi's father returned to the lounge to find three faces turned towards him in expectation.

"My daughter's turned up."

"Daughter?" They all responded together.

"I didn't know you had a daughter!" exclaimed Ivor, craning his head towards the door. "Where is she?"

"Will we meet her?" enquired Kate eagerly.

"Well, she's having some trouble at the moment," started Bill cautiously, knowing how nosy people could be.

"Married?"

"Yes, but..."

"Children?"

"No."

"How old is she?" said Sylvia, trying to recall if she had ever guided her across the road in the past.

"Oh, now let me see."

"Fancy you having a daughter!" whistled Ivor, chortling. "You're a dark horse, Bill Baker. Where is she then?" he repeated.

Sylvia's stomach chose to erupt with volcanic ferocity at this moment, promoting many apologies from her. It served as a pause in the interrogation, during which Kate noticed that Bill had gone rather grey.

"Perhaps we should leave the chess until another time," she suggested, staring hard at Ivor.

"What? Oh yes, yes, maybe another time would be better."

"Yes of course," fluttered Sylvia, rocking herself into a standing position.

They all seemed to take a long time leaving, not least as Kate insisted on taking everything out into the kitchen and washing it all up. Each of them lingered, hoping for a glimpse of the mysterious daughter. When Bill returned alone to the lounge, he was thoroughly exhausted and in some discomfort, and forgetting all about Bibi sank gratefully into a chair and fell fast asleep.

Bibi heard them finally leave as she lay in the bath. Thank God for that, she thought impatiently. By the time she had messed about with her hair and make-up it was past six and her father had been slumbering for a good hour. Feeling somewhat revived, she trotted down the stairs and put the kettle on.

"Dad?" She shook his shoulder, and he opened his eyes with effort. Then looked at his daughter, struggling to remember where he'd seen her before.

"Bibi?"

"Tea? I've just put the kettle on."

"Oh dear, must have nodded off. Yes, Lizzie love, thanks, I'd love a cup."

Lizzie? Bloody hell, he thinks I'm my mother, thought Bibi, then put it down to him having just woken up.

She was feeling much better, having made up her mind to stay here with her dad for a few days and let them all wonder where she was. That should give them something to worry about.

She brought in the tea and flopped down into a chair. Taking a careful gulp of hers, she sat back and sighed. "Aah, I needed that."

Her father had nodded off again, tea leaning perilously on the arm of his chair.

"Dad! Your tea," said Bibi, nudging his foot with her own.

"Oh, sorry love."

"Are you alright?" she asked, finally noticing how drained he seemed to be. This wasn't what she had expected, she wanted him to listen to the story of her awful day and sooth her with devoted murmurings.

"Yes love, just had a busier day than usual."

She relaxed and announced what a hell of a day she'd had, preparatory to unburdening herself.

"I thought about everything you said, and I decided you were right, that I should try to save my marriage. I met Wendell for lunch, but he was so... hostile, it was horrible. He—"

"Wendell? What kind of name is that?" he interrupted sleepily.

"A stupid pretentious one that's been in his family for generations apparently. Anyway, he was awful to me! The things he said!" She had assumed a martyred expression and now stared into her cup like a starving puppy in front of an empty bowl.

When no sympathetic response came, Bibi looked around. He was asleep again! The tea was ready to spill into his lap. She got up impatiently and removed the mug from his hand.

"Dad! You're not listening," she said loudly.

"Oh? Sorry love. What did you say?"

Bibi was still talking at ten o'clock and suddenly felt ravenously hungry.

"Do you know, he ordered me steak and kidney pie!" she cried indignantly, wrinkling her nose at the memory. "I *hate* that sort of food and he knew it, he did it out of spite. I knew it was hopeless, so in the end I said it was better to call it a day and get a divorce. Sad, I know, but he wasn't willing to even give it a try."

"Think about it carefully," was all her father could manage to reply. He was exhausted and in pain, wanted nothing other than to lie down in a warm bed but was unsure if he had the energy left to accomplish the stairs. Bibi had left the room and was clattering about in his kitchen. She returned with two plates of cheese and biscuits and offered him one.

"No thanks love, I'm not hungry."

"But you haven't eaten anything," she said with sudden concern. "You look very pale. Are you alright?"

"Past my bedtime and I'm more than ready for it." He got out of the chair with difficulty. Bibi watched, unease creeping over her as she saw him wobble slightly.

"Well… can I get you something else? I could boil an egg or something if you like. You should have something."

"My pills, I forgot them. That's all."

"I'll get them." Bibi got up. "Where are they?"

"Kitchen cupboard."

She strode into the kitchen and was taken aback by the amount of medication in front of her, so she took the whole lot back and let him select what he wanted, then wash them all down with the remains of the tea.

"Night love."

"Night Dad, sleep well."

Bibi listened to her father shuffle upstairs and found herself sitting there silent and alone. Tears stung in her eyes for them both. While she nibbled mechanically at the cheese and biscuits, her thoughts wandered back to Wendell. No one, certainly no *man* had ever rejected her before, and she didn't like it one bit.

Oh Wendell! Why did I ever leave you? She asked herself, taken aback by her feelings. Tears fell down her face. I want you; I do want you!

She pushed her plate away, threw herself to the floor, rested her head on the arm of her father's chair and wept.

Wednesday

Charles' week was also moving from bad to worse. What had he done to deserve all this? Unable to bear the thought of another evening alone, willing the phone to ring, he had gone to stay at his parents' where his mother, with undisguised pleasure, was catering for his every whim. His parents were a God-fearing middle-class couple, on the surface mild and polite but inwardly critical and disapproving, like so many others of their ilk. The house was prim and orderly in a controlled, flowery sort of way (Mr Waterman had been a navy man and liked things ship shape), although a faint smell of cooked veg had never quite been eradicated, and now the couple were completely immune to it. All their friends and neighbours were similar types, veneered with conservatism and correctness. It was in this rather dull setting that Charles had grown up, an only child indulged completely by an overprotective mother, and had been moulded into the man he was today—unimaginative, old-fashioned, and rather naive about life in general.

Mrs Waterman was a plain and washed-out thing, the wearer of sturdy, sensible shoes and clothes. She adored her only son and was secretly delighted that he was free of that dreadful woman at last. A married woman! What had he been thinking? Men! His father was just the same, could never resist a pretty face. She had put up with a lot through the years, but if he stayed with her, she would suffer it. He probably had no idea she knew; it was just another of many secrets she retained about others' lives.

Charles' pulled into the driveway, and she opened the door. "Cup of tea?" she offered.

Charles kissed her cheek in passing, threw his keys on the hall table and proceeded wordlessly to the lounge.

"Charles," acknowledged his father with a nod from his chair.
"Dad," replied Charles, sinking into the sofa gloomily. He'd been dragged over the coals by the headmaster this afternoon, over the events of Saturday. The motorbike incident had circulated the school gathering momentum as it went, and by the time the head got to hear it, Charles had been involved in an ugly street brawl with twenty Hell's Angels and been arrested kicking and swearing by a posse of uniformed policemen.

After Charles had given his own version of the incident, Mr Robinson regarded him thoughtfully for a moment, coming to the jealous conclusion that he was far too handsome for his own good, and there must have been more to this incident than was claimed here. Sly, untrustworthy. Hadn't he heard recent stories about his exploits with women? One of the other staff here? Half the females in the place had a crush on the fellow, no you couldn't trust him. That this opinion sprang from a small, wispy haired man with a large nose and bandy legs had nothing to do with it of course.

"Just remember, Mr Waterman," he said pompously, elongated nostrils quivering, "that when you are away from this establishment, you are still an ambassador for it."

"Sorry," replied Charles, uninterested, fidgeting in his seat. His trousers were uncomfortable. Where could he get another pair of nice baggy cords from?

As he left the office he wondered if he would ever enjoy his job again. The head didn't like him, he was scared to go into the staff room in case he bumped into Eve, and he didn't much care for all the attention he suddenly seemed to be getting from the pupils, even ones that weren't his. They kept asking how he 'duffed up' a hundred Hell's Angels by himself, was he a black belt and similarly unanswerable questions. And there was another love letter in his desk this morning from a disturbingly precocious fourteen year old.

He sighed loudly.

Mrs Waterman appeared with tea and biscuits. Charles grabbed a chocolate digestive before the tray even landed on the table and began chomping mechanically.

"Mmm chocolate digestives," said his father, taking one also. Neither thought to thank the bringer of the goodies.

"Did you have a good day?" His mother enquired of Charles as she poured the tea.

"No," he grunted. His father tutted.

"I'm doing a nice steak for your tea," she announced eagerly. Charles looked up, crumbs all around his mouth and smiled. "Thanks Mum."

Mrs Waterman was happy and returned to the dinner preparations with a spring in her step.

Later, Charles tried Bibi again.

"Don't stay on that thing too long, I'm not made of money," called his father as he heard the receiver being lifted.

"I won't."

Elizabeth answered, "Hello Charles. No, she isn't. I haven't a clue, dear. I'll tell her, goodbye."

He replaced the phone with a slightly clammy hand. What was it about Bibi's mother that was so intimidating? He would ring Antonia. He lifted the receiver again and was halted by his father's voice.

"Charles! Only one call an evening in this house, you know the rule."

"For God's sake!" Charles hissed under his breath and put the phone back.

"It's cold in here, Dad." Charles rubbed his hands together. "Don't you want the heating on?" He moved towards the fire.

"I never put the heating on before the end of October, you know that."

"But it's cold now." Charles had forgotten all these petty rules.

"Go up to bed then or put that blanket over you," he waved a hand towards a neatly folded tartan square which Charles regarded with distaste.

"You know Charles, you shouldn't let a woman affect you like this."

"What?"

"Don't say what."

"Sorry." Charles looked at his father's knees sticking out at him from the chair, a gap of sock between the trousers and the leathery slippers, and wanted, for a moment, to hit him. "It's alright for you to say, you've got Mum, things are easy for you."

"Easy? That's what you think is it?" Charles' father fondled his neat moustache and stared at his son with raised eyebrows.

Charles pulled a face.

"Don't pull that face at me!"

"Sorry."

There was a pause.

"Your mother is a good woman," Mr Waterman emphasised the word 'good', "salt of the earth. Reliable, faithful, respectful. That's why I chose her."

"You sound like you're talking about a pet dog."

This was ignored as Mr Waterman carried on.

"Find a good woman and marry her, someone like Antonia. You can always get a little excitement elsewhere." He tapped the side of his nose with a conspiratorial finger.

Charles' face snapped sideways in shock. "What!"

"Don't say what."

Charles stared at his father in disbelief. Excitement? Other women? His *father*? Surely not. He wanted to ask what he meant but wasn't sure he wanted to hear the answer.

"I'm going to bed," said Charles crossly.

"Night then. Don't leave the radio on."

Christ! Did he think he was still a teenager? Charles shut the door slightly harder than he was supposed to in a small act of rebellion but there was no reprimand this time, as his father was becoming a bit hard of hearing.

Charles couldn't sleep. Partly because of his father's words which kept coming back to him and partly because it was still only ten o'clock. His mother had gone to bed at nine, the habit of a lifetime, and now just as he was finally beginning to drift, she had got up and was peeing loudly in the bathroom next door. It sounded like a bucket being emptied from a height.

He stared out at the crescent moon through the gap in the curtains and thought about Antonia. Why had he left her? Bibi had convinced him completely when she showed him that note and told him how awful her own life was. He'd been completely bewitched by her. She had made him feel heroic saving her like that, and now it seemed more and more as though she wasn't coming back. Quite suddenly Charles didn't care. Was that because he was in his childhood home or that he was thinking of Antonia?

The following day, he tried Antonia again during the mid-morning break. He didn't expect her to be there, but it was as good an excuse as any to stay out of the staff room.

At lunch time he darted in and out to see if there were any messages in his pigeon hole. The first face he saw was Eve Tate's, sipping a mug of coffee and chatting with another young teacher. They both looked up as he entered.

"Hello." Eve nodded to him.

"Hello," said the other woman, whose name escaped him for the moment.

"Er, hello." He didn't look at them and departed swiftly. Was it his imagination or were they laughing, he thought, as he shut the door? He listened for a second.

"I still would though," came Eve's voice and laughter.

"You'd have to fight me first!" More laughter.

That was ok then; for a minute, he had thought they were laughing at him.

He gobbled down a sandwich (made by his mum) and marked books at the same time, giving himself wind for the rest of the afternoon.

On the way back, he stopped at the flat.

"Bibi?" He could smell her perfume, was she back?

She had been, but was long gone, along with the microwave oven and a lot of other things, he soon discovered.

"Bitch!" he hissed between clenched teeth as he stared at the crumby square once covered by the microwave. He'd bought that. He stayed until Antonia was sure to be back from work, then called her number.

"Hello?" came the sweet, familiar, and dare he believe, hopeful, voice.

"Toni!"

There was a pause.

"Hello Charles," now she sounded disappointed.

"Don't hang up, please," begged Charles, having finally got in touch. "I'm sorry about Sunday, I didn't know what I was doing. I'd been drinking."

"You scared me. Don't please ever do that again, will you? Promise me."

"I'm sorry Toni. But I'm so down," he began. Antonia interrupted him sharply.

"Listen Charles, if you've called to tell me how awful you feel I'm not interested. As I said on Sunday, I know how you feel and I'm sure you realise I'm hardly going to be sympathetic."

"Oh, no, no, sorry," he spluttered, having hoped that was exactly the response he was going to get. "Look, can I see you, Toni? Just for a friendly chat, that's all."

"Well… is it a good idea?"

"Please Toni. I can be there in ten minutes."

"No, not here," her eyes rolled skywards, and she tutted. "Alright then, but somewhere neutral, a drink or something. And that's all."

"Oh, alright then. You mean go out?"

Of course I mean go out, you fool.

"Yes. How about eight at the King's Arms, the local one to here?"

"Oh, thank you Toni, thanks. I'll make it up to you," he enthused.

"Don't get excited Charles, it's a friendly drink, and nothing more."

"Eight at the King's Arms then, you won't regret it, darling, you don't know what this means to me."

Darling again! She let it pass without comment this time. "Right then, I must go, my dinner will be burnt to a crisp. Bye."

"See you at eight at the King's Arms."

"Yes, bye."

She hung up and sighed. After Sunday's fiasco, she had been wondering if it would do some good to clear the air finally, it felt like a relief.

Charles, meanwhile, grabbed some clothes and jumped into the car. Back at his parents, the smell of food pervaded the downstairs rooms, particularly cooking vegetables.

"Charles, there you are, I was worried." His mother looked visibly relieved, all kinds of things had been going through her mind.

He kissed her cheek. "Mmm, that smells good," she glowed with happiness. "Will it be long, I'm going out?"

"Out?" she replied quickly. "Where are you going?" but he was already leaping up the stairs in his haste for the bathroom.

Where's he off to in such high spirits? she thought suspiciously. Surely not with that awful woman again! She looked up the stairs with pursed lips and shook her head.

"Dinner's ready," called Charles' mother up the stairs. She was holding two steaming plates of food with crisp white tea towels. Hearing no reply, she continued her journey to the dining table where her husband sat ready and waiting.

"Thank you," he said politely as the plate was set down in front of him, "delicious."

"Be careful, the plate's hot," she warned, already bouncing out to fetch the final meal.

She called again, "Charles! Dinner's on the table."

"Coming," he called back, hurtling down the stairs, now dressed in clean, neatly ironed clothes and with his wet hair combed backwards.

"Where are you going?" she asked again as they seated themselves.

"Mmm lovely," he mumbled as he forked food into his mouth like someone loading coal into the furnace of a moving train.

Mr Waterman regarded him with disgust. "Slow down son, you'll give yourself indigestion. Well? Where are you going?"

They had both stopped eating and were looking at him still shovelling in food.

"Out," he managed between mouthfuls, without looking up.

"Out where?" demanded his father.

They waited in vain and with an irritated grunt his father resumed eating. That boy had bad table manners; he hadn't been brought up to behave like this. He would speak to him when the meal was finished, no point in letting a nice dinner get cold over it.

The sound of knives and forks touching plates covered the ensuing silence for a minute before Charles leapt up and looked at his watch.

"We haven't finished yet! Sit down, will you," said his father angrily. Really! What unforgivable behaviour.

"Sorry Dad, must go."

Charles kissed his mother's cheek, remembering a cursory 'thank you' and barged out.

Mr Waterman reddened, but said no more.

"What time will you be back?" called Mrs Waterman.

"Don't know, don't wait up," he leapt back up the stairs, belching loudly as he went, and returned with a jacket.

"Bye, see you later."

The front door banged shut and as they listened to Charles' car drive away Mr Waterman spoke.

"Where do you think he's off to?"

"I just hope it's not that dreadful woman."

"Hmm. I'll speak to him later, can't have him treating this house like a hotel while he goes out meeting married women. He needs a good woman to take care of him, someone like you my dear," he endowed his wife with a good-natured smile and a gentle pat on the knee.

She was content.

Wendell, like Charles, had also spent the day thinking about Antonia, and Bibi. There had been a brisk wind blowing that morning, which gusted around him from all directions, and the carefully arranged hair hung in two curtains from a centre parting by the time he got under cover. Everyone and their father seemed to be parked in the town this morning and he'd had to walk further than usual.

He was only just on time and headed immediately for the men's toilet to sort out his hair before doing anything else. He was tired and his mouth felt faintly fluffy after the spicy food of the previous night.

He wished now that he hadn't called Antonia so late last night. Where had she been at that hour? Surely not with… no, surely not that. He'd try her tonight.

If he could remember the name of that surgery where she worked, he could call her there. What was that dentist's name? O'Reilly or something? Why hadn't he taken more notice when he was there? He had a quick glance through the phone book but didn't recognise anything listed there.

"Morning Beth," he said as he passed her.

She stopped her furious typing and waved a hand about in front of her.

"Phew! Who else had a curry last night? Andrew's already been breathing fumes all over me."

Wendell cupped his hands over his mouth to test. "I can't smell anything."

"It's there, I promise you. Anyway, that doesn't work. Apparently, you have to lick the back of your hand and smell that."

Wendell did this. "Oh God, that's unpleasant," he grinned, then slumped into his chair.

"Pooh! Own up, who had a curry last night?" asked another typist as she entered the office. She looked accusingly at Wendell, who raised a hand sheepishly and smiled and they all laughed.

"I'll let you off this time. Belly wants to see you."

Wendell tutted impatiently. "Oh dear, what, now?"

"When you're ready."

"No time like the present, I'll poison him with this dragon breath."

Wendell stood, straightened his tie and headed for Bellingham's sanctum, while Beth and Pamela discussed why men always smelled worse after a curry than women did, agreeing that they were sweatier and probably oozed more.

Wendell knocked, waited the obligatory few seconds for the 'enter' instruction, then went in.

"Good morning Mr Bellingham, you wanted to see me."

"Morning Cornish. Sit down."

It was hard to see his boss against the large window behind him. The early sun was so bright all he could at first make out was the silhouette of the big chair with some vague features in it like some alien in a science fiction film.

"I'll have Lung visiting this weekend Cornish, before he returns to China. He very much enjoyed your evening, expressly asked if you would be available for another?" Bellingham raised a puzzled eyebrow at the thought.

Wendell paled; he couldn't go through all that again. And so soon. His mind began galloping.

"Oh! When would that be exactly?" he enquired with a wide-eyed smile, playing for time.

"He arrives Friday evening and leaves early Monday, so I imagine Saturday evening. Expenses as before of course."

Expenses! He'd been out of pocket by twenty quid the last time, and if Belly thought he was giving up his weekend he was very mistaken.

"Oh, what a shame." Wendell's smile slumped in an Oscar winning show of disappointment, "Normally I would love to. Of course. But unfortunately, I'm doing a flying visit to my parents—they live in Spain, so I don't see them very often. I'll be getting my flight on Friday evening and won't be back until late on Sunday. What a pity."

"Hmm." Bellingham was trying, and failing, to see some way around this. "Very unfortunate. Oh well, can't be helped. Perhaps the next time then?"

Wendell almost melted with relief. "Yes of course. Do pass on my regards to Lung. Delightful company."

"I will do that," Bellingham said, then flared his nostrils. "What is that extraordinary odour."

"Odour?" frowned Wendell, sniffing. "I can't smell anything," and left the office quickly before he laughed out loud.

He left work late after sorting through a backlog of paperwork, arriving home at about seven-thirty. He went straight up to Antonia's door and knocked.

No answer. Again.

She must really be avoiding him. Had Sunday put her off completely? Every time he failed to see her, he found himself wanting to see her more. Absence really does make the heart grow fonder, he thought. He knocked again, louder this time, and called her name too without success. No, she wasn't hiding in there, she was definitely out.

His flat was quiet and warm. And lonely. He yawned and threw off his tie. A search through the kitchen revealed an unopened loaf of bread, blue with mould inside its plastic wrapping. Another loaf wasted. He tossed it into the bin. Where was Antonia? Did all that really happen only last Sunday, just a few days ago? It seemed longer, almost a dream. Why hadn't she tried to speak to him since? Perhaps he should leave another note? On the other hand, if she was annoyed with him, he wouldn't want to say the wrong thing. Oh, how ridiculous! What was the matter with him? Just knock on the door later.

A faint burning smell snapped him out of his reverie and he was just in time to save the fish fingers from turning into charcoal. A pan of baked beans was boiling merrily. Not the best tea ever eaten but never mind. Mrs O. would see to the pan on Friday, Wendell thought, leaving it to congeal and harden on the draining board. Mustn't forget to leave her money this week he reminded himself. There was last week to pay for too.

His cup of tea spilled as he put it on the coffee table, leaving a pattern of watery rings as he picked it up and put it down again. The coaster, still gleaming from last week's cleaning, lay untouched two inches from the cup.

Wendell burped and pushed his plate to one side of the sofa, then ran his tongue around his teeth, concentrating carefully on the gap where the extraction had been.

A car pulled up outside and soon afterwards he could hear Antonia's bell ringing.

Now what? Not that idiot again surely. He shuffled across to the window. There was a large estate car at the kerb apparently full of people and luggage. The rack on top was also stacked high and covered with a sheet of plastic which fluttered in the wind, having escaped its fastening at one corner. The bell rang once more, longer, followed by two short bursts. Why did no one ever believe she wasn't there?

Finally, a small figure appeared, wrapped in scarves and coats, walking backwards and looking up towards the empty flat. After a moment it headed back to the car, climbed in and drove off.

His phone rang. He hesitated for two seconds and then scooped it up hopefully.

"Hello?"

"Wendy? It's Bibi."

Wendell groaned inwardly, then massaged his temples with his free hand. What the hell did she want now?

"Have you thought any more about our conversation?"

"I thought I'd said everything there was to say Bibi. You know what I think."

"Listen Wendell. We are married. I think we should at least attempt to sort things out."

"If you had said this nine, or even eight, months ago then perhaps there was a chance, but not now. I've moved on, I'm not interested anymore."

"Oh Wendell," she almost sobbed. "Please give it a chance, you owe me that much at least."

"What! I owe you nothing, anyone would think it was me that buggered off. It's over, finished. Just forget it."

"But Wendy, just listen to me for a moment... I—"

"No, you listen. It's over, accept it and get on with your life. Try living alone for a while, it might do you good."

"Don't tell me how to live my life," she replied coldly.

"I don't want you back, Bibi." There. He'd said it and felt slightly breathless. "We should start divorce proceedings and be done with it."

"Shut up about divorce, will you! Just one chance, that's all I ask, so you can see I've changed."

"No."

"Let's go somewhere and talk about it."

"We've just done that."

There was a silence while they both waited for the other to say something. Bibi was furious, nothing she said was working.

"Right then," she shouted angrily. "Have it your way. I'll see about a solicitor in the morning. Let me know if and when you see sense and change your mind."

With that she banged the phone down, making him pull it away from his ear. He replaced it gently and sighed. A year of nothing, during which he nearly became an alcoholic monk, and now just as he meets someone nice, Bibi wants to come back. Was it all worth the hassle?

He thought of Antonia for a moment and decided, yes, it was.

Chapter Twenty-Five
Wednesday Evening

Charles arrived early bursting with eager anticipation at the Kings Arms, like an overzealous teenager on his first date. He glanced at his reflection, checked his zip and got out of the car. Antonia's car didn't seem to be there yet, but perhaps she had a different one now. He shunted his trousers up a bit and made for the door, then walked around and into every nook and cranny to satisfy himself she wasn't already inside, receiving a few odd glances from occupied areas, particularly from men. By the time he had finished his patrol it was almost ten past.

Where was she? Give it another five minutes and he would phone her.

He sat down where he could see the car park and waited, oblivious of the stares a very good-looking man sitting alone without a drink was attracting. At quarter past he got himself a beer and decided to drink it before phoning. Where the hell was she? He looked at his watch for the umpteenth time, they had said eight, hadn't they? Or was it half eight? No, eight. Definitely. It was unlike her to be late, perhaps something had happened to her.

Antonia got herself ready and moved stealthily past Wendell's door. She didn't want to bump into him now, it would be awkward to explain. She was also cross that he hadn't contacted her. After all they had said and done on Sunday too. She felt sick when she thought of what they might have done with no thought of protection, which just showed how stupid she might have been; she had behaved like some backstreet tart, utterly demeaned herself. All she asked was some certainty, this situation was giving her an ulcer.

And now here she was about to go out with Charles.

Suddenly there were men all over the place. She'd never been so popular, she thought, and made a wry face. If this carried on, she would soon be yearning for loneliness and boredom again.

A lorry had broken down on the main road which held her up, and after diverting down several side roads, she finally pulled up in the car park at about twenty past eight. She could have walked really but didn't want to risk Charles offering her a lift back.

She saw his car and looked instinctively towards the pub window, where she guessed he would have taken up a position to scan the parking area. She felt nervous, could have done without this, although she had to admit she was curious. Charles leapt up as she entered and she moved swiftly into the seat opposite him, avoiding a kiss which she could see he was intending to plant on her.

"Antonia darling! You look... you look... you look..."

Yes? Thought Antonia, slightly embarrassed.

"So wonderful."

As Antonia was wondering when he had ever said things like that to her, Charles felt almost overcome. How had he ever thought Bibi was worth leaving her for? He must have been mad.

"Hello Charles." Antonia looked into his beautiful eyes, so full of adoration, and felt pleasure and alarm in equal measure.

"How I've missed you," he tried to take her hand, but she whipped it away. "It's so good to see you, thanks for coming, my darling."

"Please don't keep calling me darling, I don't like it," she said impatiently, and seeing his face fall, added softly, "It's not appropriate."

He was certainly still very handsome, more so than she had remembered. His hair was longer, and it suited him.

"Well, it's nice to see you, Charles, after all this time of nothing. I'm sorry about all that the other night, but really, why on earth did you come around? I did say not to."

"I've been so wretched I just didn't think, you wouldn't believe it."

"I think I would."

He glanced up.

"Oh, yes, sorry. That Bibi is a bloody bitch! God knows what I ever saw in *her*."

Antonia laughed, glad to hear bad things about Wendell's wife.

"That's the first sensible thing you've said."

Charles smiled crookedly, not sure of himself yet.

"So, what are you doing now? Where are you living?"

"I'm at my parents—temporarily, of course."

"How are they?"

"Fine, just the same, you know. I think I'll go crazy if I stay there much longer though."

Charles' half-empty glass stood on the table between them, and Antonia wondered whether she would die of thirst before he thought of getting her a drink.

"I'll just get a drink," she said, fishing about in her bag.

"I'll get them. What will you have?"

"Thanks, sparkling mineral water please."

"Oh, don't you want a drink?" He sounded disappointed.

"I thought that was a drink."

"Well, you know what I mean."

"No thank you, I'm driving."

He headed off, followed by several pairs of female eyes and one or two male ones too, and was soon back.

"That barmaid ought to be in a zoo. Have you seen her nails? She kept scratching me with them."

Antonia laughed.

"So, all the women are still flirting with you then?"

"Flirting?" Charles looked genuinely puzzled.

"Oh Charles!" Antonia rolled her eyes. "How can you still be so naïve."

There was that word again, why did everyone call him naïve?

"I don't know what you mean," he replied testily.

"Don't you realise you could have *any* woman you want? You're too good-looking for your own good," she stopped to take a sip of her drink. "It's why that bloody woman was after you in the first place; she always tried to catch your eye when we bumped into them. Don't you ever wonder why women always bump into you accidentally? Clutch at your arm? Scratch you with their nails? It's because they want to attract your attention."

Antonia smiled kindly. His innocence was, after all, one of the things that had attracted her when they had first met.

Visions of various women, barmaids, Eve Tate and others appeared before Charles' eyes, and then he remembered the number of times Bibi had 'bumped into him' on the doorstep, dropped things in front of him, smiled at him. Come to think of it, the pupils at school often blushed and giggled when he spoke to them, mostly the girls but some of the boys as well. He looked over at the barmaid and saw her watching him. She smiled and made a clawing motion with one hand. He had a small moment of revelation.

"My God," he frowned. "I've been a bit of an idiot, haven't I? Bibi was right."

"Don't become a big head, will you?" Antonia had a sudden impulse to hug him but resisted it. "Perhaps you'll be able to sort yourself out now she's gone."

"Yeah. Oh, I don't know. I couldn't believe it when she went like that. As far as I knew, things were fine and then…" He shook his head and left the sentence unfinished.

"That's exactly what you did to me, remember? I'm ok now but at the time I wasn't, I can tell you." Antonia stared at him, unable to completely hide the bitterness still within her. "What made you do it?"

"God Toni, you're not completely blameless you know. I saw the note," he finished with triumph, then grasped her hand. "But that's all behind us now. I know now I never loved Bibi, there's only one girl for me."

Antonia withdrew her hand slowly and firmly. Charles looked bewildered.

"What note?"

Charles looked intently at her.

"What note are you talking about?"

"Do I have to read it out? I kept it to remind me of why I had no choice but to leave."

"Let's see this note." Antonia had no idea what he was talking about.

Charles rummaged about in his wallet and retrieved a much-read note on thin blue paper. He began to read, "Dear W…"

"Who? Let me see that." Antonia reached out to take it from him, but he whipped it away possessively.

"Dear W, I'm desperate to see you, but Charles is going to be around," he paused and looked up at her, feeling again his horror at reading the words. "I will definitely tell him this weekend and then we can be together forever. My darling, the only thing keeping me going is the thought of seeing you again. It won't be long now, just trust me. All my love, your darling Antonia." Charles folded the note carefully and replaced it reverently into his wallet, jutting his jaw out with satisfaction.

"Well?" he demanded. "Anything to say now?" He had crossed his arms.

Antonia was dumbfounded. This explained everything; they had all been manipulated.

She had always thought it had been so out of character for Charles. This Bibi tart must have written this sloppy piece of fiction and made sure Charles got it. If she intended a quick romp behind everyone's back, she had no idea what she was getting into with Charles. She was suddenly absolutely furious.

"Right. Let me ask you something, did it ever occur to you that I would write a note like that? In that way I mean, yearning and darling and all that flowery stuff?"

"Well… I er, just thought. No, hang on, don't change the subject!"

"Charlie, I promise you hand on heart," she placed a hand on her chest. "I have never seen that note before in my life. I didn't write that rubbish; I was *never* unfaithful to you. Never."

Charles was silent, suddenly coming to the same conclusion Antonia had some minutes earlier.

"No, no, she wouldn't," he muttered to himself as he rubbed his left temple. "She couldn't possibly… said we would have to look after each other because we were both the victims… oh dear."

"It seems she did, the bitch!"

"But why would someone do such a thing? What for?" He shook his head in bewilderment and repeated, "What for?"

Antonia tutted. "She wanted *you*, Charlie, she didn't care who she hurt as long as she got what she wanted. Is it written or typed?"

"Typed," Charles answered robotically, now plucking at his neck as he realised how he had so easily been fooled.

"Well, there you are then, who writes a slushy thing like that out on a typewriter? My God, Wendell said she lied but I had no idea. Why on earth didn't you show me the note, why didn't you ask *me*?"

"Wendell?" The trance was broken. "How do you know him? Stay away from him Toni, he did some awful things…" he trailed off, wondering now whether those tales were made-up too.

"Wow. Seems like we've both been too innocent, doesn't it?" Antonia now shook her head in disbelief. "It's incredible, it's like a soap plot."

There was a silent pause while each let these revelations sink in.

"Marry me Toni." Suddenly Charles grasped her hand and this time she left it there. There was a pleasant familiarity about it.

"What!" she laughed and squeezed his hand in an effort to be friendly. "Of course not! There's no going back. I came to meet you so we could understand what happened and maybe be friends, that's all."

"But Toni… it's different now we know the truth! *I'm* different now, I know things. We belong with each other; I can see that now."

Antonia held up her other hand.

"Look, I'm different now as well. You can't turn the clock back Charles. Thank you for asking but no."

"Toni…"

"No, no. Friends, nothing more. There are plenty more nice women out there."

Eve Tate bubbled up again for a second, and he mentally trampled her.

"I don't want other women, I want you," he said earnestly.

"I'm sorry Charles. We can be good friends, but nothing more." She squeezed his hand again, then took hers away, before she said something she would later regret.

"Nobody seems to want me." He was being childish now. "Even my father hinted it was time I went."

A lock of dark hair fell across his forehead in a most endearing manner and a woman at the table behind them, who had been avidly following the conversation, only just stopped herself from crying out that she'd have him.

"Don't do the childish thing, Charles. I've just told you there are plenty of other women out there wanting you—there's one at the next table, in fact." Antonia couldn't resist saying it, having spotted the eavesdropper, who turned a shade of puce and began an intense scrutiny of her table mat. "It just won't be me."

Charles turned and caught the eye of the woman behind him who was now pretending to listen with great interest to her companion, nodding as though her head was on a spring. He turned back.

"Don't say that! It's you I want; we should be together, darling."

"Will you *please* stop calling me that!"

"But you are my darling."

"I am not. The fact is, Charlie, I've met someone else." She felt herself reddening. Charles looked horrified. He ran a hand over his hair and sat back, then looked out into the dark car park.

"So that's it. How long has this been going on then?"

"It doesn't matter. The fact is… that it, well, just is. I don't need to explain it to you, it just is. You will meet someone else I promise you."

"I don't want someone else; I want you." Charles sounded pathetic.

"For God's sake." Antonia was getting fed up now. "Stop feeling so sorry for yourself. Live alone for a while and clear your head. It was hard at first, but it did do me good in the end. I'm much more independent now."

"Yes, you are," he said with disapproval. "Bibi's fucked up both our lives for no reason other than lust, just you wait until I catch up with her," there was real menace in his tone.

"Forget it, forget her. Just start again Charles. Bitterness does nothing for you, apart from making you miserable. Believe me, I know."

Charles insisted they have one more drink and while he waited at the bar Antonia was overcome with pity for him. She felt herself weaken, could it possibly work? No, it had run its course before Charles had left, and now too much time had passed. She *was* different now, and there was Wendell… maybe. She felt sick with confusion.

The next half hour passed in nostalgic reminiscences and recent events, during which the dust settled and by the time the drinks were finished Antonia felt as though they really could be friends, while Charles saw hope that they might still get back together.

In the car park they parted with a small kiss and a hug filled with genuine warmth.

"Sure you won't marry me?"

"Tempting, but no."

"Oh well, thought I'd try it one more time."

They both smiled.

"See you sometime," said Antonia, feeling like she meant it.

"Bye Toni," said Charles, feeling happier than he had done in weeks.

When he got back to his parents' house, he sneaked in quietly. It wasn't particularly late, but his parents were always in bed early. To his surprise, the lounge light was on, and his father was in there attired in tartan dressing gown and slippers. Surely, he hadn't been waiting up for him.

Mr Waterman regarded his son shrewdly, ready for the serious talking to he had prepared for him. "Good evening?"

"Yes actually," replied Charles, full of new confidence which two pints of beer was helping along nicely. "I've been thinking about what you said earlier, Dad, maybe you're right."

Mr Waterman's eyebrows shot up to his hairline in surprise. "Oh! Yes, that's the spirit." This was unlike Charles, was he on drugs? His rehearsed words dissolved away in light of this new development. "Righto, I'm off to bed then. Don't stay up too late. Er, of course, no need to mention our conversation to your mother." He laughed awkwardly.

"I'm not completely stupid, Dad."

"No, no, of course not. Goodnight then."

"Night."

"Don't forget to switch the lights out and unplug the television, will you?"

"No Dad."

Ten minutes later, Charles was asleep on the sofa, lights on and the television blaring.

At the same time, Antonia was lying still fully clothed on her bed thinking of Charles, then Wendell, then Bibi's destructive lies. Could it possibly work with Charles? Could it? He was so gorgeous, familiar, and safe.

And boring. She knew the answer. No, it was history. Wendell, if he still wanted her, and she hoped he did, was the future. As for that bitch Bibi, if she ever ran into her again, she would do something she had always fancied doing but never had the opportunity to and slap her deceitful face. Slap it really hard.

Chapter Twenty-Six
Wednesday

It was unbearably hot in her father's house, so when Bibi woke late morning, she was dry-mouthed and all bunged up. She was surprised at the lateness of the hour, it was years since she had slept for so long, or so soundly for that matter. When she had completed her morning bathroom routine, she strolled downstairs thinking of the events of the previous day. She would discuss it further with her father today, now that he'd had some sleep. But she was alarmed to find him not yet up. Mounting the stairs once more, she listened at his door for a few seconds before tapping gently.

"Dad?" she called softly.

Silence.

Her pulse began to race. She suddenly recalled how tired and grey he had looked yesterday, how he hadn't wanted food, and all she'd been concerned with were her own troubles. She stood motionless outside the door, unable to decide whether to fling it open or leave at once. In the end she went downstairs to make tea and thought about what to do next. She hadn't expected this, didn't want it.

As she filled the kettle, she was surprised to find her hands shaking. She paced restlessly from room to room, and her eyes settled on the cups and plates of the previous evening, so she clattered about making as much noise as possible and cleared everything away.

Should she call her mother? No, not yet anyway. The scenes of yesterday were still too fresh in her mind. Why had she gone barging in there like that? It had been bound not to end well. That awful toy boy, he'd ruined everything! Why was it all going wrong? Life was so unfair!

There was a sound from upstairs and she forgot all about the previous day as relief flowed through every artery, vein and capillary. Thank God he was finally stirring, hadn't died in the night after all. She wouldn't have to deal with that at least.

When he did eventually appear, Bill seemed surprised to find her there.

"Bibi! Well, what brings you here?"

She was horrified and depressed in equal measure, surely he couldn't have forgotten about yesterday?

"Well..." she hesitated. "I came yesterday. Remember?"

The lines on his face rearranged themselves from surprise to enlightenment and he smiled at her concerned expression.

"Sorry love, of course I do. You must think I'm an old fool, time I was put out to grass."

"Tea?" she said in a slightly panicked high-pitched voice, unable to think of anything else to say for the moment.

"Now that's more like it," he sat down slowly with a grunt. "I'm afraid you'll have to tell me all your troubles again love, I've forgotten what we were talking about last night. I get tired these days."

"Oh, it was nothing really, all in the past now. I'll be doing some shopping today; do you need anything while I'm out?"

"I think I'm alright for the moment lovey. Will you be staying again tonight?"

"No," she said, rather too quickly. She couldn't go through all this again. "I need to collect some bits from the house."

"Your mother's?"

"No, where I was living with Charles."

"Charles? I thought he was called Wembley, that's not a name I'd forget in a hurry."

"Yes, I mean no. Wendell." Oh God, age and illness were horrible! This wasn't how she wanted to remember her dad.

After a shared breakfast of toast and marmalade, she said her goodbyes and hurried off, drove straight to the house and pulled up outside, checking for signs of Charles before going in. Inside, she wandered from room to room listlessly, looking with disgust at the untidiness. There was an air of emptiness and history about the place already, and gloom settled on her. She loaded up a suitcase to bursting point with all her remaining clothes and a few of Charles' things that she liked, then heaved it into the car. Returning, she picked out various ornaments and pictures that had once adorned Wendell's flat and threw them all into a bag. Finally, and with much effort, she hefted the microwave oven out and into the back seat of the car, then drove off without a glance behind her. Following that, she went to the supermarket and then headed for Clara's house.

When she got there the windows were once again wide open and a lot of noise was bellowing out. Her knocking went unheard above the cacophony until, in desperation, she hallooed in through the window. How on earth did the neighbours put up with this?

Hoovering ceased abruptly, followed by the deafening music and Clara's head, in a headscarf like a charwoman, appeared in the lounge.

"Darling!" she cried, delighted, and plunged back inside to go and open the door. "Darling, come in, oh do come in."

Bibi sailed past and into the lounge where she dropped down on the sofa.

Clara threw herself into the lotus position in front of Bibi and looked up wide-eyed like a sycophantic dog. Bibi stared over her head towards the window presenting a tragic front. Also to stop herself laughing at the sight of Clara in that headscarf looking like Mrs Potato Head.

"Darling, what's happened?" she wailed, thoroughly taken in.

Bibi slowly looked down at her. Really, she did look even more grotesque than usual if it was possible.

"I'm in trouble," she began, sniffing. "My mother's thrown me out. I've got nowhere to go."

Clara slapped two big hands to her two big cheeks in horror. "No!" then a wonderful idea came to her. "but you can stay here, of course you can!"

Bibi stared at Clara, pretending this hadn't occurred to her. "Well…"

"You must stay, there's plenty of room, stay as long as you like, darling, I insist," she grabbed at her cigarettes and lit up.

"Would you mind? Just until I find somewhere, you'd be doing me a great favour, darling."

"Mind!" Clara nearly choked. "Darling, it will be wonderful, such fun. Let's celebrate!" She leapt remarkably swiftly to her feet and returned with a bottle of questionable wine, a different label from the previous nasty offering.

"This is just super," she said, pouring out two large glasses.

Bibi gulped hers, wondering whether Clara had shares in Threshers, and flopped back. "I needed that." She would have preferred a cup of coffee really.

"So do spill, darling, what's it all about?"

Clara was actually sitting in a chair for once, large hips melting into it snugly.

"My mother's got this toy boy," Bibi began, with a disapproving frown "basically, she thinks more of *him* than *me*. She told me I'd outstayed my welcome; I was an uninvited guest and should leave."

"No! Just like that? How simply awful for you! She threw you out onto the street!"

"Yes, and he was sitting there while she said it."

"Oh, how mortifying!" Clara was indignant on her friend's behalf.

The wine was cheap and unpleasant and was going to Bibi's head. She suddenly felt lethargic, didn't want to be here, hated this homeless existence. Clara was already getting on her nerves with all her exclamations and enthusiasm. She would stay until the weekend, then go back to her mother's and see what happened. Hopefully, she would have worried about her, and with a bit of luck it would have caused a rift between her mother and Action Man.

Bibi rubbed her temples and closed her eyes as Clara chattered on beside her, then cut her off mid-flow, "I'm feeling very tired, darling, I think I have a migraine coming on. Would you mind if I went to my room for a lie-down?"

"Oh, you poor thing!" Clara rammed her cigarette into an ashtray and leapt up. "Where are your things?"

They went out to the car and Clara manhandled the bulging suitcase up the stairs with a lot of grunting and puffing.

"You must have my room; I'll use the spare as it's a bit untidy. I've just changed the sheets so it's all fresh."

Clara's room was light and airy with a pretty pink floral theme encompassing curtains and scatter cushions as well as the bed linen. An army of soft toys were displayed on every available surface and a large bowl of potpourri delicately mingled with the smell of old cigarette smoke.

"It's lovely," said Bibi, pleasantly surprised. "Thank you, darling." Yes, she thought, this would do for a few nights.

Clara was positively flushed with delight, noting subconsciously that this was a genuine compliment. "Is there anything else I can get you, darling? You know where the facilities are, of course."

"I just need a little lie-down, that's all."

"Oh, this is just *fabby!* I must call the girls over tonight."

It was the last thing Bibi wanted, but she didn't say anything that might provoke another torrent of verbal diarrhoea. Clara remained standing there as Bibi stretched herself out on the bed. Was she ever going to leave?

"Right. See you later then," she finally announced, after Bibi had closed her eyes and feigned sleep. Clara backed out like a lady in waiting and banged the door shut behind her.

Thank God for that, thought Bibi, sitting up the moment she'd gone. A few blissfully quiet moments passed before the music started again. It seemed to vibrate right around the room and through Bibi's chest and was soon in competition with the hoover which banged and thumped its way around downstairs with Clara at the helm. When her loud and tuneless singing joined the noise, Bibi tutted with annoyance and rammed a tissue into each ear. Couldn't Clara do *anything* without making a bloody racket?

She got up off the bed and began a thorough investigation of the room, opening all the drawers and cupboards and shuffling through the underwear, clothes and private papers. As she shut the sock drawer an avalanche of teddies fell on top of her, so she hurled them roughly across the room. Stupid things. In one drawer lay packs of photographs. She opened one randomly and sat down to look at them. Most were of people unknown to her, although this one was obviously Clara's parents. Her mother, the tall and elegant trophy wife, cradling her little daughter in her arms, towered above a ridiculous dumpy man who was like a male version of Clara. There was a small child holding his hand, who was also the image of the father so perhaps that was Clara. Bibi vaguely remembered them attending some do or other at the school once, and there had been a lot of tittering until they learnt that the father was some kind of millionaire. She threw the pictures on the bed beside her, where one claimed her attention at once, herself and Wendell at their wedding.

How young and, frankly, happy they both looked. She tried to feel anger towards Wendell but only yearned for him afresh. Why was this happening to her? She must have him, she always got what she wanted in the end and this would be no different.

A plan formed in Bibi's mind. She would go around there and tell him she had nowhere to go. If she could just come in and get warm, cry a bit. If she could just get her foot in the door… Bibi smiled slowly, energy returning and, with it, restlessness. She wouldn't say anything to Clara, just in case she still required a bed tomorrow night.

The hoover had finally roared its last for the day. Bibi tossed the makeshift earplugs onto the bed and went down the stairs.

"Feeling better?" enquired Clara, over another glass of the vile wine. Did she never stop drinking or smoking?

"Much. I've just remembered, darling; I've got some shopping in the car. Let's bring it in and cook up something fancy, I'm starving!"

While Bibi started on the something fancy, Clara called the twins, who arrived breathless at seven o'clock.

Bibi felt good. She had showered and changed and was dressed to kill. The atmosphere lent itself to an evening of raucous enjoyment and when she finally went to bed in the early hours of the morning, she was merrily drunk and eagerly looking forward to throwing herself on the mercy of her estranged husband.

Chapter Twenty-Seven
Thursday Evening

When she arrived home from work on Thursday evening, Antonia found a note taped to her door. She had spent the entire day trying to resign herself to the fact that Wendell really was a lying womaniser and a complete non-starter, so her heart leapt, and she tore it open eagerly.

He *had* been trying to see her! They had missed one another again. He wanted to see her tonight, oh joy! She reread the note twice before going in. Then tried to tell herself to calm down, it may not be what she was thinking.

That, and of course, she'd been here before and he had let her down.

Ozzie greeted her loudly, shouting for his dinner. She watched while he checked it warily, sniffed a bit, then settled down to eat. By the time the kettle had boiled, he had had his fill and was sauntering past licking his lips. She bent to stroke him but, uninterested now, he sunk under her touch.

What time might Wendell be home? Six-thirty? Seven? As she went back again over how she had been let down previously, she tried not to get her hopes up.

It was as she sat down to watch the news that she heard his key in the door. She sat absolutely still, heart leaping in her chest like a demented frog, then listened to him close his own door before realising she had been holding her breath and blowing it out in a rush. Ten minutes later she heard it open again and then he was coming up the stairs and was knocking on her door.

She took a deep breath, centred herself, cleared her throat, and opened the door.

Wendell stood on the threshold smiling a little cautiously. He was holding a bottle of wine, misty with sudden warmth. Antonia's face was hot, she almost felt a bit faint for a moment. They stared at one another.

"Come in."

Wendell stepped in, put the bottle on a side table and closed his arms around her. She clung to him, chin resting on his shoulder as she held him tight, eyes squeezed closed to stop tears as they stood there, both of them bound by silent emotion.

"I'm sorry," whispered Wendell, "can we just start again?"

They parted, stared at each other and melted into a kiss so glorious that Antonia really did feel faint.

"I really do think I'm falling in love with you," said Wendell simply, "there's just something about you."

Antonia smiled, wanted to say yes, me too, but couldn't. "Come on, let's sit down and have a chat; I'll get some glasses."

Wendell went into the lounge, not caring whether he had said the wrong thing again, while Antonia took a few more deep breaths in the kitchen. Bloody hell, bloody hell! Her legs were weak. She fiddled around until her heart returned to a near normal pace, had a cursory sniff of her armpits, then glided calmly into the lounge where Wendell was waiting.

"I'm afraid it's tumblers, and they don't even match. I don't seem to have any vino glasses."

"They'll do." Wendell produced a corkscrew from his trouser pocket and expertly opened the wine, pouring it out with a flourish. Antonia recalled Charles doing this once, making a complete hash of it, and everyone spitting out bits of cork all evening.

"There we are," he said, placing one in front of her on the table.

"Thank you."

Wendell held his glass up and declared a toast, "To starting again!" and they both smiled and touched their glasses.

"Yes, I'm really sorry about that too." Antonia shook her head as if to clear the memory.

"It wasn't your fault. Did he call back?"

Antonia hesitated. "Yes, he did."

Wendell hesitated. "And?"

"I met him for a drink last night." She hardly dared to look at Wendell as she rushed the words out and sipped her wine with a slightly shaky hand.

"Ah." What would happen now? Wendell wasn't sure how he felt about that. Jealous? Afraid? That damn good-looking shit, she loved him once so could she again? He couldn't let her slip out of his grasp. She hadn't said she loved him, had he already lost her?

"How did your lunch with Bibi go?" said Antonia, to divert the topic.

"Ha! It was a right farce." Wendell managed to expel a little of his emotion.

Antonia sat up and looked at him for a moment.

"Look... erm, do you think... I mean, can we... I..." Antonia began and fizzled out.

"Shall we just tell it like it is you mean? I know we haven't really known each other for very long, but it seems to have been monumentally complicated so far, doesn't it? Shall we just be honest about how we feel and move on from there? Ask me anything you like, anything at all."

"Yes, that's sort of what I was trying to say," smiled Antonia shyly. "I wasn't expressing myself very well, was I?"

"Ask away then."

Antonia plunged straight in. "Wendell," she said rather formally, "do you still love her? Do you want her back?"

Wendell thought they had already covered this one and hoped it wasn't a prelude to saying that she and her ex were going to give it another go. In that moment he felt he could suffer anything but that. She was so lovely sitting there like a little doll, big serious eyes and that magnificent hair. It would really be crushing to lose her now, back to that bloody Charles too.

"Do you want Charles back?"

"You didn't answer my question."

Wendell saw a flash of annoyance pass across Antonia's face. He liked that, that she wouldn't be a wimp.

"No, as a matter of fact I don't. I don't care if I never see her again." He took a great gulp of wine. "I told her I wanted a divorce."

"Well, I wouldn't want Charles back if he was the last man on earth. I don't mind being friendly but certainly nothing more, and I don't think he's capable of just friends so I probably won't ever see him again."

Wendell searched her face for deceit, an old habit from the days of Bibi. "Really?"

Antonia opened her eyes wide to him. "Yes, really. I... I'm not very good at this sort of thing, but I hoped we could..." she struggled for the right balance between declaring undying love to a man she didn't know very well and being too indifferent. "I want to see how it goes with you Wendell. I like you; I like you a lot, but if you have decided to try and save your marriage I won't get in the way. Apart from anything, I refuse to be second best to *her* again."

There was that delightful annoyance again.

Antonia could feel her face glowing like a light bulb. It was probably the most courageous thing she had ever said to anyone, apart from when she told her mother she had wet herself on her first day at school.

Wendell put his glass down, then took hers from her hand and put it down before speaking.

"Antonia," he took her hand. "My darling, darling Antonia," then he hugged her tight and kissed her on the neck. A tingle passed through her body. "Bibi thrives on adoring males running after her all the time. When she tires of you, she just turns and kicks you in the teeth. I used to wonder sometimes why she even agreed to marry me. Maybe she did feel something, but it was doomed not to last. Everything about her is faked, it's a constant round of mind games and subterfuge. I'm almost certain she played away occasionally but I could never prove it. You are real, with real emotions and real loveliness. I want this to work. Can we give it a try?"

Antonia hugged him to her, and they kissed. Both felt they had found something precious and longed for and did not want to let it slip away. Desire rose up in them both. Wendell pulled Antonia to her feet, and they kissed again, and both thought about the bedroom.

And at this intense point Antonia's doorbell chose to ring.

This time neither of them laughed.

"I don't believe it," Wendell said incredulously.

"Who can that be?"

They stared at one another.

"Are you expecting anyone?"

"No."

"I've got a horrible feeling of déjà vu," said Wendell, as the bell rang impatiently once more. He released Antonia and peeped out of the window. "Let's hope it's the Jehovah's Witnesses and they go away."

Antonia joined him and peered through the curtain to see her sister's car parked at the kerb behind Wendell's.

"Fiona!" cried Antonia. "She's back early."

"Who's Fiona?"

But Antonia was already gone, thudding down the stairs to answer the door.

"Fi! I wasn't expecting you until the weekend."

"Is he alright?" demanded Fiona as she and the two boys stood and bored their eyes into her, daring her to say he wasn't.

"Who? Oh, Ozzie you mean, yes, he's fine."

The boys pushed by, uninvited, and began heading up the stairs on their hands and knees.

"Ozzie, Ozzie," they called in high-pitched voices.

"Hang on…" began Antonia, not sure whether to follow them up or prevent Fiona from charging in as well. It was too late, Fiona was already in, halfway up, regaling Antonia with a sorry tale about why they had had to cut the holiday short, leaving her staring into Tom's horsey face as he approached the front door.

"Hello Toni, how are you?" He kissed her cheek. "I hope this isn't inconvenient? We probably should have rung and checked first."

"I was fine and, actually, yes, it is inconvenient and yes you probably should have rung me first," she replied with barely concealed irritation. "You'd better come up."

"Oh dear, sorry."

"Never mind, you're here now."

Tom closed the door and followed her upstairs, admiring her backside. He'd always rather fancied Toni although he would never have said or done anything about it. She looked particularly radiant today.

"Good holiday?" asked Antonia in an effort at politeness.

"No, not particularly."

"Oh dear."

When they got to the top of the stairs they were greeted by an eerie silence. Fiona and the two boys were rigid with surprise in the doorway of the lounge staring at Wendell, who was still by the window glass in hand.

"Well, hello," he said smiling towards the group.

Antonia forced her way through and shot Wendell an apologetic glance, before making introductions.

Tom stepped forward and offered Wendell his hand.

"Nice to meet you, er, Wendell, was it? Sorry to burst in like this but we didn't realise Toni had company. She didn't say."

"I wasn't given the chance." Antonia glared at her sister, but Fiona was busy examining Wendell as he and Tom greeted each other. Recovering herself from the shock, she too proffered a hand.

"Well, well Toni, you are a dark horse," she turned to face Antonia. "And here's us discussing what nunnery you were going into," she turned back to Wendell, "she never tells us anything."

"Nor me," Wendell smiled. "I think you may have been mentioned once, but I didn't know your name or anything else. Are there any more of you?"

"No just me. Nice to meet you."

"Would you like to have a glass of wine with us?" asked Wendell much to Antonia's surprise, having been used to Charles' urgent whispering, wanting to know when they were leaving.

Fiona's eyes lit up, but her reply was halted by Tom. "That's very nice of you Wren… ford, was it?"

"Wendell. Call me Wendy if you like, all my friends do."

The boys giggled.

Tom continued, "But time's getting on. Another time perhaps."

"Love to."

"Where's Ozzie, Mum?" enquired the younger child, as he dragged at Fiona's sleeve.

"Yes! Where is he?" Fiona looked around the room, Wendell forgotten for the moment.

"In his usual spot on the bed I imagine," said Antonia, leading them through. Tom stayed in the lounge with Wendell.

"Ozzie!" the boys shouted, sprawling around the slumbering cat. Ozzie stretched and yawned, accepting the sudden attention with aplomb.

"Pooh, he's got fish breath," said the older child.

Fiona bent down and dragged Ozzie into an embrace.

"Oh, my beautiful boy," she crooned, while the two boys fussed at him from below. "He looks great, Toni, thank you for having him," she kissed his head. Ozzie purred happily, recognising the usual hand that fed him.

"Where did you find *him*?" whispered Fiona, jerking her head in the direction of the lounge.

"Downstairs actually, it was his wife who ran off with Charles." Antonia laughed quietly, conspiratorially, with her sister.

Fiona opened her mouth wide. "You're joking! Toni, he's nice, hang on to him. How long have you been seeing him?"

"Not long." Antonia didn't fancy a long intimate conversation just yet.

"So how was the holiday?" she asked, changing the subject.

"It was horrible," piped up Oliver.

"Yes," agreed Fiona. "It was," her face registering they'd been through an ordeal. "The cottage had no heating to speak of; it was damp and full of bugs and came complete with a nosy old bag next door. She wouldn't leave us alone and once she was in, it was a hell of a job to get rid of her."

"She was like a witch," interrupted Matthew, "she had a hairy chin and a horrible thing on her nose."

"And no teeth," put in his brother.

"Don't interrupt boys. If it hadn't been for Tom insisting we stay I would have turned around and come straight home, I swear I would. It's a miracle we haven't all contracted pneumonia, or worse."

"When did you get back?"

"Yesterday. I couldn't stand another minute of it, cold rainy place, it never stopped. I told Tom we were going whether he came with us or not, so he came," she giggled, "we called here on the way back, but you were out." Fiona stopped and looked at Antonia expectantly.

"I went for a drink with Charles."

"Charles! You have changed," said Fiona with admiration.

They both giggled in sisterly fashion.

"Well, come on then, tell me all about it," insisted Fiona, but Antonia wouldn't be drawn.

"I can't go into it all now Fi, it's a long story."

"Oh Toni, you are maddening," teased her sister, "what else have I missed while I've been suffering on Devil's Island?"

"Rob Murphy's dead."

"What? That miserable dentist? Good job too, I'll never get over that extraction," she rubbed a finger along her jaw in memory.

At this point Tom's face peered through the door.

"Fiona, come on. Boys," they bounced off the bed in response, and Fiona followed still cradling Ozzie like a baby, whose contentment faded at the sight of the cat basket, and while the four of them struggled him into it, Antonia put all his other bits into a box. She poked her head into the lounge.

"I'm so sorry, they'll be gone in a minute."

"Relax, darling, it doesn't matter. They're very nice," Wendell smiled reassuringly.

"Thanks," she replied with genuine gratitude. Charles had never liked Fiona and had always been sullen and twitchy whenever they met.

Angry cat swearing announced that Ozzie was finally safely incarcerated. Fiona was dabbing at a nasty scratch.

"The bugger got me," she said crossly, making both boys giggle.

"Well, nice meeting you, Wendell." Tom extended his hand again.

Wendell bade them all farewell, saying he hoped to see them all again very soon. How deftly he had dealt with it all, thought Antonia, far better than she had in fact.

Finally, Wendell bent down to peer at Ozzie. "Bye-bye Ozzie" and received a spiteful hiss by way of reply.

"Charming," said Wendell with amusement, and everybody laughed.

It took a further ten minutes to eject them, with various promises of meals and drinks, and suddenly there was a content silence, the kind left after a happy encounter.

Antonia hugged Wendell hard. "Thanks," she said simply.

"What for?" he laughed.

"Just thanks for being you."

He smiled at her with affection and stroked her hair.

"Look, my darling, I don't know about you but I'm starving. Shall we order a pizza or something?"

"Excellent idea, my stomach's shrunk to the size of a walnut."

"Your flat seems to be jinxed; shall we go down to mine? I've got a list of take aways by the phone."

"Ok."

Antonia grabbed the remainder of the wine and her keys, and they transferred downstairs. After ordering the food they settled down with the wine and went properly over the meetings with their exes. Wendell listened with astonishment to the story of Bibi's forged note.

"Well!" his face was expressionless. "So she completely ruined the lives of three people without a second thought. Just so she could get what she wanted. That's how much our marriage vows meant to her then," he sighed, shaking his head in wonderment. "Selfish bitch."

"Charles was devastated. He asked me to marry him."

Wendell turned to face her; his expression serious. "What did you say?"

"I said no."

Two seconds elapsed before there was spontaneous laughter, a release of tension. Wendell leant across to kiss her just as the doorbell gave two short bursts and they laughed again. He hurried out, extracting money from his wallet as he went, and Antonia leant back and smiled. Life was suddenly looking up again.

Wendell stood shoeless on the doorstep, a limp twenty-pound note in his hand, and stared in disbelief at the forlorn figure standing there.

"Hello Wendell," said Bibi sadly. "I don't suppose I could come in for a moment?" Her foot was on the step, and she shivered.

"I, well, no, sorry you can't," he stammered, at a loss for words. What the hell was she doing here?

Bibi looked at him tragically. "I tried calling you but there was no answer."

"Bibi, I'm sorry but I've got company. It's not convenient."

"Oh." Her eyes narrowed. So he had company, probably this bit of stuff he'd been seeing.

"Barney and Tracy are here. With all the children," he lied. "They've just had a new baby." It was all he could think of, remembering her dislike of children with their sticky fingers.

"Oh!" She smiled radiantly, seeing straight through the lie. "How are they? I'd love to see them." She moved forward again and bobbed her head about to see around him.

Damn the woman!

"No, I'm sorry, this isn't a good time."

"I won't be any trouble Wendy, please, I'm freezing cold," she looked up at him with enormous eyes, then lowered them again. "My mother's thrown me out, I don't know what to do, where to turn. You were the only one I could think of."

Antonia, wondering what was taking so long, got up and looked out of the window. She saw the car first; the sporty red number Bibi and Charles had made off in. The one Wendell had fondled Bibi's thighs in.

"Shit!" she hissed under her breath, moving quickly back into the room, and then stealthily towards the open door to listen.

"Just for ten minutes, please, I need to make a few phone calls that's all. I'm not asking you for a bed for the night." She managed to convey with a glance that she was on offer if he wanted to.

"No, sorry Bibi."

"Well, I can't stand here. I'm freezing," she shivered again to prove it, "come for a drink, I need to talk to someone."

"I've told you, there's nothing more to say. And anyway, I can't leave now, I've got company."

"Yes, so you said," she looked up at him again, big eyes glistening. He thought of the fake note and was unmoved.

"I've got to go Bibi," he began to close the door.

"No, wait!" she replied quickly. "Let's all go to the pub."

"No! Anyway, you can't take kids in there."

"They're not really there are they?"

"What? Yes!" A pause. "No they're not."

"Who is then?"

"A friend."

"Oh, a friend," she said with a sneer, beginning to realise this plan was unravelling in spectacular fashion. "You men are so pathetic, scared to say you've got some floozy in there, so you make up some stupid lie."

"It's none of your damn business who I invite to my place. And by the way, you're a fine one to accuse anyone of lying after making up that note."

Bibi's face froze.

"Yes, I know all about it. You ruined everyone's lives because you couldn't get what you wanted."

"What note? I don't know anything about a note," she said with disdain.

That stupid bastard, thought Bibi, she had told him to destroy it and he told her he had! And how the hell did Wendell know about it anyway?

"Actually, I have met someone else."

Bibi glowered; she had never felt so humiliated. She lunged forward but Wendell caught her arm and pushed her back before she could slap him.

"Don't you dare! Go away Bibi."

"I am going to sit in my car and wait out here until you speak to me properly," she finished and walked away to the vehicle with as much dignity as she could muster.

The car door closed, and she started the engine, turning the radio up to full volume. Antonia was startled by the venom in Bibi's voice and scuttled back to the sofa when she heard the door close.

"It's bloody Bibi," announced Wendell unnecessarily.

"I heard."

"Are you alright?" said Wendell, concerned. Antonia looked pale and anxious.

She half-smiled. "How long will she stay out there, do you think?"

Wendell shrugged heavily, got up and peeped through the curtains.

Bibi was sitting in the driver's seat with her head back, eyes closed. He could hear the music blaring out from here, and so could others by the look of those twitching curtains over the road.

"What shall we do?" said Antonia. "Give her a few minutes to calm down? If she won't leave, I suppose you'd better go and speak to her."

"Oh God," he rubbed a hand over his eyes.

"If it's the only way to get rid of her."

Wendell sighed and hugged Antonia to him, then kissed her forehead.

There was the doorbell again. Right. Wendell surged out and swung the door open angrily.

A skinny youth in a crash helmet took a step back. "Pizza delivery?"

Chapter Twenty-Eight
Friday

After the evening with Antonia and his father's strange and revealing comments, Charles had been doing some thinking. For the first time ever, his mind had broadened beyond his everyday requirements and all the trivialities that accompanied them. Understanding he was popular and admired made a difference to his confidence. He felt almost powerful as he made an entrance into the staff room on Friday morning.

No more hiding in classrooms for him.

He quailed slightly on coming face to face with Eve over the teapot, but managed to pull himself together, although he couldn't for the moment think of anything to say and, flustered, concentrated on the tea instead.

"Morning," said Eve, "haven't seen you in here for a while."

"Morning," he hurried to a chair with his cup and began leafing through a textbook. "No, I, er, I've been rather busy."

"Can I help at all?"

"Er, er, well..." *Come on, be confident*, he told himself, *she seems to have forgotten that ghastly business.*

"Er, yes, well, you could take a look at this for me." Charles held out the textbook he had been engrossed in and realised it was upside down. He spun it quickly. "Paragraph five. Is it right?"

Eve, who had begun to regard him with contempt, fell in love with him all over again and spent the rest of the day dropping books and forgetting things.

After work, Charles picked up a local paper and drove to his own place, where he could study the accommodation for rent in peace. Antonia was right, he thought importantly, one should live alone to find oneself. It would be nice not to have to obey the petty rules of his parents or be nagged by Bibi to go out to clubs and restaurants, he could do exactly what he liked. It would be fun to live on his own and besides, he couldn't afford this place without Bibi's input. Her allowance had covered quite a bit.

He'd show them all!

And if it didn't work out, well, he would just move back home again. With this reassuring thought in mind, he scanned the list on offer, crossing through anything unsuitable or too expensive. There wasn't a great deal left when he was finished. Why didn't it say where these places were located? That was a nuisance, but never mind.

The first call he made was to a "modern one bedroom flat near shops." He started to dial and then stopped, deciding to make a coffee before he did anything. Halfway through the coffee he began again. There was no answer and Charles found himself feeling a little relieved. But suddenly it was snatched up and a loud childish voice said, "hallo?"

"Oh, hello, I'm calling about the flat for rent," he responded, not particularly keen on dealing with a ten year old. No, this was no good. The line appeared to have gone dead, then he heard a distant shout at the other end.

"Dad, phone for you."

"Who is it?"

"Dunno."

The receiver rattled and shuffled its way to the father's ear. "Yep?"

"Oh, hello, I believe you have a flat to rent," said Charles in his most polite tone.

"Sorry mate, it's gone. Bye."

"Goodbye," said Charles into the lifeless phone. He drew a line through that one, took a sip of coffee and moved a finger down to the next on the list.

After two more failures he began to think it wasn't worth it after all. Living at home wasn't that bad, was it?

But he wanted to impress Antonia. That was really what all this was about. He wanted to be able to say: "Yeah, I'm living on my own now, come round and I'll cook you dinner."

One last try. This time it was swiftly answered by an older sounding lady with a plum firmly in her mouth.

"Eight nayne four, fayve fayve two nayne," she announced haughtily.

"Good afternoon," repeated Charles for the fourth time in ten minutes. He was getting used to it now. "I'm calling about the flat to rent."

Her snooty drawl metamorphosed into a tone of cautious suspicion.

"Are you working?"

"Yes."

"What do you do?"

"I'm a teacher," said Charles, slightly mystified as to where this was going.

"Oh!" Warmth flooded down the line. "Well, that's splendid. I do apologise for the interrogation but one does have to be so careful these days."

She swept on, describing the property in loud and dramatic tones and finished by enquiring whether he would like to come and view.

"Where are you exactly?" asked Charles, when the sales pitch had concluded.

"Willow Road, Mapleford. Do you know it?"

Charles brightened immediately.

"I do actually, my parents live in it."

"Oh, how splendid! Perhaps I know them?"

"Waterman's the name."

"Waterman? Waterman?" She made a few brain functioning noises at the other end. "What number?"

"148."

"Well, I'm at 1-0-9," she stretched the numbers out in case he was hard of hearing. "I have probably seen them about. How splendid. Can you come this evening for a look-see?"

"Oh, yes, I suppose so." This was moving alarmingly fast. Charles slightly hesitantly agreed to go straight there. After all, he was only a few minutes away and it was only a look, he didn't have to decide there and then. He was sweating when he put the phone down, but there was no time to shower so a quick whiff of his armpits to check he wasn't smelling like a ferret would have to suffice.

The house was much the same as all the others on the road, 1930s semi, reasonably sized front garden, rather in need of attention in this case. He had been past it many times and never really seen it. The front door had a greenhouse-like porch surrounding it, within which lay an assortment of well-worn footwear below a shelf of limp and straggling plants. The porch door was locked when he tried it, so he pushed one of the two bells and almost immediately the inner door flew open to reveal Mrs Allerdyce-Smythe in all her glory.

A shrewd eye passed over Charles as he stood there waiting in the blustery weather. The outer door opened, finally, when Mrs Allerdyce-Smythe managed to scrape it over the coconut mat.

"Mr Waterman?"

"Yes."

"Splendid, do come in," she placed a skeletal, bejewelled hand behind Charles' elbow to guide him through, then hurried back to the door, craned her neck out, swivelled her head left and right and locked up behind her.

"Mrs Allerdyce-Smythe," the cold bony hand, rattling with plastic bangles, was held out to him and Charles shook it briefly while black beady eyes scanned him quickly from head to foot.

Mrs Allerdyce-Smythe's abundant grey hair was drawn back into an unruly bun, held perilously with various combs, which surrounded a face with pointy features pointing forward, suggesting a nosy disposition. She was wearing an odd assortment of clothes topped by a Mexican poncho which smelled of dog.

"I think I have seen your parents dear, you're very like your father," her head was tilted up towards his as she appraised his chiselled features. She smiled theatrically, revealing a mouthful of large yellowed teeth, from which an unpleasant smell issued forth. Charles need not have worried about his own body odour, as this toxic pong would have overridden it completely.

They were facing two doors. The left, she explained, was hers. The right led to the flat upstairs, so it was all self-contained. She selected a key from the large bunch she was holding, opened the right-hand door and led the way up. The flat was smallish, hardly luxurious, but well furnished, affordable and, of course, close to his parents' home. He followed Mrs Allerdyce-Smythe down the stairs again and into her own abode, which was almost unbearably hot and stuffy and cluttered with furniture and hideous ornaments. A small off-white poodle with orangey-brown ends danced about, growling and yapping in front of him.

"Now, now Pom-pom," said Mrs Allerdyce-Smythe, sending the dog reeling with a pointed shoe, "don't be rude to our guest. Do sit down, Mr Waterman."

Charles skirted around the dog and took the chair on offer.

"A deposit of one month's rent is required, refundable of course, and the rent is in arrears so that would be two months' rent, including deposit, to start. How does that sound?" She didn't wait for an answer. "Do say you'll take it, I'm sure we'll get along famously." She sat on the edge of her chair flickering her eyelids, and smiled.

Charles ummed and ahhed, looked around him and made strange movements with his mouth. He really wanted to think about it but felt quite unable to say so in case he offended her. He was cornered.

"Fine," he said at last.

Mrs Allerdyce-Smythe clasped her hands together in ecstasy, she had been trying to rent the flat for weeks. "I just know we'll get along splendidly."

Ten minutes later Charles was shaking her hand in farewell, having written a cheque that would bankrupt him if he wasn't careful for the next quarter, while Pom-pom tried enthusiastically to make love to his leg. He would move in on Saturday. Tomorrow in fact. It had all happened so fast and as soon as he was out in the fresh air, doubts began to fly at him from every angle. What if he hated it? One month. He'd give it a month and if he hated it, he'd leave. After all, it wasn't very far to go, was it?

Across and down the road a little way, Mrs Waterman stood peering anxiously through the net curtains.

"I tell you; it is him!" she snapped at her husband.

"Let me see," he replied testily, raising himself with a grunt from his TV chair.

With a sigh, he parted the curtains and looked out to where his wife was indicating.

"There! Over there, the one where that eccentric woman lives. What's he doing there?"

"How should I know?" Mr Waterman fondled his moustache and pursed his lips. "No doubt he'll be back in a minute, you can ask him yourself."

When Charles' father had suggested a bit on the side, this wasn't what he'd meant. Surely the boy wasn't contemplating a dalliance with that repulsive old crone. He felt slightly uneasy.

"That ghastly woman, what on earth is he doing there? Oh dear," Mrs Waterman wrung her hands together nervously.

"Hmm, quite," Mr Waterman stared thoughtfully for a moment before returning to his chair. Just as he had settled back into it, his wife exclaimed, "It is him! Here he comes now."

Mr Waterman hoisted himself up again and joined his wife in time to see Charles walking away while that appalling woman stood and waved on the doorstep.

My God, he must be desperate, thought Mr Waterman. It didn't bear thinking about.

As Charles walked up the path, his parents affected normality.

"Hello," called Charles. "Just me," and closed the door.

He entered the lounge to find his parents sitting there as if waiting to be called in to the doctor's surgery and expecting to be told it was terminal.

"Is something the matter?" he enquired eventually.

"Is there something you want to tell us?" said his father.

"What?"

"Don't keep saying what."

"Sorry." For God's sake! Just as well he would soon be gone from here.

"We saw you over the road just now, visiting Mrs Ponsonby-Smith, or whatever she calls herself."

"Allerdyce-Smythe," interrupted Mrs Waterman, now standing.

Charles was annoyed. So, they'd been spying on him, had they? Couldn't he do anything without a bloody interrogation? He had been going to tell them during supper, now he'd have to explain before he'd even had a moment to think about it himself.

"I'm going to rent the flat there."

Mr Waterman let out a whoosh of relieved breath. His wife began wringing her hands together.

"But Charles," said his mother anxiously, "you know you can stay here. Why do you want to leave? Why there of all places?"

"You don't approve of my landlady then?" He couldn't look at either of his parents, suddenly appalled by their snobbishness.

"Well," Mrs Waterman's nostrils flared, "she's a bit… eccentric. People talk about her."

"Seemed normal enough to me," pretended Charles, addressing the backs of his splayed hands.

"We can't have the neighbours associating us with her," said his father, while Mrs Waterman nodded her agreement.

"Right then." Charles was really cross now. "While I live there, I'll make sure I keep out of your way. You won't have to worry about what the neighbours think then."

His mother let out a small involuntary cry and put a hand on her heart.

He felt a bit sorry for her. "If you must know I took it because it was near you. I just need some time alone, alright? I'll give it a month and if it isn't working out, I'll come back."

Fractionally less anxious, his mother murmured, "Oh dear" and went to prepare the dinner.

Mr Waterman studied Charles thoughtfully. He seemed a little different somehow, perhaps he was at last learning to stand on his own two feet. He didn't for a moment think he would cope but let him try. He would probably come here for meals and be back in a fortnight.

"Get yourself a good woman, Charles," his father said again, turning back to the television.

"So you said." My God, thought Charles, it was definitely a good thing he was leaving here before he strangled them both. They must think he was an imbecile.

During a rather subdued evening meal, Charles' father offered to help him move his things. Both he and his mother looked up in surprise, his father rarely offered to help with anything.

"Thanks Dad," replied Charles, pleased.

In fact, Mr Waterman wanted to see what it was like over there.

While he was soaking in the bath later, free of questioning, Charles' thoughts swayed back and forth between dread and optimism, and he was still mulling over whether to delight in the coming freedom or forget the whole thing and lose his deposit, so he was glad to see a leaflet forcing its way through the letter box as a momentary distraction.

He picked it up. A new restaurant, the 'Bistro la Bella', was opening locally. It looked quite nice and on the opening weekend, every customer would get a free bottle of wine with their meal. Charles quite fancied a night out, but who could he take? Antonia? She wouldn't come. Bibi? Out of the question. Funny really, he'd lost interest in her completely, almost forgotten what she looked like when he thought about it. Who else was there? Eve Tate? God no. It was rather sad, but there wasn't a single person he could ask. It was a sobering thought, he needed to find some friends of both sexes. If it wasn't for his parents, he'd have no one at all.

His parents… well, why not? Fired up with this plan, he marched into the lounge brandishing the leaflet.

"Mum, Dad?" he said loudly, his heartbeat quickening. Both turned to look at him fearfully, wondering what was coming now.

"I'd like to treat you to a meal out tomorrow night, just to say thanks for all you've done for me." He found, to his surprise, a little lump in his throat as he spoke. His mother was fumbling for a tissue to dab her eye with, and his father cleared his throat rather audibly. Both looked flabbergasted.

Then smiles broke out all round and his father said, "Thank you Charles, that's jolly decent of you," then turned quickly back to the television before he embarrassed himself.

Mrs Waterman gazed up at Charles as though he were the Messiah himself, kissed him on the cheek and removed herself to the kitchen where much nose blowing and sniffing was soon heard.

Charles called the restaurant and made a booking, while his father stifled a comment when he heard the phone ping.

"6.30 Saturday night. They couldn't manage any earlier, is that alright?"

"Perfect." They were all smiles now the shock was over.

Charles leant back on the sofa with great satisfaction. Yes, things were definitely moving in the right direction.

Chapter Twenty-Nine
Friday

Friday morning swept in furiously, with high winds and monsoon-like rain. For once Antonia decided against cycling and walked to work instead. As the cars crawled by, their occupants happily preferring steamed-up shelter to speed, she was enjoying the wild weather, nicely wrapped up in waterproof clothing and warm from the exercise. This was her last day at Rob Murphy's and although she wasn't sure what her future held jobwise, she had a month's wages to come, so there was time to sort something out. She would buy a paper on her way home and have a look at the options.

Mrs Murphy, or Aoife (they were now on first name terms), appeared mid-morning. Antonia had spoken to her several times now and had discovered in her an unlikely ally. It was plain to see that her life with Rob Murphy had been a miserable one and the hard done by wife was determined to make up for it from now on.

"Hello dear," she smiled the greeting, "what a foul day."

"Hello Aoife. How are you?"

"Busy still but getting through it."

She had had her hair cut and highlighted, Antonia noticed, and was wearing make-up. The slacks and cardigan had been replaced by a smart black skirt suit, daringly short, which suited her trim figure. The dowdy wife had blossomed into a merry widow.

"You look wonderful," complimented Antonia truthfully. "You've had your hair done. It's lovely."

"I was never allowed to change it before," she responded with a carefree and slightly revengeful laugh.

"Can I get you a coffee? I was just going to have one myself."

"Oh, that would be grand, thank you," she replied, sitting down to get to work.

A short while later she rose, replaced various files, loaded her bag with yet more paperwork and held out a wage cheque. Antonia took it and thanked her.

Then she held out another.

"Here you are dear. Compensation, I suppose, is the best word for this."

Antonia stared at it. There seemed to be a lot of noughts on this one. When her eyes finally focused on it, she exclaimed, "This is way too much!"

"Take it dear, you've earned it," came the reply, followed by something that sounded like 'Having to put up with him every day of the week'.

Mrs Murphy continued, "The funeral is at ten on Monday at St Andrews here," and pointed towards where the steeple could be seen. She laid a gentle hand on Antonia's shoulder. "Don't feel you have to attend, it's not compulsory."

"I'd like to." Everyone should have a decent send-off, even Rob Murphy.

Mrs Murphy breezed out into the elements, leaving behind a sudden silence filled only by an aroma of expensive perfume. Good for her!

Antonia stared in amazement at her £10,000 cheque. It was a strange feeling; she had never had so much money in her life and to be given it like that! It seemed there were lots of benefits from the demise of Rob Murphy.

The telephone rang. It was Wendell.

"Wendell!" she said with delight, feeling the usual heat radiate through her.

"Can you talk, darling?"

"I certainly can, nothing happening here, it's my last day actually."

"Oh yes of course, I forgot. How are you feeling?"

"Wonderful actually, I've just been given a compensatory cheque." She didn't want to share all the details just yet, savour it for herself for the day.

"Christ! I wish my boss…" He began, then laughed. "Perhaps not. What an awful thing to say."

"I thought it every day about mine. I think his wife did too by the look of things, maybe she did him in."

They laughed.

"I'm sorry, darling, can we put tonight off, do you mind? I've got to pick my friend Barney up from Heathrow."

"Barney? That's the one with the brat and baby Antonia?"

"Yes, him. He had to rush off to Paris and there's been some kind of cock-up with his transport. Sounds like Barney alright. I was put on the spot, and I was looking forward to seeing you."

"Me too," replied Antonia, feeling slightly deflated. "Oh well, never mind."

"We'll go out tomorrow instead, if you can?"

"Fine. Absence maketh the heart grow fonder and all that."

"I definitely hopeth so. Miss you already, see you about seven tomorrow then?"

"Ok, bye."

Wendell replaced the phone before Bellingham got back from the toilet, knowing his post lunch visit there rarely took less than twenty minutes. He leant back, hands behind head, and smiled with satisfaction.

"Antonia?" enquired Beth with a raised eyebrow, as she continued her typing.

"Who else?" he said with a faraway look, then brought both himself and his chair back down to earth.

"You've got it bad," smiled Beth, happy to see him so contented at last.

"Where can I take her tomorrow night? Any suggestions?"

"No point asking an old frump like me for goodness' sake, I never go out," she stopped typing and tore the paper from the machine with a satisfying zip. "Here you are, that's the Clarkson Thing."

"Excellent," Wendell ran an eye over it quickly. "Thank you."

"How about this? It was on the mat when I got back from lunch." Beth pulled something from the waste paper basket and handed it to him. It announced the opening of a new and trendy restaurant "Bistro la Bella," local to him and with free wine for every new customer. Bellingham still wasn't back so he picked up the phone and made a booking. That solved that one. Just in time too, Bellingham reappeared wiping his brow with a handkerchief. Must have been a bigger job than usual.

"Thank you, Beth, I can always rely on you."

"Sounds like this girl is something special then?"

"Yes. I really think she is."

There was a pause, then Beth said, "I heard you were over the road with your wife."

"You heard about that did you? Bad news travels fast around here. I was forced into speaking to the woman last night too."

"Forced?" Beth raised an eyebrow.

He ran through the events of the previous evening, including the fact that he didn't dare get in the car with her, "she kept saying let's go for a drink and a chat. I'm not that daft, she would have driven miles so I couldn't walk away. My feet were freezing by the time I got back indoors. So was the pizza."

"I get the feeling you haven't heard the last of her," said Beth sagely.

"Oh no, I made it very clear to her, and she now knows I'm seeing someone else; so I hope we can just have a civilised divorce and move on."

"Don't count on it," she said and resumed typing.

"Wendell Cornish," Wendell answered his phone as he examined the Clarkson Thing more thoroughly.

"Hi Wendy, Bibi here."

No, it couldn't be. He let the Clarkson Thing fall onto his desk.

"What do you want?" He was tired of trying to be polite. Beth had stopped typing and glanced at Wendell.

"That's a nice way to speak to your wife, I'm sure."

"Forget it Bibi, what do you want?"

Beth shook her head, raised her eyebrows, and inserted another sheet of paper into her typewriter.

"I want you to come out with me this evening."

"No! How many times do I have to say it? No more Bibi. I can't stop now, I'm busy."

"That makes a change then."

"I've got to go."

"If you hang up on me, I'll just keep calling until you agree to see me."

Bloody hell! Why wouldn't she just leave him alone?

"I said no."

"I mean it, Wendell."

He felt defeated, knowing she probably did mean it, and rubbed his eyes in the pause.

"Tonight then," she said crisply.

"Impossible."

"Cheating on me with the little woman, are we?"

"You really are a class A bitch, aren't you?"

Bibi laughed. "Tomorrow then?"

"Also impossible."

"You're a hard man to pin down, darling," she crooned. She was enjoying this.

"Sunday evening, seven-thirty in the Dancing Bear. Take it or leave it," he finished.

"Very romantic. Well, I suppose if that's your best offer, I'll have to take it won't I?"

"It is. It's also my last ever offer," he hung up without saying goodbye and ran a hand through his hair. "Bloody woman," he hissed.

Beth cast him a sympathetic look and kept typing.

Bibi threw the telephone down, leant back and laughed. Clara was out and she'd taken the opportunity to catch up on some calls. No man was going to humiliate *her* and get away with it, least of all Wendell Cornish. The rosy warmth of love had melted and hardened into an iceberg of hate; she was mortified when she thought of the way she had grovelled to him on Tuesday and she was out for revenge. In time he would come round and then she would drop him and walk away. Until then, she would pester him.

A loud crash announced the return of Clara as she hurtled through the back door. Seconds later she blocked the lounge entrance, a lumpy, damp silhouette laden with wet carrier bags.

"Hi," she trilled. "Oh what a morning! I've been in every charity shop within a ten-mile radius, just look at the treasures I've discovered."

Clara emptied the contents of all the bags into a mound on the floor and began sorting through the various bobbly sweaters and other odd clothing. Bibi could see why it had been discarded in the first place.

Was it her imagination or was Clara actually exuding smoke? She had been walking in the rain and it turned out to be steam coming off her as she sat on the floor in front of the radiator. Combined with the second hand clothes, the room began to smell of old socks and wet dog.

"Isn't this just fabulous!" she cried, holding a gaudy Indian blouse up to view. "It's the real thing."

Bibi, unimpressed, waved a hand in front of her face.

"Phew," she said, wrinkling her nose. "Smells like Gandhi was the last to wear it."

"Oh, Bibi you are a scream," roared Clara. "Of course it needs a wash, everything does. No time like the present." She scooped up half the mound and made her way to the washing machine.

"We simply must go out tomorrow night, I want to wear all my new things. What's this? It was in the letterbox." She thrust the leaflet at Bibi, before clearing the room of the rest of the clothing. Bibi took it in a bored fashion and glanced at it. "Sure, why not."

"Fab," cried Clara and reached for her cigarettes. Bibi rolled her eyes; Clara was like an over-excited child the entire time. The sight of her marshmallow face wearing its dimply smile was even starting to get on her nerves. She wanted to return to her mother's, but the longer it went on the less she felt able to make contact. She had popped in on her father, but he was still tired and uninterested in what she had to say. She was now a bit nervous of finding him dead and had hurried away.

The novelty of rekindling their relationship had rather faded in the last couple of days. He wasn't the man she remembered. She thought longingly of having the place to herself tonight as Clara wittered on and puffed smoke all over the place. Would Charlie still be at the flat?

"I need to make a phone call," she announced, cutting Clara off mid-sentence. She wasn't interested in advising someone that pink and orange would be an awful colour combination if they couldn't see it themselves. "A private one, if you wouldn't mind?" she glared pointedly at Clara.

"Oh right, I'll go and get the kettle on, I'm absolutely gasping after all that shopping," she bounced her bulk up swiftly and jiggled away. Bibi pushed the door shut after her.

"8925072."

"Good afternoon, may I speak with Mr Charles Waterman?"

"I'm afraid he's not here at the moment, can I help?"

"Do you expect him later?"

"Yes, he should be back about four thirty. May I ask who's calling?"

"Miss Haversham, goodbye," Bibi hung up before Mrs Waterman could say more. Good, Charles was staying with Mummy and Daddy, which meant the flat would be empty. She hurried upstairs and put a few things into a hold all.

"You're not leaving?" enquired Clara, crestfallen, as Bibi glided down the stairs with her bag.

"Just for tonight, darling. My father isn't feeling too well, I said I'd stay with him tonight to look after him."

"Oh golly, the poor thing," her expression was tragic. "Can I help?" she added hopefully.

"No, it's better just me," she replied in martyred tones and after the tea she left.

"You'll be back tomorrow evening?" called Clara from the step.

"Oh yes, see you."

"Ciao!" Clara waved her off and went sadly back inside, looking like a giant jelly baby in bright yellow jeans and an orange silk blouse.

Bibi parked out of sight to make sure that Charles' car wasn't in evidence. Unfortunately, it was, but the door was suddenly flung open, and Charles hurried to his car with a suitcase, heading off to Mrs Allerdyce-Smythe's. What a waste, thought Bibi, as she took in the good looks all over again. A close shave though, that could have been awkward. She parked the car outside and went in.

Peace at last.

It was nice to be back in familiar surroundings, even if it was looking a bit sparse now. She soaked in the bath for a while, then wandered around in a robe. There was some cheese in the fridge and a box of crispbreads, unopened, at the back of the cupboard, so she sat in front of the TV and ate her way through them. It was rather nice. Perhaps living alone wouldn't be such a bad idea.

A sudden knock on the door made her drop the last crispbread.

"Damn!" she whispered and leapt up to look out of the window. Outside, in all its glory, stood Guy's jeep. What the hell was *he* doing here? Was her mother with him? She stormed to the door and opened it just enough to glare out. It was Guy on his own.

"What do *you* want?" she said rudely.

"Temper, temper," he smirked, eyeing the cleavage where the robe had parted a bit.

Bibi moved to close the door, but he already had a foot solidly placed on the threshold.

"Take your cloven hoof off my property you moron," she shouted angrily.

How dare he come around here!

"I'm here on a mission of mercy babe. Elizabeth sent me, she was worried about you."

"Right, mission accomplished. Now fuck off."

She tried to crush his foot in the door, but his big expensive boots were made of strong stuff.

"Don't I even get a coffee for my trouble?"

"NO," she shouted, "but you can certainly fuck-offee."

Guy remained where he was, eyeing her up and down with approval.

"Elizabeth must have been the image of you when she was your age."

"Go away, will you?"

"She's still a very attractive woman."

"Look, just go away, I'm enjoying a bit of peace and quiet."

"All alone?" he smiled, stripping her naked with his eyes and, in spite of everything, she felt herself weaken for just a moment, enjoying the male approval.

Guy knew the signs; he was a pro at this and knew how to take advantage of a situation.

"I'd really like us to be friends," he said with great sincerity. "I really am very fond of Elizabeth, and I would like us to be fond of one another too."

His meaning was crystal clear, and Bibi found herself staring into those rather compelling, lecherous eyes and almost being tempted. He was quite attractive in a catalogue model sort of way, and what a wonderful way to revenge herself on her mother. It was during this momentary hesitation that Guy pushed his way into the flat and closed the door behind him.

"How dare you bust your way in here!" she declared, but the heat had gone from her, and he knew it.

"Come on babe, you know you want it too."

"You disgust me."

He caught hold of her and she struggled feebly. He was very muscular.

"You smell gorgeous. It's turning me on."

"Let me go you bastard!" she continued to wriggle, aware now of how hard he was down below. She could feel it through her robe.

"It'll be our little secret," he smiled wickedly.

What a strange and enticing opportunity.

Still holding her wrist, he bent his head to her face, and she turned hers away. Gently, he turned her face back and kissed her. Bibi sighed, brought a hand up behind his neck and kissed him back. He lifted her up as easily as if she had been a child, and carried her to the bedroom.

No inexperienced virgin by any means, Bibi had just had the most satisfying sexual experience of her life. No wonder her mother had bought him a jeep.

"You are fantastic," breathed Guy as he kissed her bare shoulder. "That was bloody incredible."

For once he meant it too. What. A. Woman! For the first time in his life, he felt tempted to continue a relationship for something other than financial gain.

"We'll have to do this again babe," he was propped up on one elbow, wavy hair all ruffled, looking at her with undisguised passion.

"Maybe," she said coolly.

"You vixen," he was on her again, already aroused once more.

By midnight, their passion satisfied, they lay entwined and completely contented.

"Won't my mother wonder where you are?" enquired Bibi, full of the joy of revenge and wonderful sex.

"She doesn't own me."

"She pays for you though."

Guy smiled rather cruelly. "I'll go over in the morning."

"Do you have a place of your own?"

"Sure. She pays for it, I'm a kept man."

He laughed in a way Bibi wasn't quite sure how to take.

"What!" She turned her head towards him, and he kissed her hand. Afterwards, she lay back and laughed without humour. "My God!"

"I'll see her tomorrow morning. Tomorrow night I'm spending with you." It was a statement rather than a request and Bibi felt oddly unable to refuse.

"Not here," was all she said.

"You can come and see what your mother pays for."

"That should be interesting," she said with a dark frown, but Guy was no longer listening. "Do you actually do any kind of real work?"

"Of course. I'm an actor. Resting, at the moment."

Bibi snorted. "Huh, well some things make sense now."

Guy ignored her and continued, "Someone I know is opening a new eatery tomorrow night, I've told him I'll go to support him. It's a free meal. We'll go there and grab a bite, go to a club and back to mine. All that should get us in the mood. Yeah, that's settled then," he endowed her with a lengthy kiss.

Bibi lay beside him as he slept and wondered why she had let him tell her what to do. In fact, how had all this even happened? She didn't even like him.

Meanwhile, it had taken Wendell a good two hours to reach the airport in the Friday rush hour traffic. The inclement weather seemed to have encouraged even more cars onto the road which only added to it, that and a small collision between a bike and a car driven by an elderly gentleman who probably required glasses, which held him up locally for another twenty minutes. He put the radio on and resigned himself to it, his thoughts drifting to Antonia, Bibi, the last two weeks in general. If he was late for Barney, well, he would just have to wait. He sat back into the seat, arms stretched out to the wheel and imagined how many different words could be made from the three letters of the number plate in front.

Barney's flight was due in at 8.20, he had plenty of time. His mind shifted to the coming date with Antonia, and he remembered the leaflet Beth had given him. What had he done with that? He finally located it in a back pocket and had another look, thinking what a good idea it had been, obviously fate. Maybe it would become their favourite venue.

The crawl into the airport itself took ages. Rain began to fall again, whipped about by energetic gusts of wind. What a nasty evening. He found himself in the wrong lane for arrivals and no bugger would let him cut in, resulting in a further slow orbit of the system. Every space seemed to have been taken in the car park, the car was steaming up and he was becoming seriously pissed off. The roof offered the only vacancy which was a damn nuisance as he hadn't brought a coat, believing wrongly that he wouldn't be open to the elements.

"Damn!" he cursed. Should he try the lower levels again? He glanced at his watch and found there wasn't enough time for all that faffing about. He'd just have to make a dash for cover. As he opened the door, the wind nearly tore it off along with his arm.

"Christ!" he exclaimed and got out, quickly looking around for the exit. It was difficult to see in this spiteful rain, which pricked like pins as it hurled itself into his face, first from one angle and then from another. There it was. He began to jog towards the lighted doorway, trying to protect his head by hauling his suit jacket up over it.

Between him and shelter lay a sopping sweater dropped unknowingly, no doubt by some other person sprinting for cover. Intent on keeping the rain from completely soaking him, and by the momentary distraction of glancing up at the overhead aeroplane he failed to spot it, thereby making a spectacular and balletic leap as one foot caught it mid-run. His hands left his collar and flew out in front of him in response to falling, and his now wide open eyes watched as the tarmac came up to meet them. It was a smooth landing, hands and knees taking the brunt of the fall, helped to a halt by the gritty surface.

Wendell remained motionless for a few seconds, shocked and unaware of what he had hit in the first place, then fury took over.

"Fuck!" he screamed. "FUUUCK!" The words were whipped away by the wind and the roar of the overhead plane.

He straightened himself up and looked first at his wet and blackened palms, already beading with blood, then to the tattered knees of his trousers and finally at the lump of wet material that had been the instigator of the accident.

"Fucking hell," he shouted again and kicked at the offending article which only brought pain to his knee. His hands stung, he was filthy and ragged and soaked to the skin. He limped to the exit door; hands held in front like a piano player about to begin a concerto. It was a relief to get out of the wind and rain at least, where he could properly assess his injuries. The palms of his hands were covered in a mix of blood and dirt. They felt strangely numb now. He fumbled about and in the absence of anything better, wiped them as best he could with an old till receipt.

"Goddamnit!" he swore just as the lift doors opened, spewing out several tidy looking travellers with loaded trolleys, who regarded him suspiciously as they swept past devoid of sympathy. He smiled sheepishly, muttering that he'd fallen over; no one took any notice, miserable bastards. He darted into the lift, suffering more hostile stares as it picked up more people on its descent. Once in the arrivals hall he headed straight to the toilets. It was 8.25. The warm water stung horribly and started the bleeding off again. His knees were a mess and now felt stiff as well as bruised. The hand towels were better than tissue, which just fell apart and had to be extracted from the grazed flesh bit by bit. As for the trousers, well, they were ruined, both knees ripped open to reveal the damage within to anyone who cared to examine them.

"Fucking hell," he muttered again, as the last bit of tissue flowed away with more warm water. "What a fucking disaster."

By the time he was finished it was well past 8.30. He glanced at himself in the long mirror on the way out and saw a tramp staring back at him. Just get Barney and go home, he told himself, hurrying as best he could on inflamed knees, to the arrivals gate.

As he stood there watching the, so far, empty passengers exit he began to feel terribly cold. His sodden clothes were clinging to him, and he seemed to have a heartbeat in his hands and knees. He shivered, and a woman on one side of him sidled away.

"Come on Barney," he muttered, feeling weary beyond belief.

The first trickle of passengers emerged, and his eyes followed a rather attractive girl in tight jeans. She threw herself into the arms of an older man, her father he supposed, next to whom stood a familiar face, someone he knew from somewhere else.

As the realisation of who it was dawned on him, Wendell wondered what the hell else could go wrong tonight. Bellingham looked smart and groomed in a pale blue Pringle sweater and dark trousers, one hand in a pocket, the other clutching a bunch of keys. His eyes were fixed on the now thick stream of people flowing from the tunnel. Thankfully, he didn't seem to have noticed Wendell, who shrank back from the barrier and tried to conceal himself between a young man reeking of garlic and an older, fatter man reeking of sweat. A heady combination.

What the hell was Bellingham doing here? Why now for God's sake? If there was a worse moment to bump into his boss, he couldn't think of it. He was suddenly aware of a body moving purposefully towards him at the rail. At last. Get Barney and sneak off before Bellingham noticed him.

It was Lung.

"Corniss," he grinned enormously, as Wendell stared in horrified disbelief. He'd told Belly he was off to Spain for the weekend. How would he explain his presence here? Now Bellingham had spotted Lung and was moving towards them.

"Ah Lolan," beamed Lung, shaking Bellingham's hand over the barrier. Amazingly, he hadn't yet seen Wendell and for a fleeting moment he thought he might get away with it by disappearing backwards into the crowd. Unfortunately though, before he could move Lung leant over the barrier, grabbed Wendell's hand and pumped it enthusiastically, causing him almost to cry out with pain. Bellingham turned to him with a puzzled expression, which rapidly became a frown of disapproval as he looked him up and down.

"Cornish? What are you doing here? I thought you were in Spain."

Wendell fenced the question through chattering teeth, whether from cold or terror he was unsure.

"Fancy seeing you here, Mr Bellingham, not a very pleasant evening to fly, is it?"

Lung had progressed around the barrier and now joined them, still grinning broadly. He was holding an expensive looking holdall which he temporarily relinquished in order to hug Wendell. He seemed oblivious to the state of Wendell's person.

"Ah Corniss, jolly good fun."

"Hello Lung, nice to see you again. I'm sorry I can't take you out this time."

Lung's teeth disappeared as his lips dropped with disappointment.

"Not go out. But why?"

"You do know this is arrivals?" put in Bellingham from the sidelines. "I thought you were going to Spain. Departures is upstairs," he regarded Wendell through suspicious eyes as he pointed to the staircase.

"Oh yes, I'm off in a moment. An old friend of mine was coming in on this one, so we agreed to try and cross paths if we could. Only to say hello really, old school friend, haven't seen him for years. Too good a chance to miss."

He was babbling, Bellingham didn't believe him.

"Does he live in Paris?"

"No, just passing through on business," Wendell smiled reassuringly.

"Same for me," said Lung, resuming the smile.

"Well, time to go. I'm out of time, what a shame." It sounded pathetic as he said it and Bellingham studied him with fresh suspicion, suddenly aware of the unsavoury state he was in. Wendell saw it and said feebly, "I had a bit of an accident on the way here, a puncture on the motorway. Not the night for changing a wheel, is it?" he effected a laugh.

Why didn't they bloody well go!

"No luggage, Cornish?"

"All booked in."

"Hmm. Well, we must go." Thank God, thought Wendell. "Mrs Bellingham's got a dinner planned. Enjoy your weekend."

"Thank you. Bye Lung." He exhaled with relief as they turned.

"Wendy!" came a roar from the mouth of the tunnel and all heads turned in the direction of the shout to see Barney, paralytic with drink, staggering from it with support from the arm of a red-faced security guard. Barney's luggage hung from the guard's other hand.

"Good heavens!" tutted Bellingham. "Disgraceful! I'm sorry you had to see that, Lung," and they finally disappeared into the crowd.

Thank God they've gone, thought Wendell with relief.

Meanwhile, the security guard stood scanning the people, hoping for the poor woman who might be Wendy to make herself known.

Wendell made himself known to the guard, who was infinitely relieved to be able to rid himself of his burden. He also regarded Wendell with suspicion, taking note of his ragged condition and the fact that he was not a woman.

"Here," he handed Wendell the hold all which he took painfully with his torn hand, "he's all yours," then strode away hurriedly.

"Wendy, me old mate," slurred Barney as he slumped against him.

"For God's sake, how much have you had? The flight's not that long, is it?"

"Can't 'member me ol' china," replied Barney and followed it with a silly high-pitched giggle.

"Come on then. Can you stand?"

"Doubt it," he giggled again, "you look rough."

Wendell had had enough. He was freezing cold, hungry, tired and injured and now he had to mess about with a drunk.

They shuffled along to the end of the barrier, Wendell's hands chafing painfully against the handles of Barney's bag and his friend's arm, with Barney now laughing uncontrollably.

"Stop laughing like that, everyone's staring," said Wendell, not wishing to attract attention to his own appearance.

As they slowly progressed towards the lifts they were approached by a policeman, who was grunting something into his lapel radio. He puffed his chest out and walked sternly towards them.

"Evening Sir, having trouble, are we?" It wasn't certain which one of them he was addressing but Wendell answered quickly before Barney could get in.

"Yes, my friend isn't feeling too well. I've had an accident on the way here. It's not my day, Officer."

Barney laughed through closed lips and produced a raspberry. The policeman gave him a cold stare.

"Well, I'm sorry to hear that, Sir. Do you know this is an alcohol-free area?"

"Yes, but an aeroplane isn't, is it?" replied Wendell archly. "Look, I'm sorry, Officer, I don't suppose you could possibly give me a hand getting him to my car, could you? I've hurt my hands." He rolled his palm outwards from beneath Barney's arm and showed the man.

"Fell over, did you?" he said unsympathetically.

"Yes, if you must know," said Wendell, all fear of the law wiped away by the acidic comments of this stupid copper. He looked up into the man's face. "Went arse over tit in the car park up there trying to avoid the rain. Had to be the roof, of course. I got soaked and dirty and ripped the knees from a perfectly good pair of trousers, and the skin from a previously perfect pair of knees for good measure. Satisfied?"

With this, Wendell turned and began to drag the now hysterically laughing Barney towards the lift doors.

"Just a moment, Sir," boomed the policeman.

Wendell stopped and dropped the bag, his shoulders sagged. Now what? A night in the cells presumably.

"We need a wheelchair to lift three, arrivals please," he said into the lapel, while his eyes roamed the area.

"Thank you," said Wendell humbly as the chair arrived and Barney was positioned into it by a small man in a uniform.

"Go home and have a hot bath, Sir," advised the copper. "As for him," he indicated Barney. "Black coffee. Lots of it."

"Thank you, officer, I'm extremely grateful." And he was. Wendell could have hugged the man.

The wizened porter stood awaiting instructions at the rear of the wheelchair. He was only the size of Lung and about half the weight. Wendell doubted he had the ability to move the chair empty, let alone with Barney's dead weight heaped on it.

"Where to, Sir?"

"The roof, I'm afraid."

"It would be," he sighed.

With surprising strength and dexterity, the little man manoeuvred the chair and its floppy occupant into and out of the lift and onto the roof, then whisked along at top speed to where Wendell was pointing. He heaved Barney into the car with one deft movement while the wind cut through Wendell's wet clothes like a sword, chilling him to the bone. His hands were so cold he could barely open the door. The porter had materialised by his side and was hovering expectantly.

"Oh... yes," mumbled Wendell, fumbling in his wallet with numb fingers. The smallest change he had was a fiver, which he pressed reluctantly into the outstretched hand.

"Thank you kindly, Sir, you have a nice evening," said the porter politely, before sprinting away with the chair. He jumped over the sodden sweater graceful and gazelle-like, still lying there as Wendell had last seen it. Wendell wondered how many other unfortunates had tripped over it.

Blue with cold, he started the engine and put the heater full on, then blew into his cupped hands. The car was already misting up inside and he waited a few minutes until it was clear, by which time the heat was getting through. Barney was slumped forward, snoring, so he reclined the seat a bit, strapped him in and drove them away. As his friend's innards straightened out, he emitted a long and pungent fart. Wendell was so cold he chose to endure it rather than open the window, until he had to stop and pay for the time he had been parked. The attendant's nostrils vibrated as he leant towards the open car window with the change, which was letting out a mixture of stale alcohol and cigarettes, eggy farts and damp clothing.

"Porr! Wha' a pen an' ink," he commented, grimacing at Wendell, "sumfink 'orrible in there mate."

"You're so right," replied Wendell, turning to look at his passenger. He rolled the window up and drove away.

The charge had been almost a tenner, effectively cleaning Wendell out of ready cash. He had spent a lot of money today, one way and another, and tried now to distract himself from the present situation by mentally going over where the money had gone. Barney snored quietly at first then horribly loudly in the confined space. If this had been a normal journey, Wendell would certainly have opened a window, but the thought of cold air rushing in was worse than the fetid odour. Ten minutes from his home, Barney woke up.

"Oh, my head," he moaned. "Oh, hello Wendy, forgot you were there. You look awful, by the way."

"You stupid bastard," said Wendell, tired and irritable, "why did you drink so much? You must have been pouring it down your neck from the moment you took off."

"Oh God, well before that Wendy, well before." Although he was still drunk, some sense was beginning to filter through. "Stop the car! I'm going to be sick."

Wendell screeched to a halt and flung the door open just in time for Barney to disgorge his stomach contents onto a grass verge. Freezing air rushed in carrying the smell of alcoholic puke with it.

Wendell wound his own window down and hung his head out to inhale. By now it was nearing midnight and at least the road was deserted.

Outside his place Barney thanked Wendell wearily and climbed out. He staggered up to the door and threw up again, this time into a rose bush. A damp sounding fart came out of the other end as he doubled over.

Get me out of here, said Wendell to himself with feeling, and drove away quickly before some new disaster befell him.

When he finally got home, Wendell eased his cold and aching body into a hot bath, had a sandwich, a couple of pain killers and a cup of coffee and fell asleep on the sofa.

Chapter Thirty
Saturday

Early on Saturday, Antonia was dragged from the land of nod by the ringing of the telephone.

"Hello?" she said, sleep still in her voice.

"Hello love, did I wake you?" her mother enquired brightly. "Shall I ring back later?"

"Well, yes you did, but I'm awake now."

"Will you be coming over today? I'm going shopping now; I could get us something nice for lunch."

"Yes ok, the car could do with a run. See you later."

There was no point in arranging a time. Lunch for Antonia's mother could be anything from about eleven to five depending on how the day was going. It was useless trying to pin her down to specific times, she had learnt that one long ago. As she closed her eyes and lay back in the comfort and warmth of the bed, she recalled one childhood incident when they'd all been out somewhere and had tea at midnight, although that had been exceptional even for her. She had tried to crawl into her parents' bed in the wee small hours, miserable with stomach ache, only to find Fiona already in it and no room for her.

She arrived at her mother's just before one. It wasn't a particularly nice day, although an improvement on the previous one. She let herself in the back door and called a greeting which was answered by silence. There was a little note propped up against a cup which read:

'Gone shopping, make yourself at home, back by 12.30. Love Mum x'

Antonia groaned as she crumpled the note up in her hand. 12.30 could mean anything, it was past one now. She put the kettle on and was pleasantly surprised when her mother returned just as the tea was going in the cup.

"Oh, you beat me," she laughed, "and I'm just in time for a cup of tea by the look of it."

At this point an overloaded carrier bag broke and a tin of chopped tomatoes rolled out across the floor. They picked everything up and put it on the table, chatting amiably.

"I met your friend Jane in the supermarket."

"Jane? Blimey, I haven't seen her in ages. What's she up to?"

"Well," began her mother, "she and her husband are getting divorced."

"Doesn't anyone stay together these days?" said Antonia sadly. Her own parents' divorce ten years previously was still a source of bewilderment to her and her sister. Their father had remarried two months later and moved to New Zealand, which may have had something to do with it of course.

Her mother noticed the mournful tone but chose to ignore it and carry on with the story.

"Her husband—what was his name, I've forgotten?"

"Adrian?"

"Yes, Adrian, has got a boyfriend! All these years it seems he's been leading a double life."

"What!" Antonia was shocked, Adrian had been at school with them, and she had fancied him herself at one time.

"The poor girl looked ashen; she's gone quite grey. I really don't know what's happening to men these days. It must be the water," she frowned and pursed her lips. "In my youth, men were men. We didn't have all this going on."

"Of course you did, they just hadn't come out of the closet then, didn't dare to."

"I blame computers and the pill."

"What about the water?"

"Water?"

"Oh, never mind. Shall we have some lunch? I'm hungry."

They enjoyed a nice lunch together before her mother broached the real topic she had in mind.

"I hear you've found yourself another man."

Antonia smiled. "I wondered how long it would take you to find out. Fi told you I suppose?"

"Actually, it was Tom, he must have made an impression on him. What's he like?"

"You already know. I told you about him before."

"Did you?" her mother frowned. "I don't remember."

"Wendell Cornish, my upstairs neighbour."

"The silly name? That's the one whose wife left with your Charles."

"He's very nice," said Antonia carefully.

By the time she left, her mother knew all about Wendell Cornish, the drink with Charles and the £10,000 cheque. As she watched Antonia leave, waving and smiling, a contentment settled over her. Perhaps now her daughter could be happy. Wendell Cornish sounded nice, even if he did have a rather strange name.

Wendell greeted Antonia as she stepped through the front door. He was wearing a loose-fitting jogging suit which didn't press against his knees. He looked, to her eye, a bit pale and tired.

"I was just coming to see you," he smiled and held her to him.

She kissed him lightly and he said, "Would you like a coffee?"

"Well... I've got to get ready."

"Just a quick one," he said making her laugh, and he hugged her tighter. "What a delightfully dirty mind you have." His knees weren't the only thing feeling a bit stiff.

"What's the matter with your legs? You're walking like Douglas Bader."

Wendell showed her his palms, now crusted with little scabs. He rolled up his trouser legs and above the hairy calves revealed two knees like small policemen's helmets.

"Ouch! What happened?" She was all concern. "I thought you looked a bit pale. Look, if you'd rather not go out tonight..."

"No, no, I want to take you out. I'll forget all about my injuries when I'm with you."

Wendell outlined the events leading to and from the fall and by the time he got to the part with the wheelchair, she could barely contain her laughter.

"This friend of yours, he seems to be a jinx on you," she managed to say, "why do these things always happen to you?"

"Yeah, he can be a bit of a liability alright," Wendell replied philosophically.

He looked so helpless sitting there with his grazed palms facing upwards that she leant over and gave him a gentle squeeze.

"What was that for?" he smiled.

"Wendell... I..." She wanted to tell him she loved him, wanted him, it was almost overwhelming, and she didn't really understand it. After all, they hardly knew one another. She shouldn't just throw caution to the wind completely.

"I'd better go, must get ready."

Antonia hurried upstairs. What was happening to her? She thought again. Every time she saw Wendell, she felt all funny, a bit light-headed and weak at the knees. Then, trying to think of something different, she hoped she hadn't offended him by finding his most recent predicament funny, but she couldn't help herself.

Wendell, on the other hand, felt suddenly much better and went off to the kitchen where it suddenly dawned on him how clean and tidy everything was.

"Oh my God," he slapped a gritty hand to his forehead. "I've forgotten to pay the bloody cleaner again." He picked up the phone.

Mrs O, it transpired, had left him another, as yet undiscovered, note. He grovelled in his most charming and apologetic manner and agreed to drop the money off to her this very evening. Sadly, he could not convince her to continue as his cleaner, she 'couldn't be doing with the uncertainty'.

"Bugger," he sighed, replacing the phone.

Charles was having an exhausting and stressful day. He had been back and forth between Mrs Allerdyce-Smythe's about fifty times, at least it felt like it. It had taken much longer than he expected, he still had a great stack of books to mark and his parents to take out later. What on earth had possessed him to suggest it? He'd gone off the idea completely, especially after being in the company of his father all day, whose offer of help had proved an endurance, to say the least. His father's first glimpse of the flat had been with the expression of a vet about to tell someone their animal was for the chop. He picked at microscopic flaking paintwork and made the unwelcome observation that it was likely to be very cold come the winter, facing north as it did and with those ill-fitting sash windows. Probably damp too. The criticism carried on sporadically throughout, until Charles pointed out that it wasn't him who had to live in it so why did he keep on about it.

Mr Waterman's eyebrows had shot up in surprise and he'd replied in a hurt tone that he was only trying to help, leaving Charles feeling guilty he'd said anything.

Mrs Waterman carried over a pot plant, high up to cover her face, just for a nose around. She glanced about her nervously as she entered, not wishing to be seen visiting the house of Mrs Allerdyce-Smythe. The latter had put in a brief appearance to furnish him with a set of keys, before retreating to her hothouse downstairs, much to Charles' relief.

Unbeknown to him, she'd had a beady eye glued to the peephole for most of the morning.

By late afternoon when all his things were at last deposited, Charles went back to his parents', and they all had tea and lemon cake which his mother had baked specially. Charles was exhausted but unlike his father, now slumbering in a comfy chair, he had all those sodding books waiting to be marked. Chewing sullenly on a piece of cake, Bibi slipped into his mind. Bloody Bibi, it always came back to her. He and Antonia would probably have been married by now, possibly started a family, if she hadn't upset the applecart. Why had he believed that fake letter? Antonia wasn't like that. He wanted her back to look after him, he didn't want to live alone.

"I think I'll stay here tonight if you don't mind," he said to his mother, cake crumbs falling from his mouth as he spoke, "just in case we get back late. I don't want to disturb Mrs Allerdyce-Smythe," he added, justifying his decision.

"Of course, dear," smiled his mother, pleased.

Charles made one more weary journey across to locate the things he'd need for later and by the time he'd found everything, the small lounge was strewn with clothing and toiletries and a pyramid of underwear was enjoying the comfort of the armchair. He would have a shower here he decided, maybe it would feel more like home. After some initial difficulties getting the temperature right, he let the hot water flow over him and began to feel slightly revived. A new start, yes, who knew what might happen next.

Annoyingly, the one thing he hadn't thought to locate was a towel, so he dripped through to the lounge, shivering slightly. His father was probably right as usual, it was likely to be cold in here. He shook his head to stop the icy drips from falling on his back and bent over to rummage through a pile of stuff just as a bus pulled up at the stop outside, treating the upper deck to a front row view of his naked backside, and possibly more.

"Look!" shrieked a teenage girl to her friends, pointing towards the free show. The whole top deck turned as one and cheered. Unfortunately, Charles chose this moment to stand up and turn around having found his towel, which he clamped around him as he ran for cover.

"It's Mr Waterman!" screamed the girl gleefully as the bus heaved away.

When the coast was clear Charles returned to close the curtains. How embarrassing! What a place to have a bus stop, hopefully there was no one on it who knew him, he hadn't had time to see any faces.

Before he left, Charles looked around at the chaotic mess in the unfamiliar surroundings and hated his new accommodation.

As he opened his door, there was Mrs Allerdyce-Smythe about to knock.

"Ah, Mr Waterman," she breathed, eyelids half closed, face upturned, grinning theatrically again. "All settled in I hope?"

"Charles, please. Yes, thank you, all moved in."

She made no further comment, just remained positioned there grinning, eyelids quivering slightly.

"I was just going out," continued Charles hoping to move her.

"Fine, fine. Just checking everything is alright."

"Yes, thank you, fine. By the way I won't be back until tomorrow."

"Ah," she breathed, exhaling horrible fumes. "I hope you and the lady enjoy yourselves. Ha ha ha ha ha ha ha ha," until Charles thought she would never stop.

He smiled awkwardly and edged past her holding his breath. Once outside he let the breath out and inhaled the cooling air before going back to his parents', intending to mark the books.

Guy woke Bibi with insistent stabbing in the small of her back. Half an hour later, after another swift but passionate session, he showered and left.

"I'll pick you up at six," he stated, hovering over her in the bed, tight trousers bulging at the front. "Feel that," he smirked.

She ran a painted fingernail along the bulge, and he curled his lip. "You'll have to wait till later for that," he said, "I've got business with your old lady first."

"Don't you dare mention any of this to her," demanded Bibi, her hand gripping his balls.

"I'm not stupid," he replied, acid in his voice, then threw her hand away from him and left without another word. She lay there for another while, feeling alone and dejected. What was she doing here?

Charlie! He was bound to be back at some point, and she did not want to be discovered here at any cost. She hurriedly dressed, threw her things together and drove off to Clara's in the nick of time, just as Charles and his father turned in at the other end of the road. Halfway there she changed her mind and fetched up on her father's doorstep instead. He tottered to the door and stared at her without recognition.

"Bibi?" he said finally. "Is that my little Bibi?"

He looked awful and there was an unmistakable whiff of urine about him.

"Dad? Are you ok?"

"You've come back to me," he whispered, a tear falling from the corner of a watery eye.

Bibi hesitated, wishing now she had gone straight to Clara's. He seemed to be going downhill scarily fast.

"I was here the other day, remember? Can I come in?"

He shuffled aside to let her pass.

"Come on, Dad, let's make a cup of tea. I'm starving, is there anything to eat?" She marched through to the kitchen, put the kettle on and began opening cupboards.

"My little Bibi, I thought I'd never see you again."

Bibi stopped rummaging and looked at her father. "You're not alright, are you? When did you last eat or wash?"

He looked ancient and shrivelled, his hair was unbrushed and he certainly hadn't washed since the last time she was here.

"Sit here," she pulled out a chair for him. He hugged her and despite her disgust, she felt tears sting in her eyes. Probably the smell of wee. She could feel every bone in his body, and she contemplated again how horrible old age and illness was. He was confused too.

She poured him a cup of tea and put a spoonful of sugar into it.

"Have you eaten since I was last here?" she asked sternly. He looked bewildered.

She cooked them some scrambled eggs on buttery toast which he looked at without interest. Surely she wasn't going to have to feed him!

"Come on, Dad, you must eat," she implored him.

"I'm not hungry."

"You must be! Come on, I'll help you."

She cut the food into child-size pieces and fed him with a spoon. With encouragement, he ate the lot and even nibbled voluntarily at a biscuit afterwards.

"Feeling better now?" she asked more gently.

"Yes. I could drink another cup of tea if there's one in that pot," he smiled at her for the first time, and she relaxed a little. He was probably dehydrated.

"You're a good girl, Bibi," he said, over the rim of his cup. She looked at the wisp of a man drinking the stewed tea and not even noticing and could have wept.

"I'm not really," she said, her voice quavering a little, "anyway, I expect you need some tablets, don't you?" She gave him a couple, after rummaging in the cupboard. It probably didn't matter what he had at this point.

She forced him to have a wash and change his clothes. She had wanted him to have a bath, but he didn't want to, and she certainly wasn't going to help him with that, so she let it go. At least he was cleaner. When he had finished, she took a shower and sorted herself out. By the time she left he was asleep in the armchair, so she bent over him and kissed him on the cheek. His face was wrinkled and sunken, the slack jaw hanging open and Bibi felt overwhelmingly sad.

"Bye Dad, see you soon."

He didn't wake.

The thoughtful mood that accompanied her to Clara's disappeared as she parked outside. The window, wide open as before, emitted noise louder than usual if that was possible. It seemed Clara had company. Bibi frowned; this was becoming intolerable. Tonight, she would stay at Guy's. Maybe it was time to go back to her mothers.

As she entered the house there was a sudden lull in the cacophony. She could smell the cigarette smoke and some other unpleasant odour.

"Bibi?" came a yell from the lounge, quickly followed by thundering footsteps.

"Bibi darling, it's just too amazing!" yelled Clara, curls bobbing about with hysterical excitement. "Everybody's here and we have special guests, just come and see!"

Bibi, curious, followed her into the lounge. What oxygen was still left in there was almost unbreathable. The only purpose the open window seemed to be serving was to make the room freezing cold. It was difficult to see through the haze of smoke which hung horizontally over the group. The twins she knew, they were squeezed together in an armchair and both said "Hi" as she walked in.

Stretched out along the sofa, fast asleep, was a long stringy body dressed in rags with hair in its first stages of dreadlocks, on both head and chin. Two enormous feet hung over one end, free of their boots, which was where the strange smell was emanating from. In front of this unholy exhibit, cross legged on the floor, sat a giant version of Clara, robed in Indian cotton and closely resembling a Buddha in drag. She had plum-coloured hair, cropped short, which surrounded a fat, disagreeable face decorated with nose studs and dangly earrings. In that moment, Bibi believed she had never seen two more repulsive specimens in her life, they looked like part of a freak show.

"This is my sister, Hill," beamed Clara. "Do you remember her from school?" Bibi thought 'mountain' would have been more apt. "And that's Merv," she indicated the body. "They've just flown in from Bangkok and they're jet lagged. It's such a surprise, I didn't know they were coming! So exciting! I've told them to have my room, we can double up in the spare. It'll be such fun having so many people in the place."

"Hi," drawled Hill, between drags on her Thai cigarette as she regarded Bibi sourly. Bibi returned the look and replied, "Likewise."

Bibi seated herself in the only available chair, next to the boots. Merv's pungent feet hung inches from her. She waved a lazy hand over them, and Clara and the twins hooted with laughter.

"We've had a long flight," said the Hill angrily.

"Oh Hill, Bibi was only joking, weren't you, darling? Hill's been telling us all about her wonderful travels. It's so amazing! She met Merv in a hostel in India and they've been inseparable ever since. So romantic!"

Bibi studied the ugly pair and couldn't imagine anything less romantic, but now Hill had dismissed Bibi and resumed her monologue, managing to make quite an interesting story dull by her dreary and repetitive delivery of it. Clara interrupted frequently with rapturous comments and Bibi with yawns. The twins smoked throughout and looked faintly amused. When Hill finally paused to light another camel dung cigarette, Bibi spoke into the opportunity.

"I'll be staying somewhere else tonight, darling, so you can have your room to yourself."

"Oh?" Clara frowned. "Don't feel you have to, no one will push you out because Hill's here."

"Oh, I know that, darling," replied Bibi quickly, casting a smug glance at Hill. "It's just that I've met someone."

The piercing shriek that followed this announcement momentarily woke Merv. "Hey, who's the babe?" he croaked, struggling up on an elbow to get a better look.

Hill's spatulate hand came down violently on his head. "Go back to sleep," she commanded, and he did.

"Oh Bibi, I don't believe it! Where? How? Who? Oh my God, a cigarette," the flow stopped as Clara paused to light up. Hill looked Bibi up and down huffily, so what if this bimbo had found a new man? She had been around the world and now her thunder had been stolen. The twins were all interest suddenly.

"Oh, just a guy I met a couple of weeks back," she said with nonchalance. "While I was at my mother's."

"And you said nothing, you naughty thing!" said Clara.

"What's his name? Do we know him?" said one of the twins, Bibi wasn't sure which through the fog. Had she mentioned Guy in connection with her mother? She couldn't remember. Best play safe.

"Damian."

"Oh, cool name," breathed Clara in awe, "will we meet him tonight?"

Tonight? Oh God, she'd forgotten about that, what with everything else going on.

"Maybe," she said, stalling. She wouldn't be going anywhere with this crowd, tonight or ever.

"Oh, do bring him, darling," begged Clara, "apart from anything, it'll be nice for Merv to have another man to talk to."

Bibi almost choked imagining that thing on the sofa and Guy getting chummy together.

"We'll probably meet you there. In fact, I'd better get my things together," she rose decisively and skirted the minefield of glasses and ashtrays to the door. In Clara's room she crushed everything back into the suitcase and put it in the car then, looking in through the window and waving at everyone in general, said, "Bye Hill, nice to have met you," with a look that said she was lying through her teeth.

"Bye *darling*," drawled Hill sarcastically.

"See you later," Clara's voice sailed out after her. "Eight o'clock at Bistro la Bella, don't forget."

Bibi had forgotten already. She pulled up at the nearest phone box and checked Charles wasn't at the house, then parked her car around the corner out of sight. It was already quite late, and she wanted to look hot tonight. Now she was free of the atmosphere at Clara's she began to anticipate seeing Guy again. She was still thinking about him when she realised all Charles' things had gone. So, he'd moved back home, had he? Had he bothered to inform the landlord? Who cared, it was in his name. What a pathetic *child* he was, running home to Mummy and Daddy when things went wrong. Well, let them have him, she'd found something better for the moment. She thought again of Guy and admitted to herself she didn't really like him, just lusted for him and the fact he wanted *her* had restored her damaged ego greatly. She had completely dismissed Wendell and wouldn't bother to keep that date tomorrow night. That would piss him off.

There, revenge on her mother and Wendell!

She would move back to her mother's until she got somewhere else, and Guy would be wary of being there so that would sort that out, yes things were finally beginning to fall into place. Good.

Guy finally turned up forty minutes late, by which time Bibi was furious and let fly as soon as the door was shut.

"When you say six, you make it six; I DO NOT like being kept waiting," she stormed.

He regarded her with amusement. "I had some business to finish… with your mother," his lip curled into a smile.

"You…!" Bibi raised a hand to slap his face, which he caught mid-swing.

"Naughty, naughty little girl," his eyes were cruel.

"You're hurting me," she shouted, and it was true. He was squeezing her wrist hard. "Stop! You're hurting me!" she cried again as he increased the pressure.

"Never tell me what to do, babe," he looked down at her for a few seconds before releasing her.

Bibi had never been treated like this before. It excited her. She stood flexing her hand and they stared at each other with a mixture of hatred and sexual tension.

Guy studied her with rising desire. What a woman. Grabbing her roughly, he kissed her hard on the lips and pressed against her. Bibi would never have allowed this before, especially after having just applied lipstick, but she was discovering she enjoyed being dominated and let it go.

She wiped the colour from his lips, repaired her own and spoke as if nothing had happened.

"Shall we go?"

For a moment, she thought he was about to drag her off to the bedroom. She would have let him do it. Instead, he turned without a word and headed for the jeep, leaving her to lock up and follow him.

He drove like a maniac, the action man profile pointing forward as he sped down the streets, music blaring at a deafening level, overtaking recklessly and disregarding pedestrians as they leapt out of the way of the vehicle.

"I'm ravenous," announced Guy, holding the door open for Bibi to alight, "got an appetite for some reason."

He strode off and she followed at a dignified pace in her high heels. She wasn't about to hurry for anyone in these shoes. He glanced back at her casually, they were beginning to understand one another. He would enjoy this little interlude with a sexy woman his own age. Pity she wasn't rich. Yet.

Bistro la Bella. Now where had she heard that? It sounded familiar but she couldn't quite pin it down; no matter. They entered and were greeted with Italian enthusiasm by Guy's friend, Marcos, who turned out to be just plain Mark Smith from Bermondsey. He put on a good act, Bibi had to admit. The place was surprisingly crowded but a table had been saved for them in a cosy corner by the window, overlooking the street. It seemed Guy always got what he wanted. As they waited for service Bibi examined the restaurant, cleverly set out with various large plants and statuettes, creating nooks and crannies in an otherwise rather basic floor space. Subdued lighting, background guitar music and the smell of garlic enhanced the atmosphere. The place had her approval. On the other side of the room, shielded by a large cheese plant, sat Charles and his parents, toying with an unfamiliar starter which Charles had suggested.

"Service isn't very swift in here," murmured his father as he consulted his watch for the tenth time. He scraped most of his food to one side, then looked around in the hope of attracting a waiter.

"Don't make a fuss, will you, Gerald?" said Mrs Waterman with consternation.

Gerald muttered something and fondled his moustache.

Charles was tired but resigned. His mind refused to rest, continually bringing up thoughts about the new flat, the still unmarked books and Antonia, none of which was fodder for discussion with his parents. The result was a subdued outing at best, with his mother trying to behave as she thought she should in an Italian bistro and his father looking uncomfortable and out of place. Just get it over with and go. If only it had been Toni sitting opposite him tonight, he thought with longing. He looked at his parents and felt sorry for them and himself.

"So, what's everyone having?" he asked with fake cheer, trying to liven things up a bit.

"Well, I don't understand what half of it is to be truthful," said his father, in a rare admission of lack of knowledge, "it's all in bloody wop language."

"Gerald! Keep your voice down," came a desperate hiss from Mrs Waterman as her eyes flickered left and right. "They'll hear you."

Gerald looked at her with lacklustre eyes, as if he didn't much care if they did. Charles, tired, just wished a waiter would appear and they could get on with it and go.

When one did come, he brought with him the complimentary bottle of wine, which he poured out for them with a flourish.

"Never did like this froggy stuff," muttered Mr Waterman, sipping at it carefully.

Charles was running out of patience. "It's Italian *stuff*. If you don't like it order a beer," he snapped, and the conversation dried up once more.

At this point the door flew open and in poured Clara with her entourage, all scanning the tables eagerly.

"Christ, look what's just blown in," laughed Guy scathingly. Bibi turned to look and snapped a face drained of colour back towards him.

"Oh my God," she spluttered.

"What is it?" he enquired, interested. "Don't tell me you *know* them."

"Unfortunately, yes. We've got to get out of here. I knew I'd heard that name somewhere, now I remember, they arranged to come here. God, what an absolute nightmare!"

Guy was enjoying her discomfort. "Go if you want to, I'm staying put."

Bibi glared at him with dislike.

"Why don't you go over and say hello to your pals?" he said. "Shall I wave them over?"

"You shut your mouth; this isn't funny."

A waiter had engaged the group in conversation and Bibi took the opportunity to sidle into the toilets, fortunately placed just behind a statue of the Venus de Milo where they were sitting.

Guy scrutinised the group with distaste, what a load of deadbeats. Those twins might do for a threesome, but the others looked like they'd just trekked here by ox and cart from Mongolia. The waiter was obviously thinking the same and was slowly shuffling them back towards the exit, arms outstretched in an apologetic Italian manner.

"But we're meeting someone here," wailed Clara, "we've booked. It was all arranged."

"So-a sorry madam," he lied, "there is-a no record of your-a booking, so sorry we all full, you come-a next week perhaps?" Why didn't this shower just piss off, this wasn't the image they wanted to portray. This was an upmarket bistro, not a backpacker's drop in.

"But my friend will be waiting." Clara took another look over his shoulder. Bibi was not there, but wait a minute… surely, wasn't that the gorgeous Charles? Ignoring the fact that he had never actually been introduced to her and may not know her from Adam, Clara visualised him as their gallant saviour, asking them all to dine with him and whoever those two old people were. She had once spotted him dropping Bibi off in town and she'd had romantic fantasies about him often. Now here was a God given opportunity to make them come true, it would be just like Hill and Merv!

"Charles!" she called loudly, sweeping the waiter, only the width of one of her buttocks, to one side as she barged a path through the tables. The rest of her party stared after her in bewilderment. Hill made a move to follow but the waiter, recovered, barred her way before gliding across to where Clara towered over Charles and his parents.

"Hi, I'm Clara, Bibi's friend. They've lost our booking, and we were so looking forward to eating here this evening."

Charles and his parents stared at this strange loud woman, embarrassed beyond belief at being picked out like this.

"There is a problemo?" enquired the waiter discreetly to Charles. Before he could answer, Clara continued, "Our friend hasn't turned up, but we know this gentleman, I'm sure he won't object to us sharing his table."

Charles found his voice. "Er, just a minute, I think there's been some mistake. I don't know you."

"Well… no, we've never actually met, but I'm Bibi's friend. Clara? She must have mentioned me."

The waiter interrupted, "Sorry madam, but I think you should-a leave now please."

"Bibi's friend? We're no longer together," said Charles, frowning. "I hope she's not the friend you're meeting?"

"But, but…" she stammered. "Charles," she appealed to him. He shrugged.

The dumbfounded Waterman trio watched silently as Clara and company were hustled outside to stand in a gloomy, indecisive huddle on the pavement for a few moments, before trailing off in another direction, floaty cotton clothes billowing in the breeze. They were collectively like a galleon setting sail, with the twins making up the masts.

"Who was that dreadful female—if it was female?" demanded Mr Waterman, staring at Charles.

"Dreadful!" echoed Mrs Waterman, also staring at Charles.

"I swear I've never seen her before in my life," Charles held his palms up, "and never want to again," he finished sincerely. His parents regarded him with suspicion. Firstly, leaving that lovely, suitable Antonia for a married woman, then this flat at Mrs Allerdyce-Smythe's. Who knew what he was up to the minute their backs were turned.

"Honestly," he insisted. "I haven't a clue who she is. A friend of Bibi's, she said. I've never seen her before. She's hardly easy to forget, is she?"

"She seemed to know *you*. Called you by name."

Charles shook his head, still bewildered. "I haven't a clue," he repeated, and they resumed their meal in heavy silence.

Bibi peeked through the glass panel of the door and satisfied herself that they had gone. She slipped back into her seat, smoothing the tight dress over her thighs gracefully. Guy was leaning back on his chair, one arm resting on the back of it.

"Thought you'd gone," he said finally, watching her as she examined an eye in her handbag mirror.

"I take it they left?" she said casually, still blinking into the mirror.

"Yeah. That fat bird with the poodle hair, I heard her say she was your friend to someone over there," he nodded sideways towards the Waterman party.

"Really?" she looked around, but they were still hidden from view by the cheese plant. "Oh well, they're gone now," she picked up the menu.

"The waiter came while you were gone, so I ordered for you."

"Oh?" She was annoyed. He had a cheek, what would he have ordered? He didn't know what she liked. A flashback to that disgusting pie and chips came to her. She looked up at Guy. He was smirking at her, which was also infuriating. It was as if he could read her mind.

"Thanks," she said and smiled tightly.

Their dishes arrived, and while the waiter was shielding them, so did Wendell and Antonia.

They had dropped Mrs O's money off on their way. She had been firm of lip; had stood, arms folded, on her doorstep, prepared to defend her decision to quit if needs be. Wendell had added a further fiver to her money as 'a small token of my thanks and an apology', which thawed her enough for a rare smile, revealing a set of Rob Murphy's finest dentures.

"This looks nice," smiled Antonia, as they were led to their table by the counterfeit Italian. Wendell smiled back and neither of them took their eyes off each other long enough to notice the other diners. Had they done, from their more prominent position they might have spotted Charles and his parents.

At the latter's table, the outing was now proving to be more successful. The wine, which had loosened inhibitions, had Charles' father regaling them with wartime anecdotes. This was so unlike him that they actually found they were enjoying themselves and were focused enough to be uninterested in anyone arriving or leaving the restaurant. When they had finished their desserts, coffee, mint, Charles asked for the bill. He was flushed with success, forgetting the shaky start to the evening, and wondered if he would take them out here again. It was as he rose and shoved the receipt into his wallet that Bibi spotted him over the cheese plant. Before she could stop herself, she gave a startled gasp and covered her mouth.

Guy turned and finding Charles every bit his superior in the looks department, got childish.

"Who's that?"

She hesitated.

"Who is it?" demanded Guy aggressively.

"It's Charles."

"Charles. Who is this Charles?" he said peevishly. "Everyone seems to know him, even that ugly friend of yours did."

"I do not believe this," Bibi whispered. "Don't let him see me for God's sake."

Guy looked at her through narrowed eyes. What was going on here? He wasn't going to be cuckolded by anyone, however good she was in the sack.

"Just going to the little boys room, darling, won't be a moment," cooed Wendell. He clutched Antonia's hand lovingly, unwilling to release it. He was in love, desperately, and never wanted another woman. Antonia gazed back into his eyes. She was smitten, could hardly wait for later, even though she hadn't yet had the courage to mention condoms.

"I'll order for us if the waiter comes, shall I?"

"Yes darling, if you would."

"Don't be long now, I might get lonely without you," she joked.

Wendell kissed her fingers and they smiled, still unable to tear their eyes off each other. He rose and headed for the door marked toilets. Antonia watched him go and sighed with sheer happiness. For the first time she looked around her at the other people, including the three now weaving their way past towards the door.

"Charles!" she exclaimed, without thinking. Her eyes were like saucers.

"Antonia!" chorused Charles and his parents in unison.

"What's going on here?" said Guy under his breath, still jealous of Charles.

"Now what? Are they gone?" Bibi risked a quick look. "It's her! That's his ex-girlfriend. What's she doing here, that mousy creature? And the parents too! Oh, I get it, all out together to celebrate the glorious reunion. How quaint."

"I wouldn't say no," put in Guy, investigating Antonia from his seat, while Bibi glowered.

"All we need now is Wendell to come in and complete the quartet."

"Who?"

She gave him a swift potted history, carefully omitting any wrongdoing on her part.

"We need to leave," she said, reaching under the table for her bag.

"We'll leave when I'm ready, babe."

"Mr and Mrs Waterman! Fancy seeing you here, how are you?" enquired Antonia politely and with a forced smile. It was hard to know what to say in the circumstances. She felt at a disadvantage from her seated position, like a hostage. Rather alarmingly, Charles had eased himself into Wendell's seat and was gazing, all sheep-like, at her.

"Oh Toni," he sighed as he clasped her hand, forgetting everyone else. She pulled her hand away sharply.

"Charles," she hissed. "I'm not here on my own you know," she glanced at the parents, "and neither are you."

"I don't care."

"I do."

"Darling Toni, I've been thinking about you all week. I love you."

"Come on Charles, there's a good chap," said Mr Waterman, placing a hand on his son's shoulder. His face was purple with wine and embarrassment. Some of the other diners were happily watching the exchange; Bibi was too, but from so low down at the table that she was almost under it.

Wendell reappeared from the toilet and walked past her.

It couldn't be! She didn't dare open her mouth and tell Guy, there was no knowing what he would do. She just wanted to get out of here.

Wendell returned to the table to find Charles in his seat. Antonia looked up at him pleading for tactful help. Charles, seeing her look, turned his head slowly and found Wendell's eyes on him. The dreamy expression turned to fright as he realised who he was looking at. Wendell's own expression was rigid.

"Do you mind, you're in my seat." Wendell grabbed the back of the chair and Charles leapt from it like a frightened animal.

"Oh, er, hello. Didn't realise you were there."

"Obviously."

Everybody's heads were swinging back and forth from one to the other like spectators at a tennis match.

Charles stopped and stared at Wendell. "*Your* seat?" he said, the penny dropping at last.

He looked at Antonia, then back at Wendell, then back at Antonia. "Toni?"

"Please just go," she replied wearily.

"Hey Charlie!" came a sudden shout from the other side of the room. All heads turned towards it. Bibi, scarlet with fury, bent her head and hissed, "Shut up! Shut up, you stupid bastard."

But Guy was enjoying the joke.

"Charlie, come and see who's here," he held up a hand and pointed it at Bibi, who stared back with murder in her eyes.

"You fucking stupid bastard," she said through gritted teeth, as the others looked at her curiously.

"Bibi!" said Charles and Wendell together angrily, then looked frostily at each other for a second.

"Oh no," groaned Wendell.

"Go on then, go and say hello, don't be standoffish," said Guy, laughing gleefully.

"Goodbye," replied Bibi, as she rose from her seat. She didn't look back.

"Excuse me," she said regally as she reached the group, "you're blocking my way."

They moved back as one to allow her to pass and she found herself looking straight into Antonia's face.

"You!" Bibi turned to look at Charles. "Huh, I suppose Charlie went running back to you with his tail between his legs. You dull people deserve each other," she turned back to laugh in Antonia's face before moving on.

"Actually, she's with me," said Wendell charmingly.

"Why him?" said Charles, turning from one to the other. "Oh Antonia."

Charles' mother looked like she was about to cry, his father was so purple he may have been having a heart attack standing up.

Antonia stood up and moved in front of Bibi. "Here's dull for you BRENDA," she said loudly, so everyone could hear and, without a thought, slapped Bibi's perfect face as hard as she could, then picked up her glass of free wine and threw that into it for good measure.

Bibi stood open-mouthed and rocked backwards; wine dripped from her chin. Her eyes, framed by melting mascara, darted from one to the other.

Everyone in the place was laughing and cheering. Guy was nearly apoplectic.

Knowing what Bibi could be like, Wendell moved protectively between the two women and, taking his cue from this chap, whoever he was, so did Mr Waterman. And then so did Charles in a show of male solidarity.

"Gerald! Gerald don't!" whimpered Mrs Waterman, wringing her hands together.

All this had taken only a few seconds, but now Bibi had recovered herself and her slapping hand came up swiftly. At this precise moment, Mark/Marcos chose to pop up into the middle of the group and got a slap in the ear for his trouble.

"Madam!" he reeled back from the blow with a hand against his cheek. "Please-a madam, you must-a leave now."

Guy's laughter could be heard all over the restaurant, this was priceless.

But Bibi wasn't finished yet. "Get out of the way, you stupid man!" she cried and pushed the hapless Marcos roughly, where he landed right into someone's dining experience. His supporting hand went flat into a boiling hot lasagne, bubbling cheese squeezed up between the splayed fingers and stuck all over it, and while the couple at the table tried to help by washing it off with chilled wine, he was shrieking in a very cockney accent, "Fuckin' 'ell, me 'and, me 'and!" And waving it about, splattering bits of melted cheese and minced beef in every direction.

Outnumbered and humiliated, Bibi attempted to push past to the door.

Guy was making a break for it too and would have made it had he not called across to Bibi. "Bye *Brenda*, thanks for last night, but I'll stick with your old lady from now on, it's less trouble."

Having been unable to get at Antonia through the wall of testosterone, Bibi's fury focused itself on Guy. That posturing, womanising, gold digging bastard! And now everyone knew her real name was Brenda, oh the shame of it! She lost all control and hurled herself towards him, like an Amazon warrior pushing through impenetrable jungle, as she swept plants left and right. People shrieked and vacated their tables in a hurry knocking over statuettes, some of which were reduced to rubble. One fell on a woman's foot. Someone called an ambulance to deal with all the injuries.

"This is all your fault, you stupid twat," said Marcos Mark, swinging for Guy with his good hand, "you always was a fuckin' pratt, why dincher keep yer stupid gob shut." The Italian accent was well and truly gone.

"Shall we go?" said Mr Waterman, decisively grabbing his wife by the arm and shepherding her and Charles towards the door. While Guy was occupied with Marcos, Bibi darted back to block the Waterman's path.

"Where do you think you're going?" she demanded of Charles. "None of this would ever have happened if it wasn't for you being such a wimp."

"My fault, is it?" said Charles furiously, his face the colour of putty. "You've got a—"

Before he could finish, Bibi brought her hand up and slapped his face hard. There was a general hush, as everyone waited to see what would happen next. A spoon clinked against a background of gentle Italian music.

Mrs Waterman's sturdy leather 'going out' handbag, swung with all the power of a fast bowler, hit Bibi's head side on, overbalancing her.

The tight dress was unable to stand this sort of stress and split right down the side, revealing all the sexy scarlet underwear she had chosen for later. There was a masculine roar of delight and one brave soul even got up and offered her his jacket.

"Fuck off!" she shouted at him as she struggled to hold the dress together.

Guy had had enough of all this; he had flattened Marcos Mark easily and now wanted to go home and forget the lot of them. What a bunch of losers. As he reached out for the door, it swung open and framed in it stood Elizabeth, anxiously looking past him into the chaos. Incredibly, she didn't seem to have noticed him. He dropped vertically, melted backwards and downwards and crawled on his hands and knees to the toilet, where he somehow managed to squeeze his manly body out of the tiny window to freedom.

"Bibi!" called Elizabeth urgently. Everyone turned towards this newcomer. Bibi had a hand to the top of her head, watching little birds tweet around in circles. Her hair and make-up had been ruined by the wine thrown at it and her designer dress had been reduced to rags.

"Thank goodness I've found you, Clara said you'd be here. It's your father."

Forgetting everything else in this sudden opportunity to escape, Bibi hurried to Elizabeth and salvation, and they left the restaurant together.

An ambulance squealed to a halt outside, and paramedics swarmed into the void to attend to the injured.

"Well… goodbye," said Mr and Mrs Waterman to Antonia and Wendell. "Nice to see you, Antonia. Nice to have met you, er…"

Proper behaviour observed and a modicum of normality restored, they shuffled towards the door.

"Goodbye," they replied, returning to their seats. What was left of them.

"Antonia?" called Charles, as he was shoved towards the door. "Antonia? I'll call you."

Antonia's head lay on her arms on their table. Her shoulders were heaving with sobs.

"Oh darling, darling, please don't cry," Wendell pleaded. He felt his heart would burst, seeing her so upset.

She shook her head and he put his hands on top of hers until she settled.

It was only then, as she finally looked up, that he saw she had been laughing.

"It was Jean Waterman with that handbag," she said, wiping her eyes. "It's her going out bag, made in about 1920 of solid oak, and filled with bricks. I know because I carried it for her once," she began to laugh again. "Oh dear, oh dear."

Chapter Thirty-One
Sunday

In the early hours of Sunday morning Bibi's father breathed his last. She and Elizabeth, their quarrels forgotten, were by his bedside until the end, which came peacefully with a final deep sigh. Throughout the night, mother and daughter settled their differences again, both privately relieved to have been brought together before Bill Baker had passed on.

Guy was neither mentioned nor thought of.

They quietly left the hospital at first light, arm in arm, drained of emotion.

Outside it was cold and still, with a strange, deserted feel. The sun was just rising into a pale blue sky streaked with the muted colours of an autumn morning. The wind had died too, in fact it was so still now that every small sound seemed amplified in the emptiness, the swoosh of the automatic doors as they left the building, their shoes clip-clopping as they crossed the tarmac, animated birds singing the dawn chorus seemed to echo all around the sky.

Bibi had filled a sink with warm water and dipped her whole head into it to get rid of smudged make-up and sticky wine, then blotted it all off with paper towels. The remains of her clothes were hidden under her father's big cardigan. She looked pale and scruffy in the light. Her mother looked lined and old.

Back at the house Elizabeth produced a bottle of brandy and poured a large measure into two coffees, saying they could do with it.

"I can't believe he's gone." Bibi looked into her mother's face. "It doesn't seem real, does it?"

"No."

"Was it like this when Geoff died?"

Elizabeth's face turned white. She looked, for a moment, as if she would faint.

"Yes and no." There was a wobble in her usually firm voice. She raised her hand and pinched the bridge of her nose, squeezed her eyes tight. Then she began to sob.

"Mum!" Bibi had never seen her mother cry before. Ever. "Stop! You'll set me off." Tears spilled from her own eyes. She must look awful anyway, what did it matter. She placed an awkward hand on Elizabeth's shoulder, and they cried together.

Bibi's older brother, Geoff, had died from leukaemia when Bibi was three. She barely remembered him, more the confusion felt by the sudden disappearance of the main focus of the household, and the behaviour of the adults afterwards, not least the attention and gifts that had suddenly come her way. It had certainly never been discussed.

"I didn't think you remembered your brother," Elizabeth said finally.

"Well, yes, just. I asked you about him once I think, when I was about seven. You told me not to bother you with stupid questions."

"Yes. I remember that," she replied sadly and wiped her eyes with a tissue. "It all seems like yesterday, I was numb when it happened. I haven't cried like that since before we lost him. It made me... hard. Those tears were for him, not your dad."

Bibi stared at a stranger. From far away in her memory came an image of a beautiful smiling woman, laughing, kissing Bibi's father, handing her an ice cream. Geoff would be lying in bed or on the sofa if it was a good day, thin and pale but with the sweet face and uncomplaining nature of a little angel.

"I do remember him," she said, surprised and thoughtful, "lying on the sofa. You and Dad didn't argue then, that was later." She looked at her mother for confirmation.

Elizabeth regarded her with amazement. "I didn't think you remembered him, incredible what children take in. But yes, it tore us apart. Your father thought I should stay at home and grieve, while he went to work and got away from it all for a few hours at least. I distracted myself... elsewhere," she paused for a thoughtful ten seconds. "I wasn't a good wife. Or mother. I admit it. He was right to leave."

Bibi recalled her dad being absent a lot, then gone altogether. She remembered a series of strange men in the house. They would sleep in the big bed where her dad used to sleep, and she was never allowed into it again. Some lasted longer than others, but they all disappeared in the end.

"Oh Mum." Bibi hugged Elizabeth with real feeling, understanding at last the barrier between them. That and her own dealings with men. "Why didn't you say something? We could have been friends all this time."

"The time never seemed right, and then it was too late. After your brother died, I would have done anything to forget the pain. It was unbearable, only another woman who'd been through it would have understood, but those kind of support groups didn't really exist then. You were expected to cultivate a stiff upper lip and get on with it. I probably wouldn't have gone to one if they had." She looked at Bibi. "I could hardly bear to look at you to begin with, so healthy and pretty and looking just like him. Perhaps I was even guarding myself against something similar happening to you as well, who knows? I knew it was unfair, but I couldn't help myself. The doctor kept telling me I needed to concentrate on my living child, be a proper mother and that time would heal. Stupid man, what did he know about it? He may as well have told me just to forget my dead child ever existed." She dabbed her eyes again. "That comment probably did more damage than anything." There was bitterness in her voice which faded as she finished. "I'm sorry, darling, I really am. It's no wonder you've turned out like you have."

Bibi felt a little taken aback by this, then remembered what she had been intending to do with Guy and said nothing. It was true, look at the sort of person she was, always seeking attention and adoration, especially from men. Using people then getting cross when things didn't happen as planned. Wendell, Charles, his ex-girlfriend, Clara, her own parents, and so many others. She experienced a rare moment of remorse.

"Mum?"

Elizabeth looked up.

"I slept with Guy."

"I thought so. I was almost testing him, sending him round to look for you in the first place."

"Oh!" Bibi saw no emotion on her mother's face nor heard any in her voice. "It was his doing though." She was unable to take even part of the blame, even now.

"There was something about him this morning, I don't know, I just had a feeling. And then when that strange friend of yours said you'd gone to that new place with your boyfriend, I put two and two together and came up with Guy."

Bibi didn't like being found out; she deflected the conversation. "Where did you find Clara?"

"At Gino's, I hoped you might be there. Her sister had seen you in the other place, with a man, she said. What a monster she was, good heavens, I thought Clara was bad enough."

So, the mighty Hill had squealed on her had she, that ugly cow? Now Clara would know she'd been lied to, or maybe not… she could tell her she'd been in the loo when they came in, and that it was just a refurbishment going on at Gino's, she hadn't realised…

Bibi was already doing it again, it was ingrained into her, this lying and using of people.

"Sorry," she said to her mother. "I only did it to spite you—and him. I don't even like him. Certainly not what he put me through in that restaurant." She left out the part about enjoying it and intending to stay at his flat for a few days.

"I don't doubt it," replied Elizabeth with a wry smile. "I'm afraid we are two of a kind, darling."

"It won't happen again. Certainly not after the way he behaved."

"If he wants it to, you probably will," said Elizabeth, with a sigh, "he always gets his way, he's very persuasive. I do wield some power because I have money, but he can be pretty ruthless."

"Why do you put up with him then?" Bibi said it angrily, remembering the night of unbridled lust and wishing she hadn't given in after all.

Elizabeth yawned. "I'm going to try and get some sleep, busy day ahead of us tomorrow."

Bibi liked the way her mother had said 'us'.

Back to Saturday evening.

Charles and his parents went straight home from the Bistro la Bella, his mother spitting venom about Bibi most of the way back.

"I think that's enough Jean," Charles' father had said finally. He felt emotionally battered by the events of the evening and unusually bloated from consuming so much garlicky foreign food and alcohol. He was managing to hold it in so far, but he wanted to get back and release a lot of wind.

Charles was still in shock from what he had learnt this evening.

Antonia, *his Antonia*, with Bibi's husband! It was unbelievable, that oily bastard with the pretentious name. What was it? Wenfred? Windell? Wendell, yes that was it. The bastard. What on earth did she see in him? And what was

Bibi doing in there? She seemed to have been with that male model type, the one who had called his name out. Were they in there watching them all? Maybe she'd set the whole thing up? He wouldn't have put it past her from what he'd learnt in the last couple of weeks.

It must have been Bibi that awful woman Clara was meeting, but she hadn't jumped up to greet her, so what was all that about? He vaguely remembered dropping Bibi in town to meet a school friend one weekend, maybe that had been Clara. Seemed a funny crowd for Bibi to mix with, but there you are.

It wasn't in Charles' nature to find it all amusing and his mood darkened. This last week had opened his eyes, and he wasn't going to be made a fool of again. Bloody women, he'd live happily alone from now on and do exactly what he wanted to. His mum was only down the road if he needed anything.

For the first time that day he found himself looking forward to going to his new flat. He had better let the landlord know about the other place too, it was in his name. This would be his new start, a clean slate. If Bibi ever dared to show her face again, he would slap it so hard she'd find herself in the middle of next week. Antonia really gave it to her, he had to give her that much. And who was this Brenda? Fancy mum attacking her like that, she was the only female who never let him down, dear old mum.

"Thanks mum," he said into the silence and smiled at her, huffing in the passenger seat. Pursed lips relaxed into a wondering half smile which almost made her attractive.

"Yes! Well done Jean. That woman got what was coming to her. Well done." Mr Waterman smiled at her too.

All these years, Mrs Waterman thought, she had done her utmost to be meek and mild, a good wife and mother, never rock the boat. And now, having lost control of herself completely in front of a room full of strangers, she had earned the respect of the two people she most loved in the world. She was elated.

Perhaps she would do more of it.

Having ordered, and with the others now gone, Wendell and Antonia decided to stay at Bistro la Bella and see what happened next.

When the paramedics had finished with the various minor injuries, and some minion from the kitchen had rapidly tidied things up, normality resumed and they got a good laugh from discussing everything, especially Antonia slapping Bibi's face, throwing the wine at her and calling her Brenda.

"I can't believe you did it!" laughed Wendell. "She's deserved that from someone for years. It was wonderful to see, I'll never forget it as long as I live."

"I still can't get the image of Jean Waterman whacking her with that handbag out of my mind!" said Antonia in reply, beginning to laugh at it all over again. "She's usually such a timid woman. He'll probably divorce her now, he was such a stickler for being proper, you know the type."

Smiles and tender glances passed between them frequently. Engulfed in love, neither of them could quite believe they had only met about a week ago and yet lived in lonely misery under the same roof for so long. Antonia felt as though she had known Wendell forever. Alcohol was only adding to the euphoria. That and the thought of what was surely coming later.

She had planned out what to say about contraception and had intended to start the evening with it, but all that had gone by the wayside with everything else that had happened. Then she thought about mentioning it during the journey back, but the time didn't seem quite right and after another glass or two of wine in Wendell's flat, she had decided she couldn't say anything at this late stage and, if truth be told, didn't want to spoil the magic.

But as they lay contented in each other's arms she was sobering up, and fervently hoped her hurried calculations would be lucky ones.

What had she done? She had done what she had always scorned others for doing, namely slept with him without using precautions, the sort of thing a drunk teenager might do, and having had more than usual to drink at the restaurant she had thrown caution to the wind completely. She had not cared if she became pregnant, just wanted him so badly she was more than willing to take the chance.

She despised people who said it had been 'an accident' or 'I just got carried away' didn't she?

But now that desire had been sated, and the courage and confidence that came with alcohol had worn out of her, it did begin to worry her. Very much. She stopped being dreamy and became fully awake, mulling it over. Her stomach clenched.

What an idiot! It nearly happened once, she thought, and I was relieved to have had a lucky escape, only to do it later! What was I thinking? Oh my God, *what* was I *thinking*!

How could she say to Wendell that she had thought about it, but hadn't mentioned contraception? Why hadn't she just said it? How cowardly. How stupid, how unbelievably *stupid*! Admittedly, it would have rather tainted the moment, but would have been the sensible thing to do. But sensible had gone out of the window at that moment. Nothing had mattered.

Why hadn't it been brought up earlier?

He might think she was out to trap him. Oh dear, what a mess. She decided to wait and hope nothing came of it. The chances were very small after all.

By some sixth sense, Wendell woke.

"Everything alright?" he said quietly.

When she didn't immediately respond he turned the bedside lamp on. Antonia turned from the sudden glare and now lay, shrimp-like, facing the wall.

"Darling, what's wrong?"

A pause, then, "I've done something extremely stupid."

There was another pause, during which Wendell flipped a few ideas through his still sleepy mind. Left the car lights on? Forgotten to lock up at work?

"What thing?"

A longer pause.

"What thing?" he repeated, more awake now.

"Well… I, it's not a very romantic subject but I'm not… what I mean is I don't…" she stopped, "we didn't use any contraception."

"What!" An even longer pause ensued while Wendell fought with the horrific possibilities. "Oh my God! I didn't even think about it, just assumed."

He did blame her then.

He sounded annoyed. Her heart pounded, it was all ruined, he would think she had tried to trap him into marriage and babies. Why did things always have to go wrong when she thought she was happy? Why had she said anything? She should have waited until she knew one way or the other. It was probably alright anyway. Swamped in self-pity, tears threatened.

Wendell flopped back onto the pillow and laid a clammy hand on a clammy forehead, making the hair stand up above it.

"Oh dear," he said in a tired voice, confirming Antonia's fears completely.

A tear rolled down and blotted the pillow.

"I'll go and see the doctor in the morning, there's a pill for this sort of thing I think."

"Are they there on Sundays?" said Wendell, plucking at his lip.

There was a long silence. More tears ran onto the pillow, not just for this but for all of it. How could things change so suddenly? She wanted to be in her own bed, alone, where she could cry it out and think.

"I'm sorry Wendell," she said in a tiny voice. "I'm so sorry, I really am. I'll go."

"Go? Where?"

"To my own bed."

"Oh no, don't. Why are you sorry anyway, we're both adults? I'm just as much to blame for not checking. We must be in love or something." His words held a smile as he turned over and held her. "Oh darling, you're crying!"

This kindness made her cry more.

"Don't worry, we'll use something until you're sure everything is alright, which it probably will be anyway. Forget about the morning after pill, I don't think that's very good for you. I'm sure it'll be fine."

Could it be possible he didn't blame her? How little she knew him.

"I'm sorry," she said again. "I've never believed it when people said they got 'carried away', but that's exactly what I did."

"Glad you did though," laughed Wendell and kissed her shoulder, "fancy taking another chance?"

"No!" she half laughed; half cried.

"Well, no use worrying now the deed is done. It'll be alright, you'll see," he soothed, thinking about the number of people that didn't get caught out with unplanned pregnancies. He pushed away the thought of the other option hurriedly, after all the chances of that were very remote.

"Get some rest," he kissed her again and turned out the light and, this time, they both went to sleep.

Monday

Antonia was reflecting on what a lot had happened in the last couple of weeks as she huddled with the other mourners around the grave of the late Robert Seamus Murphy. She'd never been to a burial before and was interested to find the whole scene reminded her of several films and rather more comedy sketches. Dave Allen was prominent among these.

A fair crowd had turned out to send him off, mostly attired in the usual sombre blacks or greys, all bar a little knot of golfing buddies sporting garish trousers as a mark of respect for a man they considered to have been a decent swinger. One of them had read in the church, mounting the pulpit stairs in a smart black blazer atop canary yellow and turquoise tartan. This florid cheeked chap had sounded genuinely sorry at Rob's passing, which was more than could be said of Mrs Murphy, who had moved gaily amongst the throng thanking them for coming, and for their kind messages of sympathy and beautiful flowers. A dark veil over her face hid the newly radiant expression and absence of tears at the graveside. Antonia studied their three children with interest. Two pallid teenage girls the image of their father but with flaming red hair, and a much younger boy of about six, who bore a remarkable resemblance to another of the mourners from the golfing cohort. The trio looked uncomfortable in smart black clothes bought especially for the occasion, particularly the boy who fidgeted constantly with his collar.

Before the service, Antonia hadn't been surprised to see Susan standing there, snivelling into a ragged piece of pink toilet paper.

"Hello Sue." Antonia touched her colleague lightly on the arm in a gesture of friendliness.

"Oh Antonia, it's you. Isn't this *awful?* What terrible news to get when you've just got back from a holiday."

"Yes, quite a shock wasn't it. When did you get back?"

"Saturday. Oh, I can't believe it, poor, poor Rob! He was such a... so wonderful," she began to weep afresh. Antonia stayed with her, knowing she had adored Rob Murphy, as she was feeling a bit sorry for her.

"Do you know," confided Susan when the sobbing had been brought under control. "I don't think she..." she indicated Mrs Murphy with a nod, now in animated conversation with one of the golfing buddies, the one that looked like her son's biological father, "...even cares! The cow! What did he do to deserve her? The cow!" Her eyes lingered with evil intent on Mrs Murphy for a few seconds. "Just look at her, throwing herself at those old men, it's indecent. The cow!" She turned once again to Antonia and continued, "She offered me a cheque! Seemed to think it would make up for losing my job! The cow! I had to accept it obviously, but how heartless was that?" She looked towards Mrs Murphy with venom. "Cow!" she finished, dabbed at her eyes and blew her nose loudly.

With the nose blowing attended to, Susan turned to watch and hate Mrs Murphy afresh, and Antonia could have laughed. How different from her own reaction! At least Rob had one serious mourner in attendance.

She had stopped worrying about the repercussions of wild passion and was enjoying loving Wendell (using precautions) in the knowledge that he did love her. It was all too unreal. It would be very bad luck if she became pregnant after years of pill taking. She didn't have any signs of early pregnancy, didn't feel any different at all in that department. And anyway, it had only been once, they had been very careful since. Wendell loved her, and she loved him. That was all that mattered. She had never felt so happy and had to remind herself that this was a funeral and to not smile too much. It just seemed to happen every time she thought of him, which was often, and she was already anticipating seeing him later with mounting excitement. She loved him so much it was almost painful.

Bibi was no threat; she knew that now. She'd had a good look at that man with her in the bistro, probably the only one of them that had, so she knew the woman had not been serious about a reconciliation with Wendell.

Charles, she felt genuinely sorry for. Despite it all, she would always be fond of him, he was an innocent soul and hadn't really deserved what had happened. He'd just been a bloody fool. She hoped he had learnt a lesson and that he would meet someone to be happy with too. With looks like his he would have no shortage of choice. She would never forget the look on his face when he realised she and Wendell were together.

Wendell had later told her that Bibi was a great one for slapping faces and perhaps she would think twice about it now. She'd certainly got what she deserved that evening, between the glass of wine, the slapped face and Mrs Waterman's five stone leather handbag.

The Lord's Prayer was being recited and the mourners shuffled and mumbled their way through it, sounding like a swarm of bees. Antonia discovered she was smiling again and snapped her face into a more suitable expression. She glanced around to ensure no one had seen her and noticed that, behind the veil, Mrs Murphy was smiling too.

Chapter Thirty-Two
Sometime Later

Time does heal and people do move on.

Who can even remember much about things that happened to them a week ago?

Bibi's father left her most of his estate, and as a result she had completely gutted and renewed his house before moving into it. During the time it had taken, several months, she had remained at her mother's house and involved her in the revamp. Towards the end things had inevitably become strained, but with effort by both parties had not broken down altogether and they were still talking to one another.

Guy, who had absented himself almost entirely from Elizabeth's house while her daughter was there, came knocking at Bibi's front door the moment she was living behind it.

"How dare you show your face here!" She spat at him when she opened the door.

After they had tumbled about in bed for the rest of the afternoon, she told him to go. She never wanted to see him again.

He went, intending to return sometime when it suited him. Bibi was cross with herself and made a firm decision not to let it happen again. There was something exciting but cruel about the man and it seemed to appeal to her.

For the first time in years, she got herself a job as a receptionist at a large private gym and health club. Not that she needed the money of course, it was really just to alleviate the boredom now that she had material things but no company, and pretty soon she had embarked on an affair with a smart businessman two years younger than herself. It didn't matter that he was married with two small children, a fact she had discovered when going through his wallet one afternoon. They were all the same these men, just wanted the suitable, dutiful wife at their side and a bit on the other side for fun. Well, for now it suited her.

Guy would occasionally drop around, and they would inevitably end up in bed. Elizabeth knew this was happening, and both knew the other knew it was going on, but they engineered a veneer of ignorance to prevent losing each other again. Neither was particularly satisfied with the arrangement but realised he would eventually move on to something better, so they endured it nevertheless.

While this was the state of things, Bibi ran into Charles one day, hand in hand with a girl so like Antonia that at first glance she had thought it was her.

They hadn't seen her. First reaction was to keep going, but Charles looked so gorgeous that she thought she'd see how he would react. Probably shit himself, that would look good in front of that doe-eyed little thing he was with.

"Charlie?" she said smoothly, staring into his eyes in that seductive catlike way she had found never failed her. "Well, fancy seeing you here."

If he remembered their last encounter, he showed no sign and returned her smile with the sort of pleasure reserved for meeting an old acquaintance. With confidence in fact.

"Bibi!" he said. "I didn't recognise you; you look very well."

If anyone else had told her she looked 'well', she would have taken it to mean you look 'fat', but not from Charles. He had no guile.

"You've put on weight," he finished.

Her face dropped for a second, but she recovered swiftly.

He had not, of course, introduced her to the girl whose hand still rested in his own, that was typical of him, no social graces at all. Still smarting slightly at his remark, she asked him if he was going to introduce his friend. She eyed the girl with a look of disdain and managed to make the words sound condescending in a way only Bibi could. But she regretted it instantly. Why did she always have to be so rude? It just came out naturally and she had been trying her best to stop doing it, at the same time realising how hard it was to break the habit of a lifetime.

He turned to his girl and smiled so tenderly that Bibi almost wanted to puke, then turned back with that awful sheep-like expression she knew so well.

"Bibi, this is Hazel." Again, that soppy look between them, her with her saucer sized green eyes and waves of chestnut hair gazing up at him and Charles... well, him doing the same back with his own remarkable attributes. Sickening.

"Hello," said Hazel quietly, with a shy smile. "I've heard a lot about you, Bibi."

Was it her imagination or did that creature smirk momentarily?

"Hazel's been teaching at the school for a term now," continued Charles.

How uninteresting, thought Bibi. "Really?" she enthused.

"We're saving to get married," he grinned and went a bit pink, then squeezed Hazel's hand. Another moment passed while they stared into each other's eyes.

"Anyway, how are you?" Charles dragged his gaze back to Bibi.

She was surprised by how much more confident he seemed. It was attractive, why the hell hadn't he been more like that when he was with her? There was a tiny stab of jealousy for the insipid Hazel.

"Fine, I'm working."

"Oh!" exclaimed Charles, impressed. "Good for you, darling."

Darling? He had grown up. Maybe she would ease herself back in there, perhaps he'd be up for a fling this time.

"We saw Wendell and Antonia last weekend, went out for a meal together." He smiled, but with a look which said he knew it would surprise and annoy her to hear it. She would think they were all talking about her behind her back. Which of course they had been.

"Oh!" Bibi was completely at a loss for words. So they'd all been together talking about her had they? Bibi had had enough. "Well, must get on then. Nice to see you, Charles," she finished, purposely leaving Hazel out. "Bye."

Charles and Hazel strolled away, already dismissing her, and she watched their backs until they merged into the general weekend shopping scene.

Charles had that Hazel creature. Wendell had that drippy Antonia. Unbelievably, even Clara had found herself a man, some lothario twenty-five years older than her who had a penchant for obese women.

What did she have? Two men, one married and the other a playboy who shared himself between her and her mother. Possibly others as well. There was no love or meaning in either affair, just pretence. And sex. Why had she left Wendell? Had she loved him at all? She wasn't sure if she had ever loved anyone, but she had come close with him she knew. Why hadn't Charles just had a fling with her in the first place? Why had she gone off with him like that? Why this, why that, why the other. How stupid.

Wendell had begun divorce proceedings which were shortly to come to their conclusion. At the time of her father's death and after that dreadful episode in the restaurant, she had gone along with it all and just wanted to draw a line under everything and never see Wendell again.

Last week, the discovery of a grey hair had almost frightened her into tears; now, it appeared she was getting fat. If she lost her looks, what would be left? She really must try to be nicer to people, but it was so hard when they were all so ghastly. The days of thinking she didn't need anyone were gone, but now everyone her own age was paired off and in little cosy intimate groups or had young families. She wanted to be liked, admired, loved. She stirred all this around in her head for a few minutes then wondered what she might do that evening. Perhaps Guy would deign to pay her a visit, it seemed weeks since she had last had the pleasure.

What about Oscar? Would he manage to get away from his boring wife for an hour or two? How depressing it all was, waiting for them to call. Dammit, she'd forget them all, what else could she do? Go and see her mother? Perhaps not. If Guy was there, she would feel worse. Clara? She hadn't seen her for a while. That ancient boyfriend didn't bother her at weekends, he was always seeing his children. Yes, she would go there, the sight of that great fat sycophantic lump would make her feel better.

At the very moment Bibi was reflecting on her rather empty life, grey hair and extra weight, Antonia was giving birth to Wendell's son.

He was almost two weeks late.

"Must take after my mother," joked Antonia, as she stroked the fuzzy little head.

Wendell had been present throughout, encouraging her, and as his son's tiny wrinkly red body had been held out for him to examine, he had finally understood what Barney had tried to explain to him in his blustering way, about the feeling of seeing your firstborn. He had stared in wonderment at the tiny fingers and toes, the even tinier perfect nails, then kissed Antonia's damp forehead and told her how much he loved her. She smiled, exhausted but triumphant.

After the shock of discovering she was actually expecting and fearfully wondering what to do, she and Wendell had decided it was all fate and an even stronger bond had sprung up between them.

"We did this together," Wendell had said seriously. "It's not what I wanted, I will admit, but I love you, I want to be with you, and if you want to be with me we should give this new person a chance I think."

Antonia had been filled with such a feeling of euphoria at his words that she knew she would not do anything other than have this baby, and so it was.

As soon as Wendell's divorce was final, they planned to get married without a fuss. The baby could be the guest of honour.

"Oh, what a tiny little thing you are," whispered Antonia, as she held the new baby to her. "What are we going to call him?" she said, not looking at Wendell.

It was a subject she had been avoiding. Before all this, before pregnancies and worries, she had asked him why he had been given such an 'unusual' name. Apparently, it had been an ancestor of his, someone called Winifred Wendell who had done something great and good a couple of centuries previously, and the surname had been journeying along the family line ever since to keep the story alive. Firstborn sons were traditionally given Wendell as their name.

Antonia didn't like it. She had decided not to mention it, after all it could very well be a girl and the problem would not exist. She didn't want to offend Wendell and his family, but she just knew she could never stand in a school playground calling that out and suffering the stares and snide comments that might follow. Not to mention the poor child being traumatised by it. What would he say?

"I suppose you would like Wendell; it is a tradition in your family, isn't it?" She stared up at him with large eyes, made larger and more serious by the tired circles under them.

"What? You must be joking!" He grinned suddenly, seeing her expression. "You don't think I'd saddle the poor kid with such a ridiculous name, do you? I've been teased enough for it in my own life for both of us. He can have it as a second name. I rather like Richard myself."

"Richard Wendell Cornish," said Antonia. "Perfect."